Fractured Dream

The Dreamer Saga

By

K.M. Randall

Booktrope Editions
Seattle WA 2014

Cover Design by Greg Simanson

Edited by Kristina Elliott

Print ISBN 978-1-62015-365-9

EPUB ISBN 978-1-62015-390-1

DISCOUNTS OR CUSTOMIZED EDITIONS MAY BE AVAILABLE FOR EDUCATIONAL AND OTHER GROUPS BASED ON BULK PURCHASE.

For further information please contact info@booktrope.com

Library of Congress Control Number: 2014909252

For Sheilah, my sister and dearest friend

Thank you for sharing the magic with me all those years ago, with a book on a rainy day. Every day spent with you is always a Mermaid Summer kind of afternoon.

ACKNOWLEDGMENTS

I have many people to thank who helped and supported me on this long journey. I want to thank everyone at Booktrope for giving my book a home, especially Jesse James Freeman, who was instrumental in bringing me into the family. To Wendy Logsdon, my marketing manager, whose wonderful energy and spirit made the process a joy. To Greg Simanson, for making my words a breathtaking visual reality. And of course to Kristina Elliott and Bethany Root, my editors, my proofers, my friends.

I'd like to thank my friends and family who have supported me, especially my mother, Jeanne Randall, whose unfailing belief and loving support in me helped guide me to where I am today—including her firm conviction that I would one day actually finish this book.

For my sister, Sheilah Randall, who spent countless hours listening to me babble on about my book, gave it to me straight when I needed to change something (or kill someone off), and shared my love of fantasy our whole lives through.

To my friend TJ Clark, who played a part in inspiring several elements that made their way into these pages and lent an insightful ear during this writing journey.

I'd also like to give a special thanks to Lynn Minderman, who nurtured a young child's love of reading with her own passion and has always been that teacher you never forget.

Finally, thank you to my son, Bryson, and husband, Ron, for showing me so many moments of real magic. I love you.

"They've promised that dreams can come true—but forgot to mention that nightmares are dreams, too."—Oscar Wilde

"You may say I'm a dreamer, but I'm not the only one. I hope someday you'll join us. And the world will live as one."—John Lennon

PROLOGUE

THE ACCEPTANCE LETTER had come that afternoon. Finally, she was going to get out of this town. She had planned to leave the next day. All she'd had to do was bide her time, and she could have been on the road with her hometown and her bitterness falling far behind her. But instead of staying safe in her oppressively humid room, she'd come to the lake that stole lives. Her brother's dancing brown eyes and charismatic smile flashed through her mind as she stared into the dimly lit black waters of Lake Sandeen, which was so fathomless that even the full moon couldn't seem to cast a reflection. It had been awhile since she'd seen Peter's easy grin, but it felt like only yesterday.

The sky ignited with electricity and she stood still, eyes to the sky as if praying to the god of light and chaos. She kept telling herself that she should leave, but she couldn't. Rooted to her feet, she knew he was near. Not Peter, but the other.

Lately, when she came to the lake, she had a feeling she wasn't alone. But it never scared her. Instead, she felt comforted, as if the forest itself had wrapped her in its embrace.

For a moment, she thought maybe she'd go for one last swim, but she sensed him almost before he was there. Turning her head only slightly, she caught his profile in the light of the moon. He'd never shown himself before. Perhaps he sensed her imminent plans to go. Most girls would have run screaming as fast as they could in the isolation of the night. She really shouldn't have come on her own. But instead of running, she turned to the looming outline, the shadow that stalked her gently.

She didn't say anything—she merely stood as still as a hunted deer, sensing the predator draw near. Except she wasn't afraid. When he finally stepped into the bit of moonlight that shed its grace onto the forest-lined bank, she couldn't help but smile. He was like sunshine stepping from the shadows of the pine, with golden hair that hung around his shoulders and eyes that gleamed like amber in the night.

She was certain he was a forest spirit of some sort, his strong masculine jaw the envy of any schoolboy she had known, his full lips curved almost apologetically into a smile. It was a smile she longed to kiss.

His bare feet caressed the earth as if he'd been borne of it, not making a sound or a mark as he closed in on her. When he finally stood in front of her, she lifted her wide, dark eyes eagerly from his bare chest. She turned her face to his as if doing so were the most natural thing in the world, her own dark curls rippling forward to mingle with his golden hair. She meant to speak, but he didn't let her and drew her to him as if she were his link to life itself, pressing his lips to hers and breathing her in just as she inhaled him back. Clinging to each other, they were overwhelmed by a force she couldn't explain, until all she knew was him and a greedy need to consume and be consumed by him. The forest floor became their bed, the night air their blanket, and the lake their music.

"So the spell worked?" A shrouded figure tucked a golden strand back beneath her hood and turned to the woman beside her. Although they had emerged from the lake, they were dry and comfortable in velvet-lined robes. Such was the power of Sandeen's waters.

"There was no spell—I didn't need it," Drianna answered quietly, her inky black hair blending in with her own hood and the night. She eyed the scene that lay before them on the bank of the waters, lifting her arm so that her sleeve fell back to reveal the tattoo of the spider, a reminder of her long-abandoned loyalties. She touched it gingerly, wishing she could eradicate its presence from her skin.

Ninian pulled Drianna's sleeve down fiercely. "Cover that up! What if Racell were to see that?"

The darker woman rolled her eyes. "I hardly think he's in any condition to look across the lake and see us spying on him. He's in love. Exactly as we wanted him."

"He has good eyesight," Ninian murmured in defense before asking again, "But you didn't use the spell?"

From under her hood, Drianna turned to her friend and smiled with a calculating arch of a dark brow over gleaming eyes—one brown and the other blue, the only imperfection of her otherwise flawless beauty. "Not a bit of it. I told you, their blood sings to each other. She's the only human left bearing the Fae's blood, and he's a demi-god. Only those two could possibly have been the vessels for her return. It was meant to be, we just had to push matters along."

"So it's done." A third voice joined the two women, whose heads were arched together in conversation. Her voice was heavy with secrets and lilted with an elemental cacophony that was like water over rocks. They both turned, taking in the tall, gaunt form that took her place between them. She didn't bother to cloak her alabaster skin, nor her sharply boned features and cavernous black eyes.

"Sandeen," Drianna murmured, and both women nodded to the newcomer, showing respect.

"Did you return the boy?" Drianna asked, noticing the faint glow to Sandeen's normal pallor.

Without looking at her, Sandeen answered, "I have no plans to give him back. Besides, he is a man, not a boy."

Eyes wide, Ninian turned to her as well. "What purpose does he serve? We agreed you would return him."

Sandeen turned her pitiless black eyes to Ninian. "And I decided to keep him. Don't forget who I am."

Ninian gazed at the goddess with clear, crystalline blue eyes. "I don't serve you, Sandeen."

"No, Ninian, you don't. But you don't serve anyone anymore, do you?"

Ninian shook her head. "I serve Tressla, you know that."

Sandeen merely waved a hand at her as if to say she was done with the conversation, but Ninian met Drianna's eyes with concern. Stealing a Real Worlder had not been a part of the plan. He was always supposed to have been returned.

Drianna shook her head at her, her expression telling Ninian to drop it. Sighing, Ninian turned back to the beach, nearly blushing at the heat permeating from the bank. "Perhaps we should give them their privacy," Ninian admonished the two darker women.

But Drianna shook her head vehemently. Her multicolored eyes fixed Ninian in her place, and an anxious fervor made them glow almost unnaturally in the night. "I need to see that it's done. I need to know they've conceived."

"You won't know that for moons!" Ninian huffed, lifting her hand to pull her hood further down over her pretty features, even though it was obvious they weren't going to be detected by the two oblivious lovers on the beach.

"It's been written, and it will be so." Sandeen smiled humorlessly although her black eyes glittered with something akin to emotion.

"And now my boy will be safe," Drianna whispered, thinking of the dark-eyed boy whom she'd left under the watchful eye of her maid.

"Surely this is not the only reason we've manipulated our friend and opened a forbidden doorway." Ninian turned, standing slightly taller than Drianna, but shorter than Sandeen.

"That should be reason enough. The only reason he lives is because we have manipulated the events to bring us here!" hissed Drianna. "You may think he's only a catalyst, but he does matter."

Ninian started to protest, but Sandeen cast them both imperious glances, silencing the two women. "Ninian is right. What we've wrought tonight is for far more than just your child, Drianna. This is for Tressla. For my mother, who even now is suffering."

They both nodded, chastised, not really understanding when she spoke again. "This is for love."

PART I

Once upon a time there was girl who had a dream . . .

Chapter One

Specter, New York, Real World

STORY SPARKS'S EYES snapped open. Blinking rapidly for clarity, her eyes darted around the dim room as she sat up and tried to get a grip on reality.

Shivering in the cool morning, she pulled her sweaty T-shirt away from her clammy skin and swiped at her damp forehead. Placing a hand against her heart, she felt butterfly wings flutter frantically in her chest. It wasn't until she realized she was in her old bedroom and safe at home that her heart resumed its normal rhythm.

With shaking hands, she smoothed back strands of dark hair sticking to her face and slipped out of bed. She was definitely going to need a shower.

Peeling the sodden shirt from her skin, she squinted through the gloom of early morning and identified the shadow of another shirt on the floor. She hugged herself as the dry cotton fell around her and banished the sweaty chill from her skin. It was the simple things, really, she thought with a faint smile.

Rubbing dry eyes, she pulled the curtain back from her window, revealing a sky that had faded from black to a bluish grey. The sun was rising slowly, and the rays of light cast a glow on the neighbors' yard and their dangling collection of wind chimes. As she looked out into the neighborhood beyond, a momentary dizziness overtook her, and she had the strangest sense of déjà vu.

Story didn't think about it too hard. It was just one of those moments when you felt like you had been there and done that. She'd experienced that feeling plenty of times. Now was no different. Pressing her forehead lightly against the cool glass, she exhaled a breath she didn't even realize she'd been holding. The sigh, as it fogged the cool window glass, somehow sounded like loneliness. Or maybe that's just how she felt.

The dreams were back. Well, technically, they were nightmares. She had jerked awake enough times to the sound of her own screams, serving as a pre-dawn alarm clock. And yet, she could never remember the nightmares. Wiping her eyes with weariness, she gazed out into the coming day for some sort of hope.

"What the hell?" She wiped the fog from the window and looked again. At first it appeared to be a small shadow, out of place in a wakening world. But as the sky brightened, Story could see a small girl standing in the middle of the street, her red hair rippling as if molten under the first ribbons of rising light. Even stranger, the girl seemed to be staring right at her and waving her hand as if to say, *come play*.

Blinking again, Story shook her head and looked once more. The girl was still there . . . looking eerily familiar.

Lifting her own hand, she gave a half wave back. It must be one of the neighbors' kids. Maybe someone new had moved in? Story had babysat for everyone on her street, but she was sure she had never watched the miniature delinquent wandering the streets alone. Story's anxiety kicked in. The little girl shouldn't be out there by herself. Story should go take her home.

She burst out the front door and for a moment was caught by the perfection of the morning. It was the first true summer dawn, and the air smelled like roses—her favorite flower. A sweet wave of nostalgia tickled the edges of her memory, but it left a bitter taste in her mouth.

Licking dry lips, she desperately thirsted for a glass of water. First, she had to take the little girl home. But when she looked where the girl had been standing, no one was there. She walked to the edge of her lawn, freshly mowed grass sticking to her feet, and she craned her neck looking down the street and all around. Not a soul was humming.

Where did she go? Turning back to the driveway, Story bent down and looked under the cars for good measure. Maybe she had imagined it. Could your dreams follow you out into reality?

"It is only 6 a.m. on a Saturday," Story reminded herself out loud. "That's it, I'm going crazy. The nightmares are taking over my brain." But before she went back inside, she cast one last searching look over her shoulder.

CHAPTER TWO

Specter, New York, Real World

"SINCE IT'S SUCH A nice day out, I thought we could go to the lake and eat lunch," Edie said.

Startled, Story looked up from the painting she was working on. Her mother avoided the lake like a plague. "You hate the lake," she said, voicing her thoughts aloud. She put her paintbrush down and turned to look at her mother. It always surprised her how young her mother looked. Story supposed she *was* young. She'd gotten pregnant with Story barely out of high school.

Her mom's brown curls, so dark they looked black, were pulled back in a sloppy ponytail. Although her heart-shaped face was relatively wrinkle-free, she was aged by the worry and sadness that never seemed to leave her mother's large, dark eyes. Sometimes, when Story really studied her mother, the word "haunting" surfaced in her mind. She had lost a lot, but she never spoke of it to Story. She never spoke of it at all.

"I don't hate the lake, Story." Edie was troubled that her daughter felt that way. Perhaps she did avoid it, but she had her reasons. Edie was more concerned about Story. She had been studying her daughter closely the last few days.

Story was on summer break from her first year in college as an art major at NYU. Edie often had a sense of overwhelming relief that at least one of them had been able to get out of this town. As much as Edie had wanted her daughter home for the summer, she had wanted Story to stay in the city more. This place was a black hole. Something was in the wind, in the water. And it stole lives.

Story thought differently, Edie knew. She loved the dirt roads, the hills, and the trees. She adored the nearby farming towns and liked nothing better than to hike over to the Amish farm markets and bring home crusty artisan breads and homegrown-berry-filled pies. Story once told her she didn't think she would ever be able to stay too far from home. And it was true that when Story came home she always seemed more peaceful. Edie supposed she had once felt the same way herself.

But since her daughter's return, Edie had noticed Story acting strangely. Just this morning, Edie had seen her standing in the middle of the yard, staring at nothing in the semi-darkness. She heard screams coming from Story's room and more than once had run to find her daughter writhing in bed, or sobbing in her sleep and calling out names of people Edie didn't know.

When Story had been a child, she had often talked of people Edie had always assumed were imaginary friends. But as soon as Edie would ask her who she was talking about, Story's face would go blank, and she became tight-lipped and non-responsive to Edie's frustrated queries. Story had a lot of secrets.

As a child, she had been prone to taking long naps in the middle of the day that were nearly impossible to wake her from. Edie had taken her to doctors and specialists, convinced she had some strange sort of narcolepsy. But the doctors all said she was a healthy little girl. She just liked to sleep.

Then eight years ago, that all stopped. She had walked around like a zombie—pale, sad, and withdrawn. But she had been awake.

That's when the nightmares had started. When Story woke from these night terrors, she was inconsolable. Back then she called for a man named Faulks.

Edie questioned Story's teachers at school, terrified that some teacher or employee was sexually abusing her. But the teachers assured her that no one by that name worked in the district.

When Edie questioned her, Story looked stricken. But ultimately, she would deny any knowledge or recognition. Edie knew she was lying, but Story wouldn't open up.

In desperation, she took Story to a psychologist. Dr. Joyce Harvey was a highly recommended child specialist. But even she couldn't get through to Story. Her daughter simply refused to answer questions about her nightmares—until the day the doctor had put her under hypnosis, and Story had talked about a father and a sister in a different world.

When she awoke, Story was furious. She refused to ever go back. And that, as they say, was that. Edie couldn't compel her daughter to do something she was that set against doing. If Edie was truthful with herself, she had been relieved. There had been something about the doctor during the last session that unsettled her. She had been too intense. Story's obvious dislike of the woman also had made the final verdict. She never knew her daughter to make a bad judgment about a person.

Edie thought about taking Story to see a different doctor, but then the nightmares seemed to come less and less. Story started bringing friends home after school and joined the girls' soccer team. For the first time in . . . well, since Story had been born, Edie relaxed. She never stopped worrying, but for the first time in twelve years, she felt as if things were normal.

Looking at the beautiful young woman Story had become, Edie felt pride and dread: the nightmares were back.

Edie had allowed the memories to fade. But she knew things had never been normal. Story could never be normal. And neither could she, ever again. Now she saw that the shadows lived on.

"I don't hate the lake," she repeated to herself softly, "I think it would be fun." Edie forced a smile. "I'll go pack us some lunch." As she turned to leave, she glanced at the painting Story had been working on and shuddered. It was horrifying.

A naked man with the head of a snarling wolf was crouched over a young woman, whose long red hair blended in with the blood that stained the snow around her. He was feeding on her entrails. It looked as if Story had painted the young woman's soul into the painting, for the wolf was sucking up what looked like a ghostly apparition bearing her features. The detail of the girl's face was amazing—Edie felt agony just looking at it.

Story shrugged. "If you say so."

"Huh?" She glanced at her daughter.

"I said if you say so. If you say you don't hate the lake, then we'll go."

Story shook her head slightly as her mother left the room. "Space cadet," she murmured to herself and dipped her brush in the red paint, dabbing a little more of the crimson into the snow. She stepped back to get a measure of her work and wiped away a tear with red-stained fingertips. She hadn't even realized she had been crying. Looking up, she caught a glimpse of herself in the mirror over her bed and was chilled. Several tears had slipped from her eyes while she worked and mingled with the red paint smudged on her face and hands. Like those statues of the Virgin Mary—the holy ones that cried blood-red tears, she thought.

CHAPTER THREE

Lake Sandeen, Real World

HOW MUCH DID STORY remember from all those years ago? Edie studied her daughter basking in the heat of the day. The two of them had taken a morning hike and ended up by the lake's edge with a blanket, cold lemonade, and turkey sandwich for each.

How much had she herself forgotten? Conveniently blocked, was more like it. Shaking her head, she squinted her eyes as she looked across the lake, turning quickly away from the blinding surface and to the rolling hills, covered in trees so thick she knew the sun could barely light the forest floor.

She didn't hate the lake, or so she told herself. Contrary to Story's belief, Edie had come down to the shore from time to time. She couldn't help herself. The crystal waters and looming trees called to her. This was where it had all began.

So being near the lake gave her the chills and made her skin crawl—even now she had goose bumps on her arms despite the heat. She had reason to believe there was more to these waters than just waves. It had been a long time since she had allowed herself to admit that. And if her gaze occasionally lingered on the trees, looking for a shadow or a touch of gold amidst the green, no one but she was the wiser.

She smiled ruefully to herself, but the smile ran away from her face when she saw Story's toes making lazy circles in the cool water. "Story," she said sharply.

Her head bent over a book, Story glanced up, startled. "What?"

"You just shouldn't have your feet in the water right now. I think they said something about the lake being contaminated this summer."

She knew her excuse sounded lame, but there was a possibility Story would just let it go.

No such luck. Story arched a skeptical brow and cast a pointed glance to the fish that jumped out of the water at that inopportune moment. "Mom, it's the town's drinking water," she replied dryly. Edie didn't say any more about it, but she noticed with relief some moments later that Story had pulled her feet from the water and was now sunning them, chocolate brown polished toenails sparkling with little beads of water.

"So what's with you and the lake anyway?" Story asked before she sipped from a can of lemonade. Edie was surprised that she had asked. When Story was young, she seemed to know so much—she was always so mature. But lately, Edie noticed, Story was surly to the point of being rude. It was completely out of character and a little late—she was a freshman in college, not a freshman in high school trying out rebellion for the first time. Story and Edie had been especially close during her teen years, and her daughter had rarely done anything to disappoint her. But lately Story had just been . . . different.

"You know why, Story," she said quietly, staring off into the distance. She was troubled by her daughter's insensitivity. So, when Edie felt the light touch of Story's hand a moment later, she smiled to herself before glancing her daughter's way. This was more like the Story she knew.

"Hey, I'm sorry. I know you lost Uncle Peter here. I just . . . I don't know. I thought maybe there was something else that you weren't telling me," Story said and fiddled with her necklace. Edie had never seen her take the necklace off, and Story had always insisted she had found it lying by the house one day. But Edie long suspected there was more to her story. Indeed, she suspected that the two of them were very good at keeping secrets from one another—and from themselves.

Grabbing her daughter's hand gently, Edie met her daughter's golden gaze. "What secrets do you think I'm keeping from you?" *Besides who your father is . . . and how I met him . . . and where he is,* Edie thought guiltily.

Story shrugged slightly. Biting her lip, she looked away from Edie for a moment. Taking a deep breath as if she was steeling herself for a big announcement, she finally met her mother's eyes. "I've been having these dreams lately."

Story couldn't believe that she had told her mother even that much. It always seemed easier to keep her fears and secrets to herself. But maybe it was time to open up to her mother. She felt compelled by an unseen force to do something . . . but what that something was, she didn't know. So she lingered between reality and her dreams, waiting for something to happen. It was driving her mad. Her nightmares, from what she remembered, had taken on a new tone—they were terrifying. She had barely slept in days. She felt as if she might snap, or worse—cry. She knew she had been unpleasant since she had returned home, and she felt bad, but if something didn't change soon, she was going to lose it. Her paintings had become ghoulish, and one thought kept running through her head over and over again: she had to help Jess.

But who was Jess? A childhood friend she could barely remember? Or was she merely a daydream, a figment of Story's past?

If she closed her eyes for a moment, she could see the fiery red ringlets, eyes the silver of steel, and feisty spirit barely contained by her friend's small frame. She could hear her giggle and her voice as she called Story's name to come play. Tears threatened as the ghostly image of a child's hand slid into hers. But where was Jess, and why did she have to help her? More importantly, why did the thought of her evoke such emotion?

While Story wandered like a lost soul through her thoughts, Edie held her hand. It was comforting and gave her the strength to take a deep breath and finally meet her mother's gaze once again. "Did I ever mention a friend I had as a child? A special friend?" Story asked.

Very slowly, Edie nodded. "You mean your friend Jess?"

Story gaped. "So you know her then?"

Her mother seemed equally shocked, but for a different reason. "I know you talked about her once in a while. When I asked you who she was, you refused to tell me. Don't you remember, Story?"

Story rubbed her dry eyes, feeling tired. "I don't. I mean I do . . . I remember what she looked like, the sound of her voice, the way her hair felt beneath my fingers when I played with it—and that I used to think she was the bravest girl I knew. But I don't know where she is or what happened to her." Story looked up at her mother from where her fingers had been curling around pieces of grass. "Do you think I've gone crazy? I didn't make her up, I know I didn't, Mom."

"You're not crazy, Story. Or if you are, so am I. Be—because I'm not sure your Uncle Peter drowned in this lake."

Story sat back, digesting what her mother had said. "Like . . . what do you think happened to him?"

"I don't know Story. He disappeared, so I don't know what I believe. But I don't think you're crazy. And all those years ago, Dr. Harvey didn't think you were crazy either."

"No, she just wanted to eat my brains," Story grinned. "I think she may have been the crazy one . . . but thanks." She tucked a dark strand of hair behind her ear, feeling the curls already spring unruly. As much as she tried, a flat iron wouldn't keep them straight.

"I just feel like memories from my childhood have been cut off from me. It's like my memory card has been erased. If only I could remember where Jess and I met, it would all come together."

"Did you meet her in Tressla?" Edie was focused on picking at the fibers in the blanket, avoiding eye contact as if she thought her daughter was a wild animal she might scare off. Story knew Edie worried about her, and a pang tightened in her chest. Wait, what had she said?

"Tressla!" Story's hands went to her mouth, the familiarity of the name whispering through her soul like home and hovering on the edge of her mind, ready to be remembered. But whatever revelation was about to be revealed, it was forgotten when a man's voice called her name.

"Story!"

Glancing at her mother, she jumped up to greet the man walking toward them. But the look she gave her mother was pointed. *Later*.

"Adam!" she yelled and jumped up, hurling herself with a whoop of laughter into the arms of the young man, who had been striding toward them with a goofy grin on his face. As was his usual style, he sported cargoes and a T-shirt bearing his latest cause. The one he wore today was black and had a picture of a roll of toilet paper and said, "Save the trees, use both sides." He grabbed Story and pulled her to him so that her heels lifted from the earth.

Taking a step back, he grabbed a strand of her dark hair and bounced a curl. "Glad you didn't shave it yet," he said. She was always threatening to get rid of the unruly mess.

Story laughed. "Glad you approve." She started walking back to where Edie sat, Adam following behind her.

"Hi Ms. Sparks," he said as he reached down to hug her as well.

"You look healthy." Edie winked. Adam smirked and flexed a large bicep.

"I'm in college now. I couldn't be the wiry little guy I was in high school and get any dates. Of course," he said, smiling crookedly at Story. "Your daughter was my first love."

"You can't take the geek out of the boy." Story laughed and flopped back onto the long, inviting bed of grass where they had been whiling away the afternoon. "And please," she continued, "When we were fourteen I told you I thought I loved you. The next day you were holding hands with Amanda Grey. Broke my heart," she sniffed, brushing away a mock tear.

"Eh, what did you expect? She was the first girl in our grade to wear a bra." He flopped down next to the two women. "And for the moment, I'll let the geek comment slide because I have a bone to pick with you. But just so you know, the Death Star is a cultural icon."

"Geek," she coughed. "So what's the bone?" She took a can of cold lemonade from a small cloth cooler and tossed it to Adam, who caught it with the quick reflexes of a guy who spent a lot of time climbing up the side of mountains—when he wasn't hiking through the woods.

"How long have you been home? We're supposed to be best friends, and the only reason I knew you were even in the same town was because Lois mentioned she had seen you and your mom this morning on your way out. She said you guys had talked about having a picnic by the lake. And I said, 'Are you sure it was Story?' Because Story, who I never see anymore because she's a big city girl, would never come home and not tell her best buddy.'"

"Okay, okay." Story said and held up a hand, rolling her eyes at her mother, who was enjoying the light banter between the two childhood friends. "I'll admit, I have kept kind of low key. But I have my reasons." Story grew quiet—the humor that had lit her face moments before disappearing behind troubled eyes and a stony expression.

This was a Story that Edie and Adam were both familiar with. She would only say so much before retreating behind a shroud of mystery.

Later that day as the three of them walked alongside the road toward home, Adam grabbed Story's hand to get her attention. She had been lazily walking and scuffing her flip-flops into the dry dirt found in clumps on the side of the road. Her feet were completely filthy, but she didn't care. It felt like sand between her toes and made her feel carefree; the heavy burden of half-remembered sorrow didn't seem so real anymore. But Adam brought her out of her thoughts with his touch and serious expression.

"Let's go for a hike tomorrow. I think we need to talk." He held her hand firmly as if to keep her from disappearing.

Glancing up at him through dark lashes that felt laden with invisible tears, she nodded. "We should talk." Maybe she should finally open up.

"Come over tomorrow morning, okay?" she said and leaned in to give him a quick hug. "Love ya," she called over her shoulder, grinning as she ran off to catch up with her mother, who had forged ahead in order to give them a little privacy.

Adam smiled halfheartedly and waved. But as he lost sight of her, his face was wrinkled in concern.

The Dream

"What do you dream about?" At first she pretended not to hear the question. She was too busy looking out the window. She knew there were bars. She could feel the thick steel beneath her clenched fists. But it was like she didn't even see them anymore—like she actually saw through them as if she were a superhero. Beyond lay the courtyard. And beyond that, roads, cars, and hope. Her x-ray vision allowed her to see a life beyond this prison.

She laughed aloud and cast a glance at the tired woman as if they shared a private joke. When the woman didn't return the camaraderie, she rolled her eyes and turned back to the window.

"You know, I always eat the cake." She avoided the woman's question and picked at a hangnail before putting it to her mouth and tearing at it. Silently she cursed herself, suddenly craving store-bought, sickly sweet frosting—the kind only bakeries seemed able to concoct—and a cherry chip birthday cake. Instead, she tasted the metallic flavor of her own blood.

"You don't look like it." The woman looked up from her clipboard, humoring her for the moment.

She looked down at her bony wrists and arms, nodding. "Yes, I suppose I'm awfully thin. You should bring me more cake."

What she had meant to say was that she liked eating cake, and that she didn't want to waste her life worrying whether being a size four, six or eight was good enough. She just wanted to live it. She wanted to prank call boys she had a crush on and stay up all hours of the night gossiping. She wanted to go to college. But she couldn't.

She was always lying to herself. She wasn't a superhero. The bars were as thick as ever, reminding her they had always been there, as had she.

"I don't dream… But I do remember." She closed her eyes and pressed her fingers against them, so that spots danced behind her closed lids. But that didn't stop the memories. A haunting, beautiful medley filled the room. "Do you hear that?"

"Hear what?" The woman put her clipboard down. The girl didn't open her eyes, but she heard the woman get her syringe ready. Just in case.

She didn't care. She kept her eyes closed, but that didn't stop her from seeing the images flash through her mind: Strange and beautiful music, magic and true love. And at the last, there was death. And pain.

She didn't want these memories. She didn't want any of it because they didn't belong to her. A knife glittered, a dagger . . . When she saw blood, she wailed. Beneath her horror, the sane part of herself registered the lost, elusive sound of her own screams. She sounded like a banshee. Like a ghost. When the needle slid into her arm, she smiled and slipped into a dreamless sleep—the only place where she was whole.

CHAPTER FOUR

Specter, New York, Real World

ONCE AGAIN, STORY'S EYES shot open, and she gasped for breath, sitting up in her dim room and trembling in the early day. At least she was dry this time. "Those are some dreams," she whispered, wishing she could fall back into her pillows and get some much-needed sleep.

Even now, the dream was fading, and she was having trouble remembering all that she had learned. A part of her felt it was important, but it was slipping away so fast. She moved to lie back down when she felt something slip from her neck. Shiny and glittering in her lap was the necklace she hadn't taken off since she was a child. She couldn't quite remember where she had gotten it, but for some reason she knew she wasn't supposed to take if off. It had always made her feel safe and close to home, no matter how far away she was.

Touching the pendant nostalgically, she took in the deep blue of the turquoise carved into two overlapping circles and gilded in silver. She slid her fingers along the chain until they came to the part where it had broken. Troubled, she placed the charm on the nightstand and lay back, the soft pillows cushioning her. Closing her eyes with a sigh, she tried to get some rest, but the place where the necklace used to lie felt bare and vulnerable. Try as she might, she could not get back to sleep. Nightmares hovered on the edge of her mind's vision. Finally, after an hour of trying, she rose.

The clock glowed 5 a.m., and night was just starting to fade to day. *Might as well shower and get ready*. Adam would probably be there in several hours anyway. He had always been an early riser and had seemed especially anxious to speak with her. Glancing at her bedside table once more, she touched the place just over her breast where the pendant had guarded her heart and soul for so long. She could get the chain fixed, or get a new chain. She once read or heard somewhere—probably in a new age book or at one of the many psychic conventions her friend Elliott had dragged her to—that when a necklace or charm fell off, it had served its purpose. Try as she might to be the skeptic, she was a girl who believed in signs.

CHAPTER FIVE

Specter, New York, Real World

AN HOUR LATER, Story was stirring sugar into her coffee and had just poured herself a bowl of Honey Graham O's when she heard a knock at the door. She glanced at the clock in disbelief. Seriously, Adam was absolutely crazy. She knew he would show up early, just not at 6:30 a.m. Setting down her coffee mug, she headed to the door, mumbling under her breath about morning people.

She was just about to tell him that he could forget it, she wasn't leaving to go hiking until eight-thirty at the earliest. She didn't start waking up until then. But it wasn't Adam.

"Elliott?" She blinked in disbelief.

"In the flesh," he said, striking a pose.

Jumping about an inch off the ground in excitement, Story clapped her hands and laughed. "I can't believe you're actually here!" She jumped into his arms.

Kissing her cheek and holding her at arm's length, he shook his head. "You look . . . awful," he said emphatically, clucking like a mother hen and herding her into the house. She allowed him to steer her toward the kitchen. She felt so grateful that he was there, she didn't even wonder how he knew his way around her house so well already. She relaxed into his side and took comfort in the feel of his strong arm around her and the smell of Ralph Lauren's Very Sexy cologne.

He pushed her into a chair and began to bustle around the kitchen, pouring a cup of coffee for himself. "I have a feeling that this is going to take a while," he said over his shoulder.

"Oooh, I love the five o'clock shadow," she said, taking a sip of her now lukewarm coffee.

Turning to her, he grinned. "You like? I think it gives me a more chiseled appearance."

"Oh definitely," she agreed with a grin, feeling the brightening effect Elliott always had on her mood. "Very masculine."

If you didn't know better, you might think Elliott was a rugged sort of guy—except for the brown hair streaked with honeyed blond highlights, spiked and sprayed to perfection. Except for the eyebrows that had been waxed and the fingernails that had never seen a speck of dirt and were so polished they caught the lamplight. Except for the Versace jeans and the Ralph Lauren shirt, sleeves rolled to the elbows, untucked and stylish. His Gucci sunglasses lay carelessly on the counter. He pulled out a chair and joined her at the table.

"Tell me, tell me," he said and took a sip of his steaming coffee, the aroma of hazelnut wafting through the kitchen.

"Tell you what?" Story sipped her own coffee, brushing off his inquiries. "Tell *me* what you're doing here. And tell me," Story said suddenly, having a thought that would steer them toward a pleasanter topic, "how did your date go?"

Elliott sighed heavily. "It was positively awful. He wanted to go Dutch. I mean honestly, did he really think I had the money to dish out for an expensive restaurant in NYC? Also, he lives with his mother. I heed my warning signs, and there were plenty. It's too bad because he was absolutely delicious-looking—it was totally false advertising."

"Anyway," he continued, "don't think you're off the hook. I want you to tell me what's going on."

Staring into her coffee mug, she shook her head. "I don't know what you're talking about, I'm fine."

"Don't give me that," he protested. "I was happily on my way home—happy to get away from mama's boy—when I felt a searing pain in my head. Thankfully, it cleared in time for me to pay the cabbie, who actually tried hitting on me. I had just made it up to the loft when I began to feel dizzy, and I knew one of my spells was coming on. So I lit candles and lay down to wait. Then . . . nothing happened. So I grabbed the Carlo Rossi—why let a jug of wine go to waste?—and I popped in a movie."

"I had just started to dream of a day when Prince Charming—and I mean literally, Prince Charming—comes to get me," he continued with a dreamy smile that vanished as his green-flecked brown eyes met hers directly. "I was just starting to feel like myself again really, when the movie stopped, the DVD went blank and that song by . . . What's his name again? You know, the one that goes 'Hey there Little Miss Red Riding Hood, you sure are looking good,'" he sang in a surprisingly pleasant baritone.

"Sam the Sham?" Story offered.

"Yes!" Elliott said. "It was going to bother me all day if I couldn't remember. Anyway, that song blasted from my stereo, which I never turned on, and then that picture of you and I at the Macy's Day Parade fell and broke. I love that picture. Then the room went silent again. So I was totally freaked out. I mean, I've had visions and strange things happen to me before, but never something like this. At that point, I didn't feel like doing anything but going to bed. So I went to pick up the picture and the broken glass, but it wasn't there. It was on the shelf where it always was. So I figured I must have dozed off because the credits were rolling on the movie.

"So I went to bed. I was totally asleep when my pleasant dreams of me and, well . . . were broken by a scream. It was you."

"It was me?" Story put her coffee down, taking him more seriously.

"It was you screaming. I could hear you. I ran through the house—god, I wish Uncle Carlo was here now," he said, using his nickname for the Carlo Rossi Chablis he and Story had spent many nights sipping and talking over.

"But I looked everywhere—you know my place is a box—and you weren't there. Then I remembered you went home for the summer. But I continued to have this bad feeling, like something was going on, and that you were calling out to me even if you didn't know it. Then I dreamt that you and I were sitting beside a lake, and you fell in and drowned. That was the crux of it.

"When I woke up, I knew that you needed me. If that wasn't a vision, then what was it? You've got something going on—I don't need your subconscious screaming out to me to see it. You're pale, your eyes are absolutely bloodshot, and you look as if you were partying with Lindsay Lohan last night—gorgeous, but wrecked."

Story sighed. Elliott fancied himself a psychic. And the truth was, most of the time she believed he was. His intuitions about people were dead on. He had prophesied, in detail, the downfall of every relationship their mutual friends had ever had. He always called her before she could push the send button to call him. He knew what fashions were in vogue a year before they were in, making him the best-dressed nineteenth-century literature student at NYU.

Then there was the clincher. One night on the town three months ago, he'd saved their lives by insisting they take a cab home at the end of the night. The next morning, they'd learned a mugger had murdered a couple at their subway stop. Elliot had brought Story muffins and the newspaper, and she'd never doubted him again. She ate five muffins that morning. She ate until the emptiness was filled with food, and she could take heart in the life she still had—while mourning the two who had passed, possibly in their place.

Smiling faintly, she looked up at Elliott, who had in the last few moments placed a muffin in front of her. "Spill it." Leaning back, he peeled the wrapper from his own sugar-topped blueberry muffin and took a manly bite.

She stifled a yawn and tried not to convey how exhausted she was, emotionally and physically. "You'll think I'm crazy." She picked a crumb off the muffin, strangely not hungry this time.

"I already think you're crazy," he shot back.

"But I mean really crazy."

"Why don't you just leave my judgments to me," he replied as he finished swallowing the last of his muffin.

"Alright, well, let me begin by showing you something. I'll be right ba—" She got up from the table, but was cut off by a knock at the door.

"Oh god, I forgot all about Adam. We're supposed to go hiking today," she said.

"Hiking?" Elliott brushed crumbs from his shirt, with disdain evident in his voice.

Running to the door, Story flung it open. "You're here earlier than I expected," she told Adam, who was standing at the front door in frayed khaki cargo shorts and a Peace Frog T-shirt, sunglasses perched on his burnished head. It was still early enough that although it was fully daylight, a haze still coated the morning.

Adam, who had been looking off to his right, turned as she opened the door. He smiled rakishly. "Gotta start before the heat of the day." He stepped in past her and then paused with a frown, eyeing her up and up down. "You don't look ready."

"Adam, I know I said we would go hiking, but my friend Elliott surprised me by showing up this morning."

She could tell he was disappointed as his smile faltered slightly, but after a moment he shrugged. "He can come too."

"I don't know if it's really his thing." She felt Elliott come up behind her.

"Elliott, this is Adam, my best friend growing up, and Adam, this is Elliott, my best friend from school."

The guys eyed each other intently. Story was struck by how opposite they were. Elliott was tall and lean, his dark hair perfectly in place and his five o'clock shadow giving him a movie star appeal. He was sexy, but in a glam Eurotrash sort of way.

Adam, on the other hand was several inches shorter and bright where Elliott was dark. His eyes were a foggy gray, and muscles from all his outdoor adventures rippled under his shirt whenever he moved his arms—an all-American boy. But for all their differences, she loved them both dearly, and at once felt a sense of rightness having them together with her now. "I'm so glad you're both here," she whispered, overcome with how at ease she felt in the world at that moment.

The boys turned their attention toward Story. They seemed to simultaneously lose the bitter edge of resentment that had flared the moment they locked eyes . . . or bull horns, Story thought. In the instant Story had expressed her delight at their presence, an understanding had been reached.

"Hey," Adam said, holding out his hand to Elliott. "Good to meet ya. Story's told me a lot about you."

Elliott slid his long, tapered fingers into Adam's welcoming grip and nodded. "Likewise. Although she never mentioned how cute you were," he grinned. The tension that had smelled like jealousy dissolved as the three of them broke into laughter.

"You think you're up for a hike, Elliott? Nothing too strenuous."

Elliott sighed, relenting. "I suppose so. At least I was smart enough to bring sneakers since I remembered Story saying she lived in Hicksville."

"Yeah, I don't think I ever said that," Story replied dryly.

"I read between the lines. Where can I change?" Story led Elliott to the downstairs bathroom and then headed to her own room to change. She took the stairs two at a time, like she did when she was little and excited about the day.

CHAPTER SIX

Specter, New York, Real World

WHILE STORY AND ELLIOTT got ready, Adam busied himself rifling through cupboards and packing them lunch. A true mountain man, his backpack was already full. "Hey Story," he yelled up the stairs. "Where is your backpack?"

"In the basement," she called back.

Adam returned to the kitchen and headed through the basement door and down the stairs. Reaching the bottom, he fumbled blindly for the chain and pulled, light instantly flooding the windowless basement.

The room had never been redone and was used more as a storage unit than anything else. As children, Story and Adam used to play down there—she was the witch who would lock him in the dark for a hundred years until he agreed to marry her. Then she would turn into a beautiful princess. Like most children, they flirted with their fears. They would play pretend and create a story about an awful beast lurking in the basement. They even made a game out of it. Pretending not to be terrified, one of them would run down the steps, touch the opposite wall, and come running back up into the safe kitchen. Adam remembered racing up the steps as if a pack of howling ghosts and demons were nipping at his heels—a mixture of terror and glee racing through his veins. Then one day, he remembered, they'd pretended to be chased by wolves. Story had always had an unnatural fear of the animals. She'd come up the stairs screaming and slammed the door as if there'd really been a pack of the beasts chasing her. They didn't play in the basement after that.

Now, as he looked around, he realized this was the first time he had been down there since that day. Even as an adult, he was creeped out by the place. He had suffered a lot of nightmares because of this basement. Shaking his head and putting the thought from his mind, he noticed the backpack leaning against a painting easel.

Brushing from his pants the dust that he had stirred up, he grabbed the bag. "There you are," he said out loud to himself. "Let's get out of this place."

He started to turn back toward the stairs, where natural light shone like a soft beacon of hope, but he stopped. There was a sheet dangling halfway off a painting. Curious, he slipped it off and stared. It had been a long time since he had seen anything new of Story's. But this was different than anything he had ever seen her paint before.

"Adam! Hey, where are you?" He heard Elliott call from upstairs.

"In the basement," he yelled back, transfixed by the painting. He heard Elliott clatter down the stairs and come up behind him.

"Jesus," Elliott hissed from beside him as he looked at the picture.

"She's beautiful," Adam whispered.

"You must be on crack." Elliott shuddered. "It's positively gruesome."

"No, but just look at her." Adam's finger caressed a line over the painting of a girl with hair like flames, shooting out of her head and spiraling to the edges of the painting. The colors and artistry were so vivid that Adam could actually feel the heat from the picture. The girl's pale jaw line was a delicate matter of porcelain fragility, and her seething silver-blue eyes jumped out like quicksilver on ice.

"She looks terrifying to me," Elliott murmured, breaking Adam's crush-induced daze.

"I wish she were real."

"You couldn't handle her. She'd tear you to pieces."

For the first time, Adam looked at what the girl was doing in the painting: if silver-blue was the color of fire, then her eyes were the flames. In the lines of her expression, Adam could see that she was a killer. And of course, men lay dying at her feet, so that gave it away. Their blood ran into the girl's hair. In one hand, she held a bleeding heart that she had ripped from a man's chest. In the other hand, she wielded a bloody ax above her head as if to bring it down again and again upon her victim's broken and savaged body.

Leaning forward, Elliott silently pointed to the ax. Story had painted the man's reflection, not as a man but as a snarling wolf, muzzle and teeth tinged in red.

"Wolf men," Elliott murmured.

"You're right," Adam said after moments of staring at the nightmarish qualities of the painting. "It *is* gruesome." He turned to look at Elliott. "You know Story isn't normal, right?"

Elliott, tearing his gaze away from the painting, seemed to search Adam's face before finally nodding. "Let's make an agreement that no matter what, we get her to talk." Pinching the bridge of his nose as if in pain, he closed his eyes briefly. When he opened them again, he looked even more serious. "Today. Because I have a feeling shit is about to hit the fan. Let's make a pact, here and now, that no matter where Story goes, we'll be there for her."

After a few moments, Adam nodded, held out his hand, and shook on it. "She wouldn't like this you know. She'd say we were un-empowering her or something. Women's lib and all that."

Elliott's attitude finally returned to his expression and stance, the intensity fleeing his face. "She has more rights than I do. She can deal. Now let's get out of here, this place gives me the creeps."

Adam didn't argue with that.

CHAPTER SEVEN

Lake Sandeen, Real World

"IS IT LUNCHTIME YET?" Elliott moaned as they trudged up another hill, waving his cell phone in the air as he desperately searched for reception. "I thought this was going to be more like a meander, not a full-scale trek up a mountain."

Story laughed and turned back to look at him. She was in the best mood she had been since she came home—since the dreams had started plaguing her again. She felt light, free, and hopeful. It was actually a mood she didn't feel often—maybe not since she had been a child.

"Darlin'," she drawled. "This is barely a hill, let alone a mountain. You've got to get out of the city more often."

Adam stopped and pointed to a clearing, sweat glistening on his brow. "See that? That's the road. Once we hit it, we'll just walk it till we get to Lake Sandeen. Then we can relax as long as we want."

When the three got to the road, Elliott's energy miraculously returned as he grabbed Story's hands and danced along the asphalt with her. Her girlish laughter caused both men to stop and smile at one another with a shared relief. Maybe everything would be just fine.

The trio came to rest where the elder trees' branches reached and bowed toward the sky and cast shadows upon the placid, sunlit water. The grass was soft and lush, and the shade was a salve on youthful skin that was flushed with the heat of the day and the sun's unforgiving rays.

Adam spread a blanket he had stowed in his pack, and Story removed a bag of sandwiches. She tossed each of the two boys a bottle of water, the plastic only slightly warmer than the water inside. Just the same, when she pressed the bottle to her lips, it tasted like the purest, coolest water.

They sat in silence for a while, chewing their food in quiet thoughtfulness and enjoying the rest after hours of walking. The sun and shade soothed aching limbs and calmed the restless spirits of the young.

Story kept looking out at the water. Nightmares and her mother's own fear of the lake did not make it look any less enticing. Already she was chewing faster, imagining the cool liquid engulfing her heat-mottled skin in its embrace.

She was getting ready to shed her clothing and give in to her daydream of swimming, when she heard Adam clear his throat in such a way that she knew there was meaning and intent behind it.

She looked at him and saw Elliott shoot Adam a pointed look. Oh, this looked like an intervention of sorts if she ever saw one. She frowned intently at the two of them. They had just met, and here they were, already sharing looks and meaningful sounds and gestures?

"Yes?" Story consciously arched a brow to show her derision.

Elliott smiled at her look, unable to help himself. "Oh, attitude!"

Story started to laugh, but Adam shot a stern look toward Elliott, who comically closed his mouth and looked down at the same time. His gaze went blank as he concentrated on the grass he was idly tugging. Finally, after Story was sure he was going to pull all the grass from the ground, he looked up and met her gaze.

"What?" Feeling annoyed, she ripped out her own blades of grass, and then immediately felt bad. *Every living thing must be valued,* she heard whisper through her mind. Where had she heard that before?

"We're worried about you," Elliott began.

"We know something's going on with you," Adam finished.

"Nothing is going on with me." Story went on the defensive, taken off guard by strange voices in her head that she couldn't remember.

In response, Elliott raised his brows and tilted his head, while Adam just snorted. "Honestly, Story . . . We saw your painting in the basement. I've known you a long time. You usually paint happier scenes."

Story bit her lower lip but tried to feign nonchalance. "So?" In all actuality, she had hid it down there. She had been utterly freaked out by it herself—she hadn't remembered even painting it and had been horrified by what was creeping around her mind. The painting didn't seem to belong in her sunny bedroom, and she hadn't wanted anyone to see it. "I'm trying out different styles."

"Helloooo—remember my vision?" As Elliott spoke, his face lost all traces of his personality. Compassion, humor, strength—it just all washed away as he stared out at the water, really seeing his surroundings for the first time.

"It's beautiful, isn't it?" Story mistook his shock with natural awe. Elliott looked back at her.

"No . . . I mean yes, it is beautiful. But that's not it. This is the lake," he said emphatically, his normal expression returning.

"This is Lake Sandeen," Adam chimed in helpfully.

"No," Elliott shot Adam a scathing look. "This is the lake from my dream, Story. The one I had last night, the that's-why-I-showed-up-on-your-doorstep-this-morning lake."

"You dreamt about this lake? You've never even been here before."

"Yeah, that's the point, isn't it? I see things before they happen. I dream of places I've never been before."

Adam was following their conversation but obviously not understanding anything as he looked back and forth between the two of them.

"So," Adam finally interjected, looking confused. "You had a dream. About this lake. A lake you've never been to before. And you decided you just had to see Story? Why does all of this sound like crazy talk?"

Reaching over and patting Adam's hand, Story smiled reassuringly. "Elliott is psychic," she explained.

"Huh?" He glanced at Elliott.

"I had a vision that she was drowning in this lake."

"A vision?" Adam didn't seem to be wrapping his head around the concept, but Elliott ignored him, looking back at Story as his eyes widened like he had just remembered something.

"You were calling a name."

"A name? When?"

"When you were drowning. It sounded like Tess or maybe—"

"Jess!" Story clapped her hands.

"Yeah! Jess was probably it. Who's Jess?" Elliott finished off his water and crunched the bottle.

Adam turned and looked at Story. "I remember that you used to talk about a girl named Jess when we were young. Whatever happened to her?"

Looking down at her hands, she twisted her fingers, cracking her joints as she anxiously avoided eye contact with the guys. "I don't know. But I feel like she needs my help. I've been having these nightmares." Story felt ready. She was going to tell them everything, and when she got home, she would tell her mother.

"Tell us." Adam held her gaze with his own steady gray one and nodded for her to go on.

Story started to describe her latest dream, but the sound of splashing and yelling made the three turn to see what was going on. Shielding her eyes with her hand, Story squinted into the afternoon sun and cursed herself for forgetting her sunglasses. Despite the glare, she could see that a child was struggling in the middle of the lake, his cries already muted as his head bobbed up and under the surface while he tried to swim. There was a nearby dock he must have been trying to swim out to.

"He's drowning!" A solid swimmer, Story was in the water and moving in deep strokes toward the child before either of the boys could react.

"Story! She's in the lake!" A certain amount of terror was creeping into Elliott's voice, but Adam had already shed his shirt and was cutting across the water toward Story with strong, powerful strokes.

"Get out of the lake!" Elliott yelled after them irrationally, gnawing and destroying his perfect nails.

As Story got closer, she could see the boy's head going under the surface a little longer each time he flailed. It was Tommy, their neighbor Lois's ten-year-old son. Kicking harder, she dove under the water as she saw his head disappear again.

While she plunged deeper and deeper to grab the small figure that was sinking through the depths of the murky lake water, she felt something like a hand brush her leg, but she had no time to look back. Grabbing Tommy underneath his arms, she kicked upwards and broke through the water with the nearly unconscious boy clasped in her arms. Tilting him on his back, she started to kick toward the embankment. Adam intercepted them halfway and took a now coughing Tommy from her, swimming more swiftly to the edge and toward Elliott, who was jumping up and down and frantically waving his arms.

Story followed them, but slowed to catch her breath after her race to save the boy. He seemed to be recovering well enough.

The water felt like heaven against her skin, and she stayed calf-deep as Adam hauled the boy and himself out of the water. Setting Tommy down, Elliott crouched and patted the boy's back. Coughing one more time, he finally nodded.

"I'm okay," he told them in a raspy voice. Glancing back between Story and Adam, he cast his brown, puppy-dog-shaped eyes down. "Thanks."

Story smiled. "No problem."

Adam flexed his muscles. "All in a day's work."

Snorting, Story leaned down and splashed him with water.

"Oh, please don't get my already-soaking muscles more wet," he joked and splashed her back. They both looked at Elliott, who had wrapped a towel around the boy and was handing him a sandwich and a bottle of water. Turning away from Tommy, Elliott stood upright and noticed the two of them staring at him with goofy grins.

"What—Don't you dare!" He started to jump back but it was too late. Adam was already in mid-leap and Story had managed to grab Elliott's arm and was helping to drag him into the water.

He put up a fight, but by the time they pulled him into the lake mid-waist, he had given up and was laughing and splashing back.

They were all in the midst of their afternoon water revelry when Story, treading water fairly far from shore, was pulled beneath the lake. Choking out a scream, she clawed her way to the surface and came up sputtering and coughing, fear strangling her chest. She'd felt something grab her, she was sure of it. Gasping, she looked wildly down into the dark waters and felt dread replace the humor and fun that had only moments ago filled the afternoon. Seeing a pale white object circle underneath her, she bit back a scream of terror. Something was in the lake with them.

Starting to swim toward the boys, she waved them on. "Get out of the water," she called as calmly as she could, as flashbacks of nightmares and tidbits of memories flickered behind her mind's eye. Of course, they stayed where they were until she reached them.

"What is it?" Adam floated on his back leisurely, obviously not feeling her sense of panic.

"Come on," Story swam past them, hearing the anxious edge in her voice but not wanting to alarm them. "Let's get out of the water."

But she only got so far when she suddenly stopped. Any breeze that existed moments before had evaporated like water, any ripple on the lake had stilled. She had never seen a body of water so calm. *The calm before the storm?* She wasn't cold, but goose bumps prickled over her wet skin.

The rustle of leaves mingling and dancing in summer had stopped, and the small boy sitting on the bank watched with wide eyes as daylight dimmed and blue skies turned black. There were no stars, no moon—only the silvery radiance of the water they tread gave off any illumination. It was so still and so dark, it was if the universe was waiting. For what, she didn't know.

"Go!" Adam yelled. An overwhelming sense of danger got them swimming as if there were monsters in the water—as if their lives depended on it.

Adrenaline surged through her, and she darted through the water as if a shark was slicing the wake behind her. But it wasn't fast enough. She was behind the boys, so neither saw when she felt the slickness of a claw or hand grab her ankle and pull her under, without time for a scream or a word.

Adam, suddenly aware that he couldn't hear her, wasted no time and turned back, diving beneath the surface. He resurfaced once and locked eyes with Elliott.

"Get out of here, man." That was the last thing he said before he too slipped beneath the surface, without so much as a splash or whisper.

"Adam," Elliott whispered. "Story?" He started to turn back, his eyes locked on the boy who stood near the edge of the water, whose shadow in the darkness shivered and stared in shock as Elliott came closer. The boy bravely held out his hand to help him. But Elliott never reached him. A few mere steps from where he could have put his feet down and walked to safety, he met the boy's eyes. "Go home, Tommy, tell Story's mother!" Then he was gone, without even a ripple in the deep waters to give a clue as to where he had vanished.

Tommy stood there for what seemed like hours. He couldn't move, he didn't know if he could breathe. But when sound and light returned to the world, the thundering of his heart and the raspy gasps of his panting brought him back to earth. Once again the lake rippled with life, fluffy white clouds drew countless pictures in the sky, and the trees whispered back and forth to one another. But Tommy didn't return to normal. Wiping tears, he turned and began to run toward home—toward Story's mother.

CHAPTER EIGHT

Specter, New York, Real World

EDIE KEPT IT TOGETHER.

She kept it together when she called the police and fire department and told them calmly that her daughter and two friends had been swimming when they were dragged under the surface. The small town filled with sirens moments later as the emergency crews headed to the lake.

She kept it together as she got into her car and drove with trembling hands down to the water. By the time she got there, crews were in the lake, and divers had gone under the surface. It was only about thirty feet deep and several miles long. But she knew still waters ran deep, as the saying went.

Wrapping her arms around herself, she shivered. The last few days had been in the nineties, and the UV Index had been at about a six, but Edie was cold from the inside out. "Not again," she whispered. She was staring so intently at the water that she jumped when she felt a hand on her arm. Turning, she smiled wanly, looking up into kind, familiar hazel eyes.

"How you holding up?" His voice was heavy with compassion. It was Sergeant Miller. But she knew him as just Derrick, the boy she and Peter had shared many adventures with and who had turned out to be a man with a quiet strength and stillness.

Edie turned to him and blinked back the flood that threatened to escape. It was only a matter of time before she started crying and couldn't stop. "I can't go through this again. If they aren't found, I think I'll go crazy, Derrick," she choked out.

The sergeant put an arm around Edie, and she took comfort in the knowledge that he was one of the only people in the world who could possibly understand.

"How many times did they . . . " Derrick started to ask.

"Two times," Edie cut him off. She had known what he was going to ask before he spoke. "And they found nothing."

"It doesn't make any sense," Derrick said. He should have been barking orders to the officers. The local reporter was already there as well, hanging back a few feet away from where he and Edie stood. He knew at any moment the reporter was going to get up the nerve to come ask questions. But Derrick didn't care about any of those things right now. The divers were diving, and the emergency crews were searching the trees around the lake. They were taking care of it, and right now he was taking care of Edie.

"I still think he's alive out there somewhere," he said. "I can't explain it, but I have a feeling. Don't tell anyone I said this since I'll lose credibility—but really, how does someone disappear in a lake this size and leave no trace of themselves behind?"

"I've asked myself that a million times," Edie whispered, praying that as the divers went down, they would find some scrap of evidence that her daughter had once existed.

"They're not going to find anything in there, Derrick." She looked at him with sudden conviction. "You know as well as I do that this lake steals lives." She tried really hard to keep it together. But first Peter and now Story? Worry penetrated her soul. Derrick held her on the bank of the lake as she sobbed. When they told him they hadn't found anything, he merely nodded.

Later, after Derrick had left Edie in the capable hands of his wife, Emily—who had driven down after hearing along the grapevine what had happened—the reporter approached him.

Sighing, he turned toward her. "Make it quick," he barked.

He was usually pretty approachable; he knew reporters were just doing their job. But this hit a little close to home. Plus, a storm was brewing—he could see it in the dark swirl of the clouds. A storm had hit pretty hard when Peter disappeared, he remembered.

"What are the names of the three who disappeared?" she asked. Listing them, he gazed out at the lake as she furiously scribbled down their names and ages.

"Are you aware that twenty years ago a young man was also suspected of drowning in this lake and was never found?" she asked.

He had been waiting for this question. "Yep, I am well aware. He would have been Story Sparks's uncle." *And my best friend,* he thought as Peter's familiar laughter, laced with crazy, seemed to mock him from the depths of the lake. He whispered a silent plea at Peter to watch over her.

CHAPTER NINE

Lake Sandeen, The In-Between

STORY BLINKED HER EYES, cringing from the dull throbbing in her head. Her whole body felt as if she had run a triathlon, climbed a mountain, and taken up spinning—all in the same day. Not that she had done any of those things, but she suspected the muscle aches would be similar. She licked dry, sticky lips, rolled over on her back while stifling a moan, and slowly opened her eyes.

Blinking away the bleary fog from her vision revealed a ceiling that gleamed milky white. *What a pretty ceiling . . .* .She started to feel sleepy again. Maybe she'd just go back to sleep and wake up in a few days when her muscles liked her again.

"It's moonstone. It aids sleep."

Jerking upright in bed, she choked back nausea as the room spun around her. Pain lanced through her head while reason flooded back into her thoughts. Where the hell was she? It wasn't her room; it didn't even look like it was from this century. In fact, it looked like the kind of bedroom chamber from a castle you would see in a movie, with a huge canopy bed draped in billowing satin curtains. The room was enormous. The only difference from a castle, she guessed, was that everything seemed to be made out of stone or crystals. Even the large armoire looked like it had been cut from a giant chunk of lapis lazuli.

She shook her head in confusion and clasped her head in her hands, trying to ease the throbbing headache.

"Here, drink this. It will make you feel much better, I assure you." The woman's voice rang with an eerie cadence, like the haunting sound of chimes before a storm. It was strangely soothing.

Momentarily having forgotten the voice that had caused her to sit up in the first place, Story glanced to where a small figure sat quietly in a dark corner, her features shrouded by the shadows.

"How rude of me, I forgot to introduce myself," she spoke, but the lack of emotion in her voice made it clear she didn't care whether she'd been rude or not. The woman rose from her chair and stepped into the flickering light that illuminated her gaunt profile. "I'm Sandeen." She motioned to a silver goblet held in her bone-white hands.

Story gasped, looking into her lightless black eyes and true ivory complexion. Sandeen's cheekbones seemed too angular, and her dark eyes seemed to swallow up half her face. Yet there was something haunting about her that made her almost lovely. Story stared at her without so much as blinking, while the feeling that she had met her somewhere before overwhelmed her.

"Who are you?" Story finally responded to the weirdness, hearing her own thinly veiled accusation. "Why am I here? Where is here? Where is Elliott . . . Adam?"

Clucking her tongue in a way that was more seductive than chastising, Sandeen held out the glass. "Drink first, then we will talk." Her way of speaking, although precise, did nothing to mute the elemental lilt of her voice.

Story eyed the glass suspiciously and then glanced at the woman once more. "I guess I'm not in Kansas anymore," she muttered.

"No, Dorothy, you are not. And for the record, she's not as sweet and innocent as your fairy tale makes her out to be, so maybe you could refrain from quoting her as if she's some great heroine," Sandeen all but huffed, annoyance flashing across her pale features. She offered Story the glass once more, her satin dress clinging to her tall, slender figure and billowing around her feet like one of those sexy witch costumes they sell around Halloween.

"It's just a movie . . . " Story still didn't take the glass, convinced it was poison or something else equally horrible.

"Oh for The Green's sake, it's a remedy for your headache. If I was going to harm you, I could have done that easily enough while you were unconscious."

She made a valid point. Story relented, reaching out and taking the glass from her hands. She sniffed the liquid, but it just smelled kind of earthy, like moss. Peering over the rim down into the glass was fruitless, as it just looked black. "Oh why not, this can't get any stranger." Shrugging her shoulders, she took a sip, fully expecting to hate it. Surprisingly, the liquid tasted like it smelled—like the earth after rain, or fresh cut grass, but sweet. It wasn't bad, just different. Like a shot of wheatgrass. Almost instantly, the throbbing in her head started to subside, while the burning in her limbs was reduced to a dull ache. Setting the glass down, she pulled the blanket around her and stared openly at the woman.

"Okay, I drank—what's up? Where the hell am I? Where are my friends? And what's going on?"

The dark-featured woman inclined her head toward the sitting area. "Ah yes, always the forward one aren't we? First, why don't you go sit over there, and we can relax. Your friends will join us shortly."

Although Story felt like protesting and stomping her feet until she got some answers, she oddly didn't feel threatened, so she humored the witchy woman. She slid down from the bed, her feet touching down on a floor that looked as if it had been carved out of onyx. She expected it to be cold against her bare feet, but it was surprisingly warm as if heated from below.

She padded toward the fireplace, welcoming the warmth. At the same time, she noted with a mild frown that she seemed to be wearing a long black nightgown that touched the floor. Although she knew she should care more about her current predicament, she was more worried about who had changed her clothes. It better have been a woman, that was for sure.

She sat down, stretching her toes out so the fire's flames could cast their warmth. After talking to someone outside the door, the woman returned and sat down in a chair near Story.

"They will be here momentarily." Inclining her head, the pale woman with the black holes for eyes smiled. It could have been ghastly, but instead it was lovely, in a truly ghastly sort of way. She actually had no whites in her eyes, Story noted for the first time. *Buttons for eyes—like in the movie Coraline.*

"I'm Sandeen."

"Yes, you mentioned that before. What did you do, name yourself after the lake?"

Sandeen chuckled, her first real show of emotion. "No, my love, the lake was named after me."

Story laughed, but there was no humor behind it. She believed her. Story was about to assault her with a throng of questions, but she was distracted when a short man appeared carrying a tray with food and drink. She couldn't make out one scent that was discernible, but it carried that general hot food smell. Her stomach growled rather loudly, and she rubbed it, furtively glancing at Sandeen to see if she had heard. But she was busy directing the server.

"Please," Sandeen said to the portly man who held the tray. "Serve Story here some wine and a plate and give the boys a drink as well." Nodding, the man set the tray down and began to pour. Story forgot her hunger the moment Sandeen mentioned the boys. Hearing footfalls, she turned around and jumped out of her seat at the sight of Elliott and Adam hurrying into the room. Both looked concerned until they spotted her, breaking into equally relieved smiles.

"It's about time you guys showed up!" Story laughed as they fell into a three-person hug.

"We just woke about an hour ago to find ourselves in these fabulously medieval-retro rooms. Since the doors were locked, we couldn't leave." Elliott cast a disdainfully suspicious look at Sandeen. "And then this guy came—Story, he was beautiful—and told us to chill out. I mean he literally said 'chill out.' Come to think of it, he really didn't seem to belong here. Anyway, he told us not to worry and that we would be seeing you soon. Isn't that right, Adam?"

While Elliott talked, Story noticed Adam staring off into space, a furrowed look to his usually easygoing expression. "Yeah," he nodded his assent. Out of the three of them, Adam was probably the most logical, the one studying to be an environmental lawyer. Elliott was a psychic, so he didn't have a hard time wrapping his head around inexplicable things. He also had a love for the fantastical and unknown, always trying to convince Story to take a trip to Stonehenge, or digging into his books on the sly at night, dressed down from his stylish duds to his sweats. Secretly, he'd taught himself to speak a little bit of the Elvish language created by Tolkien, and sometimes he even spoke to her in it, but only when it was just the two of them. Elliott would be the most open to believing in the impossible. Even more so than Story, although she had grown up missing parts of her memory and often wondering why her life was a constant mystery of half-remembered paintings and strange, realistic nightmares. Being here, wherever here was, would have to be the hardest on Adam.

"The question that I think needs to be answered now is, where are we?" Story said. Like synchronized swimmers, the three pivoted and faced Sandeen. She graciously inclined her head and gestured to the three chairs circling a small table set with bowls of food.

Generally, both her boys were pretty savvy, but Story noticed right away how taken they were with Sandeen. However, they were no less suspicious, which was evident when Elliott looked down at his food and declared it inedible, even though he couldn't take his eyes off the steaming contents.

"Why is that?" Sandeen asked, something of a smile curving her thin lips.

"I'm not stupid. We got sucked into some fairy circle, and now if we eat your food, we'll be stuck here forever. I've read the stories." He managed to glare at her, despite the fact that Story knew he must be loving their strange little predicament.

His obstinacy should have been hilarious, but none of them laughed. Except Sandeen, whose chuckle was almost as disturbing as her smile.

"My dears, I assure you that you have not been sucked into a fairy circle and that the food is perfectly edible. I have no intentions of keeping you here forever, as several very important people would be quite upset with me. I also would not disservice Story so. Besides, I should think you would have guessed where you are now." It was the most that Story had heard her talk up to this point, and she wanted to hear more. But what did she mean about disservicing her?

Before she could question their hostess, Adam narrowed his eyes suspiciously at her. "Where are we then? We don't even know your name." He spoke through a mouthful of food. Obviously, he had gotten over his fear of the food. Elliott was apparently convinced, as well, and was sipping his wine and eyeing the stew with interest.

"Her name is Sandeen," Story said, blowing on a spoonful of her own stew, which tasted absolutely incredible even though she was sure she was eating seaweed.

Adam choked and started coughing. Finally, after a few minutes, he swallowed a draught of wine and stared at Sandeen. "You were named after the lake?"

Sighing, she shook her head. "What a predictable reaction. As I explained to Story earlier, the lake was named after me. None of you are as quick on the uptake as I had hoped."

"That's just not possible. This lake has been here for thousands of years and has been called Sandeen in even the earliest historical accounts. Perhaps it's a family name?" His tone took on an even and reasonable ring as if he was trying not to offend the crazy person.

"Really, I don't know why you had to bring these two with you, Story. They are truly quite dense." Sandeen said Story's name with such familiarity that her indignant retort about not bashing her friends got stuck on her tongue. A memory tickled the edges of her consciousness, but she couldn't quite grasp it. Where were they? Was she supposed to have guessed already? She lifted her hand to her neck where her necklace always rested, but then she remembered it had fallen off. He had told her never to take it off, she randomly thought.

"I apologize Story. It was against Faulks's wishes that you return, but his desires matter little in the greater scheme of things. He didn't understand the totality of your destiny."

Sandeen's matter-of-fact manner grated on Story's nerves. She stood up quickly, her tray shattering against the ground. "Don't you dare talk about him that way." Her voice was shaking and her fists were clenched. "You don't know anything about what he wished."

Looking appalled, Elliott set down his wine and exchanged a glance with Adam. The silence that followed her outburst settled her rage almost as quickly as it had come, but resulted in utter confusion.

"Story," Elliott asked quietly. "Who is Faulks?"

Still shaking, she glanced over at Sandeen, whose brows were arched in question, her eerie gaze focused intently on Story.

"Yes, Story, who is Faulks?"

Pushing back tears, Story slowly felt her calm restore itself. "I don't know," she whispered. "His name makes me want to cry, and yet I can't recall . . . "

A rattled Adam looked at Sandeen hard. "Tell us where we are and why we're here. This is beginning to feel like an episode of *Tales from the Crypt*."

"Oh please." Elliott rolled his eyes. "*Tales from the Crypt* is horror, this is fantasy. Get your genres right."

"Oh, go jump in a lake," Adam responded, his voice dropping as if he knew how lame he sounded.

But Story laughed. Two sets of eyes peered at her with concern, and she supposed they were afraid she might be cracking up. The other, darker pair looked on with a detached curiosity.

"The lake." Story met their gazes.

"I'm sorry, I don't follow." Adam seemed frustrated.

"We're in the lake. Don't you remember? We were sucked under, and we woke up here, in what appears to be a strange time and place, and to a woman who fashions herself Sandeen—the very name of the lake we thought we were drowning in." Story stopped, panting softly and trying to piece together what it all meant. Silence once more followed her revelation.

"Oh my god, you're like the Lady of the Lake," Elliott broke the quiet.

Sandeen smiled thinly, but this time with a trace of humor. "Close. She is a distant cousin who copied, you might call it, my gig—I'm the original. She just got famous because of the whole King Arthur thing." Sandeen rolled her dark eyes, looking genuinely annoyed. For an instant, she appeared to be the waif-life teenage girl she resembled. It was the most human moment she'd had since Story met her.

"Okay, so fine, say you're Sandeen, the 'Lady of the Lake.'" Adam remained unconvinced, making bunny ears with his fingers and taking on a technical, superior tone he often got when he and Story were having a conversation and he was just humoring her. It always irritated her.

"So then what does that make you? A Fairy? A Dark Queen? I mean come on," he laughed, spreading his hands and gesturing to the three of them "This is ridiculous. And for that matter, what could you possibly want with us . . . with Story?"

"What it makes me is a goddess. I am Daughter of The Green and The Will. I am Keeper of the Gates, Lover of the Lost Heroes. I have existed longer than your mortal mind could even comprehend." She smiled, but there was no humor behind it, and she rose from her seat, her gown swirling and settling around her like silken night.

"You boys will play your parts I suppose, but it is Story that is the root, the seed of this tale . . . " She turned toward Story, her thin lips parted and her expression almost loving. "It hasn't been so long since I saw you last. You were smaller—and more innocent, but also wiser in your own little way. Back then you knew who you were. No one informed me that you wouldn't have the slightest recollection of who you really are." She sighed with a shake of her head. "If only Ninian were here."

Story gaped at her, a glass of wine clenched tightly in one hand, not a drop spilled, not a sip tasted. Slowly setting it down lest it go crashing to the ground, she stared at Sandeen and willed her to say more. The name Ninian raced through her mind like something she knew. It was familiar and made her feel a wave of warmth and gratitude while also making her feel silently mutinous.

"She was your teacher, Story," Sandeen explained. "I bet she would be quite upset to learn you have forgotten everything she ever taught you. I was rather unprepared myself." For the first time, Sandeen appeared to have lost her cool exterior. Her bone-white cheeks actually seemed to be flushed with emotion.

"Yes!" Story said with more feeling than she meant. "A teacher feels about right." That would explain the mild hostility she was feeling.

Sandeen studied her closely, a flame of hope glittering in her alien black eyes—at least that's what Story told herself. But any expression the self-described goddess had was fleeting. "Perhaps all is not lost."

"Is everything all right in here?" A masculine voice said from the doorway. Story looked up to see a boy about her age with light brown eyes and shaggy brown hair. He was remarkably good looking if not a little pale—the result of living under a lake, no doubt. He sauntered into the room, bearing an air of confidence and mystery very few people owned. She realized he reminded her of someone, but she couldn't quite place it. The story of her life—or at least tonight.

Sandeen stiffened as he entered, glaring a warning that he obviously was choosing to ignore by directing a rather rakish grin toward her.

The pale goddess sighed. "I had honestly hoped to avoid it, but it seems I have no choice, do I?" She shot him another seething glare, one Story was certain could terrify even Freddy Krueger. But it didn't faze him. He just shook his head with a faint smile, and then turned to look at Story, who was startled by the intensity of his gaze.

"Hey Peter," Elliott piped up. "Thanks for all your help earlier, I think Adam was a little freaked out before." Adam didn't even take the time to roll his eyes at Elliott's flirting; he and Story shared an intense look of their own before turning to the room's newcomer. The questions waited to roll off Story's tongue.

"Story, meet your uncle." Sandeen rolled her eyes and crossed her arms over her chest with dramatic flourish. They all ignored her.

"My . . . uncle? But he's dead." Story couldn't believe it. There was just no way, especially since this guy looked her age. It had been more than twenty years since his disappearance.

But Story couldn't look away from him, recalling pictures her mother had in old albums. One photo she kept in a frame by her bedside—they were younger than he looked now, and laughing as if they shared a secret. That photo showed an identical, but slightly younger version of the man who stood before her now. It couldn't possibly be. But she knew it was true after all that had happened today. And hadn't her mother just told her the day before—it felt like weeks ago—that the lake stole lives? Here was proof.

"But you're like my age." It was the first thing that came out of her mouth, but she was feeling so much more. Her mother would be so happy to see him. She could eliminate all that pain that bore itself in the sadness of her eyes, and the white streaks that had started to sliver through her hair.

"This is the in-between place, the line between the worlds—no one grows old here, no one dies, not even mortals such as your uncle here," Sandeen explained.

Story felt that there were things left unsaid hanging in the air. But in the midst of her astonishment and creeping elation, she let it go. All she cared about was that her uncle was alive and seemingly well, although he had to be a prisoner, or why else would he still be here? She stood up and stepped toward him, a stranger who wasn't. She started to hold out her arms, but felt weird and let them drop. He looked down at her, his brown eyes shining with repressed emotion before enfolding her in his embrace.

"You look so much like her," he choked over his own words. Story hugged him back, wishing she could just drag him back to the real world at that moment, put a big bow on him, and present him to her mother.

It had always just been Story and Edie. And that had been great—she and her mother had been close. Well, as close as a mother and daughter could be when they were both hiding secrets. But now, here was the uncle she had never met, the one whom her mother had missed all these years . . . But she needed to know. Why the hell had he been down here all this time while her mother's grieving never ended? Story drew away, her eyes narrowing.

"Are you some kind of prisoner?"

"I assure you, he is no such thing." Sandeen sat motionless in her chair, watching the exchange with virtually no expression.

"Where have you been for the last twenty years?" The reality of him standing before her finally set in. "Do you know there's actually a grave at the cemetery with your name on it? Everyone thinks you're dead.

"What about Edie?" His voice was hushed with guilt.

Shaking her head, Story looked away for a moment to compose herself before turning back to him. "She didn't say anything to me, but I've heard her talking to Derrick before, and I know she never believed you were gone. I never saw her visit your grave. Every year on the same date, the day of your alleged death, she takes out her photos and just looks at them. She's avoided the lake for as long as I can remember." She shot Sandeen what she hoped was a scathing look.

Sandeen merely winked a glittering charcoal eye and shrugged with a smirk. "I do what I can."

"Sandeen, cut it out." Peter said firmly. Reaching out, he turned Story's head back toward him with one hand on each side of her face.

"It's important that you know everything, Story. But first you must understand—Sandeen did not steal me. I came willingly. While you think this may be evidence that I abandoned my sister, you're wrong. I've been watching. My destiny was to come here. Where the next path on my journey will take me I can't be sure, but I know my path will take me back to Edie at some point. I made a promise to her that I would come back. I won't break it."

"But," Story protested, "you should go to her now. She misses you!"

"I can't. Not now," he said.

"This is why I didn't want you coming in here, Peter. I knew it would only upset her and delay what needs to be done." Sandeen looked irritated again. Story couldn't decide whether she liked her more when she was expressionless or when she actually acted annoyingly human.

"She's my niece, Sandeen. You won't keep me away from her, even while you play with Fate's strings."

"You're just so unreasonable," she countered. "I am doing what needs to be done. You, on the other hand, are interfering. Your destiny was because of her."

Story's eyes bounced between the two, a thought popping into her head. She was just about to speak when Elliott spoke instead. "You two are like together, aren't you?" The arguing lovers paused and looked at him and then at each other. Sandeen looked away and then back at Peter. The love that lit the caverns of her eerie black eyes was something to behold. Although he had been angry with her only moments before, Peter's entire expression softened as he met his love's gaze with an unquenchable yearning. Story could see these two were the real deal. With issues, of course.

Wow. So that's why he stayed so long. Her chest tightened, and an emptiness and longing made her feel hollow for a few moments as if she was missing her own true love. But that was silly; she'd never even had a real boyfriend before, let alone fallen in love. Then why did she feel so empty?

"Snagging a goddess . . . Way to go, Uncle Peter," Adam drawled with a grin. Story glanced at her friends and laughed, forgetting how desolate she'd felt only moments before. And then they were all laughing, even Sandeen, whose laugh was like the ebb and flow of the tide.

Chapter Ten

Lake Sandeen, The In-Between

STORY'S DREAMS THAT NIGHT starred the same red-haired woman from her paintings. She was tall, fierce, and terrible. Her eyes flashed like chrome lit with a vengeful mercurial fire as animals ran from her, their eyes white with terror. It was her painting come to life.

Story watched from an unseen place, wondering why this deceptively beautiful night stalker made her feel so afraid—not for herself, but for the woman. The red-haired predator came upon her quarry, a hulking black-pelted wolf. She leapt with feline grace and landed on the animal, sharp steel glinting in the moonlight before she plunged it into its neck, the wolf's fur soaking up the red that leaked from his wound. She started to gut the animal and seemed intent on the task for a few seconds. Story thought she might start puking in the bushes any moment, watching the girl slice into the canine's form. She was swallowing bile back down when she realized the redhead was staring directly at her. The girl's steel eyes widened as if she were seeing a ghost, the cold glint of her gaze losing its edge. A smile slowly curved the woman's full, sensual mouth.

"Story?" she asked, rising to her feet. Story nodded mutely and was about to step toward her, questions ready to roll from her tongue, when a loud cracking sound filled the gaps in speech, and the wind started to pick up, going from zero to fifty in mere seconds. Story grabbed onto a tree's limb for purchase. The red-haired woman was trying to reach her, but the wind, which was increasing speed every moment, was keeping her back. Story felt herself slipping, waking up. Over the din of the clap that split the sky, Story heard herself scream a name as she tried to grab the girl's hand, their fingers almost grazing for a split second before it all went black.

"Jess!"

Story's eyes popped open, the cry of her own voice echoing in her mind. "Jess," she whispered, her hands clutched at her throat as she motionlessly lay in the great big bed, surrounded by the room's eerie crystalline glow. Allowing her eyes to adjust to the dim light cast by several lanterns around the room, she did her best to register what had just happened. Innately, she knew that the girl from her dreams was Jess, but not as she remembered her. Not that she really remembered much of anything at all, but the moment those silvery eyes had met hers, it was as if a door had been unlocked, and out came the mischievous laugh of the child the red-haired predator had once been.

Story sat up slowly, trying to calm the trembling in her hands and knees. Small bits and pieces of her life seemed to be coming back to her, but not in any way that made sense. She vaguely remembered Jess, but she couldn't place her at any time in her life. Meanwhile, the dream had been more vivid than real life was at the moment, and the howling of the wind and sheets of lightning haunted her even minutes after she realized she was still in one piece. But was Jess okay? She put her head in her hands for a moment, trying to rub the weariness from her eyes. It was just a dream. A very vivid, Technicolor dream.

Running a hand through her bedhead, she tried smoothing out the flipped-up ends and gave up after a few moments, hoping she was presentable. She was pretty sure she was out of luck in the flat iron department. She had an actual real life to deal with at the moment, so she determinedly decided to let the dream go. She would forget about it in an hour—wasn't that the way dreams usually worked?

With no sunlight, she wasn't sure what time it was, but her inner alarm clock informed her it was morning. From how groggy she was feeling, Story was certain it was earlier than she liked to be up. But the sooner she got going, the sooner she could find out what was going on around there.

The onyx floor was once again amazingly warm as she touched her toes to it. She yearned to look out a window and see if they truly were beneath the water—she could barely believe it and imagined what it would be like to look out upon a watery underworld. Yes, she was doing a good job at diverting her attention away from the dream, but for some reason it was still as clear as glass in her mind's eye.

Glancing around, she noticed a mug of water and picked it up, drinking deeply and marveling at how pure it tasted and how refreshing it was. Draining the cup, she swirled the last mouthful around with her tongue and was gratified that after swallowing, all remnants of sleep seemed to have vacated her mouth. "If only I could bottle this stuff," she mused aloud.

Setting the mug down, her gaze zeroed in on a dress that was hanging invitingly on one of the cabinet's knobs. But she didn't go to the dress directly. Instead, she turned toward the main exit door. She gave the door handle a twist and was relieved to feel it give. Not locked, so that meant she wasn't confined to her room. Despite all Sandeen's hospitality and the appearance of her uncle, Story was still clueless as to why she was in this place, and even more, whether she was being held against her wishes. She supposed a locked door was nothing in light of her underwater surroundings. The thought of swimming in those waters again, despite knowing the Big Bad had been Sandeen, made her shudder.

Shedding her nightgown, she turned toward the cabinet and fingered the royal blue gown. The cool, smooth feeling of satin was almost alien to her, due to her mid-range retail upbringing. Grinning, she pulled the gown over her head and relished the feeling of it sliding over her skin, molding to her petite frame. The neckline was wide, dipping down into a sweetheart shape and hanging off of her shoulders. The sleeves were billowy, while the bodice was fitted like a corset and flared at the hips. Sidestepping in front of a mirror, she swayed back and forth, admiring herself in the beautifully crafted dress. She finalized the effect by slipping her feet into a pair of matching ballet-like slippers. She checked her image out once more—the reflection's honey-colored eyes met her own and glittered with the novelty of playing dress up.

Something was wrong though. Pausing in mid-sashay, she leaned closer and stared into her own image, frowning slightly. She watched her reflection frown back at her, but that wasn't what was bothering her. Her reflection seemed so familiar, as silly as that sounded. It was as if she was recognizing herself for the first time. But there was something different as well—like it was someone she had once known. The girl who peered back at her was herself, but not. Mirror Story's eyes held far more wisdom and sadness than she had experienced in her short lifetime.

Almost as quick as it had come, the feeling faded. Her gaze was confused, leaving her unsure whether she should be happy that she looked as lost as she felt. "I'm cracking up," she murmured and turned away from the mirror and her reflection, wondering if there was some sort of magic in the glass or if she was just going crazy. Either way, she needed to get out of this room. It was all she had seen since she had first woken up there. She cast one last glance behind her, but seeing only her present self, she decided she would try to find the boys and slipped out into the hallway.

Determined to explore before Sandeen returned, she moved forward with a mission glowing in her eyes. When she stepped out the door, she was confronted with a very different picture than what she had imagined. In her mind she had envisioned the sweeping hallways of a castle, just like in the movies, with the difference being they were actually underwater or in some alternate reality. Strangely enough, none of those concepts were hard for her to wrap her head around.

Instead of the grandiose pictures she had conjured, the hallway was actually fairly low and constructed of rock, resembling the narrow tunnel of a cave. But that's where the ordinary stopped. The surrounding stone was as smooth as marble, except for the ornate designs that had been carved into the walls and ceilings. The walls glowed purple and blue, and she was able to see every tiny fracture and flawless seam.

"My god," she whispered. The entire tunnel had been carved from crystals. Lightly, she pressed her hands against the walls, feeling the grains pulse beneath her fingertips, while the grooves from each design spoke a language she only wished she could begin to understand. The tunnel didn't even need lamps—or possibly torches were their thing here—because the serene glow of the crystals lit her path completely with a delicate and welcoming soft light.

Continuing on, she took in the interesting designs and only stopped walking the long tunnel when she came to a door. Somehow she sensed Adam's presence within. Testing the doorknob, she peeked inside and saw he was still nestled beneath the covers, which was unusual for mister early riser, but she imagined his analytical mind would have been exhausted after their foray into the mystical. She contemplated jumping on him, but decided to let him continue sleeping. She had a feeling their adventures were just beginning.

At that thought, a sense of excitement mixed with nervous anticipation welled up in her. She sure as hell hadn't been looking for an adventure, but here it was and she couldn't help but feel the overwhelming sense that she would soon understand more. And there was also a feeling of homecoming. She wasn't sure where it came from because of course Edie was her home. But it was there—a certainty that she was about to embark on a journey that would tell her who she truly was. Her sense of self had been lacking for as long as she could recall, and she desperately needed answers about her half remembrances and the strange characters popping up in her life.

Softly closing Adam's door so as not to wake him, she turned and saw Elliott slipping out into the hallway, which was also out of character. But then again, she had no idea what time it was. It could be ten o'clock in the morning for all she knew. Which would actually still be too early for Elliott, but there was a first for everything.

She felt a half smile curve up her lips as he noticed her as well. He too had been left clothing to wear: black satin pants, a white shirt that buttoned up into a V-neck, and a jacket that looked like black velvet. "My, my, don't you look handsome," she laughed, feeling like some sort of princess for a moment in her fancy clothes.

"And you look marvelous." He spread out his hands and gave a courtly bow while imitating a British accent. "Actually, I feel like Lestat."

Story laughed, taking his arm. The two began to stroll down the hallway towards what looked like an intersection of tunnels.

"And where were you off to this morning?" Elliott asked, his eyes flitting about as he too admired the workmanship of the tunnel.

"I just thought I would explore a little bit before Sandeen returned and decided to confuse me some more. When I'm not busy wondering what the hell is going on and trying to figure out why I keep feeling an intense déjà vu, this experience is kind of fun. I mean, it's like we stepped into a storybook or something, you know?"

Elliott's serious nod did nothing to hide the excited gleam that lit his dark eyes. "It's been totally terramazing." Story grinned at Elliott's silly quirk. He had a way of putting two words together when he was talking fast so that he could get the sentence out faster. She knew this one meant both terrifying and amazing.

"All the same, I feel like we're supposed to be moving on pretty quickly," he added. "If I could imagine what purgatory feels like, I would say this is it."

Before Story could take him too seriously, he started talking fast again. "Canyoubelievethat Sandeenislikeagoddess? When I try to wrap my head around it, I just can't. And your uncle is so gorgeous!"

"Ew, he's my uncle. Let's leave his well-muscled anatomy out of this conversation, okay?" He barely heard her, rambling on until Story pulled his arm, stopping him as they neared the intersection of corridors.

"Well, which way?" she asked. Straight was much of the same. To the left, Story noted the stones changed from purple and blue to a pale pink light that was warming and welcoming. Two large doors encrusted in a clear crystal that must be quartz could be seen only a few feet down. Guessing the doors led to Sandeen, she turned to the right, which glowed a vibrant green. Feeling curious, Story tugged on Elliott's arm and steered him down the hallway until they stepped out into a large cavern.

What they found was a verdant land of loveliness. Fresh flowers and an earthy scent assaulted her nose while she noted the lush plant life that grew with abundance among the uncut crystals that made up the interior walls. A sense of peace stole over her at the melodic rush of the water as small waterfalls splashed into bubbling crystal-clear pools. Tall staircases built into the walls led to different levels and balconies where diminutive women gathered, laughing and talking, or were busy at work. Men of modest stature also were busy lugging boxes of crystals or chatting up the women.

Story was so engrossed with her surroundings and its inhabitants that she didn't realize the ground beneath her had grown soft until she looked down and saw she was walking on beds of plush moss that were the envy of any grassy knoll. The sides of the central cavern broke off into tunnels that resembled alleyways and streets.

"My God, it's like an underwater village," she whispered. Elliott's only response was to nod. His alert gaze was taking it all in, his chest so still it was if he thought that breathing would break the magic.

A small woman scurried by them, clutching a child's hand. Although really, they were all the size of children.

With unspoken agreement, they turned down a side street called Fisher's Market.

"I think you need to adjust your vernacular," Elliott offered, interrupting their joint silence.

"What?" Story barely looked at him, taking in the shops, pubs, and street vendors selling goods.

"You keep saying 'my God' when everyone else seems to say 'Oh The Green,' or something like that."

Story glanced at him for a moment. "The Green . . . that sounds . . . " She was going to say familiar, a word she found she kept repeating, but was cut off when a street vendor cried out to them as they passed.

"Pure cadence stones from Maya's Valley. Very rare."

She looked at the woman who was holding up what seemed like circular balls of glass. She couldn't have been taller than four feet, and she had the delicate bone structure of a ten-year-old. Her features, however, were Elven-like, sharp and dainty, while her white-blond hair curled past her tiny waist. She was quite pretty, in a spritely, pushy way, as she continued to dangle an array of the glass beads in front of Story.

Story shook her head, "I'm sorry, I have no money I'm afraid." She started to move on, but the little woman called again.

"What about a Thumbelina Rose? This one is quite tired of living beneath the water and, despite our greenery, would much prefer the surface if you're going there. I presume you are since you must be that girl everyone is whispering about," she continued.

As the girl babbled, Story realized now that this child-like elf was probably about as old as she was. Holding her hand up to slow the girl down, she smiled. "I'm sorry, but what did you say was for sale?"

Smiling knowingly, the girl held up a flowerpot containing the largest red rose Story had ever seen. It had to have been as big as a man's fist if not larger.

"Wow." She wanted the flower. She didn't know why, but it felt like it belonged to her. Entranced, she turned to Elliott. "Do you have any money on you?"

Elliott gawked at her and shook his head. "Even if I did, who knows if they would take that here."

"No, I can't use your money here." The girl interrupted.

"See?" Elliott said smugly.

Tearing her gaze away from the rose, Story shrugged her shoulders dejectedly. "Sorry, we don't have any money."

The girl giggled. "I don't get paid with your Real Worlder money. I get paid with this or that. What do you have?" Her exotically slanted violet eyes peered at them up and down.

Glancing down at herself and seeing only the dress she wore, which she didn't even own, Story spread her hands. "We have nothing, I'm sorry."

The girl laughed again. "But you do. You come from above, right?"

The two nodded uncomprehendingly at the strange pixie girl.

"Well then, you could give me a memory!"

"A memory?" Elliott asked, his brow a furrow. "What do you mean?"

Story shook her head, wondering why anyone would want such a thing from her. "But what kind of memory could you possibly want from me? I have holes in my brain as it is."

"Oh, it's an easy one for you!" she said clapping her hands together.

Story arched a brow and waited for the girl to go on. The Elven woman's delight was a little nerve-wracking.

"All I need is a little bit of sunlight."

Story and Elliott glanced around, and then both looked back at the girl.

"Ummmm, yeah, not seeing any sunlight," Elliott said.

"No, sillies!" she said again with excitement. "A memory of sunlight!"

Story let out a breath, relieved. "That's all?" She had been worried the girl would take an important memory—not that she even knew what sharing memories entailed.

The girl tossed her whitish hair and smiled hopefully. "By the way, my name is Lark." She held out a tiny hand for Story to shake. "And you're Story," Lark said, dimpling at Story before turning to Elliott. "But I don't know your name. Are you sure he's a part of the story? I was sure there was something about two brave champions, one a tracker and the other a seer, but—"

"The seer? I'm the seer, I must be," Elliott interrupted, looking concerned that he wasn't important enough to be a part of whatever story she was talking about.

But Story didn't care about any of that. She was more interested in the story that wasn't her. "What story, Lark?

"Well, you must know it. You are her, right? Story?"

Nodding evenly, Story remained silent.

"Well, I actually don't. I . . . " Nervously shaking her head as if that would change the conversation, Lark smiled stiffly. "So would you like your Thumbelina Rose?"

No, she didn't want the damn flower, she wanted to know what the girl was talking about. But when the flower caught her eye again, she felt a familiar pang and was reminded of her childhood—what she could remember of it, anyway.

"Yes," she answered resolutely. "How do we go about this? Will it hurt?" The thought suddenly popped into her head, and she imagined a drill being used to extract the memory.

Shaking her delicate head, Lark smiled sweetly. "No, of course not." She crawled out from beneath the table so that she was standing next to Story and Elliott.

Lark was so small that Story felt like a giant even though she wasn't tall. "Just bend down so that your forehead touches against mine, where our third eyes can meet," Lark commanded.

Giving Elliott a shrug, Story bent down and moved her forehead until it touched Lark's. She closed her eyes, but opened them again when Lark brushed a strand of Story's hair back from her face. "Keep your eyes open so that we can connect," she whispered.

Awkwardly, Story stared back into Lark's exotic pale purple eyes. They looked even more enormous up close, consuming her vision until it was all she saw. She was only in position for a few moments when she started to feel the nagging pain from bending over uncomfortably.

"Think of a day filled with sunlight for me," Lark said impatiently. Almost immediately memories zoomed through Story's mind before she could fully pull them to the surface—playing outside with Adam, her mother swinging her by her arms at the park, sitting by Sandeen's Lake. The memories sped by in a dizzy rewind of bright colors, and then suddenly her memory paused and her world was lit by the sun.

She was lying on her back in a field of flowers. It was an idyllic scene—the sun warmed her skin and when she held up her arms, they were tan and pudgy with the first spring of youth. A sense of purpose overwhelmed her as she recounted all that she had learned that day.

Tall grass swayed around her, and the heat of the earth cradled her. She closed her eyes and felt the breeze play with her hair, sending it to dance across her face and tickle her nose. She reached a chubby, dimpled hand to scratch her nose, and heard Papa and Ninian in the gardens murmuring together.

They actually seemed to be arguing. "She needs to be trained." Ninian's voice was fierce and wafted toward her, making her frown. She didn't like it when they argued, and they had been doing that more and more as of late. She knew it was about her, and that made it worse.

"She's only a small lass, it's too early. She's just a child." Papa answered gruffly back.

"She's a child with a destiny. You've always known that." Ninian was softer now, kindness sweeping back into her voice, making Story feel better.

"I don't know nothing." He stomped away until he was a looming shadow above Story.

"Story! I didn't know you were out here." His voice was chastising, but it was coated in adoration.

She grinned and held up her arms. "Papa, what's a destiny?"

He frowned for a moment before winking a twinkling eye and wrapping her in his strong embrace. "Nothing you have to worry about right now my little lass. Nothing right now." Story wasn't listening anymore anyway, she was too busy cuddled in his arms, stroking his coarse red beard between her fingers and feeling the comfort and security of her papa's arms.

When Story opened her eyes again, she was on the ground being supported by Elliott while a concerned Lark fretted above.

"Story, are you alright?" Elliott said in a voice that was so calm it felt forced. Shaking her head to clear it, she brushed Elliott off and rose to her feet, swaying slightly before the euphoria and confusion of her memory all but slid away.

"What was that?" Story stared at Lark. "Who was that man? Where was I? Did you plant a memory in me?"

Shaking her head, Lark's large pale eyes filled with tears. "Oh no, Story! I don't know what you're speaking of, the memory you shared with me was so lovely," she said, her eyes taking on a dreamy quality and her lips smiling with a happy secret. "The memory I saw was of you and your mother. You were at the beach and the sun beat down, and it was hot and dry." She sighed happily.

"What's the big deal with the sun here?" Story asked, still recovering and using her frustration to mask her fear. But that wasn't the question, or even questions, that were really running through her mind. Just why was she here? And did she even really know herself? And finally, had she known her father?

"I'm what is called an Asrai," said Lark with misery. "Our natural habitat is beneath the water—it is where we are born and where we live our lives. When exposed to the sunlight, we turn into water until we find darkness once again," she finished with a sigh.

"So if that's all you're used to, why do you want to see the sun so much?" Elliott asked, while Story barely listened, trying to catch the fleeting memory that had mostly slipped away at her waking.

"I see it refract through the water, and some days it reaches almost to the bottom. When I can, I bask in its light. I was never meant to be such a Fae. I believe The Green made a mistake when she made me one," Lark said.

"Oh dear, I know I shouldn't say such things against The Green," she continued, placing a delicate hand against her rosebud lips. "But I do yearn so for the sun."

Elliott and Story gaped at her, the memory episode all but forgotten. Now all Story wanted to know was who this mysterious lady was everyone kept talking about.

"Who is The Green?" Elliott asked before she could formulate the words.

Now it was Lark's turn to gape. "Who is The Green? How can you not know of The Green?"

Story was about to try to dig information out of the spritely Fae, but a robust little man approached them. He was hairier than any man she had ever seen, but he smelled nice—like sea salt and the beach.

"Good day, Gimlet," nodded Lark.

"Miss Lark," the man responded back in a gravelly voice that held an air of authority. Turning to Story, Gimlet bowed his head as if in reverence. "Lady Sandeen requests your presence in her chambers. Your friends may come as well." He turned on his heel, obviously expecting them to follow him.

Glancing at Elliott, Story shrugged and turned to follow Gimlet with a smile and nod at Lark. They only got a few feet away when Lark stopped them with a shout.

"Wait! You forgot your Thumbelina." She ran around the counter of her shop with the flower outstretched in her hands. Story stopped and took the flower from her gratefully, again feeling a strange attraction to the rose.

"She'll be so happy to be on the surface and, of course, with you," said Lark, a little breathlessly.

Story laughed. "It's just a flower." When the pot started to vibrate in her hands, she thought it was her imagination at first. But then it stopped as suddenly as it started, and she could feel her arms become still again. It was almost as if the rose had been angry.

Lark shook her head with a smile. "She's actually considered royalty among Thumbelina Roses, so you may want to watch your tongue. She's a feisty one." She dimpled again and before Story could question her, gave her a little shove. "Gimlet will be cross if he finds you're keeping Sandeen waiting."

"Well, thank you." Story nodded at the rose and smiled at Lark, who gave her a wistful smile in return.

"Wait, before you go . . . If there is ever a time that I can be of aid, go to a body of water and call of my brethren, the Kelpie and the Asrai. Tell them my name and they will call me or help you themselves. We're a fickle race, but we are good. The gift of sunlight you gave me will keep me warm for a good long while. You grace this world, Story."

Story gazed at Lark a moment before smiling and placing a quick kiss on the small woman's cheek. "As do you," she murmured before turning and joining Elliott and Gimlet, her rose clasped against her chest.

Gimlet led them back down the halls of crystal to the throne room doors, the walls now the soft pink of rose quartz.

Gimlet pushed one of the great crystal-covered doors open for them and stiffly waved them inside. Right away, Story noticed that Adam was already present and wearing clothing similar to Elliott's, except instead of black, he wore brown, bringing out the color of his auburn hair. The room seemed to be made completely from quartz, and it shone from within, casting an almost divine glow around the chamber.

Sandeen rose, her gaunt figure resplendent in folds of black satin, the sleeves of the dress hanging off her bony white shoulders. Behind her stood Story's uncle, whose handsome face looked grim, his dancing brown eyes dulled with worry. Story wondered if she should be worried as well, but again she felt a sense of rightness—that she was where she belonged. Perhaps she could finally put together the pieces of her life.

She wanted to know all the mysteries behind this underwater world and the fairytale she apparently had fallen into. As much as she loved her mother, Story had been all too aware that something was missing in her life. Even when there was laughter, she sometimes felt empty, as if a piece of her heart had been missing all this time.

Sandeen beckoned them with a short, simple wave. Not waiting for them to comply, she turned and sauntered through a doorway, Peter following her with Adam and Elliott not far behind. Story stopped for a moment and breathed in the rose she kept clasped against her, feeling her heart flutter expectantly.

Sandeen's chamber looked much like the others, only it was bigger. Behind one clear crystalline wall, fish—and, well, creatures was probably the right word—swam in the deep. Story guessed that this was not the bottom of her lake at home. Sandeen had said that it was some sort of magical in-between, and here was proof.

Elliott gasped as a creature that resembled a male mermaid swam up to the wall and peered into the room. He smiled licentiously and winked at the befuddled Elliott. Rolling her eyes, Sandeen pulled a string and a heavy drape fell down, shielding them from the eyes of the underwater creatures.

"Unfortunately, the Mer people are what you might call 'voyeuristic' and have lately become such a nuisance that I am forced to close this drape almost all of the time," Sandeen said with a sigh and gestured to several sitting chairs by the fire. "Please, have a seat."

Story sat down eagerly, anticipation and nervousness warring in her chest. Elliott and Adam also took seats, while Peter chose to stand, positioning himself by Story as if he meant to protect her.

Sandeen was the last to sit, doing so with a liquid elegance that fittingly reminded Story of the smooth ripple of water.

After they sat, no one spoke for many moments. Story was staring into the fire, lost amidst hidden memories and desires. When she finally sneaked a glance at the others, she realized that her friends had both been gazing awkwardly into the flames as well. Adam had a dour expression on his face, while Elliott crossed and recrossed his legs. Story realized she had one hand clenched around the flowerpot while she furiously chewed on her thumbnail. She glanced down at her fingers with a frown and silently cursed herself. For three months she had painstakingly restrained herself from biting them, and now they were all chipped and torn. She spit out nail polish flakes that stuck to her tongue and glanced at Adam. He was usually her rock, but instead of emanating his usual quiet strength, he was furtively looking around as if trying to find the easiest escape route.

Beside her, Peter and Sandeen were locked in a silent skirmish of wills, his coffee-colored eyes almost as intense as her cavernous dark orbs. It was obvious who won the mute little battle when she gave a triumphant smile.

Story turned to her, expecting her to speak. So she was startled when it was Peter who broke the stifling silence by coming to kneel at her feet. He took her right hand between his own, his features soft and his expression compassionate. He looked like a man who was about to tell his niece some bad news—or propose, she thought. She was betting on the bad news.

"Story…" He bowed his head. When he looked up again and met her gaze, Story could see what her mother had been talking about. His eyes burned with a fire that not many would ever understand. He was a leader and radiated magnetism. Story felt as if she should be the one comforting him, as it obviously pained him to have to tell her the news.

"Story . . . I apologize. I have tried my best to save you from your fate, but my lover here tells me I cannot. And despite my feelings, I must agree—Tressla awaits."

Story squinted at him and cocked her head in question.

"Huh?" She wrinkled her nose. "What awaits?"

"Destiny . . . " Sandeen finished. "Tressla."

"What the hell is—" Adam started to forcefully exclaim, but Story succinctly cut him off.

"Tressla . . . My mom said something like that the other day. It feels so familiar." She swallowed thickly, tears choking her throat. She couldn't explain it out loud, but when Peter had said the word, images and thoughts and ideas from her childhood had overwhelmed her. Oh, how she wished she could be there, a place she could not recall.

"Edie said something about Tressla?" Peter asked.

"I mean, she said when I was a child, I spoke of it . . . " Story said finally.

"Well, you will be returning, hopefully." Sandeen's velvety voice held little emotion as usual, but her black eyes seemed to glisten. "First, you need your memories. I'm almost certain we can access them."

Story had known for a long time that she had blank spots in her memory, but they had always seemed like dreams she had simply forgotten. She had read once that most people forgot more than ninety-five percent of their dreams, and it was then that she realized she didn't just forget her dreams—she didn't dream at all. From the time her nightmares had stopped when she was thirteen until the nightmares had begun anew this summer, her sleep had been completely undisturbed. It was almost as if all the dreams she hadn't dreamt were catching up with her now—or was it all the memories that had disappeared when she had stopped dreaming?

She had seen a TV show once that said if a person didn't reach REM sleep after a certain number of hours, they would go crazy. If that was true, was this whole scenario something she had created within her head? Was she right now drugged up and catatonic in a mental institution, unable to live, existing on a dream of hope? The thought gave her pause. She felt as if she should be remembering something. She laughed. Of course—that was the point.

Shaking her head, she glanced at Adam, who like all the others was looking at her oddly.

"Something funny?" Elliott asked, watching her as if she had been taken over by a pod person.

"What? Oh no, nothing. So how do we get my memories?"

"Well, I know it's possible for you to access your memories because of your experience with Lark today."

Adam took Story's hand, and she smiled briefly at him before glancing at Sandeen. "How did you know about that?"

Sandeen looked at her expressionlessly. Emotion was a face she seemed to wear and speak only in glimpses. "Because I have eyes all around. Now, you were very upset after the memory transfer, so we know you saw something. Didn't you?" She tilted her head inquiringly.

"Well, yes."

"Do you remember it now?"

"Not really. That's the problem. I have dreams sometimes that feel more real, more like they happened or are happening. But I don't seem to be able to recall them when I open my eyes. Although this time, I do remember feeling safe. And loved."

"Well, I believe that with a bit of crystal power, we can open whatever doorway has closed you off from remembering."

"Why don't I remember?"

"I believe there may have been magic involved in making you forget."

Story frowned. "Is there magic in my world?"

"Well, no." Sandeen looked mildly perplexed. "But that's not my concern this moment. My concern is getting past the blockage."

Story glanced at Adam, who squeezed her hand gently, and then to Elliott, who was startlingly absent although he was sitting right beside her.

"Dream. It's time to dream, little dreamer." Elliott's voice was flat, and his eyes had that opaque look he got when he was having a vision. It was so fast, Story could barely tell it had happened, but she'd seen it before. Back to himself, Elliott nodded at her and took her other hand.

She turned to Sandeen. "What do I do?"

The dark goddess rose to her feet. "You do as Elliott says. You dream. Aside from your little memory earlier today, I believe other memories have started to come back to you in the form of your nightmares—those that would take over if they could. But they aren't cohesive since you are not retaining anything. Please, follow me."

Story glanced at the others—Adam's steady strength, Elliott's comforting compassion, and Peter's protectiveness kept her knees from buckling under her as she too got to her feet. "We'll be here when you get back," Peter said with a nod.

She nodded slowly in response and then turned to follow Sandeen. "Where are we going?"

"Why, the Chamber of Dreams of course," Sandeen said, her tone exasperated as if the existence of a Chamber of Dreams was normal. As if any of this was normal. "We're in the land between, where dreams pass through into our reality. Do you think we would not have such a place?"

Story merely shrugged, not sure she understood what Sandeen was talking about.

She followed Sandeen across the room to a small stone door that she hadn't seen earlier. Story watched as the god took a key that hung around her neck, fit it into the lock, and twisted the bolt.

The door yawned open and Sandeen turned to her, a shock of her ebony hair creating a storm against the pale of her skin. Her gaze was intense when it met Story's, but when wasn't it? The occasion seemed so solemn, Story almost laughed out loud, but instead she choked her inappropriate reaction back down and tried her best to quell her giddiness.

"This room is supercharged with power, Story. It is dangerous to sleep too long here as there have been some lost forever to the Land of Dreams. Although for you that shouldn't be too much of a problem, actually," she seemed to say as an aside to herself. Story wasn't feeling any less confused than normal.

"Find out what you can and then return. You should awake once your dreaming journey is done. But beware, there will be Nightmares as well."

"Yes, but they're just nightmares, they can't hurt me," Story responded.

Sandeen met her eyes for a moment before turning. "These ones can," she murmured.

Story saw that the room was literally made out of blue crystals, glowing a mellow, soothing hue. Just entering the room made Story feel sleepy. Covering her yawn with a less-than-manicured hand, she noticed a bed draped in blue silk. A stream of water slid down one crystal wall, creating white noise that had her lids already drooping. She didn't even need to be told what to do—it was as if memories and dreams were urging her toward sleep. She was so tired.

Sandeen took her arm, guiding her toward the bed. "Blue calcite," she murmured. "It aids seers and dreamers."

In response, Story giggled. "You should bring Elliott here. I can only imagine what he might see . . . "

Sandeen looked at her sharply. "He's a seer?"

Story nodded. "Psychic, you didn't know?" she said, yawning again.

Sandeen shook her head. "We'll talk about this later," she said softly as she laid Story down onto the bed. "Now, it's time to sleep."

Even as Story's eyes closed, she could feel the pulse of the blue light behind her eyelids, urging her to sleep. The last thing she felt was Sandeen cover her with the softest blanket possible, and press her lips to her brow. "Sleep, sister, and remember, for The Green awaits." Before Story could think about what the goddess meant, she succumbed to her dreams.

The Dream

They say you see your life pass in front of you before you die, but Story wasn't dying—she was remembering. Images from her past flickered in front of her as a gentle reminder of who she was and who she had been. It was all over too quickly, ending with the death of her beloved papa by men who turned into wolves, and her waking up in her mother's arms. When it was done, she expected to wake again, but instead found herself in a bare room, aside from a bed and a chair. The familiarity of it overwhelmed her, and she knew she'd visited this place before.

Her eyes scanned the room all at once, taking in the bars on the window and the sterile sense of loneliness that permeated the sharp smell of a hospital. Her gaze came to rest on the small window, and she felt claustrophobia crush against her chest as she ran to it and tugged on the bars.

Her efforts to free herself came to a halt when she zeroed in on her hands. The hands clenching the bars looked exactly like hers, except for the scars that riddled their wrists and knuckles as if they'd been thrust through glass. Gasping, she pulled her hands back and stared down at them in horror. She was in an institution, locked in a room with bars on the windows. She remembered now the girl she'd seen in her dreams before, the one who lived here. She always looked so familiar. With a sick feeling in her gut, she ran her fingers through her hair. It felt like hers but greasier. Had she always been here? Had all her dreams, nightmares, and memories been mere delusions, figments of a sick girl's mind?

Shaking her head, she refused to believe it and ran to the door, pulling on the locked handle and banging her fists against the door until they were raw. But no one came. Orderlies and nurses walked by in the corridor without stopping, without even looking at her as she begged to be freed.

Terror mounted inside of her at the thought of being trapped. Her mind racing, she was trying to think of a way to get out when a voice spoke. "Now you know what it's like." The voice was eerily familiar.

Slowly turning, she took in the sight of the institution girl she had dreamt about. Like she remembered, the girl's hair was brown like Story's, but longer and clumped in greasy tangles. Her eyes were darker, almost bronze, where Story's were like sunshine.

"Are you me?" Story whispered. "Am I stuck here?"

The girl laughed in response, her mouth twisting up humorlessly and her eyes gleaming crazily within the four nondescript walls.

"Yes and no," she laughed again, and the impact it had on Story was heart-wrenching.

"Who are you?" Story stared at her, feeling not pity, but as if a weight had been added to her shoulders. Or maybe it had always been there, and she was just noticing it for the first time. She swallowed, her throat choked thick with guilt, although she didn't know why.

"I'm glad you came. You needed to see what you did, what you've done to me—to us—before you go on." The girl didn't look at her, but flopped herself carelessly into the hard chair and curled her legs against her chest, pressing her cheek against her knees.

"What did I do to you? I don't even know you." Instead of laughing, the girl turned her gaze so that it was staring at Story. She didn't lift her head, but looked penetratingly sad.

"I just want to be real," the girl said quietly, lifting her head and widening her eyes with a maniacal glint. "And you did this, you did this you did this you did this you did this to us!" The girl had begun to rock violently, letting out a high-pitched scream as she launched herself from her chair and ran toward Story. She slammed Story into a wall and cracked her head against the bare white surface. All Story could see was the girl's horrible bronze-hued eyes raging at her as the voice so like her own demanded that she fix it. "Fix us, fix us fixuxfixusfixusfixus!" she screamed.

Pain stabbed through her head and the girl's shrieks filled her being. Finally, wanting the pain to stop, she screamed: "I will, I'll fix it!" And then, thankfully, she knew only darkness and the healing void of true sleep.

Chapter Eleven

Lake Sandeen, The In-Between

THE CRYSTAL CAVERN cast an eerie glow on her smooth features while tears streamed down her cheeks as she slept. Elliott, Adam, Sandeen, and Peter circled the sleeping Story.

"Why is she crying?" Adam demanded of Sandeen suspiciously, the hard knot in his angular jaw bulging as he tensed.

Sandeen put a bony hand to Story's tanned cheek, ignoring Adam's fierce glare. "She is only sad, and she remembers much that has been forgotten to her. Today she regains a father and loses him at the same time," she finished cryptically.

Peter also hovered anxiously over Story, her newfound uncle a protective hen who was now shooting Sandeen glaring looks as if she was singlehandedly responsible for Story's state of emotion.

"She should be waking soon," Sandeen murmured, ignoring Peter in a dance that only a couple that has been together for a while can do.

Story's lids fluttered as she flung one arm restlessly above her head. Her eyes popped open wide and she grimaced as if in pain, the pounding in her head and the girl's shrieks following her out of the dream. "I'll fix it, I promise," she whispered, as if she were still in the room, not yet noticing the concerned faces looking down on her.

"Story?" She heard Elliott's anxious voice. Adam's hand slid into hers—she could tell it was his without looking because of all the calluses he'd gained from climbing mountains. He was such a great guy. She wondered idly why she hadn't fallen in love with him. Suddenly, she remembered the dream. She had promised to fix something, but she wasn't sure what was broken.

Blinking back tears she hadn't realized were there, her vision finally cleared and she could see everyone staring down at her.

Sandeen put a restraining hand on her. "Easy now. You've been asleep for a few days, so rise slowly."

Story nodded and sluggishly, with the help of Peter on one side and Sandeen on the other, raised herself to a sitting position.

Wiping away the last of the tears from her cheeks with the back of her hand, she thickly licked dry lips, her tongue feeling mossy from days with no water. As if he were as psychic as Elliott, Peter handed her a tall mug of water. Story eyed it greedily before downing the cool contents, positive it was the best drink she'd ever had.

Finally, when she felt able to talk, she glanced first at Adam and Elliott, then to Peter, and finally to Sandeen. "I remember," she managed to croak. She offered the mug to Peter, who dutifully hurried to a pitcher of water to pour her some more. When she'd drank another two cups and was starting to feel like herself, she spoke again.

"I remember . . . I remember that I was called The Dreamer, and that when I used to sleep at night, I woke up in Tressla, where I had a whole other life and family. Faulks and Kessie and Jemma and Jess and Ninian, I remember them all—the Pegasus and Hank and Bliss, every last one of those that I loved. How did I ever forget them?" She turned to Sandeen, dismayed that she had let go of so many people from her life. Tears threatened to spill once more, and she blinked rapidly to ward them off. "How could I have forgotten Faulks of all people—my papa?"

But Sandeen was shaking her head, her brow wrinkling in the middle as if in confusion. "We don't know Story—that is one thing we never counted on. When was the last time you remember knowing all this?"

Story frowned, glancing at Adam as if he might know. But his twinkling gray eyes were serious as he watched her, confusion clouding his gaze and questions ready to roll off his tongue.

She thought about it for a few moments, recalling all that she'd learned in her induced dreaming state and remembered waking up in the middle of the night after Faulks had died—killed by wolves, she recalled. No, not just wolves. Big Bad Wolves. The stuff of fairytales, legends, and nightmares. She hadn't gone back to Tressla after that. For the first time, she had begun to experience real dreams, which had been a disconcerting, scary experience at first—especially if you counted the nightmares that plagued her after the Wolves had murdered her papa. Then the dreams had stopped, and she hadn't had one until a few weeks before when the nightmares had begun to plague her once again.

"I don't know. I can't specifically remember if one day I knew and the next day all those memories were gone. Perhaps it happened over time? I've known some part of myself was missing for a long time. I think a deeper part of me recognized that something wasn't right, that there was more to myself than just this," Story finished, confusion at her memory loss unsettling her.

They were all silent, but Adam bore a troubled expression as well and seemed to be working something out in his head. Story watched him, finding his presence the most comforting. As her lifelong friend, he knew her better than anyone, even Elliott. "What is it, Adam? Do you remember something?"

He met her gaze, his jaw tensing before he nodded shortly. "I'm not sure, we were just kids. But when you started having the nightmares, you would sometimes mention that wolves haunted you. You've always been scared of them. You were different, scared and tired all the time. But then one day I came over to hang out and watch a movie, and you were yourself again, and you talked about normal things, like school and boys you thought were cute and books you were reading. I remember being happy you seemed more normal, but you had changed too. When I first met you, you talked about fairytales as if they were real. I always thought you had a crazy imagination. But you didn't talk that way anymore. It always bothered me, but once in a while you'd say something, and I'd know that part of you was still there."

Story felt her eyes brim with tears again, and she cursed herself for her weepiness. "I guess I became a new me when Faulks died. Did you love me any less?" she whispered.

Adam crooked a smile. "You're my BFF, Story," he said half-jokingly, his gray eyes twinkling beneath a shock of reddish-brown hair. "I love you no matter how many different versions of yourself are in there."

Breathing a sigh, she nodded and grew serious once more. "But do you remember when I started seeming normal again?"

"I never said you were normal," he grinned while Elliott murmured snarkily in agreement. "But yeah, it seemed to have happened right after your mom made you see that doctor."

"Dr. Harvey," she said, snapping her head to Sandeen, her eyes wide with realization. "I always thought there was something off about that woman. I never liked her. Sh-she put me under one time. When I came out of it, I remembered I had been talking about Tressla and Faulks, and there was just something in her look. She believed me—and it was almost as if she wanted something from me. She kept asking me how she could get to Tressla. I really didn't like her. But I had totally forgotten about her. Mom didn't make me go back for a long time, but when the nightmares started, she insisted I see someone."

Sandeen seemed confused. "A doctor?" she asked, glancing at Peter, who seemed to be thinking. It was Elliott, though, who put it together.

"You said she put you under at that last appointment?"

Still sitting on the bed, leaning against pillows and feeling weak from all the revelations, Story nodded. "Yeah."

"You don't think she could have—" Peter started to say, but Elliott cut him off with a nod.

"She made you forget by suggestion while under hypnosis. Your mind was probably already primed, having been so recently traumatized after watching your father get killed," Elliott said with no hint of his usual humor and wit.

Sandeen still looked confused, but more angrily so. "Does this doctor have magic then? I thought your world had none." She glanced at Peter, who ran a hand through his hair and shook his head angrily.

"It's not magic, it's science," he answered.

Elliott nodded. "She put Story into a trance and was somehow able to get Story to repress her own memories. I learned about it in one of my psychology classes in school. It's all theory, of course, but a faction in the psychology field believe it's possible to help people recover traumatic memories, often through hypnosis. Maybe she was able to do the reverse. But why?"

"Brink," Sandeen seethed, narrowing her coal-black eyes with frightening effect. Story shivered, recalling that Sandeen was also queen of the sirens. And yet, the underwater goddess no longer scared her.

"Who?" Elliott asked, perching next to Story on the side of the bed.

"The villain," Story whispered with a wan smile as if it was all a fairytale.

"Lord Brink rules Tressla," Peter explained. "And he wants Story. Plus, he's pretty evil."

"I'm sorry, but can we pause here for a moment? Who's evil, why does he want Story, and what the hell is Tressla?" Adam asked, looking at them as if they were all crazy and he had finally had enough.

"Tressla is another world," Story said softly, raising her eyes to meet his. "It touches our own, but they are separate. And from the time I was born, when I went to sleep here, I woke up there. I had a family there. Faulks was my papa. Jemma and Hank were like an aunt and uncle, and their daughter, Kestrel, was like a sister." She glanced at Sandeen briefly with a small smile.

Adam stared at her blankly, and Story could see disbelief clouding his eyes, despite what he'd already seen up to this point. But whereas Adam was having trouble grasping it, Elliott had begun to grin, his eyes gleaming excitedly.

"That's so cool," he said.

Story laughed in response although she worried that Adam wouldn't be able to embrace the truth of the situation. Reaching forward, she felt for his hand so he would look at her. "It's true—it's why I have that fear of Wolves and why I talked about storybook characters as if they were real. It's because they are real. One of them, in fact, used to be my best friend in Tressla—Jess. I remember that now too."

"Story . . . " Adam began, but faltered before starting again. "It's just—it's going to take me awhile, okay?"

"Well, hurry up and believe because Story is going to need you when she goes back," Peter said, shooting Sandeen a look. In a show of affection, she took his hand in hers and gave him what Story guessed was supposed to pass as a comforting smile.

"Back—back where?" Adam eyed Peter suspiciously.

"To Tressla," Sandeen answered for him.

"What?" Adam exploded.

"She has to—it's her destiny. It was prophesied, actually," Sandeen explained reasonably.

"I don't give a damned about prophecies." His mouth stuck around the words as if he felt foolish even saying them aloud.

"Adam." Story shot him a pointed look to quiet him, and turned to Sandeen. "I want to go back. I need to see if Jess is okay, and Kessie—I miss her so much. But what prophesy, Sandeen? Why does Brink want me? I don't get it. Why would he have someone repress my memories, and how was he even able to communicate with a Real Worlder? I thought the doors had been closed."

Sandeen nodded. "They have been closed—all except the lake, which I have guarded for centuries upon centuries. I don't know how he has been getting through. He is powerful, but not so much that I would not have noticed if he were traversing my portals."

"If this guy has been able to move through the worlds all this time, what stopped him from just taking Story?" Elliott inserted.

"Quite simply, he couldn't. While she was in Tressla, Story was fair game, but he was not quite sure where to find her. It must have taken him years to locate her in the Real World as well, but he would have had to be very careful."

"Also, the moment Story put on the necklace from Faulks bearing the Stone of Souls, it would have protected her from him," Sandeen continued matter-of-factly. "So there was no way he could bring her through. The charm is ancient and was forged by three magical races to keep the wearer bound to her world, in soul and in body. Its magic would have been activated the moment he tried bringing her physically through, possibly killing him and instantly alerting me."

"He probably didn't find her until after he had lost her in Tressla. Then he must have found the doctor and lured her to his side, but it sounds like she was a believer before he came on the scene," Peter explained.

"But why me?" Story looked at her uncle and then to Sandeen. "I mean, I remember the Pegasus made me train and learn all that Tresslan history, and then Ninian tried to teach me stuff as well, but what could I possibly do that would make Brink go to all this trouble? Looking for me, killing Faulks . . . "

"Story, do you remember who you are—what you are?" Sandeen asked.

Story quickly glanced at Adam, who still looked shocked and rooted in denial, and Elliott, who looked like a kid who had just caught Santa Claus on Christmas Eve. "Yes, I know that everyone calls me The Dreamer, and that I can do special things when I'm in Tressla . . . that I have . . . abilities." She could feel Adam and Elliott's burning gazes. She refused to look at them, feeling especially afraid of Adam's reaction. He didn't seem to be taking this revelation of a world with magic so well, let alone the fact that his best friend could wield this magic.

"You're not a dreamer, Story. You're The Dreamer. The First, that is. And what that means would take more time than I have to explain, but you are special. Your soul, your essence, existed before man did. Your power comes from that—don't you remember this as well?"

Sadly, Story shook her head, fighting her own disbelief at Sandeen's words. Before man? That seemed impossible. She was just a girl, really.

Sandeen frowned, the expression not unattractive on her otherworldly features. A worried light turned on in the recesses of her deep eyes. She seemed about to say something, but then shut her mouth. No one else seemed to notice but Story and Peter, who cast her a suspicious look. It almost made Story laugh, watching the way they related to each other, with annoyance and love intermingling.

"Sandeen?" Story asked, feeling as if there was so much more to learn. As a child, she'd just gone with the flow, content to go about her life living in two worlds as if it was the most normal thing in the world. Now, after years of holes in her memory, she was a little more determined to find out all there was to know about being the supposed First Dreamer. Perhaps it was the past eight years she'd spent in the real world, but she had become more skeptical—even though she knew that was crazy, given where she was and what she had experienced. Living in two worlds she could handle, but being the reincarnation of some ancient being seemed far-fetched, even to her. But she wanted to go back to Tressla, to remember and experience again. She needed to go back to make sure Jess was okay. Her dreams haunted her even now.

Sandeen glanced at her and smiled, any uncertainty fading from her features. "These two worlds were once one, a very long time ago. Brink wants you to unite the worlds, but that would only lead to chaos as one world bled into another. They have become distinctly separate entities. The Fairytales would die. He has managed to harness many different magics, from sorcery and wizardry to witchcraft and alchemy, and he believes he can rule both worlds. But it would destroy everything that we know."

"So why make Story go back if it's going to only put her in danger, let alone the world? Why lead her right into his hands?" Adam finally spoke, apparently able to set aside his doubts for the moment in order to champion his best friend.

Sandeen went to speak, but Peter held up his hand to stop her and sighed. "Brink is playing his hand, so to speak, and destroying Tressla.

He has enslaved the Fairytales and imprisoned the land's natural leaders in crystal, and he has begun to destroy the Seven Forests, the lifeblood of the land."

Story looked up at Adam, and she could see he was affected by the talk of trees being cut down. He'd always had an affinity for the earth.

"But it's not just the people and the lands that suffer. It is my mother, The Green." Sandeen spoke softly, her elemental voice weighed down uncharacteristically by emotion, by sadness.

Peter nodded. "Yes, and when The Green suffers, so does your world, our Earth."

Adam shook his head, and even Elliott looked perplexed.

"The Green is like Mother Earth—she is connected to both our worlds, and if she suffers, so does your land. Noticed any storms lately? Droughts?"

"What about the Original Mythics? Would they die too, like the Fairytales?" Story asked.

"The what?" asked Elliott.

"The Original Mythics," Sandeen repeated. "They are races you would deem mythical in your world, such as the Pegasus Story mentioned before. They did not need to be created and written down in your books to have life. They have always existed. Story, it is certain the Fairytales would die, but I believe the Original Mythics would fare just as well as you or I. And no one knows how well that would be."

Adam looked sharply at Story, then back at Peter. "But how can Story do anything? I mean I know you say she's this Dreamer, or whatever, but what can she do?"

Sandeen answered this time, turning her gaze to Story, her face softening. "Because Story is very strong, even if she doesn't know it. She has power, more power than anyone else in Tressla. And of course, there's the prophecy."

"Prophecy?" Elliott asked as Adam had once again gone mute from doubt.

Sandeen nodded. "Story is destined to save Tressla," she said simply, not moving her eyes away from Story's own disbelieving gaze.

She gave a hysterical laugh, wincing because her head still hurt from the pounding it had taken in her dreams.

"Are you unwell?" Sandeen asked.

Story shook her head, "I think I just have a headache from the long nap. I'm also probably jonesing for caffeine," she joked. Everyone chuckled except Sandeen, who looked at them all blankly.

Story wasn't sure why she didn't tell them about the rest of her dream. Her aching head told her it was more than just your typical sleep foray, although perhaps less real than Tressla. Rubbing her left temple, she closed her eyes and then shook it off.

"I have a million questions," she said to Sandeen.

"Which we don't have time for," she answered back.

"I don't know how to save Tressla. I haven't used my powers in years, and when I did use them, it was always inadvertently. They were accidents that could have been catastrophic, judging by Ninian's expression every time they happened."

"Start with finding Jess. You'll need her help with the Wolves since Brink has taken to using them as his minions."

Story shuddered at the thought and nodded, acting more confident than she felt. The overwhelming urge to find her long-lost friend gave her the determination to set aside her fears.

"I'll go see Ninian—does she still live at her cottage?"

Sandeen nodded. "And find your father, he'll help you."

Story looked at her sharply. "My father?"

"Her father?" Adam and Elliott asked at the same time.

"I thought he was dead," Adam added as if to point out the discrepancies in Sandeen's argument.

Sandeen shot a look at Peter, who shook his head as if telling her not to drag him into it. Sighing, Sandeen turned back to Story. "I apologize. I was under the impression that you knew who your true father was."

"Um, no, definitely not." Story stared at her, arching her brow, her heart suddenly beating harder in her chest than she thought possible. Here she'd been told she had to save an entire world from domination, yet finding out the name of her true father had her more on edge.

"I suppose I have to tell you now," Sandeen mused.

"Uh, yeah, I suppose you do," Elliott said haughtily.

"Right. Well, I thought that after you had spent so much time with him as a child, you would have found out by now."

Story's golden eyes widened, and she stared at her in disbelief. "The Pegasus king is my father?"

"Ober? No, don't be silly, he has been with only Landria for eons. Theirs is a very well documented love story. It's Racell of course."

Story stopped, her disbelief turning to dawning joy. She had loved spending time with Racell as a child, and they had grown quite close before Faulks had died. And all these years, she could have told her mother she had met him. Her mother, who had pined for a man she would never name to her only daughter.

Story frowned as a vision haunted her. He had kissed Ninian. She had seen it. It had been when she was living with Ninian. After waking up that morning, she had decided to take a nap in the Real World and had returned to Tressla to find them in each other's arms. At the time she had just snuck back into the bedroom and played, not thinking much of it. But now she was furious. All these years her mother had waited for him, and he'd been hooking up with other women in Tressla.

"Story, what is it?" Peter asked, seeing her expression change.

Story just shook her head and changed the subject. "I guess I shouldn't be surprised. He spent enough time at the cottage when I stayed with Ninian." Although now she suspected she hadn't been the only reason for his visits. "When do I leave?"

"As soon as you are changed. We will, of course, give you food and water for your travels, but I suspect you will soon be among old friends. I wouldn't send you back, Story, if it wasn't necessary. We need you. You were prophesied as our savior, the only one who can stop him and save both worlds from dying. But he also won't stop until he has you, so tread carefully. He may try to convince you that one combined world would be the ideal alternative. But remember, the Fairytales would die, including Jess."

Story nodded and took a quick breath as if she were about to dive into a deep pool of water, gathering air and strength for a long plunge. "Perhaps Ninian can help me remember some of my abilities."

"But it's been so long," Peter murmured worriedly.

"Do you question my family's training of The Dreamer?" Sandeen said with a reproving look. "We are gods."

"It will have to be enough," Story said as she turned toward the door that led out of the dreaming room. "I'll be ready in an hour." She walked out, leaving them all staring after her.

"Hell if that girl thinks we aren't going with her." Elliott turned to Adam, who looked back at him in disbelief.

"We are? I don't know if I even believe this place exists."

"You're going to let Story go to a world that doesn't exist without your protection?"

As if all his common sense had returned, Adam straightened up to his full five-foot-nine height, while Elliott, at over six feet, was significantly taller. "No, you're right, let's go get ready. I guess I'll have to really see it to believe it." Adam grinned crookedly, and Elliott smiled back, seeing the adventurous gleam light up in his friend's dancing gray eyes.

Chapter Twelve

Lake Sandeen, The In-Between

ONLY AN HOUR LATER, Story had eaten and had changed into traveling garb that was much more practical than the dress she'd been wearing, no matter how lovely it was. She wore soft black leggings that were light enough for warmer weather, but thick enough to protect against the elements and chafing. The tall black leather traveling boots had only the smallest heel and provided support and protection for walking. The only thing she wasn't thrilled about was the corseted, black and gold top that had short, capped sleeves and seemed more in line with Tresslan fashion than practicality—although Sandeen insisted dryly that it served both purposes, being waterproof. In her bag, she also had a change of clothes, food, and a sleeved cloak for inclement weather.

She was surprised to see Elliott and Adam dressed similarly for travel although their tunics seemed to make more sense than her medieval-retro look—but she assumed they had been given practical clothing for their return home. A pang shot through her chest as she thought of all that was expected of her, and how lonely she would be without her two best friends—who up until this point had been all that was keeping her from trying to swim home to Edie and the comfort of her safe house. Story hadn't been to Tressla in eight years, but it seemed more like a lifetime. A different lifetime. Was she even that girl anymore? Maybe she'd get to Tressla and she would have no great powers. Maybe she'd be just a girl.

Slipping her bag on her shoulder, she looked at her friends with her warm golden gaze and then turned to her uncle, who swept her into his embrace.

"Please be careful, Story. I'll try to help if I can," he murmured against her hair. Peter kissed her forehead, drew her back at arm's length, and looked at her a moment, giving Story a glimpse of the loss and love that shone in his eyes. "Maybe I was wrong to leave those years ago, but I can't regret it. I'm just sorry I hurt you guys."

Story nodded and smiled, leaning forward to kiss him on his cheek. "Just promise me you'll go see Mom as soon as you can."

Peter nodded. "I'll do my best."

Next, Sandeen stepped forward and, to Story's surprise, wrapped her arms around her in a firm embrace, her insubstantial ethereal appearance deceiving. "If you have need of me, call to any body of water and I shall help if I'm able. And do check in once in a while. Nobody ever tells me anything." Her wide mouth curved into an amused smile, looking less like a goddess and more like a young woman who was hiding her anxiety behind a grin.

Story nodded. "Thank you for helping me remember. Although I don't remember the start of all this, when I supposedly lived among you at the beginning of time, you seem familiar. From the moment I saw you, it felt like I'd known you before."

Sandeen's abyssal black eyes seemed less bottomless for a moment. She blinked her eyes rapidly and looked away for a moment before turning back to Story and giving an almost imperceptible nod. "I believe in you, sister."

Lastly, Story turned to the two boys. "I'll miss you both so much—" she started to stay, but Elliott stopped her with an arched brow.

"I hope you don't think we're going to let you head off into some alternate world to save some fictional friend of yours alone. Because that isn't happening," he said.

Story shut her mouth mid-sentence and looked from Elliott to Adam, who was shaking his head, chastising her and clucking his tongue.

"You don't get to have all the fun and march off like some sacrifice, babe, not that I believe any of this," Adam said, backing Elliott.

"But it's dangerous, and I don't want to ask you two to put yourselves at risk. There's all sorts of creatures in Tressla—Nightmares, Big Bad Wolves . . . "

Elliott stopped her with a look. "Yeah, and we're coming with you. One, because—well, how cool. And two, because I'm psychic, and we can help protect you."

Story scoffed, but smiled gratefully.

Placing one hand on Story's shoulder, Sandeen gestured with the other, black nails gleaming in the glow of the crystal-lit hall. "They are your warriors," she commented with an enigmatic smile. She stepped back and swept her arm majestically to the side, encouraging everyone to move toward the door.

They all quietly followed Sandeen down the glowing halls to her golden-lit chamber, where a doorway led to the waters that would take them to Tressla. Once they stood outside the door, Sandeen turned to Story.

"You have never been to Tressla before as a whole being—you were always split, living in two worlds. I believe it would be dangerous for you to split once you are there, but with your memories back, it would be easy enough to do.

"If you had not taken off your pendant, you would not have been able to come here at all. Unfortunately, it is also what kept your wandering soul and body together. But, we have been waiting for this moment, and we believe we have been able to craft something new that will allow you to wander the worlds while remaining soulfully and physically intact." Sandeen lifted a ring from the folds of her dress and presented it to Story on the palm of her hand. "The Kelfkis love to make jewelry."

"Kelfki?" Adam asked.

Story ignored him, taking the ring from Sandeen's hand to examine the intermingling circles. But unlike the Stone of Souls pendant, the outer edges of the circles were filled in while the center was empty, and it was bejeweled with onyx instead of turquoise. Slipping it onto her right ring finger, she noted its perfect fit. "I'll never take it off," she said. "Thank you."

Sandeen ushered them to two quartz-encrusted panels that resembled an elevator. The doors parted to reveal a platform surrounded on all sides by stone.

"You will be wet while under the surface, but dry the moment you leave the water. Story, it's been awhile since you've been to Tressla, so follow the path of broken brick and it will lead you into Locksley. And do not worry, you will not run out of air," she added to Elliott, who had peeked through the doors and was looking horrified.

"Remember what I said about bodies of water. Other than that, I can't help you. Now go, save Jess and Tressla," she finished, a tremulous smile on her pale lips.

Story gazed at Sandeen and her uncle and smiled bravely back. "I'll do the best I can," she said, feeling the weight of what they were asking her to do.

Taking Adam's and Elliott's outstretched hands in her own, she squeezed them and stepped into the chamber. She glanced up and saw only a black void above her, but she knew the depths of the lake were waiting to bring her back and take her home. The metal doors clicked shut and a portal-bearing tide of water streamed into the chamber.

Mimicking Story, Sandeen took Peter's hand, and after a few moments of staring at the closed door, turned her gaze up to his.

"Why didn't you tell her she isn't whole?" he asked, his cherished light brown eyes cloudy with concern as he looked upon his lover and keeper.

"Would it matter?"

"How could it not?"

"This is more important right now. Brink's Wolves are decimating the spirit of Tressla."

"But she doesn't know about . . . "

"If she was whole, do you know what would happen? Possibly the end of everything. No, it's better this way. She's still powerful, and she can defeat Brink."

"It's wrong," Peter said softly and without reproach.

Taking a deep breath, Sandeen shook her head minutely, her gaze dropping to their clasped hands. A pang of grief at their eventual parting almost overwhelmed her. "Yes, well, there are shades of gray to wrong. I should know, I'm old friends with wrong," she said, the self-loathing only evident enough for Peter, who had long been by her side, to hear it.

"I won't be responsible for the end of the world," she finished, finally meeting his eyes.

Tenderly, he drew her toward him and nodded. "I suppose I'll have to accept that for now," he pressed his lips to her forehead. "But one day, she's going to want answers."

"Perhaps," Sandeen murmured, reveling in the feel of his arms around her and happy he had dropped the subject for the moment.

Part II

Who traveled to another world . . .

CHAPTER THIRTEEN

Lake Sandeen, Tressla

STORY BROKE THE SURFACE FIRST, taking in a deep swell of breath more out of instinct than necessity, and headed toward the nearest embankment. She heard the boys emerge behind her, and the three of them pulled themselves onto the shore. The warmth from the afternoon sun quickly warmed their skin, and Story gave thanks to The Green that it was summer here as well. It had been a long time since she had been to Tressla, and she had forgotten that the seasons mirrored those from her own world, at least in this pocket of the land.

After marveling over how dry their clothes and the contents of the backpack had stayed, Story really took in her surroundings for the first time. Tears sprang to her eyes as she spotted the Eldridge Mountains in the distance, a familiar site that had been long forgotten.

An overwhelming feeling of returning home came over her. "I do know this place," she said, casting a goofy smile at the two boys who watched her curiously.

"We can see that." Adam smiled softly back before looking around and gesturing to the dense trees that surrounded them. "Now what?"

"Come on, aren't you like a guru of the woods or something?" Elliott asked, casting a worried glance around at the foliage that could so easily snare his shiny new medieval duds. He pulled out his cell phone from his bag and examined it for water damage, holding it up and cupping the screen from the glare of the sun.

Adam laughed and shook his head. "Sure, give me a map in my own world anytime. Here, however, I think Story is our tour guide."

"I don't have any bars," Elliott complained, tuning their conversation out.

"What, did you think you'd be able to phone home?" Adam chuckled at his own joke, glancing at Story to see if she was laughing as well.

Rolling her eyes at them, she beckoned them to follow her. "Then it's fortunate that I spent a lot of time at this lake as a child, and I'm pretty sure that the way through the woods is ingrained in my heart."

The trees from a distance looked like any old trees, but up close, they were different, unique. The bark twisted and curved up the large trunks like it had been wrapped around, while the leaves spread out like a canopy. They were large, reminiscent of the Redwood Forest in California.

Now that Story studied them as she walked through the shade of their branches, she realized they appeared to be a mix of trees from the Real World. One had the white wood of a birch but the appearance of an oak, with leaves and branches that were like a bonsai. She had missed these trees. Behind her she could hear the boys quietly following her steps, taking in the wilderness around them, which was so much more wild than at home. Here, there was no road visible through the spaces the trees created, no faint noise of cars zooming by. Not that there weren't quiet places of deep wilderness in the Real World, but there was something different in the air in Tressla. Perhaps it was magic, Story thought with a smile.

After about an hour of hiking, the trio finally broke through the trees onto a well-worn and broken brick road. Elliott jumped when he heard Story cry out in joy at seeing the road. Everything had been so quiet up until that moment. Story crouched down and touched the brick as if greeting an old friend.

"Story, why were there no sounds of animals in the forest?" Adam said.

Straightening up, Story furrowed her brow and frowned. "So that's what was different," she murmured. "I thought . . . " she started to say, but was cut off when her backpack gave a sudden jolt.

"What the hell?" Adam said, wide-eyed, and he started toward Story to assist her. But she already had the bag on the ground and open, pulling out the plant she had absently stuck inside when they left.

"Oh god, I didn't even realize, but this is my Thumbelina Rose. Oh Bliss! I do remember you! I am so sorry, I didn't think," she said petting the rose's petals.

The two boys shared a look, Adam circling his finger near his temple, mouthing the word "crazy." Elliott started to laugh in response, but he jumped when the petals opened and a little flying fairy came whizzing out.

Story was laughing as Bliss shook a finger at her and then zoomed forward to kiss her on the cheek. An obviously delighted Story gently embraced the Thumbelina to her, tears shining in her sunshine eyes.

"I would have gladly slept until we reached Jess's cottage, but I didn't want you to worry about the forest creatures," Bliss said in a surprisingly normal voice. Shooting the boys a haughty look, she smirked. "What? Did you expect Tinker Bell?"

Story looked over at Elliott, who seemed delighted, and at Adam, whose jaw was slack and face composed in an expression of unease. Story was proud of him when he was able to set aside his disbelief and come back with a typical Adam snarky retort. "I guess I expected Thumbelina to sound a bit sweeter," he assented.

"Oh please, I am not *The* Thumbelina. I am *a* Thumbelina, a little girl's best friend. Therefore I have my own name, which is Bliss," she retorted, and turned back to Story. "As I was saying, you shouldn't worry. The animals were merely quiet as The Dreamer walks. See, they gather there." She pointed a small finger toward the tree line some distance away, where a number of animals, including a large bear, coyote, and an animal that resembled a gryphon watched them from a distance.

Gulping, Elliott stepped closer to Adam. "This wilderness thing is so not my scene."

Ignoring the boys, Story stared at the animals, feeling undeserving of their reverence. She gave a little nod of her head, paying her respects.

"You honor them," murmured the fairy, flitting about and tucking a strand of Story's hair behind her ear in a motherly way.

Story smiled. "I'm so sorry I forgot you and all of this. I missed you."

Shaking her head, Bliss patted Story's cheek. "It was for the best as you would have been in grave danger had you kept returning after Faulks died." She lowered her voice when she said his name, out of respect. "And while you are still in some danger, I also missed you. A Thumbelina needs her little girl," she said pointedly.

"Now, off to find Jess," the Thumbelina urged. The foursome started forward, following the brick road in search of a Wolf slayer.

Trudging behind Story and Bliss, Adam and Elliott curiously watched the fairy converse with Story, while they also took in the increasingly unfamiliar surroundings. They were in a more open area now although they still followed the line of trees. Elliott eyed flowers suspiciously, expecting them to open at any time and start talking to him. Adam warily stayed alert to the animals and any movement around them. He had the clichéd sense of being watched, the strangeness of this new world pervading his senses.

The afternoon quickly slipped away, and the sun was beginning to make its journey downwards when a village popped up in the distance. Story was happily chatting and had just taken a swig of water when she stopped, noticing for the first time what lay less than a mile ahead: Locksley.

Her heart jumped in her chest and she turned a flushed face to look back at the boys. Flashing them a high-strung smile, she glanced at Bliss meaningfully before surging ahead determinedly. While she had spent the afternoon happily reminiscing, they all knew that once they got to the village, their journey would truly begin.

Oblivious to Story's anxiety, Adam paused mid-stride. There was something big in the air, something looming like the smell of tension before a thunderstorm. Adam tried to pinpoint it while the nagging feel that eyes were watching him only grew stronger. Elliott, who had been strolling along at a leisurely pace, stumbled into him. Unfazed by the collision, Adam grabbed Elliott's arm. "Do you feel it?" But when he looked into Elliott's face, he could see his friend was out of it—almost as if he'd been drugged. Adam's hackles rose, but that didn't stop him from shaking Elliott roughly. The taller man blinked, stared at him for a split second before he ripped himself away from Adam and broke into a gallop.

"Story! Run!" he yelled.

Adam was already picking up speed and grabbed Story's hand as he ran past her, dragging her into a run as well. He was relieved when she picked up her knees and surged forward, only checking once to see if Bliss was beside her.

The village was just ahead now. Adam bit back the urge to look behind him and see what was gaining on him. But he already knew.

It was reminiscent of their old game on the cellar stairs, except this time it was real. For all of them. It was Wolves. He could hear their slavered breathing. He could smell their feral musk. He could feel their intent—and it wasn't to honor The Dreamer. A bitter taste in his mouth could only be the fear and horror he felt in anticipation of his death. There was no way they were going to make it.

"To Grandma Red's house!" Bliss called in her spirited cry, zooming ahead of them and pointing toward a small cottage set apart from the others.

"That will never hold them back!" Adam panted. He could almost feel the heat of their breath. It scorched the earth and sapped the air of all moisture. Beside him, Story was breathing hard, but she kicked up her legs and forged ahead once more.

"No, we'll be safe—it's Grandma Red's place," she gasped. Just ahead, a cottage door yawned open. A guttural growl sounded in Adam's ears. He had started to imagine what it would feel like to be shredded by the teeth of fairy-tale Wolves, when a tall woman brandishing a fiery torch stepped in front of them. Adam shouted at her to get back, but she paid him no heed.

Instead of the massacre he anticipated, the Wolves stopped short, backing up as if an unseen force field protected the woman. It was getting darker now, and day had turned to dusk, when shadows ruled. Yet, the Wolves cowered—whether in the face of the fire or the woman herself, Adam wasn't sure.

"Get back," she cried, waving the torch around. "You're in my territory, and you know what that means."

Some of the Wolves were actually whining. Adam marveled at the display. In the dim light he could see the woman more clearly, with red and white hair plaited in a long braid that almost touched the ground. Tall and statuesque, she possessed a face lined with wrinkles, and yet that didn't make her presence any less commanding. She was old, but she looked like a proud warrior.

"You know my price," her deep voice boomed.

The largest Wolf, marked by his dark fur and strange, pale blue eyes, stepped forward. One moment he was a Wolf, and in the next moment a man stood before them. A wolfish smirk on his face, his lifeless, wintery eyes stared the old woman down. Adam felt Story shudder beside him, and he reached for her hand, glancing at her momentarily to see that her face looked pale and small, her golden eyes locked on the man who stood before them.

Bliss was conspicuously whispering in Story's ear and tugging her back toward the safety of the house. He was confused when the Thumbelina's eyes met his pleadingly. Elliott seemed to understand where Adam's intuition failed. He deftly closed the space between himself and Adam, hiding Story from view while Bliss tugged her into the house, away from the glowing eyes of the Wolves. Concerned now for Story's safety, Adam turned his attention back to the Wolves, only to feel relieved by their apparent disregard for anyone but the elderly warrior in front of them.

"What are your terms?" Where the Wolf man's eyes were flat and devoid of life, his voice was silky, dripping with condescension.

"I will release you of this obligation if you return my granddaughter to me," the older woman said.

His laugh was like the slow beginnings of a growl, and there was no mirth behind it. When he threw back his head, Adam noticed that his teeth gleamed against the glare of the light, big and white. "Oh grandma, what big balls you have," the Wolf said dryly, a half smirk on his lips. "You know I can't do that. It's either her or me, and I choose me." Sweeping his arms out, he pointed to a small brindled Wolf, who gave a whine and dropped his tail between his legs. "I don't easily part with my pack, but he's weak and I must cull the herd as the cycle of life dictates," he said philosophically, his cold gaze never leaving her.

Seeming to have recovered from his refusal to return her granddaughter, the older woman laughed as if she'd known it would be a pointless request. "And he's of little use to me except to thin your already sadly diminished numbers."

The leader's smile disappeared from his face, and his pale blues eyes glittered dangerously. "Don't test me, Killer," he growled. Amidst all this, Adam had time to marvel both at the sound of a growl coming from a man, and at the thought that he hadn't completely lost it when he saw a Wolf turn into a man. It had definitely been a long weekend so far.

"Or what?" Grandma Red said, her face tilting as if in challenge. "Will you take me on, Nigel?"

Nigel's obvious growing frustration with the woman was affecting the pack as they were almost all belly to the ground, and Adam began to wonder if she was a witch or something. How the hell did this woman have so much power over them?

"I didn't think so," she said quietly after a few moments. "So how about this. I let your pup go for today, and you agree to let my friends pass in safety when they depart here."

Nigel shook his head. "Brink wouldn't be happy. They smell strange—delicious, actually. I know they're different. I can sense their unique souls, and I'm quite famished."

"My great niece has traveled from the Isle of The Will to stay with me. These two Guardians of The Will are escorting her. Would you go against Him?" she said, brow arched.

Looking surprised, he spread his arms. "But how am I to know this is true?"

"Ask Ninian. As a Daughter, she would not lie in the name of The Will."

After a few moments of holding Red's gaze, Nigel nodded. "I'll go see her. And if you're telling the truth, your friends may pass. But it is our duty as guardians of this land under Brink's rule to keep it safe. If I were to find out they were intruders—say, from the Real World—well then I'm sure our gracious ruler would be a bit upset."

Shrugging, Red nodded. "Go then, before I change my mind and decide I need a new winter coat."

A few whines sounded in response, but Nigel just nodded, bowing his head in a mocking mimic of respect. The space he occupied shimmered, and then he was once again a Wolf, his lifeless blue eyes making Adam's stomach turn. Barking what Adam could only surmise was an order, he headed out while gigantic Wolves reminiscent of every bad werewolf movie he'd ever seen followed in their pale-eyed leader's wake. Adam shuddered—man, they were big. He was half wondering if he too should be cowering at the feet of Grandma Red, so tall and terrible she seemed. But she finally turned around and silently shooed them into the house, looking for all the world like a sweet old lady.

By the light of the candles, Adam was shocked to see that the woman was older than he had originally thought. His first clue should have been the word "grandma."

Her hair was almost pure white, except for the last glory of red that streaked like fire through her long mane. She seemed familiar for a moment, and a memory tickled at his consciousness, but he quickly dismissed it. Looking into Grandma Red's steely blue eyes, Adam could almost see why the Wolves would back down. That image shattered when Story leapt forward and fell into the woman's arms. "Grandma Red!"

The older woman, handsome face lined with age, embraced Story tightly. Tears rolled down both their faces. They stood for minutes just holding one another, until finally Grandma Red pushed Story back a bit to get a good look at her, a joyful smile cracking through her puckered, wrinkled face.

"Oh my dear, I truly didn't think I'd set my eyes upon you again after you disappeared. You're so grown up! I just wish Jess were here. She missed you so much through these hard years."

Wiping tears away, Story clutched the older woman's hands, her knuckles almost white as if holding on for dear life. "I'm so sorry. I forgot—I forgot it all. I don't know why . . . After Faulks died, I woke up, and I don't know when it happened, but I just forgot," Story rambled.

Brushing Story's hair back behind her ear, Red shook her head. "Hush, it's not your fault. I think there was probably some magic at work there, and there was nothing you could have done."

"Come and sit. Introduce me to your friends," Grandma Red continued, heading toward a fire where a pot bubbled with aromas that made Adam's stomach gurgle.

Nodding to herself, Story introduced the boys. Bliss floated from mug to mug, deftly maneuvering a pitcher of water, filling their cups, and making Adam idly marvel at her strength. Story once more lurched to her feet, looking like she was about to topple over. Adam grabbed her elbow and guided her to sit as Elliott handed her a glass. "Drink it," he instructed her.

Shaking them both off and shooting them equally dark expressions, she turned back to Grandma Red. Convinced now that she was returning to some semblance of herself, Adam sat back and took a sip from his mug, thankful for the cool liquid that slid over his dry tongue and throat.

"Did you say something about the Big Bads having Jess?" she said, growing distressed all over again.

Grandma Red nodded from where she was scooping some sort of stew into bowls. "You don't worry about her, Story. Jess can take care of herself. You know it's her destiny to take him down," she said matter-of-factly.

"Take him down?" Story lurched to her feet once more, shooting the boys both looks that made it clear they had better not even think about trying to help her.

"You mean take one down, right, Grandma Red?" Story added, her hands clenched.

Sighing, the older woman shook her head and set down four wooden bowls on the table. "No I mean take *him* down, Story. Nigel is her Big Bad. I'm sorry, I thought you knew."

"Knew? I haven't been to Tressla or seen Jess in eight years! How would I know? Unless . . . Oh my god. You're not telling me she has known this for that long. I didn't think you could know that early."

Grandma Red gestured to the table. "Sit."

Taking her seat as well, she finally turned back to Story. "Yes, she knew from the moment she first saw him. That's how we know. It's a feeling that we get deep down to our very souls. Our fingers itch and our blood rushes. Our hearts pound and the burning to kill becomes inescapable. We just usually don't first see our Wolves until we're older."

Having heard enough, Adam cleared his throat. "Could someone please explain to me what the hell is a Big Bad? And why were those Wolves so scared of Grandma Red?" he asked.

Rolling his eyes, Elliott was the first to respond. "Big Bad Wolves, McFly. And Grandma Red is Little Red Riding Hood," he finished, a smug smile curving his lips.

"That's almost right. But Grandma Red isn't *the* Little Red Riding Hood she's *a* Little Red Riding Hood. Each generation of their family has one—a woman destined to fight her Wolf at some point in her lifetime. They train their whole lives for that moment when they can take their Wolf down. Jess is this generation's Little Red Riding Hood. Usually, the odds are pretty even. But well, you saw Nigel . . . " Story finished, her voice breaking as she turned her head away from them and gazed into the fire, overcome with worry.

"She's going to win, Story," Grandma Red said firmly. "So eat your stew."

"But don't you see? I can help." Story's golden eyes glowed feverishly.

"Man, I just cannot keep up with you and your moods tonight." Elliott sniffed and arched a disdainful brow at his stew before taking a sip of the wine Red had poured.

Rolling her eyes, Story ignored him. "Sandeen said that I needed to find Jess, so we'll save her."

Grandma Red had been sipping her own wine until this point, but slowly lowered her glass. "Sandeen? You saw Sandeen? And why exactly are you back? Not that I'm not overjoyed, but it's been eight years, child, like you said."

"Yes, Sandeen pulled us through the doorway, and then I met my uncle Peter, and she said I'm supposed to save the worlds." It sounded crazy when she heard it aloud, and she decided not to go around telling everyone she was the world's savior lest she begin to sound narcissistic. She wasn't even sure she really believed it herself.

"Save the worlds? From what?"

"From Lord Brink." Adam joined the conversation, figuring that since he was the sanest of the three of them, he could help explain.

Grandma Red put the spoonful of stew down that she'd been blowing on, without even looking at Adam. "Lord Brink?" Turning to Story she shook her white head. Shadows bounced off the walls of the small cottage that was lit only by the flicker of several lanterns placed strategically around the room. "You can't think to take him on, Story my dear; he's much too powerful. Jess is a trained warrior, and I wouldn't let her go after him."

"I don't have much of a choice. Sandeen says he's looking for me."

"But what would he want with you? Where have you been all these years, dear? Maybe you should explain." She pushed her bowl of stew away and set her steely gaze on each of them one by one, brooking no argument.

Sighing, Story nodded. "I thought you already knew."

The older woman shook her head, frowning. "All I ever knew was that there was something different about you and that Jess loved you. That's all that ever mattered to me."

Story smiled softly in the dimness, nodded, and then began her tale. "I guess it started when I was born. I'm from the Real World, but when I went to sleep, I used to come here . . . "

When they were done telling Red everything, she stared at Story as if she were seeing her for the first time, her puckered lips parted as if overcome by awe. "I always knew you were different. Jess told me how you would disappear, and Faulks would never let you out of his sight for too long. But there was something else. I guess you could call it a knowing—as if you were an old soul. But The Dreamer? We all know so little about her. We've only heard whispers in history lessons and lore." Red's steel blues eyes glistened as she continued to stare at Story. "The Dreamer in my very own house—the little girl with the strange golden eyes."

Story smiled self-consciously, ripping the top of her thumbnail off with one fell tear of her teeth and looking anywhere but at Red, as if uncomfortable with the reverence. For the first time, Adam took note of how insecure Story seemed. Usually so filled with life and confidence, she seemed almost diminished, as if Tressla's burden weighed too heavy.

Running her hand agitatedly through her shoulder-length waves, Story nodded. "Yes, well, I'm still not quite convinced myself, but I've been having these dreams about Jess, and I just have to find her. If I could get to Ninian, she could help me remember how to use my powers, or the Pegasus could help. But I need to find Jess."

"And then what will you do once you find her?" Red arched a brow.

"I—well, I don't know. I am hoping Ninian can help me remember some of my past abilities. I mean Brink was even able to imprison The Three. So I guess that's what we would do next . . . " She glanced around at the boys as if for help, but they merely nodded their heads in agreement, equally as clueless as to how to go about saving the world.

"Who are The Three?" Adam asked, zoning in on the newest Tresslan piece of information.

Story seemed happy for the distraction and turned to glance at Adam. "The Three are Tressla's rightful rulers. They are called this because, well, there's three of them, and they each represent a faction of Tressla's people. Are they still the same then, Grandma Red?"

The old woman nodded, sitting back and clasping her hands over her stomach, her eyes twinkling.

"Okay then," Story went on. "If I remember correctly, the Fairytale member of The Three is the Queen of Hearts."

"Of the 'off with your head' variety?" Elliott gasped.

Story laughed and shook her head. "Well, kind of, but not really. From what I remember, she's supposed to be quite a lovely person—just a little too free with her love if you get my drift."

"Ah," Elliott grinned. "And the other two?"

"Griffin is a centaur and represents the Original Mythics, and Maggie is a human. I would imagine she's getting older now, Grandma Red?"

"Ah, yes, but not as old as you might think since she's been imprisoned by Brink in crystal for the past five years. She was the balance between the two, and the three of them together were fine rulers," Red finished with a sad drop to her no-nonsense tone.

Sighing, Story looked back at Grandma Red, the topic of their imminent journey seeming to weigh on her. "We're a bit lost I suppose, and that's one reason I came to see you. I need Jess. I need a warrior on my side while I try to figure this all out. I mean, I don't even remember being this First Dreamer. I don't know if I even believe it." There, she'd finally admitted it out loud.

Leaning across the table, the old woman took Story's hand into her own and smiled gently, her withered old face still defined by a strong, proud jaw and a bony nose. "You may not believe it dear, but I merely have to look at you—with your golden eyes like Racell's and your old soul shining out—and I know it's true. You may be lost now, but you'll find your way. Not all great adventures start with a confident hero. A part of you has been sleeping for eight years. You'll find that girl again, when you get on your way and begin to see the world you once knew."

Story looked at Red hopefully as if wanting to believe the older woman's words, but failing. "I suppose we'll go see Ninian next," she said after a few moments.

"But Ninian is a Daughter of The Will . . . " Bliss piped up from the shadows, flying out and setting down on Story's shoulder.

"A Daughter of the what?" Adam asked, shoving a piece of bread into his mouth and momentarily wishing he'd wake up from the crazy, surrealistic dream he'd found himself in.

"The Daughters of The Will are priestesses who serve The Way of The Will," Bliss explained.

"The Will is a god," Story added, glancing at Bliss. "Yes, I had planned on seeing her next."

"Wait a minute." Adam gave a sidelong glance at Elliott, who seemed unfazed by the mention of gods and had finally dipped his spoon into the stew. He slurped the contents and raised his thick black eyebrows, eyes widening with pleasure.

"This is amazing!" he said to Red. "What's in it?"

Glaring at Elliott, who was too busy eating to notice, Adam continued, "So does this god just walk around?"

"Well, I mean, how else would he get around?" Story frowned, tilting her head and looking at him as if he'd gone daft.

"Because usually gods aren't like people just hanging around downtown with the rest of us."

As if paying no heed to their conversation, Red smiled at Elliott, "It's made with Field Mice Arugula."

Elliott, eating hungrily, choked. "Field mice?" Pushing the bowl away, he turned to the conversation looking a bit green. Red chuckled in response and winked at Adam.

"Well, this is Tressla," Story finally said, shooting a grin at Elliott who was gulping wine down.

"What's the wine made from?" He seemed to suddenly think to ask, eyeing the red liquid suspiciously.

"Gryphon's eyeballs." Red's wrinkled features crinkled up even more as if she couldn't contain her mischievous glee.

Elliott gagged, sending Story and Bliss into fits of giggles. They chortled together for a minute or so before finally recovering their senses. "Gryphon's eyeballs are a kind of grape, Elliott, I swear. The wine is safe, and the stew is made with a leafy plant called Field Mice Arugula because the mice like to eat it so often."

Elliott narrowed his eyes and took another sip of his wine, but didn't touch the stew again. Adam, who had been watching the exchange with mild amusement, tried to refocus the topic of conversation once again.

"So, we could like run into The Will, and he'd be a god?"

"Well not exactly. He departed the world in physical form more than one hundred years ago. But you could run into any of the other gods, dear. Although they don't make a habit of just showing up," Red explained kindly.

"But they're gods in the sense that they're all-knowing and all-powerful?" Adam tried wrapping his head around the idea of gods just walking around.

Elliott stepped in as if he were a resident of the strange land they'd been thrust into. "They're probably more like deities, like Sandeen. Am I right, Story?"

She nodded in response, looking relieved that at least one of her friends wasn't a complete waste of an adventure. "Right. The Will is the god of free will and destiny," Story encouraged.

"Okay, so he's an embodiment of free will and destiny, and rules over that select element of the human condition. And Sandeen spoke of The Green, who she explained was like Mother Nature, right?"

Story nodded again. "Oh Elliott, what would I ever do without you?"

In response, Elliott sniffed. "At the very least you'd go insane having to explain things to this half-wit," he gestured at Adam.

"Hey," Adam growled, deciding he was done with the topic at hand since he was not getting closer to any answer that would make sense. Although he had to admit to himself that meeting Mother Nature would certainly be cool. He had so many things he'd love to ask . . . He squashed the idea, reasoning that such thinking was only going to land him in the nut house with Elliott the psychic and Story the reincarnation of some legendary dreamer, whatever that even meant.

Elliott smirked and blew a kiss at Adam while Story laughed.

"This is all good to talk about," Bliss said. "But no one ever addressed my concern that Ninian is, in fact, one of the Daughters of The Will, who have historically backed Brink's rule."

Red nodded at the Thumbelina. "Thank you, Bliss dear, you are quite right. But Ninian has lived too long off the island and has been working outside of priestess orders as far as I know. There's even talk that she has helped many of us Fairytales escape The Wolves' path of destruction."

"But you're a Fairytale, Grandma Red, and they know who you are. How have you survived so long?" Story asked with a frown.

"Because I'm a Wolf killer my dear, and even Brink can't knock out of them their instinctual fear of me. Only Nigel braves the Hood, and that's because he isn't like the others. He's true evil. He's Wolf like the rest of them, but also equally man and able to rise above animal instinct. He's been after Jess for a very long time, but I'm confident she'll defeat him in the end," she finished with steel in her voice. Adam could see the hint of fear in her eyes, but she hid it well as she rose up from her chair, back rod straight, her arms still taut with muscle despite her age. She was an imposing figure, and Adam could see why the Wolves feared her.

"Time for bed," she declared. "Tomorrow will be a new day to discuss this." Red gathered up blankets and got busy making sure they all had somewhere to sleep.

As Adam warily climbed into one of the makeshift beds, he noticed how worried the older woman looked, and how quiet Story had become. He had a hard time wrapping his head around walking gods, despite having met Sandeen. But saving the world sounded like an impossible task for anyone, let alone a twenty-year-old art major who had memory problems and a pack of steroid-pumping Wolf men on her trail.

Chapter Fourteen

Locksley, Tressla

" . . . AND DON'T FORGET THIS," Red said as she took Story's hand, slipping a silver dagger into it. "You know those Tresslan Wolves hate silver." Story looked down at the dagger and nodded, closing her hand around the intricately engraved hilt.

"Does anything around here follow the rules?" an exasperated Elliott said behind Story, causing her to smile despite her weariness. "I mean, isn't it supposed to be werewolves who don't like silver?"

"I'm no psychic," Adam said with a playful wink at Story and a sympathetic pat on Elliott's back. "But something tells me the rules don't really apply here."

Shaking her head with amusement, Story turned back to Red, a feverish glow lighting up her golden eyes once more. "We'll bring her back, I promise."

"But first," Red interjected, "you need to go see Ninian."

Story nodded reluctantly, her desire to save her friend written plainly on her features.

Red put a large, veined hand on Story's shoulder. "My dear Story, as I said before, Jess can take care of herself. Nigel is a treacherous opponent, and I would be lying if I said that I haven't prayed to Maya every night since she disappeared, but I know she's still alive. And I have no doubt in my girl. She's the strongest of us."

"Maya?" Adam whispered aloud.

"Another one of those gods you're having so much trouble understanding," Bliss offered helpfully, although Adam could see the pleasure she got from antagonizing him.

"So let's see if I've got Tressla figured out yet. If gods are like people with powers, then you're kind of like a glorified bug." He smiled back at Bliss, feeling the shit in his own grin. "I should have brought bug repellant."

"While I'm not certain what bug repellent is, I can tell you that the Oaf community of Tressla will be happy to receive a new member to their ranks."

"Oafs?" Adam asked.

Elliott glanced over at Adam. "Like big trolls but extremely stupid. They're actually servants of the trolls."

Adam shook his head in wonder. "How the hell do you know that?" Elliott shrugged innocently and lifted a book he was perusing. Adam could just make out the title: *Tresslan Races Big and Small: Before the Fairytale.*

Grandma Red and Story were still talking in hushed tones although the others could easily hear what was being said. "You may have had a nice long dream in Sandeen's caverns, but you're still missing some of those pieces. And before you venture any further into Tressla—and, I'm certain, trouble—you need to recall some of those things Ninian and the Pegasus taught you so many years ago. You know, there's a prophecy that's been whispered about for years that I'm now beginning to think wasn't just a rumor at all, but was about you."

Story nodded, "So I've heard."

"So you haven't read it yet?" she asked.

Shaking her head, Story sighed. "It was only mentioned. Sandeen didn't offer to show it to us or anything. And frankly, I don't know if I want to see it. Either I'll save the world or I won't. I don't need some ancient prediction to tell me my fate. I'd prefer to leave that up to me. But maybe Ninian knows more—she and Faulks were always whispering in corners together, and she and Racell . . . " She frowned at the mention of her real father, and Adam could already tell that daddy issues were going to be a factor on this adventure. But he was also glad to hear her decide to be the master of her own fate. He winced at his own clichéd thoughts, and shouldered his pack.

Embracing Grandma Red once more, Story turned toward the brown and white spotted horse named Tuscan, whom the old woman had given them to carry their belongings. She stroked Tuscan's nose as she gazed into nothing, seemingly in a daze. The boys both hugged Red, thanking her for saving their lives, and joined Story's side, where Bliss fluttered anxiously.

"Safe journeys, children. May The Green walk with you. And when you do find Jess, tell her not to worry about me—that I'll have felt it when she defeats him."

Story met the woman's strong gaze and nodded quietly, the thin planes of Story's delicate features set determinedly, despite the fear for her friend lurking in the golden depths of her eyes.

As promised, they didn't run into any trouble from Wolves, the prospect of which Adam was certain haunted them all as they walked. He was surprised the Wolves would keep their word to Red, and he reasoned that they must really be frightened by her, which made Adam wish he'd asked her more about her days as a young Hood.

About an hour into their hike, Story stopped talking altogether, saying little when Adam and Elliott asked her a question or commented on the scenic views around them. The only person she would speak to in a complete sentence occasionally was Bliss, who hovered as a constant companion by her side. Although bothered by her silence, Adam couldn't help but take in the lay of the foreign land they traversed. They had started their hike through dense forest, which had gradually opened up to reveal towering mountains in the distance that glittered with a silver sheen beneath the sun. The hills rolled as if out of a storybook, and the breeze on his face and skin was idyllic, making the warmth of the day mixed with the fresh air a blend of perfection—something he'd only experienced the one time he went to Hawaii with his family when he was fourteen.

The walk was mostly flat, which was nice on wearied feet. Eventually, they entered another thicket of trees, but the trees stood so far apart that light shone through the leaves and danced along the forest floor, which was covered in needles and leaves. Adam was so taken with the different plant life, he was hard put to keep up with the group—the temptation to stop and study the strange vegetation almost getting him left behind more than once. Every time he rejoined the group huffing, Bliss would send him a haughty look, roll her electric green eyes, and whisper something to Story, who continued to appear dazed.

The last time, he'd been drawn in by an odd flower that was more vibrantly red than he'd ever seen before. It appeared to be a single bud, but it was full and red like a cherry about to burst. He noticed there were white ones of the same ilk, but they were smaller, and he got caught up trying to figure out if they were the same variation or somehow different. It didn't take him long to find out. After a few moments of quietly staring at the flowers, trying to memorize them, a large insect landed on a white bud, which almost instantaneously yawned open to reveal a sharp row of teeth. It clamped down on the insect and closed up, appearing once again as a seemingly innocent flower. Startled, Adam felt glad he hadn't actually touched the flower, and he watched as the bud started to swell, slowly fading from white to pink as if the blood of its victims were coloring its petals. Shuddering, he glanced at the large, throbbing red buds and stepped back. "Little Audreys," he whispered aloud, recalling the movie musical *Little Shop of Horrors*. He noticed one that was as big as his fist and gulped, wondering what the plant had found to eat that would make it that big.

Turning away from the flowers and feeling slightly sick to his stomach—while also disturbingly fascinated—he realized he'd lost the group once again and was surprised they hadn't waited for him. He followed the direction in which they'd been headed, but he hadn't walked for long when he almost ran straight into Story's back. They were at a clearing, and she was standing motionless, staring off at a small cottage that rested on a sprawling field of gardens—some were obviously overgrown and wild, while others looked carefully pruned.

The landscape was breathtakingly lovely although Story remembered a time when it was even prettier. The aroma of flowers assaulted the senses, and she breathed it in as if sucking in air after holding her breath, her lungs expanding to take in the freshness of the scented breeze.

Bliss was hovering, anxiously watching Story's expression while the boys took in the beauty before them. Story heard Elliott murmur something about the aesthetics while Adam gushed over the foreign plant life.

But for Story, looking over the landscape only made the ache in her chest hurt worse. "This was my home," she said softly. The hum of the boys' voices paused, and Elliott found her hand and gave it a squeeze.

"Despite all this nature, it must have been an amazing place to spend time," he said.

Although wind still whistled through the hole in her chest, she laughed at Elliott's attempt at comfort.

"Well, we should move on," she said, turning to go and casting one last longing glance back, her literally charmed childhood taking shape. She thought she was seeing people from her past, like the woman making her way over to them through the Purring Posies. Story heard their purr on the breeze, and she smiled fondly, remembering how Faulks had told her he didn't need no cat when he had to contend with the Posies. If left unattended, the flowers went feral, and then you rued the day you would ever have to walk through them. She'd heard the experience was as unpleasant as getting sprayed and scratched by an actual feral cat.

Shaking away the memory, she watched the woman approach, finding her jaunty way of walking heartbreakingly familiar. It was not possible. She didn't even think they could still be here. And yet . . .

"Can I help you folk?" The rail-thin woman garbed in a simple harvesting smock asked hospitably as she pushed back a strand of flyaway hair that, once a muddy blonde, had gone mostly gray.

She looked exactly the same, only older. Where her mouth had been lined and pinched before, now it was doubly so, but Story knew those lines were from laughter and love spent. The generosity of Jemma's spirit shone in her welcoming manner and the kind glow in her tired eyes. She looked at them curiously, a basket bearing an assortment of herbs from the garden tucked beneath her arm.

"I noticed you folk standing here and wondered if you weren't travelers who'd gotten lost." She glanced at the group of four and only paused with a slight frown of confusion when she saw the Thumbelina. "Bliss?" Her lined features blossomed into a look of disbelief.

Fluttering her wings, Bliss darted forward and planted a kiss on Jemma's weathered cheek. The older woman's mouth widened into a smile of joy. "It is you! Why, what are you doing here? I haven't seen you since . . . well, it's been awhile," she said, marveling at the Thumbelina Rose's reappearance. "And who have you got with you?" She turned small dark eyes to the trio, meeting Story's gaze for the first time since she'd approached them.

Story held her breath, her hands trembling by her sides. Jemma's gaze started to slide away, but then she stopped and did a double take, leaning forward and lifting spectacles from around her neck to her eyes. Choking back tears that threatened to spill, Story smiled shakily when Jemma's dark eyes widened. Her hand clutched at her chest, and Story was terrified for an instant that she was giving Jemma a heart attack. But the woman was merely grasping at her dress, twisting it between her fingers as tears sprung forth.

If it was possible, she leaned even closer. "Story?" She whispered so quietly it was as if she was scared that if she said it any louder, Story would disappear. "Is that you? My little Story?"

Story found herself unable to even speak, never imagining she'd be able to find Jemma and Hank, having always thought they would have gone somewhere else after Faulks died. But she knew now that was foolish. The Gardenia had always been as much their home as it had been Faulks's . . . and hers. Nodding, she flung herself into the woman's arms and failed to hold back the sobs that had long been lost to the whims of memory.

Just like Story remembered, Jemma's hug was firm as she held Story tight against her skinny frame, weeping and patting her hair and arms. "Bless The Green, I can't believe it's our little Story."

After many moments of weeping on both their ends, they finally separated, but Jemma continued to hold Story's hand as if she were afraid she'd disappear.

"You must come down to the cottage," Jemma said. "Hank will be back for lunch and he will be as overjoyed as I am." Elliott started to nod, and Story could tell he was biting his tongue to keep from complaining about his feet being sore.

Wiping tears from her face and trying to regain her composure, Story smiled. "I wish we could, but our trip is on the upwards of dire. We're on our way to see Ninian for help. Nigel kidnapped Jess and we have to find her."

Jemma's lined lips turned down, her brow wrinkling in thought. "Yes, unfortunately I had heard that . . . But Jess is a Hood, and that Wolf is her destiny. You can't save her from the blue-eyed demon when he comes a'knocking."

Biting her lip, Story glanced at the boys for guidance before turning to Bliss, who was looking anywhere but at her. Sighing, Story knew she was on her own on this one. "Yes, I know. It's just, well, she's supposed to help me, and I wouldn't be a good friend if I wasn't worried about her, damn destiny and all that. Sorry for my language," she said. She'd felt as if she were talking to her mother, who mostly didn't get too upset about things like that.

Jemma gave a characteristic low, good-humored laugh. "You're a woman now, Story. I'm not going to chastise you. But why do you need Jess?"

"Well, I need a warrior." Story knew how it sounded crazy. Why did a twenty-year-old college student need a sword-wielding, redheaded Wolf killer? But she did, and for more than her supposed quest. The thought of Jess with Nigel made her shudder, and guilt weighed heavily on Story's soul, despite the fact that she knew she could have done little about it. But if she'd remembered—if she'd been around the past eight years—perhaps she could have done something. She knew Jess was strong, but in her head all she could remember was a brave little girl who knew one day she would grow up to fight the baddest Wolf of them all: Nigel.

Swallowing thickly and banishing the nightmares from her head that included Jess's beautiful red hair filled with blood, Story sighed. What could she say that wouldn't sound crazy, without giving Jemma the entire truth?

"Story is the First Dreamer," Elliott piped up from behind her, impatience in his voice. He was probably upset they weren't going to be taking afternoon tea at The Gardenia. Grinding her teeth, Story barely bit back a sharp snap at her friend.

"The First what?" Jemma asked, turning to Story again.

"You know, like the legendary muse of humanity, said to have died of a broken heart when her boyfriend was murdered in front of her. He was human of course. Threw herself into Lake Sandeen, forever depriving the world of its first poet, inspirer, and dreamer, while also setting in motion the split between the two worlds."

Story, Bliss, and Adam all looked at Elliott at the same time, mouths slightly agape. "How did you know that?" Story asked, slightly shocked and upset with herself that she hadn't asked more about who The Dreamer really was.

"That's what I keep asking!" Adam added, staring Elliott down hard. "Was it that book again?"

"Um, no. I talked to Uncle Peter, who knew because of Sandeen. What?" he asked innocently. "Hey, don't get mad at me because I ask questions, while the rest of you just blindly go forth on some crazy quest without even bothering to find out the history of the why and where."

"But you didn't tell me." Story felt slightly hurt that Elliott knew so much about her alleged origins and hadn't shared it with her.

"I was planning on it, but it's just been so crazy, I mean we were chased by Wolves, fed Field Mice soup by Grandma Red, and now we just witnessed an uber-emotional reunion with an important figure from your past. Sorry I didn't have time to regale you on the origins of your history. Also, my feet feel like they're about to fall off, and I'm dying for Godiva!" Elliott, who was a serious chocolate addict, marched several feet away to cool off.

Feeling even guiltier that she had dragged her friends into this crazy world of hers, she turned back to Jemma. "Yeah, so anyway, like Elliott said, I've been told that I'm this First Dreamer, and I'm supposed to like, well . . . " She was struggling to say it again. It sounded so ridiculous to say she was supposed to save the world.

"She's the child of the prophecy, you know the one from so long ago?" Bliss added helpfully, and Story was grateful for the Thumbelina by her side. "She's going to save Tressla from Brink."

Story sighed. That was not what she wanted Bliss to mention. "Well, we don't know that I'm The Dreamer. It's just crazy to think that I would save one world let alone two. I mean I'm an art major."

Bliss frowned prettily at her companion. "You are her," she insisted.

"It's pure speculation based on some stupid prophecy probably written one hundred years ago. I mean, seriously."

Jemma went to open her mouth to say something, but Bliss cut her off. "No, it's not speculation. You are her, Story! And that prophecy was only written shortly before you were born, by a very powerful prophetess."

Story scoffed, even though she realized she was royally pissing Bliss off and creating a scene in front of Jemma, who looked increasingly more confused. "Who? Some ancient priestess on the Isle of The Will?"

"No, she's quite young and has sacrificed her happiness to see that you were in the right place at the right time. So don't you tell me you're not The Dreamer, Story Sparks. I was by your side when you opened doorways to places halfway across the world, and I saw you make an empty barn start to burn just because you imagined it. You're her.

'Where light shifts and twilight steeps, where lines cross and a babe sleeps, a shadow looms waiting . . . With eyes like sunshine . . . '"

"Okay, stop." Story held up her hand and made a "cut" motion through the air before covering her ears so she didn't have to hear anymore. "I told you, no prophecy is going to rule my future. I make my own fate."

Bliss stared at Story for a beat and said nothing, before turning on her wing and speeding off into the distance. "Bliss!" Story called out, hoping she wouldn't go too far and feeling guilty for upsetting her. She was just having a hard time taking on the weight of not one, but two worlds—all the while being told that her life had already been decided for her.

Adam and Jemma were the only two left standing beside her, and Story decided she would avoid pissing off her remaining friend so that she didn't look like a total jerk in front of Jemma. Sighing, she turned to the woman who had helped raise her as a child and took her rough, bony hand into her own. "I'm sorry for all this. I suppose I'm having a hard time accepting certain parts of my return."

Jemma smiled, smoothing back a strand of gray that had fallen loose from her bun. "Story, I'm not sure I understand even half of what yer going through, but if I've learned anything in my life it's that accepting something don't make it real. It's real because it is. You understand, girl?"

Story had to bite back a smile, hearing her old Jemma giving her a life lesson as she had so many years before.

"Do you hear what I'm saying?"

Story nodded in response, and although she opened her mouth to argue, Jemma continued on.

"And just because some prophecy says you're going to save the world, or you're not going to save the world, or we're all going to walk on our heads in the future if you don't stop Brink, don't mean you can't make your own choices. So for Racell's balls, get yer damned head out of yer ass and make sure someone can recite the prophecy to you because it could give you some clue to yer coming trials." Story was taken aback by Jemma's insights, realizing she'd never thought of it like that. Perhaps the prophecy was only a possible outcome, and her actions would make it so, but only if she chose.

"Now I said my piece, and you'd best be getting on to Ninian's so you can save the world." Jemma clapped her hands together with a customary wink. Story couldn't help but agree with her logic and started to give her a hug, but stopped in mid-motion.

"Oh god, Jemma, I totally have been so wrapped up in my own stuff, I didn't even think to ask about Kessie. Is she still gone?"

Looking pained, Jemma nodded. "Gone many years now. We've received letters telling us she's well and that she misses us. I suppose Hank and I . . . "

Story held up her hand, quieting Jemma and noticing Elliott, who had decided to rejoin them only moments before. His gaze was blank, and he mumbled what sounded like nonsense before finally blinking and shaking his head as if to clear the last vestiges of his vision from his head. His usual jovial mood had taken a turn for the serious as he shifted and looked at Jemma.

"What is it, Elliott? What did you see?"

He all but ignored Story, but smiled gently at Jemma. "Today is a bright day for those who live in Tressla—the First Dreamer walks again and Kestrel of the Seven Forests flies toward home as we speak."

Story was struck once again by how her memories came in waves, evading her and then rushing at her with the sound of just a name. "Kestrel of the Seven Forests . . . I remember the day she left . . . " She stopped speaking, recalling when the royal Pegasus family took Kessie with them to follow a destiny of her own, naming her Kestrel of the Seven Forests. She met Bliss's equally joyful smile, their previous tiff forgotten.

Story turned to Jemma, excited to see the woman's expression, but frowned when she saw Jemma clutching at her chest again, trembling violently. "How do you know?" Her dark eyes were dry as if she didn't dare to hope.

Resting her hand on Jemma's arm, Story smiled and leaned into kiss her cheek. "It's okay. He's a seer, Jemma, he can tell the future. Oh I so want to see her!"

But Elliott shook his head. "We have a date with your Kestrel that we can't miss. But your reunion will have to wait until then. We have places to be."

Throwing her arms around Jemma, Story nodded and sucked back unshed tears, kissing the old woman's weathered cheek. She wanted to argue with him and insist they stay, but she knew better than to mess with Elliott's visions. "Tell her we have an appointment, and that I'll see her soon. Tell her I love her, and Jemma, I'll be back to see you as soon as I can!"

Squeezing Story's hands, Jemma smiled joyfully back. "I know you will! Oh! What a happy day! I must ready for her arrival. Please, Story, don't be too long before I see you once again. I would have both my girls under the same roof again."

Finishing their goodbyes, they turned to go. From behind her, Story could hear Adam and Bliss's snarky banter. "Ooooh, you got a temper for someone so small. Do you feel like a big girl now?" Adam antagonized Bliss.

"I feel like a Thumbelina, which is about the size of your hand although I assure you my emotions are full-sized. Do you feel like a man, now that you've managed not to cry for a whole two minutes about how hard it is for you to believe in Tressla, even though you continue to harass a flying fairy? If so, I assure you, you're still just a boy," she retorted.

Story sighed, noting the increasing ire in their barbs, and wondered at the motivation behind it. But their rivalry couldn't dampen her mood. Kessie was returning. As they headed away from The Gardenia, Story only looked back once at the vision of rolling fields of flowers and herbs, and finally at the modest cottage where she had spent much of her life as a child. Before she turned to move on, she could have sworn she saw a ghostly vision of Faulks lift his auburn head from working the fields and smile his gentle smile.

Chapter Fifteen

Ninian's Cottage, Tressla

IT WAS SOME TIME LATER when the group emerged from the trees to a clearing, where a cozy little cottage sat in a spotlight of sunshine.

The trek had been longer than they had initially thought, and Adam could hear his stomach growling. Beside him, Elliott looked as if a wild animal had attacked him—scrapes from tree branches decorated his arms and hands, and one even got him across the cheek.

"The trees hate me," Elliott had moaned more than once as they made their way through the thicket. Adam had told him several times that the trees were only reflecting his own feelings back on him. Trees, even in his own world, seemed to sense the nature of a person and whether they were comfortable within the wild. Adam, of course, was a rugged outdoorsman, or at least that's how he liked to think of himself. Rugged or not, he knew his way through the trees and appreciated them for the natural gift they were. He could walk through the thickest, densest trees and emerge scrape-free. Even Story, who had a definite love for the outdoors, would catch a branch with her hair occasionally. But not Adam. Elliott eyed him bitterly as he licked his finger and smeared a drop of blood away from a scratch on the back of his forearm.

Adam merely shrugged and gave a manly grin. "What can I say? They like me."

Elliott snorted rudely as Adam patted him on the back in mock sympathy. He took in his surroundings while ignoring Bliss's customary roll of her eyes when he said just about anything. He didn't know what it was about the little fairy, but he just got off on making her growl. He wouldn't admit it to anyone, but it was cute coming from a miniature woman.

The trees that surrounded the clearing cast shadows in just the right areas, allowing the sunlight to reach flowers that needed to bloom under its warm glow. But where a bench and table sat on the porch, a cool shade made it a pleasant place to sit. A woman rose from the bench and headed toward them. Adam could tell the trees adored her by the way the beams of sunlight followed her.

As she drew nearer, he was surprised to see that she was probably in her early forties. The way Story had talked of her, she had always sounded much older—perhaps because of the whole priestess thing, which made images of old Catholic nuns appear in his head. Adam stopped and glanced at Elliott, who met his eyes and stood back as well. For what seemed like the hundredth time, Story was about to have another weepy reunion. It wouldn't be the last either, he thought, as Jess's and Kestrel's names came to mind.

Story stepped forward almost hesitantly and moved toward the woman as if she didn't know whether to hug her or run, but Ninian was laughing and opening her arms.

"I could hardly believe it when Maxwell told me yesterday morning, but here you are in the flesh—the real flesh, I see." She arched a brow and winked. "Being in one world at a time looks good on you, Story!"

Story laughed and for the second time that day, threw herself into the arms of her past. "I should have known you would already know we were coming."

Nodding sagely, Ninian stepped back to hold Story out at arm's length. "It's hard to reconcile the young thing you were last time I saw you and the woman you are today. It doesn't seem so long ago you were punching holes in the fabric of reality," she said with a laugh. "I trust you have that under control now."

Story looked like she was going to respond, but Ninian had turned to the rest of them with a brisk air of urgent focus, and Adam saw almost immediately that she wasn't as laid back as she would have them think. There was an edge about her, and he knew it had something to do with Story.

Her crystal blue eyes were startlingly clear, and Adam felt his cheeks warm when her gaze paused on him—she was beautiful, a hottie. But she was also at least twenty years his senior. Her lips curled into a small smile, almost as if she knew what he was thinking, and he felt the blush creep up to his ears—an unfortunate trait of men with reddish hair.

"Oh Bliss!" Ninian exclaimed as the Thumbelina lighted on her arm. "It has been too long. But Story, who are the rest of your friends?"

"Ninian, these are my two best friends from my world, Adam and Elliott," she responded motioning to each one of them. "They're stubborn and bullied their way into coming with me."

Adam silently thanked the powers that be for the fact that they didn't have to tell Story's entire life story all over again to Ninian, who if anything probably knew more than they did. He'd heard enough times that Story was going to have to save the worlds, and it was as hard for him to swallow every time. Plus, Bliss's mockery of his disbelief annoyed him.

Elliott sniffed dramatically, but Story had said it with a smile so they would both know how appreciative she really was of their company. "And I happened to buy Bliss while we were in Sandeen's caverns," she continued. "Which was something of a lucky chance, now that I think about it."

Shaking her head and gesturing to the trees and their selective shading, Ninian smiled benignly. "Fate works in mysterious ways," she said, unaware when Story bristled at her comment. "But you all must be hungry. Your one friend here looks as if he had a disagreement with the trees. Perhaps you will think better of them on your way back through, and they will think more highly of you," she said.

Adam covered his surprise at her observation, but Elliott sighed as he picked a stick out of his hair. "You sound like Adam. The entire trip here, all he did was talk about how the trees felt what I was feeling, blah blah blah."

Before, Ninian had merely glossed over him, but now her crystalline gaze, when it met his, was measured. "Wise man," she said with a nod. "Story, I believe your friends were wisely picked. Don't forget their specific gifts." And with that, she beckoned for them to follow her.

As they entered the cozy cottage, Adam was overwhelmed by the smell of meats and spices wafting up from steaming pots. It was only after Ninian handed him a loaf of bread to quench his hunger that he noticed the man sitting at the table. As Elliott took a seat, Adam smirked and tore off another chunk of bread, noticing his friend appraise the stranger while trying not to be obvious. The man rose and held out a hand, and Adam could see he was taller than the six-foot Elliott. He wore what Adam deduced to be traveling clothes, as he was covered in dust from the road, and strands of dark hair clung to his damp forehead, so he must not have arrived very long ago.

He had a serious set to his face, a strong, tense jaw, and eyes that were only a shade or two lighter than Sandeen's black caverns although less cosmic. But he came off friendly enough. Adam nodded and shook the proffered hand as he realized he was being introduced.

"This is Nicholas," Ninian was saying. "He's B—"

"I'm a fellow dissenter of Brink's rule," he said, cutting Ninian off and pointedly meeting her gaze.

Hmmm, Adam thought, *now that was odd*. But before he could analyze the situation, another arose. Nicholas seemed to have noticed Story for the first time and had stopped in mid-breath. Unfortunately, the dark stranger wasn't the only one staring; Story seemed equally as enthralled.

The silence became thick with the two locked in a staring contest. Adam's sense of brotherly protectiveness started to ruffle. Why was this guy staring so intently at his Story?

Ninian finally broke the silence. "Nicholas, this is Story. You remember, I told you about her before," she said softly, her hand resting on his arm.

Shaking himself as if waking from a dream, Nicholas nodded and lifted the corners of his wide mouth into a charming smile. "Of course. Your beauty merely took my voice away," he amended with a wink.

Story too seemed to come back to herself, a flush creeping up her cheeks while her golden eyes glittered strangely. "Ninian, I think your friend here is a little flirt," she laughed and smiled a friendly greeting to Nicholas.

"He does have a way with the ladies," Ninian said with a laugh although Adam noticed she watched the two curiously. Adam's own curiosity was rendered obsolete by the sight of the steaming meal put out before him. A contented silence took over the cottage as everyone set to eating.

CHAPTER SIXTEEN

Ninian's Cottage, Tressla

"SO WE NEED JESS, but she's in The Capital. I'm not a warrior—I barely remember the magic I'm supposed to have—and so, I don't really know what else to do," Story finished, after explaining how she'd ended up back in Tressla and why it was imperative they find Jess.

All was quiet for a few moments while Ninian gazed between the three of them. A few feet away, Nicholas sat by the hearth where the fire flickered, seemingly lost in thought.

Ninian placed her hand over Story's and smiled gently. It was such a nurturing touch, Story ached for her mother, wondering how worried she must be. But the thought was fleeting. Ninian, who had stepped away for a moment toward her bookcase, was removing what looked like a scroll from behind a loose cobblestone in the wall.

Returning to her spot across from Story at the table, she glanced at Elliott, who was lounging happily with a mug of wine while Adam sat next to Story, and Bliss perched on an arm of her chair.

"Story, do you remember our lessons?" Ninian asked quietly although the intensity of her gaze belied her emotions.

Sighing, Story nodded, puckering her brow apologetically. "Yes, but not so well that I could recreate what you showed me."

"But didn't Sandeen take you into the Chamber of Dreams?"

Story nodded in response. "She did, but I was still only a child when I lived here with you. It's just fuzzy."

Clasping Story's hand between heavily ringed fingers, Ninian brushed a strand of Story's hair from her face in a soothing manner. "Do you remember the beginning? When you were the First Dreamer?"

"No, not at all," Story said miserably, running her hands through her chestnut hair, something she had a habit of doing when she was frustrated. She looked down at her hands, touching the ring Sandeen had given her with the tip of her index finger. "I mean, there were some glimpses—like Sandeen seemed familiar to me. But other than that, no. Sandeen asked me the same question, but she didn't say anything else about it . . . God, how will I ever save Jess?"

"You need to find Jess, Story, not save her," Ninian reminded her gently.

"But I've been dreaming about her for weeks. I've even been painting her being attacked by Wolves—I didn't even know it until the paintings were finished," she snapped.

As soon as she had mentioned the paintings, Elliott and Adam looked at one another as if a light bulb went off. For Adam, it had a different meaning. "That girl was Jess? You mean I'm going to meet her?"

"Oh lord." Elliott rolled his eyes heavenwards and took another sip of his drink. "That is so not the point. The point is, Story, that you also painted Jess tearing Wolves apart. So I don't think your paintings are particularly prophetic. Besides, we only have room for one psychic."

Story didn't know what to say. Elliott was right. She had been so consumed with the idea of Jess getting killed by her Big Bad Wolf, she had forgotten the paintings where Little Red Riding Hood kicked ass.

"Story," Ninian said. "Elliott is right. Jess's destiny is to pursue her prey and eliminate it. And she's strong; it's what she was born for. But you, my dear, were not born to slay Wolves or fight Jess's battles, you were meant to rule dreams and inspire. I'm not worried about Jess, you'll find her. I'm more worried about your memory lapse. The Chamber of Dreams should have restored all your memories."

Ninian glanced down at the parchment she'd taken from the wall and very carefully began to unroll it. "There is a prophecy of a child being born with one foot in our world and one foot in the Real World," she said softly as she smoothed out the creases.

"Yeah, so we've heard," Adam said, kicking his legs up on the table and lounging back in his chair, waiting for the priestess to tell them something they didn't already know.

She didn't seem surprised and nodded. "Have you heard or read it?"

Story shook her head. "I haven't wanted to up until now."

"Why not?" Ninian asked carefully, her hand still smoothing out the wrinkled scroll.

"I didn't like the thought of my life being laid out for me as if I have no choice, as if nothing I do makes a difference. I want to make my own choices, not try to live by some words a priestess wrote down from a vision. Elliott is a psychic, so I know that when he sees things, he sees potentials." Story glanced at Elliott as if making sure she was talking sense. He nodded encouragingly, one foot crossed easily over his knee, his dark gaze intent on Story's form.

Taking a breath, she turned back to Ninian, but not before Adam saw her golden-hued gaze slide over Nicholas about as casually as a dog sticking its nose in your groin. It also didn't fall below Adam's notice that Nicholas locked onto her for the brief moment she met his eyes, but unlike Story, he made no attempt at feigning nonchalance. Adam frowned, not liking the hunger he saw in the dark stranger's face.

"Go on," Ninian murmured, standing back against the small wood burning stove that was currently unlit, given the warmth of the night.

Nodding, Story looked down, twisting the silver ring from Sandeen around her finger before looking up. "So, like if Elliott has a psychic vision and tells me if we go to the mall we might get robbed, I can choose to do it anyway and take my chances, or I can decide I'm going to stay home and avoid the possibility altogether—if that makes any sense at all." Story stopped and laughed self-consciously, her cheeks slightly flushed at being the center of attention.

"But after talking to Jemma, I think I'm ready to hear the prophecy because I think they're kind of like Elliott's psychic visions. There's multiple possibilities, and all of those possibilities are based on my choices. So I guess I should try and find out what the right choices are, because I'd rather not be the reason Tressla dies."

Ninian's brow smoothed, and her expression of confusion faded away into a warm smile, her crystalline blue eyes clear and placid. "You are correct. Without the choices you and we all make, nothing can come about. This is merely a possibility . . . So, while we're all here, why don't I read it aloud and see what you can make of it."

They all nodded in response, except Nicholas, who seemed disinterested in the prophecy altogether and was more focused on following Story's every hair flick and nervous tic. No wonder she seemed anxious, Adam thought, what with eye stalker boy in the corner. He turned a dark look toward Nicholas, who after several moments finally seemed to realize Adam was boring a hole in his head. Adam arched his brows and tried on his most intimidating facial expression. Nicholas merely looked back at him blankly before returning to his Story stare fest.

Ninian held up the prophecy, cleared her throat, and began to read:

When Fae blood meets a golden god in another world away,
a dreamer we shall dream

Where light shifts and twilight steeps
Where lines cross and a babe sleeps
A shadow looms

In sleep a world awaits
Of her own making

Through the sacred lake The Dreamer goes
Knowing little of what she previously chose
And is surprised by the waking

Born of two worlds, The Dreamer brings the way to unite
Born of two worlds, The Dreamer fights the internal fight
And she can bring the awakening

But only when the Dream, The Dreamer and the Spirit unite

She is The Dreamer, She is The Destroyer
Standing outside the grace of The Will
She must undo, she must un-rue

The fate she so hastily ended
And the worlds she so easily bended
Into two

But in three she will be
Warring to see
Who will win?
Her or her or she?

No one stirred as Ninian finished the prophecy, not even Elliott, who Story was sure had much to say. Finally, after a few moments of subtly watching Nicholas in the corner, who had closed himself off as soon as Ninian began reading, Story asked the question that was on all their lips. "What does it all mean? I mean, some of it is obvious, like 'The Dreamer must wake,' which I assume is me coming back and remembering. But that part about 'her or her or she,' and 'living in three' . . . I don't get it," she said, hearing the edge of frustration in her own voice. That last line bothered her the most. What could it possibly mean?

"And what's 'the awakening?' And why is it telling us that Story can 'bring the way to unite' when Sandeen told us uniting the two worlds back together again would basically be the end of both worlds?" Adam asked, looking as confused as the rest of them.

Ninian raised a hand to silence everyone, resembling a teacher quieting her students. Story smiled in spite of herself, remembering Ninian's gracefully stern ways. "I have studied this prophecy for years, and so I do believe I have a few lines figured out," she said in her softly elegant voice. "At least, the part about the uniting of worlds. It's my belief," her crystal eyes flicked to Nicholas and then back to the rest of them, "that there is a way for Story to unite the worlds without destroying them. My theory, and Racell agrees with me, is that since the worlds have always been connected, the life forces could be reunited without altering the two realities that have been established separately. Without destroying the Fairytales."

Story breathed out softly and swallowed, twisting her ring around her finger. All the talk of life forces and connecting worlds had her on edge. She wouldn't dare tell anyone, but since they'd come back to Tressla, she'd felt a void, an emptiness inside her that she couldn't quite name, as if something or some part of herself wasn't quite right. At first, she'd chalked it up to everything that was going on, the revelations and the responsibility. But now she felt there was something innately wrong.

"What do you think, Elliott?" Ninian asked him seriously. His psychic abilities apparently gave him some authority over prophecies now, Story thought dryly.

"I think I don't like the part that says she's going to have to fight." Story looked up at his words and caught Ninian's worried gaze.

"What do you think, Story?"

"I think I'm tired." She heard the edge in her voice, but didn't really care. "We can sit here all night trying to figure it out, but when it comes down to it, we're not going to be able to because it's vague and written in riddles. I'm going to go with my original plan and fly by the seat of my pants. I've always been good at that." She flashed a cocksure grin she knew was fooling no one.

"Okay, but if you're going to be the world's savior, we should know at least what you were taught as a child. I know I wasn't the only one training you although I was not privy to who else did," Ninian responded.

"No, but you knew that my father also helped train me."

"Yes, but Faulks taught you herbology, nothing I would imagine that could unite the worlds."

"I thought the point was to *not* unite the worlds." Adam chimed in.

"No, the point is to not destroy the world, dimwit, something you would have known if you'd been listening earlier. The worlds would be much healthier if their life forces were united, much healthier for The Green," Bliss said from her perch on the chair nearest Nicholas, who'd remained silent and serious the entire time they'd been there.

Adam looked as if he was about to retort something as equally immature to Bliss, but Story cut him off. "I wasn't talking about Faulks, I was talking about my father, Racell." She raised her amber eyes to Ninian's, a bitter look glittering in their depths.

"So you know . . . " Lines creased Ninian's sun-kissed skin, but she made no move to go to Story, perhaps sensing that a time bomb was ticking within the girl's wearied soul.

"Shouldn't he be here greeting his long-lost daughter?" Her voice was laced with glass and discord, but mainly she just felt betrayed, the kiss between Racell and Ninian flashing in her mind. She bore Ninian no ill will—it was Racell she blamed, moving on so quickly from her love-struck mother.

Ninian sighed as if dealing with a particularly wearisome child. "I doubt he even knows you're here."

"He's a god, isn't he?" Story shot back while inwardly observing how their roles so easily slid back into that of a teacher and an angry ten-year-old.

"A god?" Elliott echoed, his eyes growing wide.

"He's a demi-god," Ninian corrected. "Meaning, he is often left in the dark just as much as the rest of us. None of us knew when we'd see you again. We only hoped."

"What's his parentage?" Elliott said single-mindedly, still focused on Racell.

Glancing at him quickly, Ninian sighed. "His mother was human, his father, The Will."

"You mean that god that up and left everyone in the lurch to be oppressed by Brink?" Elliott leaned back in his chair, a look of distaste crossing his face. He had firsthand knowledge of oppression, himself.

"See, I think you all will understand the prophecy a bit better if we had a little history lesson. Story, do you remember any of it?" Ninian directed a look her way.

Folding her legs beneath her in the chair, Story nodded, trying to act less like a spoilt brat. "Let's see, there are four gods and many lesser deities that exist in Tressla. The Green, well, like we said earlier, she's like what we call Mother Earth. She is the life essence of the very world. Then there is Maya. No one's really sure what she is, but she's kind of like chaos and wild magic. I remember her being a bit scary." A vision of the Pegasus danced through her mind, and the day they came to take Kestrel. Maya, usually appearing as a child, had shown herself as well, honoring her sister's destiny. "I first met her when I was training with Ober." Story glanced pointedly at Ninian, whose delicately arched silvery blonde brows flew up under a soft sweep of bangs.

"Then there's Sandeen, who you all remember. She is daughter to The Green and The Will. Which brings us to their relationship." Story stopped and nodded to Ninian. "I think you best tell this part; it's been so long and you served The Will, so you know him better."

All eyes turned to Ninian, excluding Nicholas's, which stared into the fire. Shadows danced over his angled cheekbones and the ridge of his jaw, which sported a shadow of a beard. Story found herself staring at him almost desperately, trying to place the familiar planes of his face when Ninian picked up the story.

"The Will was once The Green's consort, but all that changed after the death of the First Dreamer, which is perhaps a story that is more important."

The Story of the First Dreamer

The world was still new when The Green and The Will found a young girl sleeping under a tree one early morning before the sun had fully risen in the sky. They loved her at once, feeling inspired by the mere energy of her presence, even though she did not wake. They carried her back with them to show their daughter Sandeen as well as Maya.

The first night she slept near, both gods were besieged with dreams of a race that would tend to The Green's land and give The Will a purpose. This race would create and build, and the gods would watch over them. They had never dreamed before, and this was a powerful dream, one that took shape at the dawn's first light. With the first human's breath of life, the girl opened her eyes. She was the world's First Dreamer, and humanity was born from her dreams begotten by two gods.

She was also the world's first muse. Fairytales were born in the form of tales passed down through the ages, and finally written into books. Great artists were forged from the whispered words of dreams into their ears. And so the years wore on, and the gods watched humanity imagine wonderful and sometimes horrible things.

There came a day when The Dreamer, who had heard and inspired the most exquisite music to ever be played, fell in love with a simple fiddler. She had never shown herself to any human she played muse to, but one night as the man bent over his fiddle and played something particularly beautiful, she gave into her heart's greatest desire. With his head bent over his instrument, a lock of hair brushing his forehead, and his face a study of concentration in the moonlight, she reached out and placed her hand against his cheek.

The startled man looked up and was at once taken with the beauty of the vision before him. Like all those she inspired, he had been born with a dreamer's heart, but the spark in him was particularly strong. And at once, he knew her to be his muse and heart's one true love.

Without a word, looking deep into the golden hue of her eyes, he played a song she had never heard him play before. It wrapped around her like a breeze and caressed her in a way that even she couldn't describe. She had dreamed many love stories before, but until now she had never truly understood the depth of feeling.

That night the two lay together beneath the stars, and no love was ever quite so deep, nor sadly, so star-crossed. For in the shadows was a spy.

The fiddler's greatest rival across the land was insanely jealous of his talent and renown. He himself had once been the most sought-after musician, until the young fiddler had been discovered. Referred to as the Master Fiddler, he had followed the fiddler, trying to glean some of his techniques for creating his beautiful music, and he was shocked when the First Dreamer appeared. He felt cheated out of his rightful place, and bitter that The Dreamer had passed him over for the other fiddler. He felt that surely if she just heard him play, she would lend him some inspiration, or give him a dream of a song.

So while they lay sleeping, the fiend crept closer and stabbed the fiddler in his sleep. As his life bled out from him, The Dreamer cried out in grief—their love dashed before it had barely begun. Clutching her hand, the fiddler stared up at her, the stars in his eyes. As he gazed at the one he loved, he promised her before he died that one day his soul would find hers.

With no will left to go on, nor no will left to dream, she walked until she came to the shores of Sandeen's Lake. There, she threw herself against the rocks. Slipping beneath the dark waters, she closed her eyes and for the first time did not dream.

Her actions, her death, succeeded in ripping the world in two, creating two vastly separate and yet connected realities. Where one world lost man's creations and civilization, the other lost magic. At first, the gods thought the dreams were gone. They soon found that in the Real World, dreams remained on the pages and canvases of their mundane existence. But in Tressla, which is what we named our world, those dreams came to life, known as the Fairytales. And while the humans had no solid memory of what the world had once been, the shadows of its existence can be found in their storybooks and superstitions.

Story listened intently as Ninian retold the tale of the First Dreamer, her life, her love, and her death. She felt she could almost visualize the events, but not as if she'd been there—it was more like she was watching a movie. Only when Ninian came to the part where The Dreamer threw herself into Sandeen's lake and died of a broken heart did Story feel any sort of emotion. Something akin to grief welled up in her chest, filling the emptiness for a few soundless moments before disappearing altogether once again. When the sadness had leaked out of her as if it had never been, she realized something was missing from Ninian's version of events, but she didn't know what. It just felt like she wasn't telling the whole story. A pang of inexplicable guilt tightened in her chest, but Story had no idea why.

She searched Ninian's face for any falseness, but saw the same elegant features as always. It was hard to believe that it was Story she was talking about—this being that had existed at the beginning of humanity was supposed to be her. She didn't have that power; she couldn't have existed so long ago. She couldn't be the one responsible for the splitting of the world.

"I know you feel lost, and you feel as if you don't know how to defeat Brink," Ninian said. "But there is one thing I have learned recently. He has a fiddle, a fiddle we believe to be the one that belonged to the original Fiddler. It's thought to be powerful and perhaps the tool that gives Brink much of his strength. If you were able to get it, you may be able to handicap him."

"What happened to the other musician? The one who killed the Fiddler?" All heads swiveled to Nicholas, who had spoken for the first time since dinner. For Story, it gave her an excuse to stare at him once more. She'd been painfully aware of his profile that was just out of reach for her to comfortably stare at without drawing attention to herself.

Ninian shrugged slim shoulders and lifted a candle to blow it out. "No one knows."

Chapter Seventeen

Ninian's Cottage, Tressla

EVERYONE WAS ASLEEP SAVE STORY. Her straw-stuffed mattress was itchy and uncomfortable, but more than that, she couldn't get the story of the First Dreamer out of her mind. And if she was honest with herself, she couldn't stop thinking about Nicholas. His presence disturbed her. She didn't know why, only that the lines of his face and eyes felt like a painting she'd seen a million times, as if she could draw him herself without looking. It was on the tip of her tongue like a name barely forgotten. Had she met him in Tressla before? It was hard for her to think about it because then she would have to admit that, despite her experience in the Chamber of Dreams, memories still escaped her.

Sighing, she rolled over once more in discomfort, pausing only when Elliott stirred in his sleep and rolled closer to the fire. Despite her earlier exhaustion, she knew sleep was far off. She quietly got up and grabbed her blanket, wrapping it around her as she slipped out the front door. She sighed as the night air hit her bare feet. Even as a child, the natural world had called to her. She couldn't explain her affinity for it, but she loved hiking with Adam in the deep woods. It made her feel free. "All good things are wild and free," she whispered. It was a quote from Henry David Thoreau, one her mother had often said to her as she tore out the door on a sunny afternoon, headed for the lake.

The fresh air was a boon to her anxious soul. It was spring-like, but the chill had softened, carrying with it a hint of summer warmth. She lowered herself onto a bench and inhaled the scent of Gargoyle blossoms and Night Boggles, which kept Nightmares at bay and also smelled similar to lilacs.

The night air and bright stars cleared her head, and Story suddenly found herself recalling the nights she had slipped out here when she was a child. Days when she napped in her own world and awoke in this one. God, how had she not just been exhausted all the time? She never really slept. And yet she was supposed to be The Dreamer of mankind or something insane like that.

Despite feeling exhaustion creep up on her and settle like a weight on her limbs and eyes, the plan they had put together continued to run through her head. Just before Ninian had blown out all the lights, they had decided to head toward the palace where Nigel was holding Jess. But their real mission at the moment was to track down Racell. Her father. The one her mother had never gotten over, despite the occasional date or month-long boyfriend.

Meanwhile, he was here in Tressla hooking up with poor unsuspecting Ninian. Her eyes narrowed but she shook the thought away, refusing to let her absentee father disturb her further.

Gazing off into the thick shadows, she wondered how in the world she was supposed to go up against some sort of sorcerer and unite the life energies from two worlds. It sounded ridiculous even to her. She didn't notice right away when a shadow joined her on the porch. She blinked her eyes against the glow of the lantern that hung on the porch just behind him before she realized it was Nicholas. By gods he was quiet! He actually kind of creeped her out while also making her pulse quicken every time he was near.

"Would you mind if I joined you?" He gestured to the seat next to her on the bench.

Dumbly, she shook her head, but then wasn't sure if he could really tell in the dark. "Uh, no, go ahead," she said clumsily and wondered at her own demeanor. This wasn't like her. While boys seemed to like her, and she liked them quite well, she was never tongue-tied or shy. But Nicholas made her feel all fluttery inside.

She slid over so he had room as he lowered his tall frame down next to her, his bulk taking up more than half the bench and sucking the chill from the air that immediately surrounded her. For a moment, she was reminded of Faulks with a pang that went straight to her heart. He had been a large man, quite a bit larger than Nicholas, but a very gentle and graceful giant.

They sat in a strangely companionable silence for a moment, despite the tension that was rife between them. When he finally spoke, he skipped the pleasantries and turned to her, the planes of his face made sharp by the shadows and lending him a certain beauty.

"I would like to come with you."

She opened her mouth in surprise, but before she could respond, he continued. "I don't think you're aware of who your enemies are and I'm pretty sure whatever powers you had as a kid, you don't know how to use anymore."

"Well, I haven't even tried . . . " Story started to protest, but stopped when he held up his hand.

"Maybe not, but even if you could access them, do you remember how to use them? A leader should not be leading her troops to war without the smallest knowledge of combat skills."

Trying to keep up, Story finally held up her own hand mimicking his gesture from only moments before. "Combat skills? Leader? War?"

The slow curve of his lips in the dim light made her shiver, a cleft in his chin adding to the seductiveness of what Story could now tell was an easy grin, even if he often seemed serious. Heat prickled against her skin, and when he shifted his leg so that it rested against hers, she couldn't stop herself from being aware of his closeness. As if she had a fever, she found herself shivering and pulled the blanket around her. Glad that the night hid any blushing she might be doing, she tossed her hair back reflexively and cursed herself for the flirtatious gesture. He was going to think she was a total spaz.

"You're the girl in the prophecy and what you're doing is heading into a war against not only a powerful sorcerer, but Big Bad Wolves and any other darkling they can pull to their side. Besides, every hero needs an army—small or large. Until you can figure out how to harness your abilities, I think you might be happy to have me."

Story stared at him in the darkness, a million questions running through her head—namely, *who are you and why do you make me feel like this?* But she didn't ask it, nor did she ask who her enemies were. That would all come soon enough. Instead she asked another nagging question. "What makes you qualified?" She smiled inwardly, congratulating herself for playing it so cool. Usually it wasn't so hard.

Staring off into the trees, Nicholas finally met her gaze and when he did she nearly swooned. She immediately hated herself for her reaction. But she kept his gaze, steady and unwavering because that's how she rolled.

"Because my mother is the prophetess who wrote that prophecy, so you're going to need someone along who can help you translate it. Good enough?"

Silenced and slightly in awe, despite the way she felt about prophecies, she inclined her head. "Then I suppose I should be honored by your most gallant offer," she teased. But while he smiled in what Story took as good humor at her gentle jibing, his eyes were serious and intent on her.

Perhaps it was the way he was looking at her, or the ray of moonlight that fleetingly splashed across his face, illuminating his beauty and an unseen vulnerability. She knew she had met him before and she could see in his face that he knew her. It was this that finally gave her the confidence to lean forward, her breath splashing against his and mingling in the air. "Who are you?" she spoke softly, heady with the closeness of him.

In response, he too shifted his body and face closer so that she could feel the heat of his moist breath against her mouth. Her anticipation mixed with the sensuality of the moment caused her to gasp for air. If he kissed her, she didn't think she'd have the strength to stop him even though they were practically strangers. He seemed about to answer, drawn to her as much as she was to him. But at that moment a Night Boggle squirted its attack fumes into the air. It was lovely but overpowering, and it instantly assaulted their senses. Story jumped up and peered warily into the dark.

"Nightmares." Nicholas pointed at moving shadows that would have blended completely into the night if not for the shifting of their movements. They were also much darker than normal nighttime and creepier than any normal shadow. So if you knew what to look for, you could spot them easily enough.

Story nodded, watching the shadows slink away as another Night Boggle let loose the fume that repelled Nightmares.

"Strange there would be so many of them," he murmured before turning to Story. "Looking for you, I bet. And that's not good because it means your enemies are already aware you're here."

Story shivered, but this time it wasn't from Nicholas or the cold, but the sense that unseen eyes were watching her. As they turned to go inside, she looked behind her to catch Nicholas cast one last searching look across the dark glade, but the night was once again peaceful and pure. No, it was the look of fear that gleamed in his dark eyes that made her heart lurch. *What aren't you telling me?*

CHAPTER EIGHTEEN

Locksley, Tressla

STORY WAS EAGER to be on the road, so the next day they were up early. The day was bright, and the trees rustled along the breeze with happy titters, offering a welcome start to their journey. Elliott's excitement, despite his disdain for anything involving nature, made Adam smile to himself. It *was* sort of exciting, and it did feel as if they had stepped into a movie or book, but he also knew that like in any good story, danger was ahead. He eyed Story worriedly and Elliott more so, as he was more likely to run off with some Fairy Prince. Inwardly, he puffed up his chest and promised himself he'd protect his friends as best as he could. So he was a little peeved when he realized Nicholas appeared to be joining them.

In an offhand way, he recognized he was merely irritated at being denied his place as the token protector male of the group. Nicholas was an actual seasoned fighter, while the most action Adam had seen was in his Tae Kwon Do classes. But he was strong, had climbed mountains in fact, and felt as at home in a crowded bar as he did swinging from trees. It was definitely a guy thing. But none of his self-awareness made him less prickly when Nicholas announced they were leaving Tuscan and Cobble, a brown gelding Ninian had offered them.

"I'm sorry, we're what?" Adam asked, already feeling the backache he was bound to get from the many miles of carrying a pack with no reprieve.

Nicholas barely glanced at him as he heaved his own backpack on his shoulders. "We're leaving them," he said shortly as if Adam was beneath his notice.

"Who elected you leader of the group? Those horses will save us time and our backs." Adam was startled when Story put a hand on his shoulder. Although there were circles under her eyes, she looked fresh in the morning light. Her silky brown hair was pulled back into a ponytail and she sported a similar outfit to the one she wore when she'd departed Sandeen's lake. Tresslan styles were definitely different, and seemed to be a mix of anything from contemporary Real World styles to medieval and Goth. Story's tight black riding leggings clung to her shapely legs and fit easily into the tall riding boots that were also somehow stylish. Once again, she wore a fitted top with short, puffed cap sleeves. You had to love a fairytale world.

"You could totally pull off that look in our world too," Elliott chimed in before Story could say anything to Adam. "Rider chic."

Story merely shook her head with a small smile, her good humor hopefully having returned, and met Adam's gaze with a furrowed, chastising brow. "I asked him to take the lead, Adam. He knows Tressla much better than I do and can help us identify our enemies before it's too late. And he can help us," she said, catching Nicholas's eye and sharing a small nod with him before she went on, which annoyed Adam even more. "I didn't want to alarm anyone last night, but Nightmares paid us a visit. Thankfully the Boggles scared them away."

"Story, Nightmares may not often come this way but it's been known to happen, especially if they sense there's more than one person sleeping here." Ninian explained with a small frown.

Story shook her head. "Yeah, I know; but there wasn't just one or two, there were a lot of them. They almost covered the night. Nicholas and I were out on the porch and I can tell you, it was like watching a horror movie."

Ninian's brows furrowed at the mention of horror movies, and Adam realized she probably didn't know what Story was talking about. But she knew about Nightmares, and he could tell by her reaction that it was not normal for them to come in a hoard.

Ninian turned to Nicholas, who gave an almost imperceptible shake of his head, while Ninian frowned in response. Adam continued to stare at Nicholas even as Ninian turned to address the rest of them. Testosterone feuds aside, Adam didn't trust him. There was something Nicholas wasn't telling them. Who was he anyway? Ninian had merely introduced him as a fellow dissenter. Adam suddenly started to feel as if they weren't all that informed.

"Before you leave there are a few things you must know. I'm sorry I didn't tell you this much earlier. Brink, as you know, is very powerful. The important thing to remember is although he is powerful, much of it is borrowed power. It can be taken away."

Adam sighed loudly, but no one looked at him except Bliss, who rolled her eyes before perching on the back of the brown gelding. Navigating the ins and outs of Tressla was proving to be exhausting—with fairytale characters who lived and breathed, prophecies, and humongous Wolves with the intellect of men, hot on their trail. Now they had the ruler of Tressla sending some sort of phantom-like nightmare creature to get them in the middle of the night. His last-minute internship at the law offices of Kipke & Lennon never sounded so inviting. At this rate he'd never make law school.

"And yet, the power he does wield is significant, and it comes to you, Story, to stop him."

She rose from her seat on the cottage's stoop and shook her head agitatedly. "Seriously, the gods must have more power than me."

Ninian shook her head, the soft blonde of her hair hung over her shoulder in a long braid. "I'm afraid you're it, Story. It was your death that set all this in motion."

Story's pixie-shaped face so often seen with a smile was hopelessly solemn, while doubt shone within the golden depths of her eyes. "I can't do anything," she muttered and turned to grab her pack from where it lay on the ground.

"You can tear a hole in the fabric of reality," Elliott pointed out softly, obviously remembering when Ninian had greeted them and mentioned the bizarre incident.

"But I can't right now," she protested.

"You've flown with The Pegasus," Ninian said, her voice laden with envy despite her gentle smile.

"You can pass between two worlds with ease when even I cannot visit the ones I love most," said a new voice from behind Adam. Startled, they all collectively jumped and took in the man who had joined them.

He was larger than life. His eyes were as gold as honey, and his long blond hair was tied back in a band. He was taller than even Nicholas, but that's not what made him stand out. He had a presence that you could almost hear—it thrummed with a gentle pulse. Adam immediately took to him, realizing he gave off a certain sort of earthy energy.

"Racell," Ninian said, breaking the quiet gawking as she stepped forward and embraced him as an old friend. He chivalrously kissed her hand before turning his intense golden gaze back to Story.

"I am sorry I did not come sooner. I only just heard from the trees that The Dreamer had arrived. It took me a few minutes to realize it was you, as I have rarely thought of you as anything other than little Story."

Her face had softened initially, but she quickly recovered and her amber gaze—so like her father's—narrowed like a hawk's, nursing something akin to hostility. "Racell," she nodded politely.

Ignoring her obvious snubbing, Racell moved past them and enveloped her in a hug from where she sat on the wood post. He held her tight for a few moments, while she stiffly returned his embrace. Holding her out at arm's length, he beamed at her. He had a strong and steady presence, and Adam was hard put to join Story on her I-hate-my-father crusade.

But as she looked back at him, her gaze was unwavering and also unrelenting. Racell released her with a sigh, but not before brushing a tender hand against her brow.

"Don't judge me before you hear me out," he murmured to her, so only Adam, who was standing right behind Story, could hear. And then addressing the rest of them, Racell spoke in a voice that reminded Adam of a stag. Not like he had ever heard a stag talk before, but he sounded like the stag that was Bambi's dad. His voice seemed wise, and Adam felt better knowing he was on their side.

"I bring some unfortunate news. You may have avoided the Big Bad Wolves for a moment, but they're back on your trail and they are looking for Story. They're not sure of who you are yet, but word is you're newcomers. And the impossibility of traveling between doorways has them riled. Ninian, they know you lied to them, so you're going to have to go into hiding."

Ninian merely shook her head, a peaceful smile on her lips. "They daren't lay a finger on me, or they would lose the support of the Daughters of The Will, who may be blind to what's going on around Tressla, but would never take the murder of one of their own without retribution." Racell turned a furrowed brow to her, but obviously knowing her, didn't push the issue.

"So how do we avoid getting torn to pieces?" Elliott said, voicing all their thoughts aloud.

"We need a witch," Nicholas interjected. "We have to appear to be someone else."

"Yes, and the moment you step off Ninian's property, the Big Bads will have you, so finding a witch is out of the question," Racell said seriously.

"Well, thank The Green I have just the thing. I may not be a simple Hedge witch but I am a Daughter of the Will," Ninian said dryly, and dashed into the cottage.

Moments later she returned with a box that she set down on the small gilded garden table, lifting the lid and pulling out a flower.

"A flower?" Elliott said with an arched brow.

"Ah, but this is Tressla," Racell admonished with a smile. "Nothing is just a mere flower."

Ninian held up the flower, which had silver petals and looked like someone had poured glitter over it. "This is an Incognitos Silver Bell," she said. "Whoever ingests its petals will take on the appearance of someone else. Even your scent will be different, which is important given who's tracking you. All the witches of old used this flower when pretending to be an old woman knocking on a kingdom door, or poisoning young girls they thought were prettier than they. However, I only have one and its petals will only replenish themselves three times."

"How does it wear off?" Nicholas said, asking the obvious question as he tore his intense gaze from Story for a mere few seconds to ask. Adam was relieved to see his attention was elsewhere for the moment.

"Good question. Since these petals are all from the same flower, they are connected. If one of you wanders off too far, or worse, dies, everyone else's disguises will disappear. So it's imperative you stick together if you want it to work. The illusion will also wear off if you eat some of the stem," she paused a moment, gazing at all of them, and then nodded to herself. "Everyone ready then?"

In response, they all nodded. "I better still look good," Elliott murmured. Story rolled her eyes before plucking a petal and laying it on her tongue. Elliott, Nicholas, and Racell all did the same. Adam followed suit and was surprised when the petal dissolved almost instantly and left a sugary aftertaste.

They all looked at each other, waiting for something to happen.

"Nothing is happening." Elliott stated the obvious.

"Join hands," Ninian instructed. Adam found himself between Racell and Elliott. Adam saw Story wince when she wound up next to Racell, but that was quickly replaced by a mild blush when Nicholas took her other hand in his, their eyes locking deeply for a few seconds before they turned back to Ninian. No, Adam was not relishing this development.

Again, nothing happened at first, and then Adam, who was still staring at Nicholas, noticed the man's eyes fade from black to an ordinary brown in a shimmering flicker. His square jaw narrowed and his wavy dark hair shortened to a light blond. Next to him, Story's hair had also lightened and turned a straight, strawberry blonde, while her pixie-like features had rounded out. Her face was wholly unrecognizable.

Adam was a little surprised they still looked so young. He had expected they'd become hags after Ninian's description of old witches. Elliott didn't get as lucky, which made Adam chuckle. He appeared a great deal shorter and was a nondescript middle-aged man with a sagging belly and overgrown graying facial hair.

They all laughed when Elliott peeked at himself in the glass of Ninian's window and gasped in horror. "This is so not fair!" he complained.

Ninian smiled. "The petals have a sense of humor it would seem."

Racell had become a young boy, around nine or ten, with freckled cheeks and bright blue eyes. Bliss actually had taken the form of an owl, giving Adam no end of amusement. He could hear her cursing up a storm.

Adam was curious to see what he looked like and peered into the glass as Elliott had. Turning, he directed a glare at his friend and sighed. He was ancient-looking, and he realized he was going to have to hobble around when anyone was nearby, in order to play the part. "At least you're not an octogenarian, Elliott."

CHAPTER NINETEEN

Locksley, Tressla

IT WAS ONLY LATE MORNING when they finally got on the road, despite their long discussion and Story's reluctant reunion with her father. They had decided if confronted, and when stopping in towns, Story and Nicholas would pretend to be married, Racell would be Story's younger brother, Elliott would play the part of her father, and Adam her grandfather. Adam had remarked with a sly grin that Bliss could be their pet, and now she wasn't talking to him. Which was fine with him since all she had done since they left was complain about looking like an owl.

They were on their way to the Festival of Wares, should anyone ask. It was apparently a big event held every year in The Capital, and people from all around traveled there to sell and trade goods. Adam was in good spirits. Since their story hinged on them traveling to sell, they needed to look as if they were hauling goods. So Tuscan and Cobble now trotted slowly next to them, hauling a cart filled with herbs.

Story had shot a longing glance as they passed by her old home, now Jemma's place, but it was too risky to stop there. Plus, they didn't want to lead the Big Bads to her doorstep in the event their disguises didn't work.

They had been on the road for a couple of hours. As he moaned and complained about what the walking was doing to his perfect feet, Elliott was beginning to look more like an old man than Adam. Story had been uncharacteristically quiet, avoiding her father so efficiently that Racell was now chatting up Elliott while Story and Nicholas led the way, walking closer than Adam liked.

Adam glanced at Bliss, who was perched on Cobble's back and winked. "Looks like it's you and me, pet," he said, laughing.

She scowled with her owl's beak before responding. "I'll have you know that I'm a Thumbelina Rose. I'm magical, a fairy if you will. I have fairy dust that will make you sneeze every time you look at me." Although hard to smile with a beak, he could hear in her voice the pleasure she got from the threat.

Adam's retort froze on his tongue, but it wasn't because of Bliss—although she seemed to think so for a minute, given a triumphant flap of her wings.

When Bliss finally noticed what was ahead of them, she gave a startled squawk and took flight into the trees. It certainly wouldn't do for them to be traveling with an animal most well-known for being a companion of the Daughters of the Will, as Adam had learned in his brief history lesson.

"Racell's balls," Racell hissed and Story actually looked at him and laughed.

"Really? You couldn't find a curse that didn't involve yourself?"

Racell looked up at her with twinkling eyes from the face of a young boy and shrugged. "I've heard it shouted and whispered so many times over the last thousand years, I can't help it."

Story laughed again, and Nicholas joined her as they approached a group of Big Bads, who, dressed as men, had blocked the road off ahead of them. They were directed to stop by the same Big Bad leader who had accosted them at Red's house. Nigel, Adam remembered. The one with the dead eyes.

Nigel stepped forward with two of the Wolf men flanking each side. "State your business," he said shortly. He sniffed the air, his disconcerting Wolf gaze pausing on Story a moment longer than Adam felt comfortable with. But he moved on quickly, his gaze resting on each one of them. Adam could see he was counting the number of people in their group. Thank God for Racell, although he wondered if he should be thanking the *gods* since he was in Tressla. Smart—Nigel had counted their group knowing there was a possibility for disguise. Adam hoped the fear they probably smelled emanating off of him was something the Wolves were familiar with, since he was sure they all smelled that way, except for maybe Racell. Which, when he started to think about it, might give them away as well. Wouldn't that be strange?

As if thinking it made it true, all slitted yellow orbs and one pair of winter blue focused on Racell, low growls emitting from their human throats.

Adam was sure they were totally, to put it mildly, screwed, when Nicholas bowed his head in greeting.

"My Lords, we are heading to the festival to sell our wares. Is there a problem?" Wiping a backhand against his brow and smearing more dirt, he looked for all the world like an honest farmer sweating beneath a brutal sun.

Nigel held up his hand, silencing the Wolves' growls for the moment. "My men are put off by your boy. There is something strange about him," he said with a nod toward Racell, who was quietly standing with one hand on Cobble to calm her.

"Yes, well, our boy has never seen the Wolves of Tressla. His grandfather has regaled him with tales of your adventures, as he is a staunch loyalist," Nicholas said, shooting Adam a look that said he had better give an Oscar-worthy performance or they were all dead.

Adam really didn't like him, he decided once again before nodding his balding head and stroking his long white beard, the act of the motion calming him as he played the part. He fleetingly considered growing a beard himself for the meditative benefit of stroking it.

"I fought beside the Wolves in the Battle of the Wills." Elliott had been filling him in on the Tresslan history he'd been reading about during their travels, and Adam had paid close attention to the parts dealing with the Big Bads. He'd learned about the war and how after The Will had left the world, the Wolves along with loyalists began their Brink-directed oppression of the Fairytales. The Fairytales had fought back at first, but as their numbers fell, many had gone underground or given their allegiance to Brink.

Adam decided to go big—who would question a crazy old coot anyway? He started to dance around using his cane like a sword and cackled, but then remembered that he shouldn't act too confident since they could smell his fear, so he stopped as suddenly as he started, heaving an old man sigh. He thought his performance must have been pretty good because even the Wolves looked aghast.

Nigel arched a brow and grinned slowly, the turn of his wolfish smirk ghoulish even in the light of the day. "We then thank you for your service. Tell me, how many Fairytales did you kill yourself?"

Adam rubbed his beard again, croaking as well as he could like an old man. "Eh, there were twelve before I got wounded." Adam nodded at his knee, hobbling for performance. Nigel narrowed his keen stare, his pointed features sharper than Adam had recalled, his startling gaze too aware. Adam forced himself to remain as calm as possible and only relaxed when Nigel finally tore his gaze away from him and nodded.

"Are we free to pass then?" Nicholas asked smoothly, gripping Story's hand so tightly his knuckles had turned white. Story had been quiet and was staring at Nicholas as if he was the second coming.

If he wasn't saving their asses, Adam would have gone on an inner Nicholas tirade, but he was still too scared to be anything but grateful, especially when Nigel turned back to them sniffing the air again as if something wasn't right. The alpha sensed something although the rest of the pack seemed bored. The hairy behemoth men with their wrestler-like arms and long beards and hair chatted in low murmurs along the side of the road, passing around flasks and laughing in low, chillingly canine-like chuckles. If Adam didn't know any better, he would have taken them for regular soldiers, until you saw their yellow wolf eyes.

Showing how adept he was under pressure and the intensity of Nigel's distrustful stare, Nicholas spoke again after a beat of silence in which the alpha did not wave them through to pass. "We would hate to disrespect, but would you be willing to let my son here shake your hand?" Nicholas asked, clapping Racell on the shoulders and pushing him slightly forward.

Racell smiled timidly at the Wolves, his gaze wide and open. Nigel turned the force of his gaze onto Racell, his face breaking out in a Wolfish smile. All he needed was his tongue hanging out. He laughed and pushed one of his men forward. "Go for it, Darvish, shake the boy's hand."

Darvish's deep brown skin glistened with sweat beneath the heavy heat of the air. His well-muscled, taut form was a dark, hulking presence in the afternoon daylight. His features were strong, and his head was bald, unlike the other Wolves who were usually adorned with long ponytails. The only hair he had was a dark, well-kept goatee that curved around his strong, boxy jaw. But it was his eyes that were the most interesting because like Nigel, they were different than the sickly yellow glow of the others. But unlike his alpha's, Darvish's were a bright, clear green.

"I'll do even better," he chuckled in a voice that boomed deep, resonating against the thickness of the oppressive air. "Your boy can even pet me." There was a shimmer, like glass melting, and then he was standing in front of them in his looming Wolf form. His fur was a shiny, rich brown that rippled like chocolate when he lay down so Racell could pet him.

Racell reached out his hand and stroked the Wolf's thick coat. For a moment, his face registered surprise, and then it was gone, replaced by a child's wonderment. At the same moment, Darvish's massive head turned sharply toward Racell, sending a spear of fear straight through Adam's gut as visions of glistening, dagger-like canine teeth ripping at his flesh already danced in his head. But as fast as Racell had recovered, so did Darvish, and Adam wondered if he had really seen anything at all.

A few moments later, Darvish stepped back, morphing into a man. He smiled his own wolfish grin at Racell, his big white teeth, which should have been threatening, almost friendly between the curve of his lips. Adam stared at the dark Wolf and wondered: was it possible for a Big Bad to not be bad? He quickly vanquished the thought, desperately hoping they'd passed the test.

Nigel grinned toothily for a few moments, his intention obviously to disconcert them. "I wouldn't try petting us on a regular basis, boy," Nigel snarled for show. Racell gave the appearance of being startled, and Adam was impressed by Elliott, who put a hand on his shoulder as if protecting the boy.

Nicholas held Nigel's gaze for but a moment before lowering his own in what Adam suspected was a show of passivity. He imagined backing down to anyone wouldn't be easy for the man, and he felt a moment of earned respect for his survival skills before his resentment returned.

Nigel nodded and waved them through. "You can pass. But if you see a strange group of travelers—a woman with two men and a Thumbelina Rose—report them. They're wanted by Brink for stealing."

"What did they steal?" Story asked, making Adam's jaw tense. What the hell was she doing, engaging them in conversation? But she merely looked slightly interested, tense but unafraid.

Nigel turned to her and sniffed, causing Adam's heart to beat erratically in his chest, while he yearned for the normalcy of reality.

"You could say they've stolen his muse. So if you see them, detain her without hurting her." Losing interest, he stepped back and gave a flickering wave of his hand as if dismissing them.

"But how will we know what they look like?" Nicholas asked.

A mangy-looking Big Bad sidled up and pounded a fist against a broken-down wagon that looked as if it had been discarded on the side of the road. Four pictures hung with the likenesses of Adam, Story, Elliott, and Bliss.

Elliott gave a small gasp, and while Adam hoped only he had heard, he knew from the way all eyes turned to his companion that Wolf hearing was the real deal for these guys. *Damn.*

But Nicholas was already covering, and Adam couldn't help but admire the guy once again. He was quick on his feet, which of course made Adam more suspicious. Who exactly was he again?

Nicholas nodded thoughtfully. "I'm sure we saw them on the road, back that way," he jerked his head back the way they had come. "That guy," he pointed a finger at Elliott's picture, "specifically stood out to me because he kept crying about how his feet hurt when we saw them in the tavern getting a bite to eat. If you don't know how to walk, then you're obviously not from these parts." He finished with bravado, shooting Nigel a comradely smirk.

Nigel nodded to the men and the lot of them morphed into their Wolf forms. "Brink will be pleased by your loyalty," he said. But Nigel's icy Wolf gaze stared at them all a moment longer than Adam would have liked, before he too joined his pack and took the lead. All that was left was dust in the road when Story's growing following had finally gathered their bearings.

Nicholas was furious. "You fool, how long do you think it will be before they realize we lied to them, and they're on to us? Our disguises will be worthless and we'll be torn to shreds."

Elliott, who normally had a lot to say, was quiet, and Adam felt an unexpected rush of protectiveness toward him. "Hey man, lay off. He was just surprised. It could have happened to any of us."

"No, what should have happened is Story should have come here alone without the baggage," Nicholas said with a sharp snap of his voice. Racell was trying to intervene, but his will didn't hold much weight. Demi-god or not, he looked like a ten-year-old at the moment.

"You arrogant schmuck," Adam started to say and stepped toward Nicholas in his indignation, feeling bottled resentment boil up and spill out. But before he could poke his finger aggressively into his chest, Story stepped between them. Up until this point, she had seemed unlike herself—small and vulnerable, someone to protect. But now Adam could hardly remember that girl as her eyes were spitting sparks. She turned one chastising look on Adam before turning her attention to Nicholas, her nose almost touching his as she glared up at him.

"Back off, Nicholas. These are my friends and you're lucky they're here with me. Did you know Elliott is a seer, or that Adam can track almost anything? But besides that, all that should matter to you is they are my friends and without them I might not be here. So back the hell off," she finished through gritted teeth.

Nicholas looked as if he was going to say something, but he shut his mouth in the wake of Story's outburst. Her inner fire had been relit.

Nicholas, looking as if he'd been slapped as well as properly chastised, stalked off down the road, leaving them behind. His large boots hit the dirt road with force, kicking up a trail of dust behind him. No one moved at first, allowing him the space he probably needed.

Sighing, Story stared after him and nodded to the others. "We should follow him. He knows where we're going and we need to decide what we're going to do now that the Wolves are bound to come back looking for us."

"Story." Adam touched her arm. "What was that about a muse?" Her face may have been someone else's under the illusion, but he could see her shining through, the worry etched on her features.

"That's what they said they were looking for when they killed Faulks . . . when they killed Papa," she whispered and shook her head, ridding herself of the tears before they could spill. "They killed him because of me. And now, they're going to pay."

"She's starting to embrace The Dreamer," Racell whispered. Adam wanted to ask what he meant, but Elliott interrupted, his voice devoid of emotion.

"Broken girl can't save the world, can't save anyone, least herself." Elliott's eyes looked sightless, like a blind person's as they stared into something beyond earthly vision. He blinked and the spell was broken. Adam shot Story a look, but she was already walking to catch up with

Nicholas. Bliss hovered nearby, her agitation written in the way she flapped her wings, feathers dropping.

"Broken? Is that about Story?"

Elliott looked from Racell to Adam and then back to Bliss, nodding. "Yeah, I think so. At least, that's who I felt I was talking about, but I didn't see anything else."

"Can't save herself?" Racell murmured, his boyish features barely able to hide the fatherly concern etched in the wrinkles of his furrowed brow, the firm set of his mouth and the clench of his small fists.

"Sorry to break up the discussion." Nicholas had rejoined them accompanied by Story, his expression soft and apologetic, but his voice brooking no argument. "But we need to head into the Eldridge mountains if we're to steer clear of the Big Bads, who will be coming for us the moment they realize we're not back there—the real us, I mean."

Bliss was shaking her owl's head. "It's too dangerous; there's too much at stake. The mountains will kill us."

"But why, what's wrong with the mountains?" Adam asked. "Besides Elliott here, the rest of us can handle it." Elliott glowered at Adam, but said nothing as they waited for a response from their resident Tresslans.

Story sighed, a sound she made a lot lately. "The Eldridge Mountains are home to the wild magic of Tressla—the Fairytales gone wrong and Fae who make chaos their home. Maya rules there, but she is unpredictable."

"Capricious," Nicholas said nodding.

Adam didn't really like the word so much. "Well then what are our alternatives?"

Nicholas answered with a grimace. "Wolf teeth, shredded flesh, and certain death, except for Story, who will be taken to Brink and used in whatever way he sees fit."

Adam was already eying the mountains that loomed ahead. "What makes you think we can get away from them there?"

Bliss impatiently flapped her wings, losing more feathers. "It is chaotic and unwieldy, but the Capital's Big Bad Wolves are not welcome within Maya's Valley, nor do the Fairytales there take kindly to them. You see, we could very well die in the mountains, but evil is not allowed there beyond a certain point . . . They're afraid."

"So basically it's 'we might die' versus 'certain death'?" Elliott summarized.

Nicholas, Story, and Bliss nodded in unison.

"Ok then, let's get going." Adam shouldered his pack. Much to Adam's chagrin, Story took the lead even before Nicholas.

They started to trudge forward but Adam had to stop. "But why is Story taking the risk by leading us in?"

She turned back to him and smiled. "Maya might not let you enter, but she'll let me. I'm the First Dreamer." A wistful smile floated across her face for a moment, and then she was leading them up the trail to the mountains.

Chapter Twenty

Eldridge Mountains, Tressla

AS THEY ENTERED THE FOOTPATH that would take them to the brink of the Eldridge Mountains, Story stopped and paused.

"Ready?" Nicholas lifted his blond eyebrows and jerked his head toward a path that looked dauntingly steep. "The faster we get ourselves established in the land of Maya, the faster we secure our safety from those bloodthirsty demons."

Story nodded mutely and started forward, a glimmer of trepidation in her eyes, but also a look of determination firmly etched in the stubborn set of her mouth. Nicholas put his hand on her arm and stopped her, a gentle smile curving his lips as he stared so intently at Story. Adam wondered if he'd forgotten everyone else's existence. A flush crept up her cheeks, and a look passed between the two that was filled with heat, before she nodded and started to climb.

Adam frowned while taking hold of a sapling and steadying himself, pushing himself up the steep side of the hill with a grunt. It was not going to be an easy climb, but he'd scaled worse.

The trail became easier, but only after about a half an hour of climbing. They all expressed wearied joy when they got to the point where the hill leveled out. Everyone glistened with sweat save Bliss, who had annoyingly fluttered above them shouting words of encouragement. Adam had thrown a rotten apple he found along the way at her, missing on purpose, but also solidifying her enmity toward him.

The climb not only became easier, but increasingly wooded. Eventually, they found themselves in a forest with the only sounds their panting and the chirrup of the birds. Adam was comforted that the birds at least sounded like home, and he could imagine for a moment he wasn't in another world, a place so foreign there was nowhere in his own world that could compare. The birds seemed to be calling for something unseen, and for a fleeting moment, he almost could see the shadow of his own world touching this one.

"They're searching for their shadow mate." Adam jumped and glanced at Nicholas, who had somehow come to walk beside him. He didn't know what surprised him more, the fact that Nicholas was talking to him as if he was worthy of attention, or the fact that his words echoed Adam's own thoughts.

"What do you mean?" he murmured, quiet because the birds had started to creep him out instead of comfort him.

"Here, the birds are mere shadows. They sing, but they don't fly. They are not whole. In your world there is a mate for every shadow of a bird that exists in Tressla. Our birds here spend their whole lives mimicking what your birds are doing in your world."

Adam thought on this a few moments, trying to catch a glance of these shadow halves, but he was unsuccessful. "I don't get it, the birds in our world seem normal."

Nicholas smiled wryly. "But how would you know? Were you there when the worlds began? It is said that birds used to be brilliant, soaring creatures—how could they not be? They learned how to fly." Nicholas glanced at the sky before meeting Adam's quizzical glance with a smile.

"When the worlds split, creatures were either here or there, either real or mythical. But birds, they were torn in two much like the world. And no one really knows why. Perhaps they were a bit of both—real and magic. Here, their intelligence has been kept intact, but they're ugly, horrid little creatures that slink along the earth with wings but without the ability to fly. In your world, they are dumb creatures, but they can fly. Funny, because the most magical thing I can think of doing is soaring through the clouds."

"But what about owls? They seem normal enough." He lifted his eyes to Bliss's form sailing above them through the trees.

"Yes, they retained their ability to fly, but notice how our owls take flight through the daylight, while yours only come out at night. They once lived in both sun and dark, and were by far a creature of immense intellect, thus often being a symbol for wisdom."

Both men were silent for a moment as Nicholas cast another longing gaze to the sky while Adam searched the ground for the sad shadow of Tressla's birds.

"I don't trust you," Adam said without really thinking.

Nicholas stayed quiet for a moment, nodding thoughtfully before meeting Adam's gaze. "It's good Story has you here," he responded quietly. "And I apologize for my earlier outburst. Even if you don't trust me, perhaps we can learn to work together."

Nicholas nodded once and then picked up his pace to match that of Story, who had been politely holding court with Racell. Adam searched the forest floor for the birds, but didn't see any. In his mind's eye, he kept trying to picture what they must have been like once, intelligent and majestic. No wonder there were people who found birds creepy. They could probably sense something was off with them. He was pondering this when Elliott nudged him and jerked his head toward Nicholas.

"What do you make of him?" Elliott asked.

Adam glanced at him and shrugged slightly. "I'm not sure, I just know there's more there. But, I don't think he's trying to hurt us; I think he's on our side." As he spoke, Adam was surprised by his own feelings. But despite his resentments and questions, he felt that Nicholas was there to help.

"He's hiding something," Elliott observed. "But I think you're probably right. I hope he reveals whatever it is soon . . . Story doesn't need any more secrets or problems to figure out."

"Do you know?" Adam asked, his fingers glancing over bark and bough as he walked, as if stroking the trees. They had always grounded him.

"No, just a feeling . . . Are you petting the trees?"

Adam caressed a leaf and smiled. "They like it, it soothes them when strangers walk through their midst. I do it back home, but the trees don't speak as loud there."

Elliott looked at him strangely for a moment before rolling his eyes. "You know, Adam, I think you have your own magic working here. You might want to look into your lineage. Are there any dreamers there? Any demi-gods?"

Adam chuckled. "All you have to do is really listen and you'll hear it too—the forest talks, even in our world."

They decided to stop just after the sun had risen its highest. They were all tired and hungry from the climb.

Story was resting against a tree with her knees drawn to her chest, chewing thoughtfully on a piece of bread baked fresh for them by Ninian before they left, when Adam dropped down next to her. Elliott and Bliss had gotten caught up in a conversation having to do with Tresslan style trends, while Nicholas and Racell discussed their next move through the mountains.

"You doing okay?"

"Yeah, I'm okay," she said with a smile, taking a sip from a canteen. She swallowed, licked her lips and passed the water jug to him, debating whether to unload on her longtime friend. Deciding she'd go crazy if she didn't, she shook her head. "I just feel different."

"I've seen a difference." He nodded for her to go on.

Smiling gratefully for his support, she bit her lip. After years of holding back her secrets, she wasn't sure that it was so easy to break the habit, but if he'd noticed a change, then maybe she should mention it. "I don't know how to explain it, except that I don't feel . . . " she struggled with the word, her molars grinding and her jaw clenching, "I feel like something's missing."

She stared down at the grass and moss, picking up a piece of bark and rolling her thumb over its roughness. "It's like, I was always like this but now I'm just noticing." Peeking a glance through her lashes, she was disturbed to see Adam's brow furrowed deep, his jaw pulsing.

Seeing her looking at him, he flashed her one of his typical cocksure smiles, and all traces of worry fled from his face. "Maybe you should talk to your dad, he might have some insights. Isn't he like centuries-old or something?" He nodded toward Racell, who was still cloaked in the illusion of a ten-year-old.

Story followed his nod and rolled her eyes, the image of Ninian and her father kissing all those years ago making her almost physically sick to her stomach, especially when she thought of her poor mother loving him all these years. "No thanks, I'll figure it out without him." She stuffed a last bit of bread into her mouth, effectively ending the topic of conversation. He opened his mouth to say something, but she cut him off with a mere look and shook her head. She just wasn't in the mood to go there about her father.

Adam, who'd been her friend long enough to know when he'd been bulldozed into silence, changed the topic. "Story, we're going to get the answers we need. And it will be soon. Color me intuitive—Elliott already has the title of psychic." He was rewarded with a quick grin from Story before he went on.

"Joking aside, we should come up with some sort of plan of action once we get to The Capital. In the meantime, you might think about getting your boy Nicholas to clue you in. I don't trust him."

Story nodded. "I know, I think he's hiding something."

Adam was not thrilled to notice that Nicholas's secrets didn't keep Story from blushing at the mention of his name. But he wasn't going to get into it unless he saw something to worry about.

"I just wonder what the prophecy meant by 'in three she will be'." Sighing, she rose and brushed her pants free of crumbs and ground debris. "We should get going. The faster we're through these mountains, the happier I'll be."

"What exactly is so scary about them, besides that valley you mentioned?"

Lowering her voice, she closed the distance between their heads. "Faulks, my papa, used to say that Fairytales would even go crazy there, and they don't tend to be the most grounded sort of people. What with all those tragedies followed by happy endings, they're all just a little bit askew."

"Isn't Jess one?" Adam asked.

"I didn't say Jess was sane. She's crazy—who else would go wrestle one of those Big Bad Wolves? I'm going to go round up the troops. Could you grab some more of those berries we picked before? We can snack on them as we walk if we get really desperate."

Adam nodded. "Sure, I have to take a leak anyway."

Rolling her eyes, Story nodded and started toward Elliott and Bliss. Adam headed toward the bush where they had found the berries, but they had cleaned it out. Looking around, he noticed another bush not far ahead, so he walked to that one, dropping berries in a basket, again provided by Ninian. He had only ventured a little further when he heard the tinkling of laughter.

The sound was rich and warm and made him thirsty for a glass of red wine. Enthralled, Adam found himself moving deeper into the woods, barely glancing at the deformed creatures covered in feathers singing like angels and scuttling along the ground, although he'd been hungry to see them before.

Like a siren's call, the sound lured Adam into a grove. His usually calm eyes, gray once more since he'd traveled outside the flower's effectiveness, widened at the sight. Two women lay asleep upon platforms encased in glass in the middle of the clearing. Glancing around quickly in bewilderment, Adam could see there was no one else about.

He took a few steps toward them against his own volition, and he only stopped when he was close enough to see their features. "Oh man," he breathed, clutching his chest and feeling his heart hammer. They were by far the most gorgeous creatures he had ever set his eyes on. The first had hair like night that curled around her shoulders, contrasting sharply against her milky white shoulders and lips as red as blood. A vague recognition flickered in his mind . . . "Lips as red as blood," he whispered, and then he shook his head, breathing in the entirety of her beauty.

Her long black lashes rested against her cheeks, making him yearn to stroke his finger down that soft, sensual curve. The second woman was equally as exquisite although her beauty was like summer compared to the other's wintry loveliness. Where the first had skin like ivory, hers was sun-kissed. She had golden waves that reached to her waist and her lips were plush and pink. Where the dark beauty had been soft curves, this one was sharper with her high cheekbones and sweetheart chin.

Adam stared at the two women for a few minutes longer, silently enchanted. He came back to himself momentarily, examining the cases they slept in. They couldn't be dead, their youth and energy was too palpable. He could see the flush to their skin although their breasts seemed strangely still. He was wondering what he should do when he noticed an inscription decorating each of their domes. The first read, "Snow" while the second read "Beauty."

"My god," Adam whispered as he ran a hand through his auburn hair, the old fairytales dawning on him. "It's Snow White and Sleeping Beauty."

He awkwardly stood there, shifting from foot to foot, wondering how he could help. As if under a spell, all thoughts of Story and their quest were forgotten. All that existed was Snow White and his Sleeping Beauty, both of which he intended on waking since he was meant to be with them. But he didn't know how . . .

Adam stopped, tilting his head as he listened to something whispering in his ear. "What?" he said aloud.

"True love's kiss." The soft sound rustled over the leaves and danced across his skin.

"True love's kiss?" he asked.

"True love's kill," the breeze assured him.

"Ah," he whispered, remembering the movies and how the prince always saved the princess by kissing her. "Well, I can do that."

Entranced, he lifted the casing that contained Snow White and slowly lowered his lips to hers. Her lips were plush and tasted like maraschino cherries. He could have gone on kissing her forever, but Sleeping Beauty still needed his kiss as well.

Turning toward her, he lifted the glass case and met her silent lips as well. In a matter of a few seconds, he felt a sharp sting at the side of his neck. Beauty had wrapped her lips around his own and kissed him back, her teeth sinking into his lips. But Adam didn't mind, he only felt bliss as he imagined himself lying on the soft grass of the forest with the two most beautiful women on earth for eternity.

He only startled when the two women pulled back. Racell, now looking like his golden demi-god self once more, was standing at the start of the clearing, ordering the awakened princesses, who Adam groggily noticed looked even more beautiful with their fangs, away from Adam. As if from far away, he noticed they looked hungry, and their lips, both sets now beaded red with his blood, were parted sensuously in hunger.

"Oh Racell," Snow White said sweetly and wiggled her shoulders coquettishly while dark eyes glittered beneath batting lashes. "We just want to play for a little bit. He's so yummy."

"He is the First Dreamer's dearest friend. Release him."

Beauty shook her long golden tresses and positioned her wide blue eyes on Adam before turning back to Racell. "We are not obligated, no matter who he is. He is ours for the time being. Out of respect for The

Dreamer, however, we will not drain him. But he woke us with the intention of true love, which means he's ours for now." She stroked Adam's arm, her voice low and sultry while Snow's was like spun sugar.

Adam barely heard their exchange, feeling like jelly—like he wanted to fall into their arms forever.

"Adam," Racell said. "Remember Story?"

Adam felt the fog lift away for a moment at the mention of his best friend. He started to step forward but was stopped when Snow White's small hand slipped into his and she leaned in and stroked her tongue against his neck. Then the fleeting image of Story was gone.

"Story will be fine without me," Adam responded, never taking his eyes off the girls. In turn, the bloodthirsty duo had wrapped their arms around him and were alternately peppering him with sensuous kisses and even more lusty bites.

"Adam," Racell's voice boomed. "Story will be waiting when you decide to find us." And then with a sigh, Racell was gone and Adam was left alone with two very beautiful princesses who wanted to suck his blood. For a moment, Adam was overcome with the need to leave them, to get back to Story and the group, to meet the fearless Jess. But the haze of his own lust overcame him and he laughed, holding the two Fairytale vampiresses to him and laying down and laughing. "What shall we do?" he asked them.

Beauty chuckled throatily and nibbled at his ear. "Oh so many things, my prince."

CHAPTER TWENTY-ONE

Eldridge Mountains, Tressla

STORY WAS DOWN by Chaos Creek when Racell found her. She had been gazing into its rolling depths, looking for answers to her life. The most pertinent question in her mind was who she was. She was supposed to know. So why didn't she? Why was there a void where her self-identity was supposed to be? And then there were the million questions she had running around in her head about Nicholas. Like for one, why did he seem so familiar when she was sure she had never met him in her life? His eyes had a dark compassion that made her feel . . . protected. And yet as Adam and Elliott had pointed out, he was keeping secrets. But she trusted him. Shaking her head, she skipped a rock against the relatively quiet surface of the river. One, two, three times. Ahead, above the trees tops, she could see the steady rise of the mountain they were intent on climbing. A hybrid of colors, from turquoise to brick red and sea foam green, colored the leaves that adorned the trees of the Eldridge Mountains. Like fall turned psychedelic.

This life was coming back to her gradually with every day that passed. But why not that other life, where she had been this divine dreamer? Honestly, she felt about as divine as a cockroach. She could call for Sandeen to take her back. But Story knew she would never do that, not when they were counting on her—her other family, the one she had forgotten. How could she have forgotten?

Racell appeared as quietly as a whisper in that moment, interrupting her thoughts. He didn't look like a little boy anymore. In fact, when Story turned quickly to glance at the stream, she could see by her reflection that her glamour had also disappeared, her strange golden eyes peering back at her.

Turning quickly to Racell she jumped to her feet. "What's happened?" Racell held up his hand in a calming motion.

"There is no cause for alarm, but yes, we are now without our disguises. And while what I'm about to tell you is surely going to distress you, I want you to rest assured that it's not permanent.

"What is it?" she said, feeling more alarmed despite his reassurance.

"Your friend Adam took a walk and found Sleeping Beauty and Snow White."

Not understanding, Story tucked a dark strand of hair impatiently behind her ear. "So?"

"Well, you know how Fairytales in Tressla aren't always what they seem to be . . . They're not like the stories in your books. In Tressla, Snow White and Sleeping Beauty sleep within the forest and lure young men to their clearing, much like sirens. When a man kisses each of them, they wake up and then he is bound to them."

"What?" Panic fluttered in her chest, and also protectiveness, as she got ready to go catfight the she-demons to the ground.

"Hold, Story. There's more." Story crossed her arms and nodded, waiting for him to go on, feeling anything but calm.

"So Adam, of course, kissed them—because not only are they very beautiful, but there's also all sorts of magic and enchantments encased around them. And, there's something else," he said glancing away, looking uncomfortable and steeling himself. "They're also what you would call vampires." He looked back at her, an apologetic expression creasing his godly features.

"What?" Story repeated herself once again, but much more vehemently, turning to stalk up the hill and rip her friend from the bloodsuckers' clutches. She didn't get very far before Racell's long legs carried him to her side, and he stopped her with one iron grip on her shoulder. She knocked his hand from her shoulder and glared at him.

He sighed. "Story, you can do nothing. I found him and tried to help, but it was too late."

"You mean to tell me that you, a demi-god, were there while this all was happening, and you didn't put a stop to it?" She could feel herself losing her cool exterior. Adam was her rock, her strength. She needed him to be there with her, to see her through this strange journey. She didn't mean to sound as nasty as she did, but all her unease, insecurities, and fear manifested in this one moment, and Racell was the easiest scapegoat since she already felt betrayed by him.

"Oh, the big demi-god," she seethed through her teeth. "Everyone loves Racell in Tressla, don't they? Little do they know you're nothing but a fake. You have immortality and that's about it. Wait until they find out what a shameless coward you are. You, who think it's okay to knock up pretty young girls and then break their hearts when the relationship doesn't suit you anymore. Here's a news flash, you're not Zeus. And how long did it even take you to find me when I came here? I was like ten years old before I even met you. You're obviously useless here, so why don't you take your pointless immortality and ridiculous fatherly overtures to someone who cares. Because I don't.

"You're not my father. The only man who deserves the title of father is Faulks, and you aren't even half the man. He was godlier than you ever could be." She stared at him through narrowed eyes, breathing quickly and startled by her own outburst. She knew he rubbed her the wrong way, but she hadn't meant to go so far.

Racell, for his part, remained quiet, although she saw hurt flash in his eyes so like her own, which made Story even angrier. How dare he make her feel bad for his shortcomings?

Very quietly, he spoke, "I'm sorry you feel that way. I was only going to say that I tried, of course, but I have no dominion over such creatures. Those that were created from Fairytales and walk in Maya's Valley often come back changed. A part of chaos comes with them. Only Maya can help. We can try calling to her, and she may answer. Eventually, however, the princesses will tire of him and send him on his way. They are Fairytales after all, and so they are still confined to the Happy Ending rule of The Will, which means Adam will not suffer."

"No, in fact, he'll probably love it," said Nicholas, who had sauntered from the woods into their conversation. "Those ladies are something else," he added with a smirk, nodding at Racell, who took the moment to exit the scene. Story could feel the waves of his hurt as he walked away.

Sighing, Story kicked at a clump of grass with her booted toe and peeked up at Nicholas. "Too harsh?"

Nicholas gazed at her for a moment, the calmness of his dark eyes like a boon to Story's wounded self-worth. "Yes, but he'll get over it.

He's lived many years and you don't live as long as he has without gaining some grit. Besides, what kind of father-daughter relationship would you have if you didn't tell him you hated him at least once," he added with a wink.

Story smiled. "It sounds like you have had personal experience with the vampire princesses."

"Ah, indeed I have. And don't worry, they come off like succubae, but deep down they're just little Disney princesses at heart."

Story started to laugh, but stopped, her body growing very still as she looked at Nicholas. "Disney? How do you know that? Have you been to my world? Why didn't you say anything?"

Nicholas sighed and then unexpectedly took Story's hand between his own capable, strong ones. She tried hard not shudder at his touch. His hand on her own sent sparks of electricity running up through her fingers, up her arms and through her body, so that she felt her cheeks warm and her body temperature skyrocket. She wanted to bottle up what he had and take him home for those cold East Coast winters.

"Yes, I have been to your world. They say all the doors are closed, save Sandeen's lake, but one door was surprisingly created about ten years ago. A little girl was playing in her mentor's backyard when she poked a hole through the fabric of reality. The teacher may have thought she did a fine job closing it up, but it's still open and no one knows about it but me."

Staring at him with her mouth agape, she slid her hand from his although she more than anything wanted to continue to feel his warm, strong grip. "How do you know about that?"

"My father and I were passing through the area when I saw it happen. We had been camping, and I wandered away. I was young, maybe nine. I saw what you did, and some years later when I was passing through the area, I decided to check it out. When I came through, I was lost for a while. I got so hungry, I stumbled into a diner and the waitress took pity on me and bought me dinner. She brought me home and her kid, who was about the same age as me, introduced me to your world's TV."

"But how long were you there?"

"Only a month or so, but I learned a lot about TV in a short time," he joked with a smile. "But seriously, that was all the kid did was watch

TV, so I did it a lot too, and I have to confess, I found your world's fairytales the most wonderful thing of all."

"Why? You have the real thing here."

"Because where you live, they're only stories, but they're beloved. Here, they're treated as second-class citizens." He shrugged and squeezed her hand, which he trapped within his own again, his dark eyes penetrating hers as he drew her an inch closer. Her breath caught in her throat, and she dropped her eyes, unable to keep up the intimacy of their eye contact. She didn't believe he had yet told her everything, but every time he touched her, she felt hot, her muscles twitched, and she couldn't take her eyes away from his lips.

"Story," he said, his eyes dark and filled with a storm she couldn't yet name, as he traced circles with his thumb on her palm. "There's something else I should tell you."

She swallowed hard, the tingles he left from his tracery exploration of her lifeline causing the blood to rush to better-unexplored areas. If he only leaned forward, she was sure she would just collapse into his arms, the thought of his mouth haunting her all day. But she wasn't ready to hear any more from him. Snatching her hand back abruptly, she turned and started to make her way towards camp.

"We should get going if we're going to get anywhere before dark. I also want to see if we can find Maya. I need Adam," she called over her shoulder. She thought she would have been relieved to escape his overwhelming presence, but instead she only felt the loss of his warmth.

CHAPTER TWENTY-TWO

Eldridge Mountains, Tressla

STORY CAST ONE MORE desperate look behind her, searching the clearing for the princesses and Adam, but they were nowhere to be seen. Racell cleared his throat and patted her shoulder awkwardly. "Nicholas told you the truth. They will release him eventually, and he'll stumble from there with some fond memories."

They had begun the easy part of their trek, in terms of physical effort. But Maya's Valley was not far ahead, and none of them wanted to spend the night within it although they knew they'd have to. It was really a matter of prolonging the inevitable. So the debate had begun: whether to push forward and try to make it across as far as they could before dark, or stop before crossing and make camp. If they left early enough the next day, it was possible they could get to the other side by nightfall, but it would be a hard pace. Elliott was dead set against going across the valley only a few hours before dark, terrified that if they got trapped at night, he would go crazy due to his "psychic sensitivity."

Racell was somewhere in the middle, while Bliss took Elliott's side. Story was hopeful that if they stalled, Adam might break from the spell he was under and find them. Only Nicholas wanted to push forward, afraid the Big Bads would sniff out their trail and get them before they could enter the valley.

When Story had informed Elliott of Adam's situation, his remark had only been, "Oh god, vampires are so on the way out."

"This isn't pop culture, Elliott, this is Adam's neck being bitten by two actual vampires."

"Well, they're probably only vampires because fiction is so rampant with them nowadays; it's just a matter of time before vampires are passé." Story was about to give a snarky reply, annoyed by Elliott's apparent lack of comprehension, when the thought occurred to her that he was on to something. What if the Real World's tastes in literature were somehow affecting the way Fairytales translated here? It was an interesting thought, but she still wanted Adam back lest the two princesses suddenly become zombies.

She turned to Racell anxiously. "But how will he find us?" Her hand clenched one of Tuscan's halters so tightly her knuckles turned white. Her father squeezed her shoulder and then let his hand fall away.

"I don't speak for Maya, but I'm pretty sure she'll help make sure he finds his way to you. You're the First Dreamer, after all. She once called you sister and walked through moonlight when it was still new with you."

Story shook her hand. "No, no, no!"

Racell looked at her quizzically, and even Nicholas and Elliott up ahead glanced back.

Lowering her voice self-consciously, she sighed. "I'm sorry . . . I just don't know who that person is. I don't feel like her, I don't have her memories . . . I'm just me."

"I know it must feel that way, but you are her. Just wait. Tomorrow we will cross Maya's Valley, but without you the way would be barred to us. Only those with a sacred purpose can cross with welcome," Racell said softly.

"And you wouldn't be welcomed," Story stated flatly, turning to look at him finally. It was strange to be here walking and talking with Racell . . . her father. As much as she wanted to loathe him, and the hard edge of resentment still seethed under her polite exterior, she had to admit to herself that she felt safer in his presence. She had also been told multiple times that Racell had never wanted to leave her mother, and that Sandeen had banned him from the Real World by closing the doorway to him. But she still couldn't lose the image of him kissing Ninian, even though rationally she knew that believing he couldn't go back may have made him turn to another woman. She could tell he was still sad, however. It was written in his features, in the shadows that muted the eyes she had inherited from him.

Despite this awareness, the anger wouldn't resolve itself, but she felt she at least owed him an apology for the harsh way she'd spoken to him. "Hey, Racell—I'm sorry . . . for what I said back at the camp. I was just worried about Adam, I shouldn't have taken it out on you."

Racell shook his head and smiled at her, the corners of his eyes crinkling, and the shadows disappeared for a moment as the color brightened. "And that's because you're a good friend. You don't owe me an apology."

Story cut him off with a jerky wave of her hand. "But I do. I was harsh, and you've done nothing but try to get close to me since I was a child and you realized I existed. And I guess I can't fault you for wanting to find someone else, and Ninian deserves happiness—it's just that my mom never did . . . find anyone else, that is." Story looked away when she mentioned his and Ninian's relationship, so she was confused by Racell's startled expression.

"Me and Ninian?"

"Yeah, I came back one night when I was napping, you know, in my world, and I saw you two . . . kissing. It made me angry when I found out that you were my father, because I could only think of my mom."

"Oh Story," he breathed, taking her hand between his massive ones and holding it like it was a delicate gift. "I'm sorry that you saw that, but you have to know, I have never stopped loving Edie. She's all I've ever dreamed of since I was forced to leave her all those years ago. It was just complicated. When I found out you were my daughter, I tried to get to know you, but Ninian didn't want me upsetting you, and so she asked me to keep my parentage a secret for the time. We grew close, she and I, trying to decipher the prophecy and watching your abilities grow stronger and wilder. And one night, yes, we kissed. But the moment it happened, I knew it was wrong, not only because of my feelings for your mother, but also because I knew I did not have those feelings for her. I love her, yes, but as a dear friend. And so we have remained ever since. Every year, I go to Sandeen and I ask her to allow me to pass, but she always refuses."

Feeling those final sticky remnants of ire toward her father dissolve like cotton candy touching the tongue, she felt well-being settle over her, the happy and safe feeling any child gets knowing their parents are in love.

"She never stopped loving you either. She doesn't talk about it, but I've seen it my whole life. Whenever I figure out how to use these powers, I'll send you back, I promise." She turned her hand within his own so she was holding his left hand back, and was gratified to see the lift of light in his eyes.

Racell stared in silence at her, his gaze unwaveringly gentle, and Story knew at that moment that she could accept him as her father someday. "You can do anything here. Story, don't you realize that? You created this world. You're its master."

Blinking her eyes against his beaming smile, she swore she could see dots shift and dance before her eyes, like she was coming inside after being out in the bright sun without sunglasses. Although the idea that she could control Tressla seemed beyond the extreme, in that moment, she felt more right than she had since the nightmares had started again, since she had come home.

CHAPTER TWENTY-THREE

Eldridge Mountains, Tressla

THEY REACHED THE ENTRANCE to Maya's Valley just as the sun's light started to fade away into night. As they made camp, Story found that between looking behind her in hopes of seeing Adam and sneaking glances at Nicholas, while also worrying about crossing Maya's Valley, her appetite was almost null.

Both Racell and Nicholas could hunt, and soon enough they brought back a rabbit, which Racell seasoned with wild herbs. The smell wafted around them and Story's mouth watered. Perhaps she could eat.

Taking a swig of water from her canteen, she capped it and looked up in time to see Elliott start toward her. Bliss took to the trees, probably to forage for roots and berries since the smell of meat always made her slightly sick, as her species was vegetarian. Story had noticed how on edge Bliss had been since Adam had disappeared, and she wondered if the Thumbelina was actually worried about her chosen nemesis.

"What's up?" Elliott lowered his long form down beside her, and Story noticed that his stylish stubble was growing into a beard, and how different he looked than his usual New York City fashion-plate self. He still managed to cock an air though, picking up a few pieces of bark that had clung to his clothes between two fingertips and dropping them back to the ground with a cluck of his tongue. "I swear, I will never take a shower for granted ever again."

Crossing her legs out in front of her at the ankles, she admired the black leather boots Sandeen had provided for her, thanking the goddess for the comfort. She didn't have one blister, and she wondered idly if there wasn't a little magic or charm at work in the footwear.

"I hope Adam comes." She bit her lip and glanced at her friend, trying to quell the worry eating at her.

"What if he doesn't?" He asked the looming question without pause.

"I can only hope that Maya shows."

But as the night wore on, it became evident that Maya wasn't going to entertain them with her presence. As exhausted as she was, Story doubted she would sleep at all. Especially since the sounds had begun.

Right on the edge of Maya's Valley, the chaos within could not be contained. Noises reached them that were hard to describe, like a discordant symphony of out-of-tune pianos and crashing cymbals, while the haunting sound of wings rushing around them made it near impossible to sleep. The dark seemed so complete, despite the glow of the fire, Story felt a chill consume her, and she shivered, digging down deeper into the sleeping roll.

She was lying close to the fire, and although the warmth and light were welcome and comforting, the blackness that surrounded was all-pervading. Occasionally, a burst of light would shoot forth from the valley's entrance. She couldn't believe how anyone could sleep through the racket. But looking over, she saw motionless lumps and heard soft snores while Bliss nestled quietly in a tree. Story startled when she realized the dark lump that had been Nicholas was gone. She started to sit up and nearly shrieked when a hand wrapped around her arm.

"Hey, sorry to startle you," Nicholas whispered. "I don't know how anyone can sleep, though."

Recovering from her surprise, Story glanced up at him and nodded, sitting up fully but pulling the blanket around her as best she could to keep in the heat and ward off the moonless chill. Illuminated only by the fire, his dark eyes gleamed soulfully into the night while the strong planes of his face and masculine angular jaw made Story start to feel a little better. Smoothing down her mussed-up hair, she slid her butt a few inches so that her back rested up against a large stump that had earlier served as Racell's chair. Following her lead, Nicholas dropped down next to her.

"When I came through here before, I was a child. So this didn't scare me. I still had that innocence, you know, that fearlessness that made it seem amazing."

"Are you scared now?" Story asked, turning so she could study his profile in the waning firelight. Their shoulders banged together as

Story jumped nervously when a melody broke through the darkness, eerie and beautiful at the same time.

"Even chaos can be beautiful, eh?" Nicholas said and patted her leg beneath the blanket as if to calm her. Turning to her with a rakish smile, he seemed unfazed by the periodic booms that were grating her nerves raw.

"And to answer your question, no, not scared, just startled at times. The truth is I remember feeling as if the music of the valley understood me—that its chaos actually had a melody, like it was in tune with me. What about you, are you scared?"

Story shook her head, trying to find a way to break the eye contact they had going on, and break the hold on her erratically beating heart. She cursed her body for reacting to his physical presence like a freshman girl in love with the cutest senior boy in school. Except this was so much worse. If she looked down, she knew she'd see her hands tremble slightly. They always did when he was near.

"Just unnerved I suppose." She forced an assured smile, hoping he couldn't see how he affected her.

Her arm accidentally brushed his and he smiled, his strong, large hand wrapping her small one in his own. His touch startled her more than any sound had. Swallowing thickly, she realized she had lost all desire to break their gaze. Her shoulders relaxed downward as she started to give into the pull that was calling her home to him.

"You know," Nicholas whispered, using his other hand to tuck a stray strand of her dark hair behind her ear. "I've been waiting for you."

"What?" Story whispered back, leaning toward his hand before she consciously knew what she was doing. He cupped her chin in his hand, his fingers slightly caressing the arch of her neck and making her tremble, her eyes fluttering at the warm sensuality of his touch against her skin.

Her eyes flickered closed and then opened again, and she leaned forwards, her body rebelling against what logic told her was a bad idea.

"I've been meaning to tell you something," he whispered, his face so close to hers his breath shivered across her skin.

"What?" She whispered back.

"We've met before," he said, pausing as if he were about to say something else and then instead giving a quiet growl and pressing his warm mouth demandingly against her own.

Story vaguely head him, but fell into the kiss, only wondering for less than a split second what he was talking about, before he consumed her. His arms encircled her and drew her in close, so that her breasts were flattened against his chest and there was no room for even air between their bodies. She didn't feel the chill of the air as her sleep roll slipped to her waist, and they entwined their bodies around one another completely. His lips were soft, and yet demanding, his tongue flicking between her lips without caution.

His fingers slid along the small of her back that was bare between her cropped top and low-waisted pants, making her breath catch in her throat as she slid her tongue against his more bravely. Her own fingers clutched his shirt, and his lemony, woodsy smell made the world spin behind her closed lids. She cried out when his lips left her mouth, whimpering only in satisfaction when his moist mouth started to work on her neck, his lips blistering against her skin so that she lost all thought of anything but him. The still night broke when the wind came to play, slowly at first, whipping trees and branches into a dance, but even the growing whistle of the wind was not enough to awaken them from their embrace.

He bent her back and lowered her to the ground, hunger lighting up his eyes as his long form pressed down against her, her legs sliding apart to admit his hips against her own. It was then in the back of her mind that she felt something rustle, an awareness flicker that urged her on, feeding on the lust that drove them.

She wrapped her legs around him, the fever of his body against hers all that she could feel. But it was more than just the physical. The sense that she knew him grew greater, and as it did, so did her own hunger for him. They might have made love right there on the forest floor if the rustle in the dark corners of Story's mind hadn't made her gasp and wonder at its presence. The break was enough so that Nicholas was able to hear what was coming, his head jerking up from her mouth, both their lips swollen from the mutual abuse.

"Did you hear that?" His eyes looked pure black in the night, and only the dim firelight showed the widening of his pupils as awareness flooded back to him.

Story gaped, pressing the back of her hand to her lips. Barely heard above the din of the growing wind was the howl of a Wolf.

"How close?" she managed to choke out between quiet gasps as she tried to regain her composure. Her body was still humming, throbbing with his touch and how far they might have gone, her hair beginning to whip into her face.

"Close enough. We can't stay here any longer. The Big Bads may not enter Maya's Valley, but they'll come here to get us before we enter if they can," he said looking at the trees that whirled around them. "And a storm is coming, and we don't want to be sitting around for that either."

She wasn't ready to enter the valley when the sky was still thick with night. And Adam, he was still lost somewhere deep within the trees with two bloodsucking princesses from hell. Story sighed, feeling the weight of guilt press on her chest. He had come here because of her. If anything happened to him, she would never forgive herself.

"Story," Nicholas whispered, his lips brushing her cheek and his strong hand wrapping around her own in reassurance. "It's going to be alright. You're the First Dreamer, you can do anything."

The wind was picking up. By now Racell had roused and was packing them up while Bliss was flittering frantically for purchase as the wind grew stronger and louder, although not loud enough to block out the triumphant howl of the Wolves on a trail.

"But I can't . . . " she whispered, her response lost to the wind.

Nicholas roused a groggy Elliott, who slept like the dead.

"Story, they are almost here," Bliss hissed, her fluorescent green eyes wide with urgency while she held onto a branch that whipped her about. "But you have to enter first, we must not delay!"

Story nabbed her from the tree and handed her to Racell, who secreted her into a pocket where she wouldn't blow away. He handed Story her pack and she shouldered it. She turned toward the entrance, stumbling against the power of the storm and bearing down lower to the ground in an attempt to gain stability.

The valley entrance was nothing obvious, merely two trees that bowed together like a doorway. But through it Story knew they were about to encounter chaos, although the howling of wind and Wolves around her couldn't be better. Exhaustion seeped into her bones and she almost wished she had spent the last couple of hours sleeping. But when she remembered Nicholas's kisses, she felt hot, the feel and smell of him still wrapping around her body and soul and encasing her in its warmth, and she hungered for more.

Shaking her head free of all such thoughts, she looked around at the group as they tried shielding their faces from the wind, ducking while branches snapped off and flew at them like daggers aiming for their eyes. Sucking in a deep breath, she gathered her bearings and committed herself to being strong.

Her hair flung into her eyes, and she pushed it back, hearing the sounds around them grow more ominous.

"Story!" Elliott shouted over the growing growls and storm. "You ready, because I am totally not going to have it say in my obituary that I died so I could be dog food."

Story glanced at Racell, who nodded, practically shooing her through with a mere look. "Just step through and we'll follow. Once we're through they won't come after us, and we can deal with the gatekeeper then."

Taking a deep breath, she narrowed her eyes with determination and gave her friends one last glance. Then, she stepped through the tree boughs, disappearing as if she had been erased.

When she came out the other side, she was greeted by a cacophony of sounds so overwhelming she dropped to her knees and covered her ears. She could never dream such horrible noise and she heard herself screaming, demanding that it end. It seemed to go on for a while, the noise, her screaming. Her eyes were clenched so tightly shut that it wasn't until Elliott shook her that she realized the noise had stopped. Slowly opening her eyes, she rose to her feet and glanced around. "It's so . . ."

"Beautiful," Nicholas murmured and stepped next to her to take her hand. Racell took her other hand and she glanced at him, meeting his honeyed gaze. She knew then she didn't hate Racell any longer, that she never had. She squeezed his hand and smiled, happy to be sharing this moment with her father.

They had left the storm behind, but were confronted with something entirely different of an elemental nature. Never in her life had she seen a sight like the one before her. The sky was awash with color, and lights danced over their faces. The only thing Story could think to compare it to was from one summer when she was a little girl, when she and Adam had walked outside after dark to play a game of Ghosts in the Graveyard and had been awed to find the night sky illuminated by an array of colors. It had been her only glimpse of the Northern Lights. This was reminiscent of that, but also much more.

There was no need for a flashlight because the sky was red, gold, blue, purple, pink, cerulean, and any other color Story had ever seen in a Crayola crayon box and more. It made her chest feel funny. Empty. She missed her mother. She should be experiencing this with her.

Feeling the pressure of someone's stare, she glanced over to see Nicholas watching her. His intense gaze reflected the lights, and she felt the familiar rush of heat, glad that no one would be able to tell under the rainbow in the night.

She swallowed, trying to bring her focus back to the task at hand and not the lights, and definitely not Nicholas. Story didn't really believe in love at first sight, and she'd like to think she was much too pragmatic for such things, but here she was, falling for him. And it was ridiculous. He was from a different world, literally. And they barely knew anything about one another, and yet . . . his gaze sent a thrill through her entire soul that made her shiver. And she knew that she couldn't fight it. But she could ignore it. For now. Because she had things to do, a world she was apparently supposed to save and he had nothing to do with that. Or did he? She turned to him beneath the colorful aurora to study him, but he was oblivious to her examination and kept her gaze soulfully, his full lips curving into a faint smile as if they were sharing some secret. Against her will, she noticed her lips start to return the smile, but thankfully, they were interrupted.

"Who comes to cross Maya's Valley?"

The voice was light, musical, like a breeze might talk if it could formulate normal speech. Story stepped forward to meet the source of the voice and was surprised to find that he was Fae. He had almond eyes that seemed to shift with the colors in the dark sky and silvery hair that curled at his neck. He was also tall and slender like the rest of his race, but unlike some of the other Fae she had encountered, his skin was a light caramel brown. Story stepped forward and tried drawing herself up to seem more imposing. Inflecting a modicum of self-importance into her voice, she said, "Story Sparks."

"And why should I allow you to cross, Story?" he asked in his eerie breeze of a voice.

Story anxiously glanced back at the others, but Elliott nodded, giving her his support, and Bliss came to light on her shoulder, a solid companion against one of her own species. Again, Racell's presence gave her strength and she turned back to the Fae. He was Elvish, if she were being politically correct. He was beautiful as most Fae races were. Although not all—she'd seen gnomes and fairies that were grotesque. But the Elvish were the royals of the Fae, and his pointed ears and general gorgeousness were enough of an indicator. What Story wouldn't do to hear Elliott's thoughts right now—he was probably salivating over the sentry.

"Because . . . I am the First Dreamer . . . and we're being hunted by the Big Bad Wolves of Tressla, and we need to get to The Capital."

The Elven barely flinched when she said who she really was, but Story noticed his eyes widen slightly and a hopefulness spark where it hadn't existed before.

"If you are who you say you are . . . " His voice trailed off as Racell came to stand by him.

"Oh, forgive me, Son of The Will, I did not see you there. You travel with this self-proclaimed Dreamer then?"

"She is not self-proclaimed, the gods have called her so. She is also my daughter." There was a quiet command within his voice and Story was startled by it. He was a demi-god after all, she remembered.

Bowing his head in respect, the Elven nodded.

"Then perhaps she is who she says she is. But I am the gatekeeper and I must . . . "

"Give it a rest, Berk."

Startled, Story turned sharply to the new voice, and memories of her first encounter with it rushed back. She had been with the Pegasus, and the goddess had resembled a child with brown curls, dimples and the deepest, unwieldy gaze. Like Shirley Temple on drugs, she thought to herself. This time she didn't appear to be as childlike, having taken on the form of a young teenager, her body barely in bloom and her face still softened by childhood, yet more angular and mature than before. She wore deep purple leggings, long black boots and a matching corseted top, with long, see-through balloon sleeves. A crown of blossoms also rested on her head, making her look like a flower child.

It was on her lips to respond first, but Racell beat her to it. "Maya, good of you to come," he said formally.

"Oh Racell," the goddess sighed. "Save your bitterness for your stubborn family."

Turning to Story, Maya rested her intense violet gaze on her. The irritated glint she'd had when addressing Racell vanished and was replaced by something far more tender, almost alien to the chaos goddess.

"Sister," Maya said softly.

"Don't call me that," Story said before she could stop herself. What had come over her? Why would she say that? Maya might look like a sweet preteen, but she was scary.

Maya merely arched a brow in response.

"I mean, no offense, but I . . . I don't know. I'm not her. I'm just Story."

Berk, who had been respectfully standing back a distance stepped forward. "So you lied?"

"No, she didn't lie," Maya said, never taking her gaze off Story. "She just doesn't believe in herself." Walking toward Story, she stopped right in front of her. Crooking her finger, she motioned for her to come closer.

Story stepped toward the goddess and met her cerulean gaze. Wait . . . blue? They had been violet only moments before. Shaking her head, she focused on the goddess, who pressed two ring-clad hands to Story's face.

"You are her. You may not remember, and your power may not be the same, but I was your friend, and you were like my sister. And I remember you. I recognize your soul," she said, peering deep into her eyes.

Story was struck by the swirling depths of the goddess's eyes, and felt herself falling.

Some time later, Story opened her eyes. Lifting her head, she slowly pulled her body from the position she had been lying in and looked around. Everyone was sleeping. Elliott curled near a fire, as close to Berk as he could get. Racell was on his back, tall and strong even in his sleep. Tiny Bliss had made a pocket for herself in the earth, so that she was sleeping peacefully within the grass and leaves. And right beside her lay Nicholas. He had been curled around her for warmth, and Story touched his brow gently, loving the handsome planes of his face in sleep. Men were always the most beautiful when they slept, she thought. When they dreamt . . .

Rubbing her head, she looked to her left and jumped a little at the sight of Maya, who was sitting up cross-legged and staring intently at Story. Wiping her mouth with the back of her hand self-consciously, she blinked and met the goddess's gaze, just not too directly.

"What happened?"

The goddess shrugged, looking all too human. "Oh you looked too long into my eyes and passed out, it happens," she said. Maya went quiet again, staring at her in that way someone does before they tell you bad news.

"What is it? Did something happen?" She looked around for her pack, dying for a sip of water, but Maya must have read her thoughts because she passed Story a coconut filled with milk.

"A coconut?"

"Wild magic," Maya murmured as if that explained it.

Not caring where it came from, she sipped the contents hungrily and sighed at the sweet taste. After she drained it, she set it aside, combing grass from her hair and blinking in the darkness. The lightshow had grown fainter, but still cast a glow over the sleeping party, sending eerie shadows across Maya's deceiving features.

"Is something wrong, Maya?"

The god shook her head, her pretty round face turned down in a state of perplexity, her sweet brow drawn and lips pursed as she seemed to contemplate Story. "My mountains call the young Shadow Fae every year to come find their Fairy Spirits. Split from their spirits at birth, they must traverse the dangers of my wild world and search out their kindreds. Without them, they are only half alive, unable to live to their full potential."

Nodding, Story glanced distractedly at Nicholas sleeping, remembering the way they had acted together. Had it only been earlier tonight?

"Yeah, I remember hearing something about them when I was younger." She turned back to Maya, instantly overwhelmed by the force her of hypnotic gaze, and the disquiet she read in their luminous depths. "What's your point?" She didn't mean to have such an attitude, but she was tired and all she wanted to do was lie down for a little while and remember the feel of Nicholas's hands touching her—and the fervor that had lit her body and soul in such a way, she wasn't certain she'd ever be able to put out the fire.

Maya was a patient god, though, and ignored Story's rudeness, sitting more still than Story could imagine possible. "I did not notice it when you were younger, but having seen the shadow that follows a split soul, I know what it looks like. Tonight, perhaps because you are here in flesh, not just a wandering soul, I saw that in you."

Irritation bubbled up within Story, and she shook her head with a jerk, throwing one arm to the side in question, her palm dangling in the air, and then dropping when realization struck her. "What are you saying? That I'm like the Shadow Fae, and I have to find my Fairy Spirit?"

Unblinking and still as the rock she sat against, only Maya's lips moved. "I do not know; I only see what I see, that like the Shadow Fae, there is a shadow of your missing spirit, unseen to the naked eye, and only catching mine by the glance."

"That doesn't even make sense." Story heard the annoyance thread through her voice, but she couldn't help it. How was it possible that a piece of her just wasn't inside her? Her spirit, no less?

"I do not know myself how it feels, but I have overheard many of the Shadow Fae on lonely nights such as this, when they quest for their Fairy Spirits, unable to go home if they fail. They say it is like an emptiness in their chest, an inner loneliness. They say that the lost spirit echoes, calls their name, and waits, unable to live a life of its own without its missing counterpart, the soul. Have you," Maya peered at Story through the darkness, "ever experienced this?"

Story started to deny it, but she stopped, her inner voice reminding her of all the times when she hadn't felt quite whole. She didn't answer Maya right away, and the goddess, who could sit for years without speaking, didn't push her.

Finally, after some moments of contemplation and staring into the trippy night sky, she nodded. "Yes, I guess I've felt that way at times, as if I wasn't living up to a certain potential, that something was missing. But I wouldn't even begin to know where to find a Fairy Spirit." Not meaning to be so loud, she quickly glanced at the others and envied their uninterrupted sleep.

Curling her knees to her chest, she noticed it was getting lighter out and could tell sunrise was not far off. She briefly wondered what the sun's climb into the sky would reveal within Maya's Valley. But all she could think about was her other self—this self that possibly existed elsewhere. How could that have even happened?

"I do not think it is as easy even as finding a Fairy Spirit, but I do believe that you will not be able to fulfill your destiny in full until you have been reunited with the part of you that is missing." Maya shifted, ever so slightly, and Story could see that the strange, chaotic goddess looked disturbed.

"Well, what can I do? Who can help me? I don't know what to do." If being a legendary figure of a prophecy hadn't been enough pressure, now she'd found out that an actual piece of her might be missing—had maybe always been missing—and the depth of what that meant eluded her. Ignorance really is bliss, she thought. Because now she could feel that something was missing, almost as if she was looking at a puzzle and couldn't find the middle piece, that one cardboard-shaped cutout that revealed what the picture really was.

"I do not know, sister, but we will discuss this more tomorrow. Please sleep. You have a long journey ahead of you, and a spirit to find."

Story didn't expect sleep to find her so quickly, given all that she had learned, but even as the sun started to rise, she found oblivion calling her fast. Before she closed her eyes, she made a request: "Don't tell the others. Not yet," she whispered and finally allowed her lids to droop. And when they did, she dreamt.

The Dream

"Oh, it's you." The girl looked up, pushing back tangles of stringy brown hair from where she sat huddled on the bed, her gray sweats and plain white T-shirt hanging off of her frail form. Story eyed her warily. A phantom headache throbbed where the girl had banged her head against the wall the last time she'd dreamed herself here. She was beginning to think there was something more significant to this dream. Otherwise, why would she keep coming back?

"Are you bringing me here?" she asked.

"You're The Dreamer," the girl muttered back, tearing the top of her nail off her right middle finger and spitting it to the ground.

"You know who I am? Or what they say I am?"

"You're her." The girl's voice released in staccato bursts as if she was little more than tolerating Story's intrusive visit to her institutional room. Story felt like shaking loose any truths the girl was hiding, but she was hesitant after what happened the last time.

Eyeing the girl, Story noted her pale face and chapped lips, and noticed her toenails colored a now-chipped cherry red. "You haven't been here long, have you?" Story was saying the words out loud before she could stop herself.

Lifting her bronzy brown eyes to Story, she stared unwaveringly at her with a blank expression on features that would have been pretty had they not been twisted so bitterly. "Long enough."

"Why do I keep coming here?"

"You haven't figured it out yet?" The girl leaned back, and fishing underneath her pillow, pulled out a cigarette and a lighter she was obviously not supposed to have. She lit it, the ember glowing as she took a long drag. The last time Story was here, the girl had been a raving lunatic, but now she was a world-wise smoking badass.

The girl shrugged in response and took another drag of her cigarette, causing Story to notice the bandages on her wrists. "Did you try to kill yourself?" she asked, wondering if that was really the PC thing to be asking a crazy girl. Unwarranted anger built in her chest. How dare she!

The girl glanced at the bandages, turned her chalky lips up in something resembling a lifeless smile, and shrugged again. "What do you care?" she said, but Story saw a challenge light up her eyes.

Story didn't know what to say. This was all a dream, and yet, she did care. Shaking her head in frustration, she glanced around the stark white walls, the bars on the windows, and then back at her. "It's just . . . life is precious. Why would you ever try to end it so soon?"

"You don't live in here." She gestured to the prison she lived within, but Story noticed her eyes had softened as if she recognized that Story truly did care, even if she was only a figment of her imagination.

"So what are you going to do?" institution girl asked. She pulled out a jar filled with cigarette butts from beneath her bed and dropped in the still-burning stub, cutting off the oxygen to the Parliament Light by twisting the lid on tight.

"How the hell did you get glass in here—and cigarettes?" Story shook her head, bewildered, but then reminded herself it was a dream.

As if reading her thoughts, the girl smirked. "It's just a dream, right? So what are you going to do?"

"About what?

"Brink . . . "

Taking it in stride that the girl knew so much, Story mimicked her and shrugged. "Get the fiddle and cut his power source before he hurts any more people, all without letting him use me to unite the worlds."

The girl nodded, leaned back on her bed, and crossed her hands behind her head. She closed her eyes, almost as if she were basking in the sun on a beach instead of lying atop the rough, sterile sheets on her bed in the psych wing of a hospital. "That's a good start, but you need to watch out for the other one. She can help you, but she also likes to be in power."

Confused, Story stared at the girl's peacefully composed face and tried to spy any avarice, but she only saw the gaunt features of a girl who was trying to imagine herself away from her prison. "Who's the other one?"

The girl lifted one eye and smiled. A sadistic turn of her pale lips seemed to take delight in Story's obvious discomfort. "Oh, you'll know soon enough. Like I said, let her help you, but don't let her rule you because then we're all screwed."

"Can't you tell me who you're talking about? Is it someone working with Brink? Someone I know?" But the girl didn't answer, merely turning her back to Story as if she was planning to go to sleep.

"You should probably wake up now," she murmured. As the girl closed her eyes, Story's world went dark, and sleep took her firmly for its own.

Story awoke with a start. The sun had risen but she could tell through slitted eyes that it was still early morning. The others were rousing. Coffee was bubbling over an open fire, and the aromas sifted around her in the cool morning air. But she needed some time before greeting the group, so she kept her eyes closed to get a quiet moment with her thoughts.

This wasn't the first time she had dreamed of the institutionalized girl, but she realized that each time before, she'd forgotten it almost as soon as she woke. Who had the girl been talking about at the end? And who was the girl? Why did Story keep going back there, and why did she seem so familiar and yet a stranger at the same time? She was getting tired of the nagging feeling that accompanied her interactions with people, awake and in dreams, but before she could put much more thought toward it, Elliott was shaking her arm.

"Story, get up, breakfast is ready and the sun is up. That means get your ass up because I want to get out of this valley today."

Sighing, Story blinked her eyes open and rolled onto her back so she was looking up at him. The sun wasn't high yet, but it was moving and she longed for her cheap, eight-dollar red-rimmed sunglasses.

Without missing a beat, Elliott continued, "There was some crazy stuff going on out there last night. Like, did you not hear the trumpets that trumpeted the sun rising? I mean seriously, it's like some trippy crap out of *Fantasia*. Not to mention the winged horses that flew over our heads like twenty minutes ago." Elliott continued to babble on about dancing stars and talking strawberries, but Story had stopped listening.

"Flying horses?" she asked, tearing her gaze from him and scanning the Crayon-colored sky.

"Which way? Which way were they headed?" she asked urgently.

"Ummm, I guess that way," Elliott said, pointing beyond the boundaries of the valley. Story popped up and shouldered her pack, focused intently on the edge of their destination.

"Didn't you say I had an appointment to keep with my sister?"

Realization flashed in Elliott's eyes as he recalled his vision from only a few days before. He glanced back at the sky and nodded, a hint of a secret smile curving his lips and making Story wonder what he knew.

She flashed him a smile and clapped her hands together like a kindergarten teacher trying to get a classroom of post-toddlers to attention.

"Alright, everyone, let's get it together. We're going to push it and make it out of here before we have to endure another night, especially now that Maya is gone." Story didn't know when Maya had left, but she was nowhere to be seen now. "We need to get to The Green's Solace by tonight."

"Story," Nicholas said, turning and pausing from packing up Cobble with their supplies. The horse had been finicky since they entered the valley, so it was no mean feat to get her to be still.

"Story," Nicholas said again, and she felt herself thrill at the sound of her name leaving his lips. *Damn, damn,* she thought. *Not what I need.* So she did what she was able to do best: ignore what she was feeling and confront the situation at hand.

"What's up?"

Nicholas paused for a moment, probably not as familiar with casual lingo, but he recovered quickly. "The edge of the valley is at least a day, and there's no way we'll make it, especially not through the Trees of Thanos."

But Story was determined. The flying horses must have been The Pegasus, and she desperately needed to see them, and more than that, Kestrel. Her chosen sister had left with them when Story was a mere child, and Story knew she still traveled with them. They had named her Queen of the Seven Forests, and the Trees of Thanos were included in that seven. Surely, Jemma had informed Kestrel that Story was back by now, and Story knew—trusted—that Kestrel would not allow them to get lost within the timeless trees. But it had to be today. Time was ticking fast and Story had never been more aware of it than now. Elliott had said it was an appointment she couldn't be late for.

"We'll make it," she insisted, pushing hair from her eyes.

"Story, there's no way." He tried reasoning with her, but she wasn't having it.

Turning on Nicholas sharply, Story pierced him with an intense stare. "We. Will. Make. It."

CHAPTER TWENTY-FOUR

Eldridge Mountains, Tressla

ADAM WAS IN THE MIDST of every man's dream, snuggled between two gorgeous princesses. It seemed like a mere few hours he had been wrapped within their spell, only waking from his daze when Snow White recoiled from where her lips had been locked around his wrist. "He's starting to go bad," she sighed.

Beauty looked up from his other wrist, her lips stained dark, and dropped his hand so that it clunked against the earthen forest floor. "That means we're taking too much," she agreed with a frown.

Laughing, Snow picked up his wrist again and winked. "I'm still hungry, though. No one will know if we take what we want."

Beauty tossed strawberry-golden curls and smiled slyly. "Yeah, what's one boy?"

Adam frowned as his consciousness resurfaced, wondering what they were talking about. He actually didn't think he liked the sound of it all. He worked his tongue around in his mouth, trying to find his voice so he could complain, when a young teenage girl walked into the clearing. She was a sweet-looking little thing, but through Adam's half-closed eyes, she also looked a bit creepy.

Snow was the first to react to the new presence and dropped his wrist again, trying to hide the fact that she'd had it at all. In response, he flexed it, feeling blood rush back into his limb.

"Maya," Beauty whispered, bowing her head in respect.

"I am going to overlook the fact that you were even thinking about draining him because had you gone through with it, the very trees would not only have ejected you from this valley, but from existence. Happy endings, remember, girls?" Snow darted dark eyes at Beauty and then looked down.

"But I cannot overlook the fact that you took the BFF of the First Dreamer."

"BFF?" Beauty asked, testing it out on her tongue.

"Best friend forever," Maya nodded casually.

Adam grinned hearing the goddess's stiff use of the phrase while his consciousness returned. As his vision cleared, a stormy violet gaze greeted him, and he was glad he wasn't those particular princesses. Or any princess actually, he reminded himself.

"You may rise, BFF Adam." Maya nodded toward him again.

"So does a person only have one BFF?" Snow White asked curiously, smiling sweetly at Beauty before glancing back at Maya. The blonde princess frowned.

"I'm your BFF, Snow," she said. But Snow ignored her and cocked her head coquettishly.

"I'm pretty sure you can have more than one, because Story has another BFF called Elliott," Maya answered conversationally.

Now it was Adam's turn to frown. "Wait a second, I'm Story's original BFF," he exclaimed indignantly, realizing how ridiculous he sounded the moment the words left his lips. Man, it was good to have his willpower back although his limbs trembled from loss of blood.

"Never mind," he muttered, sitting up and seeing that three pairs of eyes were quietly staring at him.

Maya finally broke the silence. "Adam, Story needs you, so it is time you were done with the two succubae here and got on your way."

"Succubae?" Snow said with a frown while Beauty preened, apparently flattered by the title. Maya merely turned a violet gaze on them for a moment before turning back to Adam, who at this point was beginning to realize what a jerk he had made out of himself. Lured by Fairytale princesses, he had abandoned Story after he had promised himself he would be there to protect her.

"Where is she? Is she okay?" Feeling panic rise in his chest, he ventured a glare at the girls, who batted their lashes back.

Maya nodded. "She is fine, but they are in my valley, and she is trying to push through to the other side today. You must meet her there."

"But how? They have a huge head start on me. I'm a strong hiker, but even I can't make up that distance."

"A friend was running late to her destination, but she was nice enough to offer to escort you above the valley."

"Above?" Adam asked with a mild frown, turning to look up at the sky just as a massive shape came hurtling toward them. Adam had just enough time to pray he wouldn't die, when the shape touched down gracefully and snorted.

Adam blinked. Of all the fantasies he never even thought to see, this would be one of them. Standing in front of him was a flying horse, er Pegasus, he thought. Its wingspan was wide—wider than Adam could calculate in his amazement, but even then he knew that in the real world it wouldn't support a horse's weight in flight. No, this was magic. Real magic, as if that should surprise him. The Pegasus was a dappled white and gray with sparkling silver wings, and he had a rider. Adam swallowed hard as he stared up at the woman who slid down from the animal's back and hugged Maya. She was really one of the most gorgeous creatures he had ever seen, even compared to the two blood-sucking princesses. At first he noticed her height—she was exceptionally tall for a woman, standing taller than his own five-foot-nine form. She was slender, but her stomach swelled out against the thin, white top she wore, and her cheeks glowed with the blush of pregnancy. Her flaxen hair was plaited closely to her head and fell loose in ripples over her shoulder. A dark fringe of lashes ringed large aqua eyes that sparkled with laughter as she greeted Adam by placing the tips of her two index fingers to her lips, almost as if she was double shushing someone, and bowed.

"So you're Adam—a dear friend, I hear, to my sister, so long gone from my company."

Awkwardly, Adam returned her bow and peeked up at her to see her laughing with the horse. Adam's brow furrowed and he huffed for a moment before smiling back.

"Yes, I guess I am. I've heard about you too. Story was sorry to have missed you."

Kestrel smiled warmly and nodded. "Yes, I am sure she was. Well, we shall just have to go see her now." Turning to Maya, Kestrel kissed her cheek and expressed her apologies at not being able to visit.

"Your mission is ahead, but Kestrel," Maya said, her own smile vanishing, "be careful—prophecies aside, free will can always override destiny."

Kestrel shook her head. "This is what I've been training for, what it's all been for." She smiled and Adam noted the light freckles that dotted her nose. "Lance is my bow and I am the arrow, we make a good team," she finished, stroking her fingers across the Pegasus's midnight mane and gazing at him with such love that Adam was uncomfortable, briefly wondering at the nature of her relationship with the animal.

Jumping back onto the Pegasus with ease, Kestrel held out her hand. "Come on up!"

"Huh?" Adam asked, not sure he entirely comprehended, and still amazed at the way she had scaled the beast given that she looked to be about nine months pregnant. "You want me to fly on the back of a horse, with no seatbelt or helmet?" Adam was by nature a risk taker, but even this made him stop for a moment in a prequel to fear. When Kestrel merely nodded with a laugh, he shrugged.

"No one will ever believe me," he lamented as he took her hand and boosted himself up, pushing his foot off a nearby tree to settle on behind her. "But this is going to be awesome."

"If awesome means amazing, then you bet it will be," she said over her shoulder. He started to adjust himself and turned to wave goodbye to Maya as Lance began to flap his wings, slowly at first.

The Pegasus beat his wings, a torrent battering his riders from both sides. Adam clutched Kestrel's waist, clenching his knees tightly as the beast's haunches moved beneath him and they lifted up into the air, instead of taking a running start as he thought they would.

He kept his eyes tightly shut, unable to grasp for a moment that there was nothing but air between him and the ground, which he was sure was falling away fast behind him. *I am so going to die.* He pictured the horrified look on his mother's face if she could see him at that moment. Adam had been bungee jumping, skydiving and cliff diving, but there had always been some sort of safety net.

"How you doing?" Kestrel called to him.

"Scared shitless," Adam said with no shame.

Kestrel laughed. "Open your eyes! Lance wouldn't ever let you fall, I promise."

Slowly Adam lifted his head from where he'd ducked it behind Kestrel's shoulders. Feeling the cool air against his face, he cracked open one eye as if watching a horror movie, unable to keep himself from looking. But what he saw was beyond imagining.

The wind rushed against him while they soared through the air, the land stretching out beneath them for miles as clear as could be. He had been on the back of a motorcycle, and he had always felt that experience and skydiving would be the closest to flying, but this was in its own league. They were so high he could smell the moisture in the air, and he knew later they should expect rain. Breathing deeply of the freedom, he avoided looking directly down and laughed, the wind carrying it away on its back. *We need Pegasus in our world*, he thought and laughed again.

CHAPTER TWENTY-FIVE

Maya's Valley, Tressla

THEY HAD BEEN HIKING through what seemed like a never-ending plain of grass and wildflowers, with no more than one break for six or seven hours. Everyone was exhausted, but no one more than Story. She had ceased to care about how beautiful the foliage was, here where trees didn't need a change of season to be colorful. She didn't even notice the symphony of music that accompanied them from a source that was undeterminable. Her legs were heavy, her feet hurt, and sleep had never sounded so good. She had no doubt the rest of her group felt the same, especially Elliott. But she was determined they would not only get to the Trees of Thanos by the end of the day, they would get through it. Story couldn't explain it, but she knew Kestrel needed her that night.

She gave a cursory look at the others, the effort nearly bringing her down. Elliott was quietly suffering, his easy lope now stilted and limp, while Bliss seemed to sullenly bop along the breeze. Nicholas was looking haggard as he joined her, his growing facial hair giving him a chiseled look that made Story weak in the knees. Or it could have been her weariness.

Only Racell still looked untouched by the long travels. His strong figure set a pace for the others that would hopefully get them where they needed to be before the sun sank into night.

Story gave Nicholas a sidelong glance. "I hope you don't hate me for insisting that we make this trek all in one day."

Nicholas curved an arm around her shoulders and chuckled. "While I may certainly be cursing your name under my breath right now, I can assure you I could never hate you—in fact, it's just the opposite," he said softly, his dark gaze heavy with meaning, holding her own longer than she could handle. Feeling slightly self-conscious with his arm tucked around her, she shrugged him off and felt the comfort she'd gained from the touch slide away like water.

It didn't matter though, because she had to get to The Capital and overthrow Brink and worry about some woman, if her dream girl was to be believed. But she wanted to lighten the frown that had replaced his smile so she laughed, "Did I tell you how you remind me of someone, I just can't put a name to it."

Story was surprised when Nicholas visually blanched, his normally tan face losing its healthy color. He quickly shot her a smile, but he didn't say anything for a few moments, the silence growing awkward.

"I'm sorry, did I say something wrong?" She searched his features as he looked away from her. Finally, Nicholas found her hand and entwined his fingers with hers. Story swallowed, and this time she held his hand back, unable to deny him twice and not really wanting to.

"No, nothing's wrong. I tried to tell you before, but I never got the chance . . . ." Story itched to stroke the stubble of his twenty-four hour shadow. About to give into her more lustful impulses, her hand was in mid-air when the world went dark.

"What the . . . ?" she hissed, hearing Elliott whisper similar vulgarities while the resident Tresslans like Bliss and Nicholas spouted out oaths that included "Racell's balls" and "Damn The Will," which in Story's opinion were much worse since one of the curses involved a person in their present company.

"Nightmares," Nicholas whispered beside her, his breath dancing along her cheek as he leaned in and then tugged her forward. "They've come for you."

"But it's daytime. How the hell did they get here and break the barrier between day and night?"

"Brink," Nicholas said, his figure barely an outline in the growing darkness. "You have to get out of here."

"Story!" Racell called. "Are you okay?"

"Yes, yes, I'm fine," she replied, more annoyed by the inconvenience of this newest development than scared. This would only slow them down. Apparently, she wasn't showing the proper amount of respect for their situation, because Nicholas started pulling her into a run. The Trees of Thanos were still a ways ahead. Perhaps if they could make it to the pinnacle of rocks, which was supposed to be a sacred spot to Maya, they would be okay. The darkness wasn't so complete that she couldn't make out the shadowy outline of the rocks ahead. Story was pretty sure it was like Tressla's version of Stonehenge. In good shape, Story kept pace with Nicholas, calling out Elliott's name anxiously, and was comforted when she heard his panting response just ahead of her.

The Nightmares were gaining on them. She could feel their cold, dark presence on the edge of her consciousness. They were trying to get in, but she kept pushing them out although she wasn't quite sure how she was doing it. She just knew that she could not let them into her mind. The rocks were so close. She picked up the pace and just as she did so, something caught her foot and she stumbled, her hand slipping from Nicholas's strong grip. Of course she would slip, she thought, but she managed to keep her balance and reached out for his hand once more.

"Story!" he shouted, his gravelly voice laced with panic.

"Nicholas," she panted, and felt relieved when his hand found hers once more. Only this hand wasn't warm and firm, it was intangible and clammy. As it tightened its chilly grip around hers, she felt herself grow cold and heavy.

"Story, where are you?" She heard Nicholas call through what had become an all-encompassing darkness. The clammy hand curled tightly around her own and she sighed.

"Damn," Story managed to curse before the darkness became complete.

When she opened her eyes again, it was light out and she could tell from the distinct lack of music surrounding her that she was no longer in Maya's Valley. Confused, Story glanced down at her hand. It still felt cold where the Nightmare had touched her, but her hand looked normal.

In fact, the location she now found herself in looked much like the area where they had stopped previously right before losing Adam. Glancing around and seeing no one nearby, she decided to head north toward Maya's doorway in hopes that she could figure out how she had ended up back there. Why would a Nightmare merely eject her from the valley unless they were keeping her from something? Yeah, her reunion with Kestrel, she thought bitterly, beginning to feel slightly depressed. They would all be freaking out, especially Elliott. She liked to imagine that Nicholas also would be quite upset at her disappearance, but she probably shouldn't worry too much about them at the moment, assuming the Nightmares had come mainly for her. Just as she was about to become immersed in the multitasking feat of walking and feeling sorry for herself, she heard a thin echo caress her ear as it floated by on a breeze.

Stopping in her stride, she cocked her head and heard it again, the hint of it tickling her eardrum. It sounded like a voice. When it came once more, she ducked under trees and limbs, and then she started to follow the trail of its resonance.

A few minutes later, she bounded out into a clearing and stopped at the edge of the trees, trying to take in what she was seeing. Two of the most impossibly beautiful women were hovered over a sleeping man. Unable to tell who it was, she leaned forward, but a branch ripped at her hair. Growling under her breath, she started to untangle herself when she realized who the man was: Adam.

But why was he so pale? She managed to free herself, not without a few casualties from her tangled curls, when she saw Adam's neck. There was a gaping gash. The two women turned toward Story and flashed smiles that were covered in red.

Blood, she thought. "Adam," she cried uncertainly, with no regard for her own safety. When he didn't respond, she ran faster than she thought possible and shoved one of the girls out of her way, oblivious to the vampy snarl she received. "Adam," she cried, shaking his shoulders and watching his head flop unnaturally around. Pressing her cheek to his, she felt the frigidness of his skin.

"He told me you wouldn't hurt him!" she cried, turning to the two princesses, who watched her in detached silence.

"Who, dear?" asked the blonde—Beauty, Story thought—wiping her mouth with the back of her hand.

"Racell . . . "

"Oh him?" Snow laughed. "He's just a washed up demi-god who still thinks he's important. All the gods are washed up, even Queen Green herself."

Story stared at them. "But why?"

"We were hungry," answered Beauty with a shrug.

Story thought she would lose her mind, and she pressed Adam to her, feeling her own helplessness set in as tears streamed down her face. This was a nightmare come true.

Nightmare . . . She stopped suddenly and looked up. Both girls were smiling darkly at her and moving closer as if they were gliding along the grassy floor—like monsters sometimes did in the movies.

"This is just a nightmare," Story whispered as they closed in.

"Don't be so sure," Snow whispered, her breath like frost as she wrapped a hand around her neck and squeezed.

Feeling her ability to breathe being cut off, Story glared at the dark beauty, clamping her hands around her wrist and digging her fingernails into her ivory arm. "This is a nightmare," she choked out with more certainty.

Snow smiled. "Lucky for you, you're smart," she said as she grabbed Story's hair and yanked her head back to bare her neck. "But before you go, I want a bite." Story raked at her face and suddenly could breathe again.

Her throat felt a little sore as she blinked open her eyes and glanced around. Where was she now? She had fully expected to wake up back in Maya's Valley, but it looked as if she had made it to The Capital early.

That couldn't be right, she thought, peering blearily through the gray of dawn and running her hand over her throat, checking anxiously for any bite marks. *Adam's not dead, Adam's not dead*, she told herself, attempting to ease the grief that was trying to grip her heart. "This. Is. A. Nightmare," she whispered aloud.

In the distance, the white pillars of The Capital House caught her eye while salty air wafted through the morning mist, coming from the bay of the Silver Sea.

The streets were quiet this early in the day, but the city was beginning to wake up. A young, well-dressed man strolled leisurely through the streets, his suit coat, trousers, and fedora reminiscent of the early twentieth century—except it was all made from leather, giving it a retro-contemporary style that seemed to be the rage in Tressla, and which Story was finding exceedingly random given her medieval-Real World modern state of dress.

Glancing away from the man, she noticed a woman, her head covered in a scarf, bent forward as if propelling herself and her child, a little girl dressed in the rags of a street urchin, through the semi-darkness toward The House of Destiny. The tall, brown building was rustic in appearance, set against the backdrop of shops and businesses, and it was only discernible by the glittering gold engraved spider that had been sculpted for eternity to depict the arachnid weaving its own web. It housed a sect that worshipped The Will, following the ideology that although their lives were predestined, they had a measure of free will while following their destiny. The sect had gathered a larger following from those who were unwilling to dedicate themselves to The House of Fate, which adhered to the principle that life was predestined, and there was nothing you could do about it.

Story started to follow the woman and child, thinking they were perhaps her sign in this particular scene, when she heard the screams. She paused for only a moment, until she heard the piercing cry of a curse slam into her chest. It was Jess. She headed down a corner street, winding through alleyways. Turning on pure instinct as if she were a Wolf herself, buildings and a blur of faces flashed by her, but all she could think of was Jess. She had to get to Jess.

She stopped so fast she almost went toppling over her body. Her breast was heaving as she gasped to catch her breath. She wiped the back of her arm against her moist brow and sucked in a breath, trying to understand what she was seeing. She had run to The Capital building without a thought to where she was going, almost as if she had decided to run right into Brink's hands. But that's not what bothered her.

A platform had been erected, or perhaps it had always been there. Story had never come this far north before, even when she lived in Tressla part-time. The untreated, unsmoothed wood had been used to create what looked like a scaffold for hanging. On the platform stood Jess. The little girl she'd once known and loved had grown—a lot. She was Amazonian at best, and she was shackled as a dozen vicious Big Bads jumped at her, scraping her flesh with their claws and sharp fangs. Bit by bit, they would bleed her dry, Story quickly saw. She nearly choked as another Wolf went to take his part in the torture.

"Stop," she screamed, unable to take a moment more. Wolves turned and snarled, their hackles rising, but Story only had eyes for Jess, whose arms dripped blood and whose face was black and blue, probably from the hands of the Big Bads' human counterparts. But who was Story kidding? There was no part to those beasts that was human.

"Leave her be!" she cried, walking toward the Wolves without any regard to her own safety.

"Story," Jess croaked, her battered, swollen face serene as if she had accepted her fate.

"I won't let this happen, Jess," Story said, staring into the sparkling chrome of her friend's eyes, the only color of her countenance that was still true, that wasn't bruised—that, and the flaming red of her hair, now ratty and matted with blood.

"This is what's supposed to happen. The Will has said," Jess said sadly.

"I don't care!" Story cried, paying little heed to the Wolves moving in on her. "I should have been here. I should never have left. It's because of me you're even here right now." A deluge of desolation hit her as she stared at her battered but beautiful friend. It was all her fault, it really was.

"No." Jess protested, her face a mask of tears mingling with blood. She looked beaten. When she spoke, a Wolf took the moment to swipe razor-sharp claws down her back. Jess convulsed, although appearing brave as the claws shredded her back to the bone. Her gargled shrieks of pain crept into Story's soul like a shadow, sinking her further into a dark hole. Seeing no way to save Jess or herself, she welcomed the death that was sure to come. She had failed. She had deserted her poor mother, been cruel to her father, led the enemy straight to her papa, and allowed her best friends to fall into harm's way. She deserved to die at the claws of these nightmares.

Nightmare. And then she remembered. A bit too late, because Nigel, the pack's leader, had her by the neck, his guttural snarling deafening to her ears. He wrapped his hands, smaller in comparison to other Wolves, but still big by her standards, and started to squeeze—his strange, pale blue eyes devoid of humor, joy or love.

Not this again, she sighed inwardly as she felt herself running out of air. His chokehold was stronger than Snow's, and she couldn't even speak. Her eyes grew wide as his feral smile widened.

"Die, Dreamer," he growled through his human mouth, his frosty gaze fading from her vision.

As her final breath swelled into her lungs, and the world started to fade, she grabbed onto Nigel's words like an anchor as they echoed in her head.

Wait, if I die here, I might as well bank on not waking up again. Ever. Well, maybe in the afterlife. Or actually . . . haven't I already been reincarnated?

That's right, she was The Dreamer. The First Dreamer to be correct. She was supposed to have all these powers here in Tressla, but really, it was so silly. Or was it? Nightmare . . . Dream. If she had dominion over dreaming, she should sure as hell be able to combat a Wolf in her nightmares. Right? What did she have to lose but to embrace the birthright? And if it were true, well then she would live another day.

Her eyes popped open, and she smiled as she took a deep breath. Despite the fact that Nigel still had his massive hands wrapped around her delicate neck, she was breathing fine. Story wrapped her much smaller hands around his and pried them from her neck with the ease of a superhero, then tossed them back at him, planting a foot into his chest and shoving him away. He snarled, falling back into his canine minions. Turning to Jess, Story smiled, realizing her Jess would have never given up so easily. "I'll see the real you soon." And then she walked away from death into nothingness.

This time when she blinked her eyes open, she found herself in a room. It was prepossessing if for only the musical instruments that hung glittering from the ceiling and walls, and atop tables and trunks that otherwise cluttered the room. There were ornately detailed oboes and guitars and a harp that looked as if it had been pieced together by cavemen. But the instruments themselves gave the stone walls an artistic beauty, and she imagined the symphony that could be created from these tools.

"I'm sure you can tell, but I like music," came a voice from behind her. Startled, Story turned to the shadows, which parted to reveal the form of a man. Until now, when she heard the name Brink, she had been picturing a tall, skinny man with a long beard and madness glittering in his crazy black gaze. Or at least a man of god-like beauty like Racell. But this man was none of those. And yet she knew he was Brink.

This man was well-groomed, dressed in dark pants and what looked like a freshly-ironed tunic. His dark hair was cropped short, and instead of sporting a long beard, he was clean-shaven. He was handsome enough; he had a strong jaw and smooth, olive-toned skin. But he wasn't as beautiful as Racell. It was his eyes that made her uncomfortable. They weren't outwardly cruel-looking, and although their color was close to black, neither was the reason for her discomfort. He reminded her of someone. But she couldn't quite place her finger on it—really, the story of her life since she'd come back to Tressla.

"Ah Dreamer, do you have no words for me? No exchange of greeting? I had so hoped we could meet face to face."

She sighed, realizing she was going to have to talk to him too. Would she ever get out of this Nightmare, or was she stuck here until she finally succumbed and died? There had to be a way out.

"I never would have allowed you to be killed, my dear, not totally," he continued. "This is merely a tactic to make your friends give up hope and give my puppies time to come collect you."

"Why do you have all these instruments? It's quite the collection. That one, for instance, looks as if it's as old as Tressla," she responded, ignoring his antagonisms and studying the ancient, weathered fiddle that rested against a guitar with gleaming wood. The fiddle! She needed to look for the fiddle, but there were so many instruments! Story quickly turned her eyes to trace the contents of the room, searching for one that exuded magic.

He ignored her attempt at distraction. Narrowing his eyes with a shrewd smile, he shrugged. "So it's true, you don't remember everything. That's just too sad, but it might work in my favor." He had the audacity to wink as if they were in on some secret together.

"Why do you want me?" Story asked bluntly, turning toward him and trying to calm the racing of her heart. She had always been a good actress, so now she was going to play the part of the strong heroine, even though all she wanted to do was fall to pieces and beg to go home. She wanted to collect Adam, Elliott, Jess, and everyone else, and go somewhere with them that was safe. She was tired of feeling so scared all the time, as if she was forgetting something, missing the point, and failing an entire world on a quest she wasn't really sure belonged to her.

"Let's just say, little Dreamer, that you have some abilities that would be very helpful to me, and I have ways of helping you tap into them."

"Well, all I can say is that I don't care much for your agenda. I'm not coming to you so you can 'tap' into my powers, as I'm pretty sure I can tap into them myself, and when I do, I'm going to kick your wannabe-bad-guy ass," she finished with much bravado and little confidence.

"Oh?" he asked, laughing, circling the room and running a delicate and loving finger over a glittering violin. Her eyes darted to the instrument like a hawk, watching the way his fingers danced over the instrument as if it were a precious jewel. That must be it. She was pretty sure a violin was the same thing as a fiddle.

"Do you like my violin?" She cursed herself for being so transparent, but he was going on. "It belonged to my mother, passed down through the years as one of the only known relics to survive the Great World Divide. It meant a lot to her. You could say it was all she had left of her hopes and dreams."

"Well, that's pretty sad, placing all your hopes and dreams on an inanimate object," she retorted, trying to keep him on his toes but not really feeling the derision she put into her tone. She was too busy worrying about getting out of there and to Kestrel before it was too late—and she was admiring the beauty of the violin. It had been intricately carved from the most beautiful wood, and it was almost silver, while the detail was exquisite. As an artist herself, such beauty and talent touched her deeply. It had to be what she was looking for. If only she could take it with her through dreams. She didn't notice right away that Brink's expression had grown dark. Gone was the mocking smile and the hungry expression. Instead it had been replaced with pure, unadulterated malice. Story hadn't really felt fear before, but now she was nearly choking from it. She couldn't show it though, so she put on her best nonchalant expression and met his gaze unwaveringly.

"Did I say something?"

"Little Dreamer is so self-righteous," he said, setting the violin down with tenderness as if it were a living creature. His fingers were quite beautiful, like a musician's, she thought. They were long, and she could see calluses on his fingertips. But when she lifted her lingering gaze from his fingers back to his face, all thoughts of music and beauty were eliminated by the fury roiling in his dark, familiar eyes.

"You think I'm evil," he said conversationally, moving closer to her. "But you're no better than I am. Do you even know what you did?"

Story grew still, tearing her eyes from the violin and staring at him with a growing amount of discomfort. Frowning slightly, she felt something nag at her repressed memories. She shook it off and narrowed her eyes and stuck out her chin. "I *am* better than you. I don't oppress poor Fairytales or make a whole world miserable. I don't destroy trees and sign off on the certain death of the Earth itself."

Brink threw back his head and laughed, his grimace as bitterly twisted as his features. "Story dear, you are the very reason Tressla exists. Didn't anyone ever tell you what a naughty thing you did?"

Shaking her head, Story laughed. "Yes, I know, my former self died of a broken heart, and when she did the worlds ripped into two."

"Oh this I wasn't counting on. I thought at least one of your little friends, your father even, would have told you why we're all here in this predicament today. Don't you know about the curse? Back when we were one world, our little Dreamer, so beloved by the gods and humans alike, stripped a young fiddler of his hopes and dreams—for-ev-er," he said pronouncing the last word so that Story could make no mistake as to what he was saying.

"But that . . . that's awful," she whispered. The fact that she ever had held that kind of power seemed impossible, but that she would have ever used that power for something so horrible—well, she didn't know if she really wanted to embrace her destiny if that was who she needed to be. Shocked, she lifted her eyes back to him. "But how does that have anything to do with the splitting of worlds?"

Brink smiled slowly, cruelly. "You stole someone's dreams and hopes. You were a powerful being meant to create, not deprive people of a future. You alone are responsible for this mess, for The Green's slow death and needless separation of humanity from dream. You, Story.

"But if you come to me, if you surrender to me, I can show you how to heal our worlds and save everyone within it. Because believe me, the worlds are dying, both of them. I alone can lead you to your full potential." Brink held out his hands and Story stared at them, his beautiful hands. "Come with me. I've been misunderstood. All I want to do is restore Tressla and the Real World to their original state, and make them whole."

Could a man with such beautiful hands really be evil? Looking up at him she nodded to the violin. "Do you play?"

Seeming flustered, he nodded sharply, "Of course I play."

"Can you play for me? I would love to hear you play from your violin. You have a musician's hands." She tucked a strand of dark hair behind her ear and stared up at him solemnly, resembling the child she once was.

Thrown off, Brink turned toward the violin as if unable to keep himself from it, clenching his hands into fists, and then after a pause, relaxing his fingers enough to touch the strings of the violin. Stopping, he turned to her. "If I play, will you come with me?"

"If you play beautifully," she amended, wondering at the gamble she was taking. But she had a gut feeling, and she followed it.

Smiling slowly, he nodded. And then his fingers reached out and delicately coaxed the strings.

Story closed her eyes, but she was jarred when what she heard was catastrophe. Her eyes flew open and she stared at him, her hands flying to cover her ears from the awful noise. How such sounds could come from such a beautiful instrument she wasn't sure, but she did know it was his touch that brought forth the clanging disharmonies.

"You," he hissed, looking at her. "This is your fault."

Story nodded. "I thought so. You're the Master Fiddler, the one I cursed, aren't you? The one who killed my true love? I have no idea how you're still alive, but it's easy to figure out that you can't play because I took away your hopes and dreams. There's no way in hell I'm coming with you."

She looked desperately around for a way out, her thoughts racing as she wondered how no one else had figured out Brink's true identity. And that's when it came. She felt her air being cut off and she cursed in her mind. Again? How many times did she have to get strangled today? She had gotten some really bad news about her inner nature and she just wasn't in the mood. It wasn't Brink who was choking her though, it was a Nightmare. She knew because she could feel the clamminess of its dark hand leaving behind grime on her neck while Brink stood in front of her with a smirk.

"Like I said, I won't kill you. Not totally anyway. I need you. But I need your friends to think you're dead so they'll give up guarding you." Story knew this time the Nightmare could really do what Brink was saying. But if she was going to ever right the wrong she had committed in another life, then this was just not going to work for her. So instead of curling up inside herself and moaning in misery at the revelations that had been revealed to her, she fought back, feeling that strange flicker in the back of her consciousness once again as her eyes snapped open.

Unfortunately the Nightmare was choking her from behind, but it wasn't that much of an inconvenience. She may not be able to remember her past life as The Dreamer, and she couldn't even recall all of her childhood, but she could do one thing, and it was so simple. All she had to do was believe. She had believed as a child, that much she remembered. She was powerful, and it was time she remembered that. In fact, the Nightmares should be answering to her, The Dreamer, not Brink, the failed musician.

Reaching her hands up, she grabbed the cold Nightmare's fingers and stroked them gently. At once they began to dissipate and she felt air return to her lungs. Smiling slowly, she cast one last glance at Brink. "I'm afraid you'll have to come and find me if you want me . . . And you might want to practice your violin playing. I think it needs a little work."

Glowering at her, he snapped at the Nightmare to regain control, but Story had already taken the helm of the dream. "I'm The Dreamer," she said turning toward the Nightmare, whose shadowy form had taken the visage of a black steed. "The Nightmares are mine from now on." Story grabbed the shadowy horse's mane and pulled herself onto its back, casting one last look at Brink.

"See, I don't need you to claim my birthright," Story said, nudging the Mare to take her back to Maya's Valley and back to her friends.

As she turned the horse shape toward a now-looming doorway, Brink spoke, "Don't be so sure you and your split soul don't need me. You haven't claimed anything just yet."

Ignoring him, Story plunged forward, but his words echoed in her head even as she felt blessed, peaceful sleep embrace her.

CHAPTER TWENTY-SIX

Maya's Valley, Tressla

AS AWARENESS SEEPED BACK into her consciousness, Story at first thought she was still traveling through the dream world on the back of the Nightmare. But she quickly dismissed the notion from her sleep-addled mind. This horse felt much too corporeal to be the shadowy, cold mist of a Nightmare. Next she became aware of the hard body behind her, and it didn't take her long to realize from the scent of earth and pine that it was Nicholas. What had been a trip into hell was starting to look up.

Blinking the sleep away, she slowly raised her head and blearily peeked through eyes that felt swollen with sleep. Almost immediately Nicholas pulled back on the reins, his arms sliding across the side of her body, and halting the horse.

When Tuscan finally wandered to a slow walk and then stopped, his sides heaving in and out beneath Story's legs, she glanced back at Nicholas. He had been holding her hard against his chest as they rode, but now his grip loosened and he slid down off the horse, pulling her down with him. She wobbled on her feet, and he reached out and steadied her with a hand on her shoulder, his dark gaze searching her face.

"You're awake!" He grinned, looking relieved and enfolding her in a hug. "We were so worried, we decided your best chance was for me to ride ahead with you and see if the Pegasus knew of any way to bring you out of the Nightmare-induced sleep. But you're back. How?" He still held her tightly, his mouth speaking against her hair. Still wobbly from her adventure, she barely kept herself from sinking into him and letting him hold her for real.

Finally, he pushed her back with his hands so he could get a good look at her. "You look different," he murmured, his dark brow furrowing and casting wrinkles up his forehead.

Story recovered enough to brush his comment off with a wan smile. "No big deal, I just had to take the bull by its horns, or I guess the mare by its reins." She flashed another smile, rubbing her neck, which felt sore despite the fact that her physical body had been with Nicholas the entire time.

"You're hurt," Nicholas observed, a wounded note lacing through his voice as he stared at the black and blue marks that had followed her out of her nightmare.

"You should see the other guy," she quipped, and then she grew more sober. "How much time did we lose?"

Nicholas reached out and gently tucked a strand of her hair behind her ear and smiled. "Barely an hour—we made a quick decision. Elliott and Bliss are safe with Racell and should be able to meet us by midday tomorrow. I . . ."

Story held up her hand, more to break the spell he had over her than to stop his words. She needed to concentrate on the task at hand, and this boy kept invading her thoughts with his ruggedly unshaven jaw and his dark, penetrating eyes. His gaze was so intense she often wanted to squirm beneath it, but when it was gone she always wanted it back. She was struck once more by his familiarity, a face flashing in her mind so fleetingly it was gone before she could fully grasp what she had seen—perhaps the memory that would unlock the mystery of Nicholas.

Shaking her head free of her thoughts, she glanced up at him while avoiding the heat of his stare. "I feel as if we don't have much time. We have to get to Kestrel and the Pegasus tonight."

Nodding seriously, Nicholas handed her a brown-skinned canteen of water, and she gulped thirstily, feeling the dry, caked dust of sleep wash from her mouth. God, what she wouldn't do for a toothbrush. As they mounted Tuscan, Story asked Nicholas if he carried one with him. He merely chuckled, and wrapping his arms tightly around her, he grabbed the reins and pressed his rough cheek against hers, making Story shiver, despite her resolve to focus on the journey. In her mind, she could hear Brink telling her she was the reason for not just one, but two worlds' problems. Despite knowing she shouldn't listen to him, she had heard the truth in his words, and his appalling music. She had stripped him of his hopes and dreams, a truly awful fate. Death would have been kinder. Feeling the onset of a headache, she allowed the speed of the horse under her and the bouncing scenery to distract her.

She may not remember her wrongdoings, but she could right them. And at this point, she wasn't even sure she wanted to remember the person or Dreamer she had been. But perhaps she could be a new Dreamer.

Story must have fallen asleep because it was starting to get dark when the jostling of the horse's pounding hooves woke her. Blinking her eyes, she took in the dry landscape and the darkening sky, which was already beginning to swirl like the Aurora Borealis.

Straightening so that Nicholas no longer had to bear so much of her weight, it did not pass without notice that one strong arm held her firmly against his body, his breath blowing in her hair. Sighing, she looked out ahead and couldn't stop the smile that slipped fleetingly across her lips. They were entering the Trees of Thanos, which could ultimately decide their fate, depending on how the trees were feeling. Time worked in funny ways in the forest. An hour could go by, but it would feel like a minute. Or only a minute would go by and it would feel like an hour. If they could get through the forest, they would emerge from the chaos of Maya's Valley into The Green's Solace, one of the three sacred groves in Tressla. In this particular grove, earth and rock would soak up grief to give the bearer a brief respite from their pain.

Turning to Nicholas as the horse slowed to a trot, she asked the question she had been wondering. "You think Thanos' trees will let us be?"

Smiling, he leaned and grazed her lips with his own, the momentary union sending a thrill through her. "I would bet my life on it." He sat back and winked knowingly.

As they entered the forest, the tall, luminous, silvery trees swayed against a breeze that hadn't existed in Maya's Valley, but blew gently around them now, bringing coolness to the heat that had permeated the night.

It was so easy, Story found it hard to believe the tales that had preceded the forest. But when a buck pranced up to them and stepped in stride with them, Story knew something mystical was afoot. Its nose was surprisingly warm and dry when it snuffled against her hand. Startled, Story looked into his large, liquid brown eyes and smiled despite herself. He honored her—without words, she could tell what he was about. He was the king of the Trees of Thanos and had proved himself a timely escort. He would make sure they made it through the trees quickly. She was almost disappointed when they neared the clearing, as riding beside him had been so lovely.

Turning to the stag, who paused next to them, Story placed a hand on his head, stroking it softly and feeling like Snow White. Well, the pretty innocent one from the fairytales, not the bloodsucking fiend of Tressla. "Thank you for your guidance. I have friends . . . they're coming close to the trees I'm sure as we speak. Could you possibly make their journey through the trees short as well? We're trying to stop Brink from hurting any more Fairytales, but we need to do it quickly," Story said softly, feeling her face turn hard.

Lifting his great head, the stag dipped in obeisance, his antlers curved like massive limbs from a tree.

"Thank you," Story exclaimed, leaning to the side and throwing her arm around the stag's neck. "Thank you. I won't forget your kindness." The stag bowed its head, looking up with his large eyes only once more before turning and dashing gracefully back into the hands of time.

As they walked into the clearing, Story looked back once more and smiled at the stag as its white tail bobbed away. She glanced up only when Nicholas chuckled. "What's so funny?" Story asked, stiffening despite the warmth of his chest against her back.

"You. You're funny," he murmured with a smile in his voice. "You sound so old world, so Tresslan actually. 'We won't forget your kindness,'" he mimicked in a high-pitched voice.

Elbowing him lightly, Story smiled. "How would you know? You spent like ten minutes in my world—how do you know we don't talk like that? Besides, according to your prophecies, I'm the reincarnation of someone much older than even Tressla itself, so don't make fun or I can send a Nightmare your way," she joked. "Would you rather we wander around for hours, or days even?" she added.

Nuzzling her neck from behind, he gave a soft sensual growl near her ear. "I wouldn't have minded if I got to spend hours wandering with you. Days would have been even better. I've been wanting to get you alone from the moment I saw you."

Shivering despite the heat of the day, Story tried to keep herself from melting back against him. Instead she didn't respond, which made Nicholas chuckle again.

It took every fiber of discipline she possessed to pull her body away from Nicholas just enough to create a little space and calm her nerves. She didn't resist when he pulled her back against him, refusing to let her push him away. Swallowing thickly she didn't dare look back at him, and instead she focused on the thicket of trees ahead, which bent and arched, parting ways as they drew closer and making a gateway into what looked like a land of grass and flower. Blossoms bloomed peacefully next to trees that slumbered while butterflies and Thumbelina fairies bopped along on the breeze. And in the middle of the grove was the Pegasus family in their human forms, creating a circle around the shrieking and writhing half-naked form of a woman.

"Oh my god," Story cried, jumping down from the horse and running toward the group, heedless of anything else but the cries coming from Kestrel. Was she hurt? Dying?

But when she managed to squeeze herself between Ober and Adam, who she flashed a quick smile of relief without even thinking about how he had gotten there, she found a very pregnant Kestrel on the ground screaming as she bore down.

Aside from being pregnant, Kestrel was just as she had remembered—wild and free, only older. Lance, the Pegasus prince, held onto Kestrel's hand as she pushed again, emitting a wild scream.

Frozen, Story stared, not knowing what to do until she felt a firm hand come down to rest on her shoulder and give it a squeeze. Turning, she looked up into the wise and comforting silver eyes of the Pegasus king. "Ober," Story whispered, flinging herself into his arms and feeling the black raven-like feathers of his wings caress her hands and wrists softly. Only the royal Pegasus family could shift between horse and human form, with their signature wings the one shared identifying characteristic between both shapes.

"Will she be okay?" Story asked, looking up into his eternally youthful features. Man, was he beautiful—something she hadn't fully appreciated as a child when he'd been her teacher and forced her to learn how to fly on the back of a Pegasus. She remembered riding on the pearly pink back of Ophelia, the Pegasus princess, soaring on fear and the joyful rush of freedom.

"The first royal child in a thousand years is being born within this grove. Bear witness, Story. It is a great honor for you to be here and to witness this new life." Gazing up at him, she felt like scoffing. Her? Honoring the baby? Then she remembered her commitment to have confidence in her legacy. It had saved her from Brink, hadn't it?

Looking back at Kestrel, who was crying out again, she realized that her sister was staring directly at her with a broad grin and tears in her darkly fringed aqua eyes.

"Story," she murmured stretching out her fingers to her.

Story smiled once more at Ober, glad to have seen his face once again, and she glanced at Lance, who nodded his assent with a strong yet gentle smile. Moving back toward her laboring sister, Story took Kestrel's other hand and squeezed.

"I . . . ," she whispered choking up and swallowing the lump back in her throat. "I'm so happy to be with you. I've missed you. I can't believe you're having a baby!" she finished with a hysterical laugh.

Kestrel smiled serenely despite the briefness of this respite. "I always knew you'd come back," she whispered, taking Story's hand and cradling it against her cheek. "My sister." Then another contraction came and she hollered into the growing night. For a while, that's all there was—the sound of whispered encouragement and a woman pushing new life out into the world.

She was so focused on Kestrel, she didn't even notice when Racell, Elliott, and Bliss joined them quietly in the clearing. But they were all there to witness when Kestrel's son came screaming into the world.

The little boy had a full head of flaxen hair and wide-open eyes the color of silver. Story brushed away tears as Kestrel cradled the new babe to her chest and pushed his mouth onto her breast. The new mother looked up at her husband and smiled wearily. "Say hello to your son, Daddy." Lance smiled tenderly and brushed his hand against Kestrel's cheek. Story choked up just watching.

"Hello, baby," Lance whispered with tears in his own eyes.

Story stepped back a little distance to give the new parents their private time, observing from a distance.

"I wish I could have been there when you were born," Racell's deep voice came softly beside her, his hand coming down on her shoulder.

The old Story would have jumped back at the familiar touch, but she found she liked her father. He was a good man, she decided. And a good demi-god. He had merely been caught up in circumstances, and she could understand that better than anyone. So instead of pulling away like she normally would have, she turned and smiled up at him.

"You were." His golden eyes met her similar gaze with gratefulness and love. His eyes for a moment looked stock-full of tears, and he smiled as he sucked in a deep breath and squeezed her shoulder. Nodding once, he turned and clapped a fatherly hand on Adam's shoulder in passing.

Turning around, Story threw herself into Adam's arms and hugged him tightly. "Don't you ever do that to me again, you hear? I mean seriously, hot girls are one thing, but vampire princesses who day-job in children's stories is something else completely."

Adam laughed and hugged her tightly back. Finally, he stepped back, looking sheepish. "They do have magic, you know. It's not like I'm completely devoid of self-control."

"Yeah, yeah, I think you need to start thinking with your brain instead of your you-know-what," she teased.

Adam wrapped his arms around her shoulders and squeezed, and that was enough for Story. She was just relieved to have everyone back in one place. Now, if they could just find Jess.

Story and Adam stood together, both lost in the rapt faces of Kestrel and Lance as they gazed lovingly down at their new son. Even amidst all the joy, Story was haunted by the dark thoughts of her past. She had to make it right. She remembered Ninian saying she believed there was a way to reunite the essences of the two worlds, but the thought of stopping Brink, let alone healing the world's spirit, was daunting.

"There must be some way," she said, not even realizing she had whispered it out loud until she saw that Adam was staring at her questioningly.

"Some way to what?" he asked.

Biting her lip, Story stared at the ground, feeling her chest tighten with anxiety and guilt. "I . . . found out some things about myself—about why we're possibly here today—that I'm not proud of," she said finally, looking up at him to meet his gaze.

"What is it? Does it have anything to do with that evil dude? Brink?"

Nodding, Story bit her thumb, watching Kestrel beckon to her. "I have to go, sorry. I'll tell you later. It's a long story anyway, and everyone should hear it." Casting an apologetic smile at Adam, she made her way back to Kestrel, who lay on a cushion of straw and leaves, her back propped up by Daisy Pillows the Thumbelinas had gathered for the new mother.

Smiling widely, Story peered down into the sleepy face of her new nephew, his eyes as silver as his grandfather's. "Say hi to Aunt Story," Kestrel spoke in that high-pitched voice women reserve for babies and little kids. "Do you want to hold him?"

Story nodded eagerly as she took the baby from Kestrel, nestling the infant in the crook of her arm and cradling him against her chest. Tears crept unwarranted to her eyes as she stared down at the child, his little mouth a rosebud, his chest rising and falling while a shock of flaxen hair slipped against his forehead. After many minutes of just staring, Story looked up at Kestrel.

"Will he grow wings?"

Lance laughed as he joined Kestrel, who smiled benevolently. Her cheeks were flushed happily, and the joy of new motherhood glittered in her eyes. Story knew she must be exhausted, but Kestrel didn't complain. She just glowed.

"Yes, he will most likely be Pegasus," Kestrel explained as Story handed the baby back to her, so she could feed the now-fussing child.

"What's his name?" Story was surprised that hadn't been the first question on her mind, but this was also her first birth, so she was cutting herself some slack regarding proper question etiquette.

"Robin," Kestrel smiled gently, and Story could see the spirit of the nurturer take hold.

"He is actually the first royal Pegasus child to be born in a thousand years. It's a very auspicious occasion," Kestrel added, growing quiet. Almost as if her words had power themselves, the grove suddenly seemed more crowded. It took Story a moment, but then she noticed Bliss flitting about with other Thumbelinas. Meanwhile, a couple who appeared to be the Elven king and queen congratulated the new grandparents, Ober and Landria, the Pegasus queen, who had touched down into the grove only moments before. Story met Landria's gaze for a brief moment and was met with warm amethyst eyes and a soft smile before she turned with a quiet laugh back to the Elven queen who was saying something to her.

Maya had even joined them, looking like a sixteen-year-old young woman now instead of an early adolescent. Story wondered, if she were to look in a pool of water, would Sandeen also be nearby? The trolls had come as well, their elemental energies clanging and melding in opposition and harmony, along with several wolves—wait, wolves?

Startled, Story looked up at Lance, feeling fear rise in her throat, but he just smiled. "Just ordinary wolves. But I wouldn't let them hear me say that or they might get a complex. They're just honoring us with their presence. They harbor no evil, unlike their shape-shifting fairytale brothers."

Nodding reluctantly and eyeing the silver-pelted clan with suspicion, Story took in a tall figure moving so gracefully it was as if she had inspired the word. Her long chestnut dreadlocks trailed behind her, while her eyes were a deep hunter green. All around the grove, Tresslans dropped to their knees in honor. The reaction was so silent, Story didn't even realize at first that she was the only one left standing aside from Kestrel and Lance, who were holding the honoree. Dropping to her knees like the others, Story stared unbelieving at the essence of Mother Earth walking around as a person. Only in storybooks did stuff like this come true. But of course, they had basically come to the place where all the storybook characters go after being created.

Story's head was bowed, so she only noticed the bare feet that stopped in front of her, with brown ankles circled by little pink and orange flowers, and ivy. Slowly glancing up, Story took in The Green's willowy figure and her rich hair color, streaked with the burnished reddish brown of the earth. Flowers were threaded through the thick twists of her hair that fell to the forest floor, and her indescribably beautiful features were touched by weariness and sadness. "Rise, Dreamer. I would not have you bow to me."

Lifting her gaze, Story rose so that she was standing in front of the embodiment of Earth, the top of her head barely reaching The Green's chin. Even the woman's voice was magnificent, clear like the tinkling of water and a cool summer breeze, and yet deep and throaty like the earth. Meeting her green gaze, Story smiled and sighed. The air seemed fresher somehow.

"I'm honored to meet you. I didn't think I'd ever see you," Story murmured.

Shaking her head, The Green smiled gently at Story. "You are very dear to me, and I would not let you walk through Tressla without at least seeing you once. Do you not remember?"

Frustrated, Story shook her head and tucked back a strand of what used to be a flat-ironed straight strand of hair, which had boinged back to its usual curl.

"I didn't remember anything, but then Sandeen took me to the Chamber of Dreams, and I did—I remembered what happened here, for the most part. But the part where I was this Dreamer? No, I don't remember that."

The Green frowned slightly, and Story marveled at how beautiful she was when she wasn't even smiling.

"That is unexpected, but I'm sure your memories will be revealed in time. Until then, I welcome you back to Tressla." Then to Story's total surprise, The Green stepped forward and embraced her, resting her cheek against Story's hair and squeezing her lightly. In turn, Story gingerly embraced her back, inhaling the soothing smell of rain and moss.

"I have missed our little Dreamer," she whispered tenderly. Story felt all guilt and anxiety slip away as the strength of stone and sea cradled her in its grasp. Even when The Green stepped back with a fond smile and turned toward Kestrel, Lance and Robin, Story could feel strength infuse her limbs, and she felt more confident than she had since she'd come back to Tressla.

Elliott joined Story and Adam, who still stood nearby, and the three looked on as The Green bowed her head and brushed her lips across the suckling child's forehead, bestowing a blessing from the earth.

She didn't stick around long, but her presence seemed to have a centering effect on the entire grove. Elliott wound his arm through Story's as The Green departed, going out as she came—in grace.

Casting him a smile, Story shared the moment with him and then looped her arm through Adam's as well. Here she was in this magical place, a place that had been a home to her once, and she was with two of her best friends. She couldn't ruin the occasion with her sob story. For all she knew, Brink was probably lying. He was the bad guy, right? His beautiful, talentless hands invaded her mind for a fleeting moment but she pushed it away. Tonight, she would dance.

CHAPTER TWENTY-SEVEN

The Green's Solace, Tressla

STORY FELT AS IF she was drinking the best wine in the world as she observed the revelry. It was like a scene out of a movie, except in this medieval-type grove, the majority of the attendees were either Pegasus or of some other magical variety. For a moment, she stood alone enjoying the night lit up by a bonfire and stars. It felt like a mild summer night, the perfect kind when it wasn't too hot or chilly, and the breeze rustling through the leaves on her bare arms and upturned face felt like freedom.

Story laughed to herself as she watched Elliott, who was wearing his signature smolder-face, gaze deeply into Berk's eyes. Much to Elliott's delight, Berk had accompanied Maya to the party, and when she had departed, she had let him stay behind. Now the two sat close together by the fire brushing hands. That would be Elliott's absolute fantasy, to hook up with a real Elf, Story thought with a giggle.

Adam, on the other hand, hadn't even looked at the pretty Elven girls or any of the female Fairytale Extras, which were the characters in stories that never got much play, but existed nevertheless. He'd sworn off women for good, he had grumbled earlier. Instead, he joined some trolls who had taken to drinking heavily and playing some sort of game using golden coins, where the purpose was to bounce them off of stone into goblets. The result was some very drunk trolls along with a very drunk Adam.

Seeking a moment of solitude to take it all in, Story found a spot on a nearby hill overlooking the festivities and took a seat on the forest floor, swilling back a few more drops of the wine she'd been given. Story's smile grew softer when she observed Kestrel and Lance, who looked happy in the firelight, with their heads bowed together over their sleeping bundle.

Story knew they weren't long for this night, and just as she thought it, the two rose, begging weariness, and slipped into the night. Kestrel cast one glance out and caught Story's gaze with a smile and mouthed: "Tomorrow."

Story nodded and shooed the tired new mommy on as she stifled a yawn herself. She felt just a tad bit woozy and her eyes drooped a bit from sleepiness.

"You look like you're about to pass out. Did the Elven Queen give you some of her wine?" Nicholas's warm whisper and beard stubble against her ear gave Story a start and she jumped apart from him before recovering her senses.

"Oh, it's you," she said, putting a hand to her chest and shaking her head at him as he chuckled, his warm velvety laugh making her chest ache. "You nearly scared me to death," she said, but she smiled at him, feeling her already warm cheeks grow rosier as his strong hand found hers and squeezed while he scooted in closer to her.

"Sorry, but you looked like you were about to fall over. Dew Drop Wine?"

With her back against a tree, Story had nowhere to go, and she was increasingly aware of his closeness, his one arm snaking around her to draw her to his side while his other hand played with her fingers, drawing caresses along her palm. He turned to look at her, their faces only inches apart as his dark gaze stared intently into her own.

Swallowing, she looked away quickly and then met his eyes once more. Goose bumps rose along her arms as her skin responded to his lightest of touches. Unable to tear her gaze away from his, she managed to shrug and smile lamely. "You know, dew drops—they're water. I thought she was just giving a fancy name to water."

He smiled darkly and Story knew she was done for. Elliott had nothing on this guy's smolder, she thought. Quest and responsibilities aside, she couldn't be expected to have this much willpower. If he kissed her, and she suspected he might, she would probably just melt and demand he ravish her right there.

"But when you started drinking it, you must have known better," he teased her with a whisper, his lips so close to hers the warmth of his breath beat against her own parted lips.

"Yeah, but it was so yummy," she whispered back, staring up at him like a deer in headlights.

His only response was a smile before he swooped down on her like an owl in the night, his strong arms pulling her close. When their lips met, she felt she would burn alive, his passion and hers connected in an all-consuming blaze. She slid her arms around him as well, and they pulled each other so close that a normal fire between them would have been quelled by the lack of oxygen.

Her logic slipped away and all she could do was feel. Feel his sullen lips upon hers, feel his hands moving down over her back and hips, caressing the small of her back and up her sides.

When she felt the absence of his mouth, she realized she was on her back, cushioned in a bed of the softest grass. Breathing hard, Story looked up at him, feeling as if she wanted to wrench his lips back to hers and keep on going.

Nicholas looked down at her and around, almost as if he was as surprised as her to find himself lying on top of her. Stroking her hair and staring down at her, he slowly sat up and pulled her toward him so they were both sitting on the forest floor, his arm wrapped gently around her, while his other hand softly smoothed away moistness from her cheeks.

"Story, why are you crying?" he broke the silence. Snapping out of her post-kiss daze, she touched her cheeks and looked down in surprise at the salty drops clinging to her fingertips.

"I don't know," she said, glancing from her fingers to him. "It was just . . . What was that?" she breathed, barely daring to hold his gaze longer lest they lose control again. She could only imagine what sex with him would be like, and then she was glad it was dark, so he couldn't see the blood rush to her face.

"It was powerful," he finished for her, nodding.

"I just feel like I know you," she said when he didn't continue.

Again, Nicholas seemed uncomfortable with where the discussion was headed, but Story brushed it off.

"No, I mean it. Ever since I met you, I've felt as if we knew each other, except I don't ever remember meeting anyone like you here or there. When I look into your eyes, it's like I know you. And when you kissed me, it felt like . . . " She paused, not sure she actually wanted to expose as much as she was feeling; she hated the vulnerability of it.

"Like what?" he urged.

"Like I've been missing you," she finished, although that wasn't quite all. What she really wanted to say was that it felt like they were meant to be together, as if they were destined. But even as she thought it, she wanted to bat the thought away. Although destiny was better than fate, she liked to think most things happened by chance, despite the prophecy naming her as the world's savior.

Nicholas had a look on his face she couldn't read. He nodded as if what she said made sense to him as well, then looked away, but not before she saw something like guilt flash across his face. She knew the expression well, having worn it herself as of late. He was silent for a few moments, and Story started to fear that she'd scared him off by coming on too strong with the you're-my-soul-mate bit. But then he turned to her, his gaze intense and serious. He took her hands back into his own and held them tight.

"I've been meaning to tell you something."

"No, first let me tell you something," she said in a rush, the Dew Drop Wine making her bold enough to tell him. She wanted him to know what kind of person he was dealing with before they got any more involved. She wanted a clear conscience.

"Okay." He nodded slowly, turning his dark gaze to hers and holding it with a soft smile.

Taking a deep breath, she met his eyes, unwilling to show fear even though she was terrified he might reject her if he knew she had such darkness within her. "When the Nightmares took me, I ended up in Brink's music chamber. I . . . I spoke with him." Story sifted her fingers through the dewy grass and was comforted by the smell of the burning bonfire, which made her think of camping with her mother when she was young. Before she could lose her nerve, she told him what Brink had said and how she'd cursed him.

For a few moments Nicholas was silent, but he never let go of her hand. Finally, when she thought her heart would explode from her chest, it was beating so anxiously within her, he smiled. "Story, you have nothing to be ashamed of. That wasn't even you."

"But it was," she insisted. "I mean, if you believe I'm the First Dreamer, he has every reason to hate me."

Nicholas smiled again, his soft gaze piercing her with its gentleness. "Yes, I do believe you are very much so. But I do not believe you are the exact same. You have lived a different life. And I also do not believe the act, although certainly cruel, came from an evil place. It came from pain. Then The Dreamer died, so who knows if she wouldn't have retracted the curse, given some time to think and heal."

Story gazed at him and felt relief wash through her, while a rush of longing so strong made her dizzier than the wine, and the desire to lead him further into the woods for more privacy dominated her thoughts. She was just about to suggest they do just that, but he spoke again.

"Now my turn."

Rapt, Story nodded, waiting for him to go on. But instead of talking he turned, distracted by a commotion going on near the bonfire. He rose slowly, helping Story up next to him.

"What is it?" Story asked, standing on her tiptoes and peering over his shoulder since he had moved to block her from harm, which gave her pause for a smile.

"It would seem someone else has joined the party," he said, nodding to the figure stepping into the spotlight of the fire. Laughter and exclamations of welcome carried up toward them, and Story squinted to see who it was.

Holding up a massive Wolf's pelt, the Amazonian-like woman laughed, her hair as fiery as the dancing fire behind her. "Behold the pelt of Nigel!" she cried, and cheers followed from the gathering crowd. "My Big Bad is dead!"

"Story," yelled Elliott, beckoning her excitedly. She glanced at him briefly but her stunned gaze went back to the chrome-eyed warrior who was now staring in disbelief through the shadows right at Story. Although she must have only been a shadow to everyone else standing a distance away, Story remembered that Jess had the eyesight of a Wolf herself, the better to hunt them with. At that moment, the Wolf killer's gaze zeroed in on her with confusion at first, and then a smile split her wide lips.

Dropping the pelt as if it was a carcass and not the prized trophy it really was, the woman stumbled forward past the crowd that parted for her. "Story? Is that you?" The girl asked through a sob.

Choking back her own sobs of surprise and joy, she stepped toward Jess, forgetting for the moment her brief passion with Nicholas. All Story could see was her: this generation's Little Red Riding Hood and her very first best friend. "Jess!" she cried, gasping, and ran down the hill, almost tripping from the Dew Drop Wine's effects but making it safely into the taller girl's slender, but iron-like embrace.

The two girls cried, holding each other back and touching one another's faces, marveling at the changes the years had brought and blubbering into each other's shoulders until they wiped their tears away. Forgetting everyone else as if they were children again, they took to a corner near the fire to talk. Everyone else returned to drinking and dancing, but the girls clasped hands and stared at each other as if the other might disappear.

"How did you get back?" Jess asked.

"It's a long story. But I kept having these dreams that you were in trouble, and well, they led me here."

Smiling, Jess shook her head and cast a saucy wink toward Story. "Come on, you should know I can take care of myself. I told you I would beat him down one day, and I have, haven't I?" she asked, her silvery blue eyes twinkling.

"I know, I guess I should have trusted that, but I thought I was supposed to come help save you, and now I find you're here and whole and you killed that evil bastard."

Jess laughed, her wild red curls floating around her like a halo of fire.

"You got pretty hot, Jess," Story smiled.

"Hot? I'm not hot," she responded, confused.

Laughing, Story shook her head. "It means you're beautiful."

Jess smiled slowly, her lips curving up wickedly. "You didn't turn out so bad yourself. And besides, I saw you up on that hill with a boy. Who was he?" she teased.

Laughing in response, Story shook her head. "Nobody," she said with a blush.

"Uh huh," Jess said leaning back and smiled knowingly. "I'll bet."

Story opened her mouth to change the subject, not ready to discuss Nicholas yet, when she saw Jess's gaze lift above her. Adam and Elliott were standing in the shadows like two little lost boys, and Story realized she'd forgotten them.

"Oh!" Pushing herself quickly to her feet, Story gestured to them to come closer, and when they stalled, she grabbed their hands, dragging them forward.

"Jess, I would love for you to meet my two best friends from the Real World: Elliott and Adam."

Rising and brushing dirt off her leggings, Jess shot them a feral smile and nodded. "You pick some nice-looking company," she observed in a sultry tone.

Laughing, Story nodded. "They are a couple of lookers," she agreed.

Rolling his eyes, Elliott faked modesty. "Please, I'm lucky Story hangs out with me," he said, giving his best smoldering look at Jess, who cackled in response. Adam, Story noticed, couldn't seem to take his eyes off her.

"Is the other one mute, Story?"

"Hardly," she scoffed, leaning up towards Adam and giving him a hard nudge. "Aren't you going to say hi?"

Adam seemed to shake himself, and finally nodded. "You're the girl from the painting."

Arching a fiery brow, Jess looked questioningly at Story. "Painting?"

Story frowned at Adam and then it dawned on her. "Oh, you see, I'm an artist. I make paintings, and lately, I have been painting some of my dreams, and in them you're usually fighting with Wolves," she explained.

"Right, Adam? You saw Jess in one of my paintings?" she added.

Adam nodded again, unable to tear his gaze from her.

Waving one hand in front of Adam's face, Elliott slapped him on the back. "Get with it man!"

Shaking his head, Adam seemed to come out of his surprised daze and broke into a rakish smile. "It's a pleasure to meet you, Jess, we've heard a lot about you. Excuse me for my temporary loss of words, I just didn't realize you were so much more beautiful than the painting gave you credit for," he said with a wink.

Jess grinned. "Oh, well, I'd probably be speechless if I saw paintings of you too," Jess shamelessly flirted.

"Really?" Adam asked, momentarily caught off guard.

Jess laughed and shook her head. "No, not really, but I wanted you to feel better."

Adam blushed, making Story stare at him hard. She'd never seen him quite so out of sorts with a beautiful girl. Adam was usually pretty smooth and confident, but he looked star-struck.

Uh oh, just what she didn't need—a romance between Adam and Jess on top of her own blossoming one with Nicholas. Actually, where was Nicholas? In her elation at seeing Jess, she had forgotten all about him. And that was hard to do since she thought about him constantly. Even now her heart beat hard in her chest at the thought of their wild kiss.

Where was he? She cast a glance around the clearing and squinted into the darkness.

"Story," Jess said after Elliott and Adam had slipped away to give them some time together. "Let's go down to the lake and talk. Are you tired?"

Although sleepiness nagged at her slightly, she was so pumped from being with Jess and had so much to talk to her about that she shook her head.

"Yeah, let's go. I just wish I knew where Nicholas went off to since I wanted to introduce you."

"Ah, the love interest," Jess said with a pause, her eyes flickering strangely for a moment. She gave a chuckle and took Story's arm as they headed toward the path that would take them to the Will's Waterway, which eventually led to the Isle of The Will.

"I'm sure he'll pop up. Until then, tell me more about your friend Adam."

Story laughed and rested her head against Jess's shoulder for a moment as they headed toward the water. Now if only her mother were here, Story felt as if life would be next to perfect. That is, if the worlds weren't dying because she had cursed a musician a long time ago. Dammit.

CHAPTER TWENTY-EIGHT

The Green's Solace, Tressla

THE DAY DAWNED TOO EARLY. Actually, it dawned before Story had even gone to sleep since she and Jess had spent the wee hours of the morning reminiscing and catching up on their lives. There had been laughter, but there had been tears, and Jess had held Story as she wept over Faulks. And in her turn, Story had lent her shoulder to Jess, who sobbed over the ruin of the Fairytale villages closer to The Capital, detailing the oppressive measures that were taking place. But the aggression had moved beyond Fairytales, and even Real World descendants and the Original Mythics were suffering as Brink grasped for power with The Three out of commission. He was obsessed, Jess had said quietly. Obsessed with finding a girl, The Dreamer, she had heard whispered about throughout the kingdom. So Story launched into her own story, with Jess listening intently as she told her everything that had happened since she started having nightmares. And in those sacred moments, Story had relayed to Jess in whispered tones what Brink had told her about her horrible deed, feeling relief as the burden of the secret was lifted once more.

"But Story," Jess had whispered vehemently. "That wasn't you, and yes, I know it is supposed to be you, and oh this is confusing, but it was a long time ago. I hardly think Brink would give you the full story anyhow, especially if he was trying to convince you of his innocence. Oh Story, don't feel guilty, we'll figure it out."

Story had grasped onto her words as she had Nicholas's earlier that night, hoping she could right what had been a horrible wrong that was now costing everyone.

The smell of food cooking and smoke rising through the trees first roused Story, but Bliss quickly finished the job. When Story's eyes blinked open, she saw Bliss's small figure standing in front of her, hands on hips and foot tapping.

"You overslept Story. Kestrel has been waiting to see you for hours."

Sitting up quickly, Story moaned and caught her head. Stupid Dew Drop Wine.

It seemed like she hadn't seen Bliss in forever, and she remembered the Thumbelina had been flitting around on the forest floor all night like the bell of the Thumbelina ball. But now she just looked pouty. Not far behind her was Adam, who cocked a smile and winked as he looked at Bliss.

"Hey Thumb," he said casually and turned his gaze back to Story. Bliss's fists clenched and she fluttered up to Adam's face and shook her finger at him.

"It's Bliss, not Thumb, for the last time!" And then throwing her little arms up into the air she fluttered off toward camp, where Story could hear the murmurs of voices and the occasional cry of a baby.

Adam laughed and smiled wickedly at Story. "I love getting a rise out of her; it's so easy," he said, laughing. Shaking her head, Story rose to her feet and sighed. He really didn't get women very well did he?

"Where's Jess?" she asked, looking around and cringing as the pain shrieked through her head.

"Oh, she's up at the fire eating. Man, can that girl dig in. It's almost as if she has the appetite of a Wolf."

Story nodded. "Yeah, she does. She literally has the appetite of a Wolf as well as the metabolism. She'll always be that annoying girl who can eat anything she wants."

Adam grinned, looking back to the fire where Story could see Jess laughing at something Lance had said. "You hungry?"

Story ran her fingers through her hair and stretched. "Yeah, I could eat, but I think I'm going to walk down to the water and splash my face," she said.

"Adam, Story," Jess called, beckoning them over.

Adam looked back, the longing as clear as day on his face. Love was in the air, Story thought.

"Do you want me to go with you?" he asked.

Shaking her head, she smiled at him and patted his shoulder. "I know you're pining for a certain Fairytale. I'm beginning to see you have a type here, and it's called unattainable since they're all storybook characters. Except here, they're not so hard to find, huh?"

Adam grinned. "Think she likes me?"

Grinning, Story nodded. "Oh, I'd put money on it."

Lighting up, Adam cocked a wink and grinned, and then he started back toward the camp.

Turning to head toward the water, Story paused and called back to Adam, who stopped to look at her. "Hey, have you seen Nicholas? I haven't seen him since before Jess showed up."

"Uh, yeah, he was wandering around this morning looking kind of down. But he did mention he needed to talk to you, so I'll let him know where you are if I see him."

"Thanks," she said, heading down to the water.

She took her time strolling toward the picturesque bank, breathing in the air and trying to clear the pounding in her head. But even the ache in her temples couldn't keep her from finding delight in the morning. She idly wondered what Nicholas wanted to talk to her about. She vaguely remembered him telling her he wanted to tell her something, but then Jess had appeared and he had perfunctorily disappeared. Funny he didn't even come say hi since he must have known by now how much Jess meant to her.

Finding the water's edge, she dipped her hands in the water and splashed the cool liquid against her grimy face. Shivering slightly from the cold, she ran her fingers through her hair in hopes of smoothing the wild mess it had become. She really should take a bath one of these days, but not in this water she thought, cringing from its frigidness.

The Will's Waterway was always cold, at least since he had departed the mortal realm anyway.

She splashed water once more over her face and closed her eyes, feeling refreshed.

"Sister," Story's eyes popped open and she looked wildly around.

"Hello?" she asked slowly.

"Sister, down here."

Slowly, Story looked down into the water and jumped, her heart stopping and restarting. Staring up at her from the water were hollow sunken eyes in a familiar gaunt and yet hauntingly lovely face.

"Sandeen," Story gasped. "You startled me."

"My apologies, sister," Sandeen said with a slow smile that made Story think she wasn't really all that sorry.

"Is something wrong?"

"No, nothing like that. I was just curious as to how you had been doing on your journey. Have you figured out how to stop Brink yet without letting him unite the worlds?"

Shaking her head, Story bit her lower lip. "You know, Ninian seems to think that it would be better if the worlds were united," she said.

Sandeen narrowed her gaze, resembling a wraith with her bottomless black eyes. "That is not wise, sister. Too much time has passed, it could destroy everything," she said.

"Yes, but aren't the worlds dying without one another? I mean, there have been a lot of storms and droughts, and supposed Biblical signs of the end-of-the-world. Ninian also said she thought that there was possibly a way to unite the energy forces of our two worlds without disrupting timelines. You said yourself that The Green is suffering because of the rift."

For the first time, Story thought Sandeen looked guilty, her gaze flittering away as if trying to avoid Story's.

"Sandeen? I mean, do you know anything about this? Do you think it's possible?"

An expression wavering between hope and fear played along her usually composed features, intriguing Story. "What? What do you know? Sandeen?" she urged, feeling as if another piece of the puzzle might suddenly be revealed.

Sandeen shook her head in agitation, causing a geyser of water to erupt a few feet away, droplets of water spraying down on Story. "I know nothing, sister, but that even combining life forces could upset the balance of everything, of everyone. You must do nothing they say, Ninian does not know everything. Do you hear me, sister? You will stop Brink and that is all," she commanded, the elemental quality of her voice taking on an eerie tone of power, her corpse-bride-like features unforgiving.

But Story was having none of it. Who did she think she was, trying to command her? She'd sent Story off to save the world instead of going herself, so whatever power Sandeen had aside from stealing people out for an afternoon swim, Story didn't have much faith in it.

"Listen to me, sister," she said, sarcasm weighing her own voice. "I don't take commands from you, especially when I can tell you're not giving me the whole story. I will find a way to stop Brink, but you better move over, lady, because I'm not going to stop there. I will find a way to save both worlds from the unbalance I created. You got it?"

As soon as the words left her mouth she knew them to be true. She had felt helpless and grief-ridden from the moment Brink told her how the worlds had come to be the way they were. But now she felt a glimmer of power in her soul, and she knew that she could do something to fix what she had screwed up in the first place.

Sandeen hadn't flickered during Story's tirade, but now she seethed. "Who have you spoken with? Did Brink tell you something?"

"I know how I broke the worlds, Sandeen."

A flicker of unease glittered in her ink pools for eyes. "You do?"

"Yes, Brink told me about the curse I put on him when he was the Master Fiddler, and how it upset the balance of the world because it was so horrible. So why don't you stop with all the cryptic crap. Until then, I don't want to see your image in any bodies of water."

"A curse on Brink? He's the Master Fiddler?" Sandeen frowned, realization brightening up the sharp planes of her face. "Sister, what has he told you?"

Story ignored her question. "Sister? You don't even know me," she said firmly and flicked Sandeen's image so that it spoiled in the surface of the lake. When the water became placid once more, she was gone.

Sighing, Story sat back for a moment staring, at the place where Sandeen had disappeared. She hadn't meant to fly off the handle and insult her. The truth was that out of all the gods she had met, Sandeen was the one she felt most familiar with. But she was sick of the riddles and secrets. There was something more to this whole story and no one was being completely honest with her. She could barely believe that Sandeen didn't know Brink's role in how it all started, but then she really had looked surprised when Story had told her Brink was the Master Fiddler. Until all the gods and Daughters of the Will and anyone else who wanted to evade her were truthful, she was going to save Tressla and the worlds on her terms. Not because of what some stupid prophecy said, and certainly not because an exiled goddess who really needed to eat a hamburger told her what to do.

She was pulled from her reverie by the persistent growl of her stomach. The alluring scent of meat cooking pulled her from her thoughts, motivating her to head back to camp, fill her stomach, and figure out a game plan. She was about halfway back when she heard her name. She didn't need to turn because his voice alone could send little thrills racing through her limbs while making her heart work harder. She swallowed, trying to rid her face of all telltale traces of desire and nervousness. She must not let on how much she liked him lest he reject her. And yet the hunger in his eyes for her assured her he wanted her as much as she wanted him.

Assuming a nonchalant air, she turned and faced him, hoping he couldn't tell how much he affected her. Aside from his stormy dark eyes and brooding good looks, he had an easy smile that was warm like the sun's rays on a cool day. He was one of those people who seemed serious most of the time, but when he finally smiled, it lit up his face, making Story want to be the reason for that smile.

"Hey," she said, meeting Nicholas's gaze and offering a friendly smile. "You disappeared last night."

Glancing away, Nicholas nodded. "Yeah." His tone dropped like a rock and Story started to wonder if she had done something wrong. Had she hurt his feelings? They had been making out pretty hardcore. Actually, now that she thought about it, their make-out session had been more than just a little intense. Had her total lack of regard for him when Jess showed up upset him?

"Sorry about that," he said after a few beats and gazed off into the trees. "I just needed to think about a few things."

She nodded and they stood in awkward silence for a few moments while Story worried that he'd changed his mind about her, and she felt her heart wither.

"Nicho—" she was cut off when Jess approached. Finally, she was going to be able to introduce them. Turning to Jess with a bright smile, she faltered when her friend broke the happy moment with a dead look toward Nicholas. Her chrome-like eyes grew frostier if that was even possible, and the stance she took was on the defensive.

"What are you doing here?" she asked, her voice thick with suspicion.

Nicholas's eyes widened almost imperceptibly before they returned to their usual hooded state. "Helping Story," he said evenly, his face composed like stone.

"Story." Jess turned to her, her hands on her hips and her brows arched as high as they could possibly go. "What are you doing hanging with this low life? Do you even know who he is?"

Frowning in confusion, Story looked to him for a response, but Jess was going on. "What are you, a spy, Nicholas? Did you come here for Daddy? Didn't you think anyone would recognize you?"

"No, of course not. You may think you know me, Jess, but you do not."

"Oh don't I? Daddy said, 'Go help the Big Bads, go get Little Red Riding Hood,' and you jumped. You helped them drag me across an entire kingdom so Nigel and his crew could torture me."

"Did they torture you?" Nicholas asked, with an arch of his dark brows.

"Well, no, but what does that matter, Nicholas? The point was you helped them abduct me."

Horrified, Story turned on Nicholas. "Is this true? Why would you do that?"

"Story, didn't you know? This is Brink's son," she said, crossing her arms and glaring at Nicholas.

Story gasped. The news hit her like a baseball to her chest, the air blown out of her as she tried to catch a breath. She turned toward Nicholas, wanting to beg him to tell her that Jess was wrong, that it was a mistake.

"Is this true?" she was finally able to whisper. But she knew it was. Brink's deep dark eyes flashed in her mind, and she remembered how disturbed she'd been by them. Because they had reminded her of Nicholas, she just hadn't put the two together, the thought had been so abhorrent.

"Story," Nicholas said, turning to her, "You don't understand, I helped them to kidnap Jess so I could help her. I knew if they went on her own, the chances of her making it back in one piece were slim. At best, they would have raped and tortured her. I knew I could keep her safe."

"Why would you care about me?" Jess scowled.

Not even looking at Jess, Nicholas stared at Story with the dark eyes that she still loved despite who gave them to him. Yes, loved, she realized. She was hopelessly in love with him. She couldn't help but feel herself soften, gazing into his rugged features usually composed so confidently, but which were now pleading with Story to understand. And she wanted to, but she felt like she was stepping through a web of lies, and she already had enough mystery in her life. So she hardened her heart and with her hands on her hips stared him down.

"Answer her question, why would you care about Jess?"

Sighing, he turned and ran his hands through his hair in frustration, not saying anything for a few beats. Finally he turned and met her gaze, his dark eyes softening. "Because of you, Story."

"Me?" She whispered, confusion rushing over her. "But we just met."

"Oh please, what a bunch of . . . "

"Jess," Story snapped, holding her hand up and perfunctorily silencing her friend.

Both ignored Jess as she snorted unattractively, while Nicholas managed to offer a faint smile.

"You know how you keep saying I look familiar? Well, I've seen you before, when you were younger. We didn't exactly meet, but, well, I . . . I was there when the Big Bads killed Faulks.

"You were?" Story asked in disbelief, trying to recall those horrifying moments. "Oh my god," she whispered, looking sharply back at Nicholas. "You were the boy . . . You saw me hiding beneath the floor and you didn't tell them."

Those horrifying moments eight years ago played out in her mind—the Wolves growling and demanding to know where Story was, where The Dreamer was, while Faulks stared them down with honor and courage, never giving her away, sacrificing himself for her. She remembered them closing in on him like the beasts they were. And then after as she stared in mute horror up through the slats, a dark-eyed boy who had stopped one of the men from discovering her beneath the floor, holding her gaze as she blinked out of Tressla for the last time.

Nodding, he took a step closer to Story. "I've never forgotten you, and in all these years I've been working to overthrow my father. I'm not on his side. My mother is the prophetess who created the prophecy. We've always known it was you it was talking about, and I've just been waiting for you to return. I've been trying to help you, and when I heard they were going to get Jess, I knew I had to stop them because she was your friend. So I made sure she wasn't overly abused—because she might be of the legendary Riding Hood family, but seven Big Bads against just her weren't good odds."

"Oh, please," Jess interjected. "Are you going to believe him?"

Staring at Nicholas hard, Story finally nodded. "Yes, I believe him."

"Then are we okay?" Nicholas asked, stepping closer to her again, relief flooding his strong, handsome face.

"Could you give us a minute?" Story said, turning to Jess.

Nodding sullenly, her friend turned and walked off, giving Nicholas a dark look as she passed him.

"I do believe you, and I want you on our side. But I can't do this."

"Do what?" he asked, his brow furrowing as the relief that had been present earlier disappeared.

"Us," she whispered, casting her eyes down for a moment and wishing she wasn't saying these words.

"Story," he said as if reasoning with a child.

"No," she said more firmly, and met his gaze. "Since I returned here, I've gotten nothing but vague ideas and absolutely no answers, except from your father, who's supposed to be the enemy. No one is leveling with me, and now I find out that even you, who I could easily tell was harboring some secrets, had a whammy to lay on me."

"I tried to tell you . . . "

"Yes, I realize that you tried to tell me last night. But Nicholas, why didn't you just let Ninian introduce you truthfully and explain to us that you're a good guy? How hard would that have been? Did you think I would freak out? So what if you're Brink's son? I'm not so naïve to think you couldn't have a different path. And so what if you're the boy from the day Papa died? You saved me. I would have welcomed you no less than I did not knowing these things. But you lied. And I am sick of lies and evasions. So I'm done. I need to be concentrating on our next step anyway. I'm supposed to save the world, I can't be making out with the enemy's son in the bushes when I should be coming up with a plan. I'm sorry," Story said, gazing at him for a moment before turning on her heel and heading back to camp, leaving Nicholas standing behind her with a forlorn expression and a sadness in his deep, dark eyes.

Her heart hurt as she trudged away, and she angrily swiped at tears. Gods, she'd cried so much since she'd come back, it would be amazing if she didn't have permanent bags under her eyes. But she had to be strong and be a leader, she realized. So she gathered herself, and by the time she reached the camp, she was tear-free and determined.

Elliott met her when she arrived, holding a bread cake and some water for her. Thanking him and refusing to meet his knowing eyes, she nodded and looked to the rest of her entourage. "We're heading to The Capital, and when we get there, we're going to take down Brink. Who's with me?" She was surprised when Lance and Kestrel volunteered, the baby slung in a sack around her chest. Forcing a smile, Story nodded gratefully and bit into the bread. It tasted like sawdust and heartbreak.

CHAPTER TWENTY-NINE

Breman, Tressla

THEY HAD BEEN WALKING for a few hours, but Nicholas barely noticed, he was so lost in his own despair. He couldn't have lost her already, not when he had just found her. If she only knew how perfect they really were for each other. She was all he could think about since he'd laid eyes on her at Ninian's. So when Racell took up his pace and joined him on their trek, he barely noticed.

"She'll get over it soon," Racell said with a comforting smile.

Nicholas grunted and then glanced at the demi-god. "I'm afraid neither one of us can claim to know Story too well, so I'm not optimistic."

Racell chuckled and nodded. "Well, if it's any consolation, she's angry with me too."

"Why?"

"I may have mentioned that I was aware of who you really were, so she's decided we're no longer on speaking terms. Unlike you, I am optimistic. She's just angry and unsure, and she has a lot to handle right now." Reaching out and patting Nicholas's arm, Racell smiled, his golden eyes more like sunshine while Story's tended to be darker, like honey.

"She'll get over it, trust me. And even though it's been twenty years since I've laid eyes on Edie, I think she'll forgive me when I finally see her again," he said longingly.

"Why don't you go now?" Nicholas asked. "I'm sure if she tried, Story could make a doorway."

Shaking his head, Racell sighed. "Story needs me. And if you hadn't noticed, we need Story," he said.

Glancing around, Nicholas noticed for the first time that Story had amassed a small following. They were a diverse bunch. A couple of Elves had followed along, looking more ethereal than ever. They were brother and sister, Nicholas remembered—Sylvester and Sylvaine. He recalled that the twin elves were known particularly for their stealth, and he could tell why. The two barely spoke, riding on twin horses with heads held high, Sylvaine with black hair and Sylvester with white. A few Fairytale Extras had followed along as well as a smattering of trolls and some other Original Mythics. Nicholas could see a young female tree dryad accompanied by a male diwata, his skin pale next to the young dryad's nut-brown complexion.

Shaking his head, Nicholas sighed and glanced back at Story, who walked beside Jess and Elliott. It was all he could do to keep himself from spiriting her away so that she'd be forced to talk to him, to admit the connection they had couldn't be denied. It was all he could do to keep from touching her, most moments. The gap between them now was nearly killing him, and he felt tight with restraint and grief.

She was smiling at something Elliott was saying, but the smiled quickly faded when she caught Nicholas staring at her. He locked on to her gaze almost beseechingly, willing her to reconsider her decision. But she merely shook her head and looked back at Elliott, pasting a forced smile to her face.

Nicholas looked away and wondered if he had merely imagined that she looked sadder than normal. Regardless, he wasn't going to give up. He'd often felt an emptiness in his life, a desire for more, but it wasn't until he saw Story that he realized that what was lacking had been her all along.

Nicholas had been angry at his mother for a long time for making him into a warrior when his passions lay elsewhere. But when he'd first laid eyes on Story when he was only fifteen, all had been forgiven. He'd known at that moment what he was fighting for, and he knew deep within that it was worth it. He'd never been a quitter, and he wasn't about to now.

He looked back once more and saw that Story had moved. Adam joined Jess and Elliott, making doe eyes at the red-haired Wolf killer.

Behind them walked Kestrel and Lance, who had decided to stay in human form to help Kestrel with Robin. Lastly, was a procession of trolls who had decided to join them, along with some rogue Thumbelinas who had followed Bliss's lead.

Nicholas wished Ninian was there. Perhaps she could have talked some sense into Story. He blinked as Bliss nervously flitted by, her small face in his, her large electric green eyes glittering with worry. "Have you seen Story?"

Nicholas glanced around and behind him once more. "No, I was just wondering where she was as well. Perhaps she's with the trolls? I can't see that far back."

Shaking her head, Bliss wrung her hands. "Oh, what kind of Thumbelina am I? I can't even keep track of my little girl?" she cried, flitting over to Racell and talking to him.

Nicholas started to get a bad feeling in his chest. He dropped off from the procession and turned toward the back, passing the small army in search of Story. Nothing. Turning around once more, he joined the best friend clan. "Where did Story go?"

Jess glared at him. "As if I would tell you." Adam and Elliott glanced at Jess curiously before looking back to Nicholas.

"She was here like ten minutes ago," said Elliott, rolling his eyes towards Jess and mouthing to Nicholas, "Drama."

Nicholas's heart warmed at this bit of kindness from Elliott, who had no reason to care about him.

"I saw that, Elliott," Jess snapped, tossing her wild red mane.

Adam, who had always seemed to resent Nicholas and was walking closest to him, clapped him on his shoulder like they were old friends. "She just said something about needing some alone time, and she walked off toward the back of the group. She's probably just taking some me time," he said quietly.

Nicholas felt his jaw tense. Now he knew something was wrong. Locking his gaze on all three he shook his head. "That's just the thing, Story is not back there or anywhere."

"Maybe she ducked into the woods to relieve herself," Jess suggested, although her expression and countenance had taken on the alertness of a warrior. "I'll go check the woods."

Elliott and Adam also looked concerned and with good reason. "I'll go talk to the Elves," Elliott said.

"Let's go talk to the trolls," Adam said to Nicholas.

Nicholas nodded. "But let's be discreet. I don't want to alert the whole bunch just yet. Nodding in agreement, Adam followed Nicholas as he jogged toward the back, where the trolls shuffled along at a slower pace.

Nicholas eyed them as they approached. Unlike what contemporary fiction would tell you, Trolls were not altogether unattractive. They were actually elemental by nature, each one possessing a trait and belonging to a tribe of its specific element. There were often squabbles and fights between the tribes when dueling elements were forced together. In this group, there were three trolls altogether, two of which were ruled by fire and one by earth. Their bickering voices had been a constant noise in the background since the three had joined their party a few days before.

Story's army had stopped moving altogether at this point. Jess, who had taken Tuscan, returned having seen no sign of Story, and she was consulting with Racell.

Turning to the three Trolls, Nicholas nodded to Adam. "Have you seen Story? We can't seem to find her."

One of the fire trolls—Gordon, Nicholas remembered—spoke first, "She walked back here and had a few words with us," he said slapping at a spark that flew from his red, crackling beard, "but then she said something 'bout using the forest's natural amenities," he gruffed.

The other fire troll, shorter and slender with bright ruddy cheeks, also spoke. "Yeah, she took off that way and we haven't seen her since." Nicholas glanced at Adam, who nodded.

"Thanks, Grady. Jasper, did you see anything?" Adam directed his question to the black-haired earth troll, who had a rippling beard and an olive complexion. Jasper only shook his head, a frown creased into his wrinkled features.

Jess came riding toward them, sniffing the air. "Wolf," she said.

Nicholas felt bile rise in his throat, and he coughed. He should have been more on guard. He could tell Jess and Adam felt the same way.

"I don't know how I didn't smell it before," Jess moaned. Nicholas could hardly believe it when he saw tears spring to Jess's eyes.

Meeting Adam's and Jess's eyes, he nodded firmly. He had been trained and groomed to lead after all, and he couldn't lose his cool now. "Jess, you have to start tracking now before we lose them."

"I'll go with her," Racell said, having joined them at the back of the procession. "I can talk to the naiads and call the nature spirits if need be."

Nicholas nodded curtly and watched as Racell jumped on Cobble to follow Jess and Tuscan into the woods. Turning back, Nicholas noticed the entire following had circled around them, looking serious and determined. Smiling inwardly, Nicholas realized how proud he was of Story. She was a true leader. She had an entourage that would risk themselves to save what was precious: her. And because of that, and because he loved her, he admitted to himself, he would be the leader in her absence, and make sure that she was found. Then they would stop his father together.

"The Big Bads have taken her. We need to set up camp. We need a base. Because when we find out where they're located, well, we're bringing her back no matter what," Nicholas said firmly.

Adam's jaw was locked hard in agreement while Elliott nodded vehemently.

"Those Big Bads are going down," Elliott said, looking angrier than Nicholas had ever seen him.

Sylvaine put a hand on Nicholas's shoulder for a moment and met his gaze. "Brother, we follow your lead. Make use of us as you will, and we will see that The Dreamer returns safely."

"Thank you."

Sylvaine nodded slowly, silver eyes glittering, and moved on to help her brother find a suitable camp.

It was dark before they heard any word from Jess and Racell, and when it did come, it was only Racell who showed up.

Nicholas was sitting by the fire talking softly to Gordon, who was discussing battle tactics with him. He had spent most of the night cursing himself for not having gone with Jess and Racell, pacing with the need to do something, to act.

"We found it," Racell whispered, almost a ghost in the darkness, his sunny golden eyes more like a tiger's in the night. "Jess is waiting outside camp. I had to convince her to wait for help because she's determined to get Story out of there as quickly as possible."

Rising swiftly, Nicholas grasped Racell's shoulder. "How far?"

"Not far at all. They're camped about two miles from here, but deep in the valley so their fires won't be seen."

"Who would have thought that Wolves would like fire so much," Adam grumbled.

Looking at him, Racell met his gaze intently. "You must never forget Adam, these Wolves were men first. The same rules do not apply. But you are right, Wolves do not usually need fire."

Chastened, Adam nodded, his handsome brow furrowed. "You know, Bliss would be great at the sort of recon needed for this kind of thing. Anyone seen her?" Adam asked.

Racell nodded. "Yeah, she followed us there. She's Story's Thumbelina, a little girl's best friend. She was invaluable—she was able to get into the compound and find out that there are two Big Bads watching Story's tent."

"Thank Maya's Chaos that Nigel is dead," Nicholas murmured, rubbing his face with his hands.

"Was he that bad?" Adam asked.

"Yes," Racell and Nicholas said at the same time.

"Jinx," Elliott called anxiously.

"What?" they both asked again at the same time.

"Double jinx," he said. "I'm going with you. I'm our group's psychic, you need me."

Rolling his eyes, Adam turned to them as well. "I'm going too," he said.

Shrugging, Nicholas nodded. "Let's go then. We have The Dreamer to save."

CHAPTER THIRTY

Big Bad Wolves' Camp, Tressla

SHE COULDN'T BELIEVE how stupid she had been. What had she been thinking, going off alone into the trees like that? She had been so confident since defeating the Nightmares. *Over-confident,* she berated herself.

She had just needed a moment—a moment to relieve herself as well as a minute away from Nicholas's deeply intense gazes that still made her feel hot, despite her resolve to focus solely on getting to The Capital and defeating Brink. Instead, here she was in some dingy tent, guarded on all sides by creepy Big Bad Wolves. Ms. Confident, who supposedly had all this power and yet couldn't think of one way to get out of the mess she now found herself in. They hadn't even bothered to tie her up, that's how sure they were that she wasn't a flight risk.

Sighing, she got up from the small cot she'd been sitting on, and she was trying to discover a way out of there when the flap lifted, and one of the guards entered. Darvish, she remembered, was his name, the strange one with the green eyes that Racell had petted. He didn't seem as bad as the rest, but she supposed that wasn't saying much. Deep down they were all soulless killers. Faulks's face just before the Wolves tore him apart so many years before flickered in her mind, and she clenched her eyes shut for a moment, trying to stomp out the image.

"I've brought you something to eat," Darvish said, reminding Story he was there.

Unclenching her eyes, she stared at him stonily. Her stomach rumbled, but she refused to even look at the food, and instead she continued to hold his gaze in the challenge she knew it presented. But instead of the usual reaction, hackles raised, a growl, a challenge back, he lowered his gaze and set the tray of deliciously aromatic food down on a low-lying table next to the cot.

He stood for a moment silently, and Story studied him, confused by his lack of presence. Big Bads, if anything, were aggressive—all of them. Their very nearness whispered predator, and you couldn't help but want to run screaming in the opposite direction. But Darvish had a quietness about him that was curious. Story found she wasn't frightened, and none of the ordinary symptoms were present. Her heartbeat remained steady, her pulse didn't race, and she could breathe just fine.

Crossing her arms against her breast, she eyed him for a moment before speaking. "Thanks for the food, I suppose."

"Your humble thanks is most welcome," he responded with a flourish so that Story almost smiled. Was he actually joking around with her? Must have come trying to get some sort of allowance from her. Yes, it was a trick.

"Can I help you?" she asked, wondering why he just stood there without leaving.

"I'm supposed to stick around until you eat," he said, nodding at the food.

Crossing her arms, she glared at him, noticing that he was rather good-looking, with dark chocolate skin, a strong determined jaw, and piercing green eyes so unlike those of other Wolves—they almost seemed pure against the usual sickly yellow. He was bald, but as if he had shaved his head. It suited him, adding to his handsomeness instead of detracting from it. She had never really looked at a Wolf before. Their snarls and evil eyes were usually all she could see. But Darvish's gaze lacked that certain flavor of darkness she was used to.

Ignoring the food even though her stomach protested, she nodded at him. "You're different from the others."

"Are you asking?"

"I'm stating a fact," she said, rising from the cot and taking a step toward him. She stepped closer, sort of as a test to see if he would start to creep her out. But there was nothing. She suppressed a smile. Elliott would have laughed at her daring.

It was actually Darvish who seemed to be the uncomfortable one when she took another step closer.

"So what's your deal?" she asked. "Are you a trick?"

"A trick?" he echoed her, raising thick black brows. "No, I just came to bring you food."

"Okay, because my gut feeling here is that one of these Wolves is not like the other."

He moved away with the grace of a predator, but with a certain nonchalance. "Don't do that," he hissed. For the first time, Story got a glimpse of the Big Bad inside of this Wolf as his green eyes diamonded out.

"Do what?" she asked, feeling the familiar heart surge start up.

"Use your Dreamer sense on me."

"Dreamer sense? I have Dreamer sense?"

The snarl ran away from his face and was replaced with disbelief and the deep rumbling bark of laughter. "I can see now you have some catching up to do before Brink will get anything amounting to inspiration from you. So in the meantime, maybe you should stop trying to punch holes in the tent. You're not going to get away," he growled, and then winked.

Story was just about to respond with a confused but sharp retort about how she hadn't been punching any holes, when she realized that was the point. She wasn't going to punch any holes in the tent, but she'd definitely punched a hole in the fabric of reality before. She would bet anything she could create a doorway out of this tent that would lead her back to the woods. Now if she could just figure out how to do it.

She watched the flap of the tent swing shut after Darvish and frowned, deciding she'd ponder this strange meeting with a Big Bad when she had more time. She didn't really think he was all that bad, although he had been quite big. Shaking her head, she started pacing, trying to remember how she had punched holes in reality before.

Closing her eyes, she could almost smell the aroma of pumpkin and cinnamon wafting from Ninian's spice garden, containing flowers that came in all varieties and smelled of various foods. Her stomach growled at the memory, but she concentrated more fully. Jess, Bliss, and Story had been playing in the garden. Story was pretending to be a courtier, while Jess was the princess. Story almost laughed at the thought—warrior Jess a princess. It really had been make-believe.

Story had held Jess's hand as if she was helping her cross a bridge, and had told her royal highness she was opening a gate to the most magnificent gardens. But instead, a piece of the landscape had disappeared, and trees and flowers that didn't exist in Ninian's backyard could be seen. It seemed so wrong, Story had jumped back and screamed.

The door had yawned open from one landscape to another. A butterfly flitted from the doorway into Ninian's backyard, and Story had rushed forward trying to shut the intangible door. After that day, Ninian had started to really work with Story, but her knowledge had been minimal and she hadn't been able to fully show her how to control her gift.

Story opened her eyes, looked around the tent, and sighed. "But how do I open it?"

"Just think where you want go," said a voice near her ear, making Story jump.

"Bliss!" she whispered, plucking the Thumbelina from the air and pressing her small form to her cheek. "But how?"

"Shhh," Bliss whispered, all business. But Story could see the delighted gleam in her Day-Glo green eyes. Story realized she had been neglecting Bliss and hugged her again. "I'm so sorry for not spending any time with you lately."

Shaking her head, Bliss swatted at Story's hand as it came in again to grab her. "Enough of that; you're going to need to open that door because you are guarded on all sides."

"But I don't remember how," she sighed.

"Yes, you do, all you have to do is will it to be there. That's what you did that day at Ninian's."

"Yes, but how do I know where we'll end up?"

"Just concentrate on where you want to go, and it will open up."

"How do you know?"

"Story, where were you thinking of the day you opened the door in Ninian's gardens?"

"I was thinking of Faulks's gardens," Story said, thinking back to that day. "I remember thinking Ninian had pretty ones, but that Papa's gardens were so much prettier. More fit for a princess," she finished with a smile.

"And when you opened that door, where did it lead?"

"To a garden," Story said slowly, tilting her head and thinking for a moment. "But that could have been any garden."

"But it wasn't. Don't you remember?" Bliss said excitedly, her ruby-colored hair dancing around her curvy little figure. Thumbelinas were pretty much always gorgeous, Story thought with a distracted sigh, touching her own tangled brown mess. She was definitely on her way to dreads.

Dropping her split ends, she thought hard for a moment and realized Bliss was right. Those flowers hadn't just been anyone's garden. There had been Bellow Dings, a yellow flower that gave a loud bellow when intruders happened into the garden, and a beautiful ding when friends came to visit. She remembered those flowers so well because Faulks had made a point of always telling Story to play near that specific area. That way he would know if someone was approaching.

"Oh my God . . . or gods—whatever. All I have to do is think where I want to be and pretend to open a door. I can do it . . . maybe," she said, losing the air in her sails as she remembered how ludicrous opening a door out of thin air really seemed.

"Story, don't pretend, really open it. You might still have a hard time grasping this, but I've always known who you were," Bliss said quietly, her gaze intense as Story turned to meet it.

"Faulks gave me to you so that I could help take care of you. Since I was first budded, I knew I had been given the most very important task a Thumbelina could be given—to protect the First Dreamer."

Shaking her head, Story stared at her. "No, you're wrong. Faulks didn't even know I was supposed to be this legendary being. He was always trying to get Ninian to tell him."

Bliss smiled softly. "Faulks didn't know for sure, Story. But he had a very strong suspicion. He had seen and heard a lot of things in his time, and one of those had been the tale of the First Dreamer and her hopeful return. Not long after you showed up at his cottage, Faulks went into The Capital for trading. It was a big event, so he went with a wagon of plants and herbs to sell and trade. There, he met the prophetess who told of your coming, and after that his purpose in life was to keep you safe."

She shouldn't have been surprised, Story thought, since Faulks had laid down his life to save her. Her thoughts went on mute when she heard talking right outside the tent. She knew the Big Bads' new alpha was finally going to pay her a visit.

"Now, Story!" Bliss urged.

Nodding, she took a deep breath and held out her hand. In her mind she imagined a wooden door knob, inlaid with ivy and leaf that would take her into the woods outside of camp. But at the last moment, another thought flashed through her mind, so that when they stepped through the gaping hole in the room, they landed just far enough from the Big Bads to be undetected.

Story's elation over her triumph would have to wait. She turned to examine her surroundings when a hand went over her mouth and dragged her down to the ground behind a crag of rocks.

Hot breath met her ear, but it was the voice that caused her heart to lurch. "Quiet, we're waiting for Jess and Adam to return from creating a distraction, and then I want to hear about how the hell you got out of there," he said, his lips lingering near her face a little longer than necessary, which only served to make Story flush, once again grateful for the dark.

"But what's the distraction?" she asked once his hand had dropped away from her mouth.

"Oh, well Jess is going to wage a vendetta against all Wolves," he said a bit less confidently.

Story heard Bliss gasp in horror, just as she did. "What? I'm right here, we could leave now and they wouldn't even know. We have to stop them, that's like a death sentence."

"Well, Adam and Jess feel as if they will be able to get out after I set fire to the entire camp. Elliott and I covered the area just outside the camp with Slow Bloomers."

Story gasped again. "Adam is down there too? And where's Elliott? How could you let them come, Nicholas?" Story asked accusingly.

He was stopped from returning a sharp retort when a breathless Elliott joined them from behind.

"Oh Story, like he had a choice, sweetie?" he said, kissing her quickly and shaking his head in the darkness as if chastising her naiveté.

Feeling her anger dissipate, she nodded. She supposed he was right—neither Adam nor Elliott were good at waiting or following orders. They were also profoundly loyal, and Story wrapped an arm around his waist quickly and squeezed. "Thanks for coming," she whispered quietly.

"And thank you," she turned to both Nicholas and Bliss. "But I can't let Jess do this. It's too late for the Slow Bloomers, so we'll just have to use the fire as a distraction. I'm going in for them."

"Don't be ridiculous. We came here to rescue you, not let you walk right back into, literally, a den of Wolves," Elliott argued.

Nicholas nodded in agreement. "There is no way I'm letting you go back in there, Story. You're what matters."

"And Jess and Adam matter to me." Story met his gaze and smiled slowly. "Anyway, it's not as if you could stop me."

"Story, so help me, I will if I have to."

Balking at his tone, she stood. "I'll just be a minute. Don't follow me." Nicholas started to grab her, but Bliss slapped his hand away.

"Let her go, Nicholas. She can open doorways now, and she's the best chance we have."

His eyes widened slightly in the darkness so that the whites of his eyes caught the moonlight. "I should have known by the way you appeared from out of nowhere."

Nodding, Story turned, and concentrating on Jess, imagined a doorknob, this one bright red and hot to the touch. Although she only had to turn the knob and she was through, her hand stung from the brief heat.

Just like before, she was in one place—standing beside Nicholas ready to smack him or kiss him, she wasn't sure which—and then she was behind Jess, who was standing on a rock and yelling to all the snarling Wolves that she would kill them all if it was the last thing she did.

"Damn," Story whispered. Before Jess could say another word, she grabbed her so fast even the warrior in Jess didn't react until it was too late and Story had propelled her through the doorway without a backwards glance.

Looking at Adam who was staring at Story incredulously, she jerked her head to the doorway. "Go, now. I'll be right behind you." Adam looked as if he would argue, but she stared at him fiercely. He must have thought better of it because he glanced once at the slavering Wolves and then dashed into the gap in reality.

She turned to the Wolves, who were just now realizing what was happening.

"That's The Dreamer," one snarled. "How did she escape?"

All through the crowd, Wolves started to turn and the word "Dreamer" began to seethe from them as they crawled closer.

Story smiled. Although she felt like she could do anything in that moment, she knew she had to make this quick. They all looked pretty pissed, and her heart was beating double time.

"That's right, I am The Dreamer. And you can't trap me, bind me, or give me away. I can get into your dreams, and I will make you wish you never had to sleep again if you don't leave us alone. Pleasant dreams!" she called as they started to rush forward, and then she slipped through the door, closing the opening right before they reached it.

Turning, she found her friends gathered close as well as one fuming red-haired warrior. She was opening her mouth to go off on Story, but she cut her off. "We don't have time."

Turning, Story reached out her hand, grasped a doorknob as golden as her father's eyes, and thought of Racell.

"Let's go," she whispered urgently, hearing the sounds of Wolves tracking them and drawing closer. Story had never felt as relieved as she did when she slammed that door shut on the howling beasts.

Shaking, Story turned to Adam and met his gaze. "Just like when we were kids," he whispered, looking a little pale and shaken. "Except real."

"That was real too," she whispered. "Just a different real."

He nodded and looked down, the breadth of their journey finally seeming to take its toll. But she couldn't worry about that now.

They still didn't have much time. Story turned into the waiting arms of her father and all her previous anger at him disappeared as she gazed up into his eyes so like her own. "Hi Dad," she whispered and smiled.

His sunny gaze misted over as he kissed her forehead. "We've got to go," he said. "I can hear them."

"I know," Story said turning to her followers. "We're going to The Capital. Now."

Chapter Thirty-One

Racell's Rood, Tressla

IT HAD BEEN TWO DAYS since they had stepped out into Racell's Rood, a clearing that existed in the Forest of Sylum. It was idyllic, a peaceful sanctuary in the midst of a dying, repressed world. There, a bubbling brook sang them to sleep and provided them with the sweetest of water. But only a mile or two away lay the hovels the Fairytales were forced to keep, their happy endings a sad joke in this story.

Story and her companions were protected in the Rood. Elliott had informed Story they could remain undetected within the circle of its protective arms. How he knew she wasn't sure, but he had been making a lot of friends lately, she noticed. She glanced over at his tall, lanky form as he shared what he had deemed the best coffee ever with those two stuffy elves. At least, that had been her impression of them, up until she witnessed Sylvaine throwing her head back and laughing at something Elliott said.

Story smiled to herself. He was getting more comfortable here than she ever thought possible. Glancing around at the group, she thought it funny how they were supposed to be in this big secret place when townsfolk, Fairytales and all manner of Tresslans had been showing up pretty much since they had arrived. If Story had been looking for an army, she was certainly building one. They said they had come to join The Dreamer on her quest to take down The Capital. When she had asked Racell about the veil hiding the Rood, he had mumbled something about the veil only keeping out those with dishonest intentions.

Concerned, she glanced at her father, who had been quiet since they'd arrived. She felt closer to him than ever before, so it wasn't hard for her to tap into that Dream Sense Darvish had been talking about and figure out what it was. She could open doors now, and he must have realized what that would mean for him. He could see her mother again. She had tried to suggest that he go see Edie, but he refused to leave her side.

Sighing, she looked back down at the parchment where the prophecy had been written and tried to decipher the words. Scrunching up her eyes didn't really help, but she felt it might put the words into perspective.

Twisting a strand of hair around her finger, she glanced up from the paper and heaved another sigh. If only Racell would see that his depressing presence wasn't helping anyone—and how it would give her peace of mind, knowing that her mother had someone there with her. Edie must be going out of her mind with worry. If only there was some way Story could get him to go back. Shaking her head, she pressed her back against the rough bark of the tree she was leaning against and anxiously pulled at a hangnail with her teeth. If only she could figure out how she was supposed to get the fiddle from Brink without getting caught and destroying the world. Again.

"Ergh!" she said, not meaning to be so loud. Looking around quickly, she noticed the only person who had witnessed her frustration, of course, was Nicholas. Yes, give him another reason to stare at you, Story, and drive yourself crazy with the want of him. She held his gaze for a fraction of a second too long before she looked down.

With her eyes averted back to the prophecy, she could pretend he wasn't getting to her, pretend he wasn't almost all she could think about. They hadn't had a chance to talk since they had returned from the Wolf camp. And although she was no longer angry with him, she didn't know what to say. The truth was, she was there to right the wrongs she had allegedly committed as this First Dreamer, and she really didn't think indulging in a crush was the best idea right now. Look what he was doing to her with just one glance.

Flustered and annoyed at herself for her lack of focus, she stood up, brushed off bits of leaves and grass, and headed through the camp of people. She walked toward a trail that would lead down further toward the Three Brothers River, which emptied into the Silver Sea. She needed to get away and clear her head.

As she passed, people bowed their heads and murmured their blessings, which Story found disconcerting. Yes, she did believe that there must be some truth to their beliefs because she could definitely do some cool magic, and she wasn't the same girl now. But The Dreamer sounded like a being from a storybook, and Story just felt . . . human, with superpowers.

She hadn't even gotten to the trail when Kestrel called out to her. "Story, wait up," she said from her spot near Lance and Jess. The two girls had probably been trading battle stories. Handing Robin to Lance, Kestrel jumped up and came trotting toward her with a flip of her long yellow braid.

Story wanted to be alone, but she and Kestrel had enjoyed little time to talk since they were reunited, and she welcomed her sister's company. Story laughed as Kestrel linked arms with her and whispered, "I saw you making your getaway, but I figured you could do with some venting. You've been alone enough in your head lately."

"True enough," she said and squeezed her friend's hand.

As they meandered quietly toward the bank of the river, Kestrel cleared her throat, and that's when Story knew that this was no innocent little walk. "You know, I thought it was strange that when you opened that first door, you were supposed to end up outside the perimeter of camp, but you didn't, right?"

Story shrugged. "Beginner's mistake," she answered, avoiding Kestrel's piercing gaze.

"That's interesting because when you had to make the jump into the bowels of the Big Bads' camp and then out to our camp, and then again to Racell's Rood there was no hesitation," she said, getting warmed up. Story gritted her teeth, hearing the familiar know-it-all tone creep into her sister's voice, just like when she was thirteen.

"I don't know, Kestrel. Like I said, it was a mistake, it was my first time," she answered, failing to keep the edge from her voice.

Shaking her flaxen head, Kestrel smiled prettily, blatantly ignoring Story's irritation. "I think not. Even when you were a child and opened doors by mistake, you never missed your mark. So tell me, how did you end up where you did?"

Jerking her arm from Kestrel's, Story turned to her in exasperation. "At the last moment I thought of Nicholas," she finished lamely, losing her fire quickly. "He popped into my head and that's why we ended up with him. Is that what you wanted to hear? Now you can see why it's so bad for me to get involved with him when I have so many other things on my plate right now."

"Wrong," Kestrel said softly but firmly. Story could tell her big sister syndrome was only about to get worse, and she regretted not making a break for privacy when she could have.

Grasping Story's shoulders, Kestrel smiled and locked their gazes. "Your insistence on staying away from Nicholas is what's causing the problems. You keep saying he's bad for you, but the times you've allowed yourself to give in to your emotions are the times when you've been the most focused. Once you gave up on him, the Wolves captured you, and now you can't figure out how to defeat Brink because you keep sneaking looks at him. You haven't trained to learn any other powers you might have, and you still haven't come up with a plan. We've been sitting here stagnant for days now, and I think a lot of it has to do with this major distraction. If anyone knows any tactical maneuvers that could help us get into The Capital, it would be Nicholas, but you avoid him. Story, you're more grounded when you're with him. You can't allow yourself to feel guilty that you found love."

"Love," Story scoffed, feeling her cheeks color. "I barely even know him."

Kestrel smiled. "That doesn't matter. Love knows no rhyme or reason. Trust me, I know."

Story looked up into Kestrel's beautiful face and for a moment remembered the child she once was, the one with the wild straw-like hair and knobby elbows.

"You really believe that?" Story whispered.

"I do," Kestrel said. "You can save the worlds and be happy too. It's okay."

Picking up a rock, Story snapped her wrist back and skipped it against the calm surface of the wide river. It skipped, once, twice, three times and then disappeared beneath the water's surface.

Turning back to Kestrel, she nodded. "I'll be happy when I can right the wrongs my former self-created with her selfishness. And to do that, I first have to stop Brink from destroying Tressla."

"He'll do more than that if he gets his hands on you," said Nicholas from behind them, making Story jump. She hadn't heard him creep up on them amidst her own misery.

Facing him, Story nodded and sank down on a convenient boulder. Her legs were getting tired from standing. "Yes, I know he wants to use me to open doors into the other world and unite them."

"That's a big part of it, yes, and when those doors open and stay open as he wants them to, the worlds will melt into one another, and order will be replaced by chaos. But before he does any of that, there's something even more important to him that he wants you for."

"What?" Kestrel asked, her brow furrowed in confusion.

"Yeah, I thought the goal here was power," Story said. "Like it usually is for all the bad guys."

Shaking his head, Nicholas's serious dark eyes met Story's. But this time she didn't look away. "Revenge." Shocked by this new bit of information, Story laughed nervously. "Come again?"

"You said it yourself, Story. You stole any possibility for him to hope. Wouldn't you hate that person too?"

"Well, it's not like I thought he wanted to be BFFs, so I guess you have a point. Why should I be surprised? I'm horrified The Dreamer cursed the Master Fiddler like she did, and I'm supposed to be her," she sighed. "Of course he'd want revenge."

"Wait, Brink is the Master Fiddler? The Master Fiddler, the one from thousands of years ago?" Kestrel asked, trying to catch up.

Story looked over at her and nodded, the guilt catching in the back of her throat. "He told me when the Nightmares took me. When he killed The Dreamer's Fiddler, she—*I* was apparently so distraught, I cursed him by taking away his ability to dream, or hope, or wish for anything better. He has every right to be angry, and he's been stewing in those bitter juices for a long time."

Kestrel shook her head, her flaxen braid moving with the motion, her aqua eyes wide. "First, Story, do not blame yourself. You don't even remember the person you were all those years ago. And I can't say I wouldn't have done the same if someone were to take Lance from me. The Dreamer you were reacted from the heart, and while there are consequences, you're trying to fix them. So do not let the guilt I see in your eyes consume you, okay?"

Story nodded, grateful that her sister, like Jess and Nicholas, didn't seem to blame her. But she still blamed herself, despite their reassurances.

Kestrel was going on, "And second, how in Maya's Chaos is he still alive? He's human, right?"

Story glanced at Nicholas, and he shrugged. "He's human. But he's stockpiled every item of power he could get his hands on through the years. If you want to know where Excalibur is, you'd have to get through Brink. He has amassed a well of dark power. And the Tales the items were stolen from are locked beneath The Capital, hidden away, chained, held captive. So perhaps he was able to steal immortality as well."

"Wow, great news," Story muttered sarcastically. "Stealing immortality? How will I ever defeat someone who has power like that?"

Glancing at Story, Kestrel laid her hand on her shoulder and squeezed. "I think I should get back, I need to talk to Lance about this. No one, I don't think even Ober, knew that Brink is actually the same man who killed the Fiddler."

Nodding, Story made to follow her, "I'll come with you."

"No," Kestrel interrupted, glanced back at Nicholas, and then whispered, "Talk to him." Holding her gaze for a moment or two, Kestrel finally turned with a nod at Nicholas and headed back to the camp.

Story watched Kestrel hurry off before finally, and reluctantly, turning her gaze back to Nicholas. He wasn't staring at her with his impenetrable black eyes as usual. He seemed lost in a reverie, gazing out at the grassy knoll that sat on the opposite side of the river. From here, Story could see several wild Thumbelinas flitting about the other side. After a few minutes, Story thought maybe she should head back. Maybe he had forgotten she was there, or maybe she had imagined all the longing stares he had cast her way, the stolen moments between them when their eyes had met. When it came to Nicholas, she found she was usually at a loss, with no direction, no thought as to what was right.

Slowly rising from her seat on the hard boulder, she started to turn back to camp. "So that's it?" Nicholas's voice stopped her.

"What?" she asked, her breath catching in her throat as she met his deep gaze once more. She could feel the tension between them building.

He took three quick strides and was in front of her, his hands enfolding her own in his large grasp and pulling her close enough so that his breath was moist on her cheek.

"You're just going to walk away with no other word? Will you never forgive me?"

Pulling back just slightly, although it was almost physically painful to do so, she looked up at him and sighed. "You're already forgiven, Nicholas."

"Then what? I know you want me the way I want you," he said, closing the distance once more so that his chest, his lips, his presence invaded her personal space. He didn't give her time to respond. He pressed her yielding form to his own and found her mouth, stealing her breath with his impassioned kiss, his lips like a cool balm.

Kissing him was like no other experience she had ever felt, and every last ounce of self-control flittered away like a Thumbelina on the breeze. Kestral was right. She couldn't fight this. Not anymore. His hand wound in her hair as he pressed her even closer, as if he would consume her. She didn't want him to stop, ever, as his strong hands held her up, supporting her weight against him.

His fingers slid up her spine and squeezed under her corset-style top, which thankfully she had loosened. As his large, calloused fingers seared her body and soul, she thrilled at his touch on her bare skin, her own breath growing ragged. She wound herself around him, her breasts pressed into his chest, one leg hitching around his waist, all but daring him to take her on the grassy bank. Words of pleading were on the roll of her tongue, words begging him to touch her more, but as if he anticipated her need, his mouth buried itself in her neck while one hand crept over the curve of her hip.

"Story."

"Nicholas," she murmured, but then realized it hadn't been her lover's voice. He pulled away first. She blinked her eyes against the daylight, wondering why it had felt like deep twilight in her mind. Her arms were clutched around Nicholas's neck. She quickly pulled her arms away and got around to straightening herself up, but she could barely get herself together at the sudden absence of his warmth and his spirit that had so lit up her soul.

She felt ragged. But more than that, her heart was sick with this denial of him once more. Collecting her bearings, she finally focused enough to see that it had been Adam who had disrupted their lovers' tryst. Her cheeks flushed as she darted a quick look at Nicholas, who was grinning and had an arm wrapped protectively around her.

Feeling a growl in her throat, she looked back at Adam, who appeared to be as embarrassed as Story. "Er, yeah, so anyway, sorry to interrupt your, uh, moment, but we have some shit going down back at the camp. There is a messenger from Brink. We tried to find out what he wants, but he will only talk to you, Story."

Story shot a look at Nicholas, who nodded his understanding. Turning, she quickly followed Adam toward camp, glancing back only once to see if Nicholas followed, which he did. She only hoped the heat in her cheeks and fervor in her eyes would abate by the time she made it back to the camp.

As they trudged quickly up the hill toward their small village of people, Story muttered about the veil. "I thought we were hidden. I thought only those with honest intentions could follow us," she muttered, quoting Racell, who was walking toward them.

When Racell joined them, he waited for Nicholas to catch up, and then he directed his gaze at Story. "His intentions are perfectly honorable. He is here to deliver a message. When he leaves, he will be unable to give directions back to us. Only because he has no other intentions in mind was he able to find us in the first place."

Mollified, Story nodded. "What else do you know?"

"Not much," Racell sighed, running his hands through his long blond hair, which hung loosely past his broad, thickly muscled shoulders. He looked better than he had the last couple of days, now that he had something to take his mind off the doors that his daughter could generate out of thin air.

"We know he's Brink's personal messenger, who came here to tell you something, which I'm positive we will not enjoy."

Nodding seriously, she jerked her head toward camp. "Well, no use in waiting. Let's find out what he has to say."

When they got to the clearing, Jess and Lance held the messenger at a distance with spears while the trolls and Elves stood in a loose circle behind him. They looked as if they were just hanging out, but Story knew they were ready for action should the messenger try anything funny.

Story looked around the group and caught sight of Elliott, who was staring at Kestrel and Robin with a distant look in his eyes. She frowned, recognizing the look, but she put it in the back of her mind and turned to the messenger.

He had lanky brown hair and wore Tressla's basic style of riding dress—leggings, boots that reached the calf if you were a guy or the knee if you were a girl, and a fitted tunic-like shirt. His facial features were plain, nothing more than a larger-than-average nose, ruddy skin that was probably from too much drink, and thin wiry lips that were set in a straight line devoid of expression. But there was something in his eyes that gleamed with a wrongness. Her Dream Sense, which now seemed to kick on at will, told her he was creepy.

"Okay, I'm here," Story said, walking slowly toward him with her head held high and wearing what she hoped was a superior expression. She was supposed to be a leader here, so some airs might do her well. "So what's the story?" she said flippantly.

Smiling in phony benevolence, the messenger bowed. "Lord Brink has asked me to deliver this message to you."

Crossing her arms over her chest, she rolled her eyes. "I'm sure he did. Things haven't worked out for him so well the last couple of days."

He smiled, sending a chill of worry racing through her. What was he going to do? Kill all the Fairytales? How could she stop that? She took a deep breath, trying to release the knots that had suddenly tied up her chest. But she knew she couldn't show weakness, so instead she glanced at Nicholas, whose solid form stood just behind her to the right, and she took strength from his presence. He was her home.

"Brink wanted me to tell the First Dreamer, named Story in this lifetime, that if she surrenders herself of her own will, he will make sure the Wolves don't kill The Witch of the Will and the horse lover's mother."

The knots seized her again while her heart thundered in her ears, making Story wonder if she was going to have a heart attack at the tender age of twenty. She stared at him, uncomprehending for a moment, although panic made her gasp for breath. "The Wolves have Ninian and Jemma," she said, only after she knew she could speak without her voice wavering. It wasn't a question but a statement. She deciphered the unpleasant nicknames easily enough and with mounting horror. Oh, Ninian. And Jemma—she was getting up there in age—at the mercy of those slavering beasts . . .

Behind her Kestrel let out a cry, with Robin quickly following suit at his mother's distress. Bliss's "oh no," echoed in her ear. She almost gave herself up on the spot, but then she remembered she could open a doorway and just take them back.

As if reading her thoughts, the messenger smiled slickly. "Oh, and don't get any ideas about using your power to open any doors. Brink has spelled it so that if you were to try to locate them, you'd end up in the belly of the Wolves' den," he said, his smile growing wider to show crooked, brown-stained teeth.

Of course he did, she thought with an inward moan, ready again to give herself up. Nicholas put a restraining hand on her arm as did Racell, both having guessed what she might do.

The Messenger's grin never left his face, and Story's fist itched to pound it, even though she'd never been in a physical fight in her entire life.

Turning to Nicholas, she whispered, "Let me go, I have to do this."

But Nicholas merely shook his head while Kestrel slowly walked to the front, nodding at Nicholas to step away for a moment.

Story turned toward her sister. "I'm sorry," she mouthed.

Kestrel lifted a hand to smooth back flaxen flyaways that had come loose from her braid in an anxious gesture, and cradled Story's cheek with her other hand. "Jemma would not want you to give yourself up to Brink for her. She would be devastated if she was the reason you did not stop all of this."

"But Kestrel, I can't just leave her."

As a flash of pain crossed Kestrel's face, Nicholas chimed in. "Ninian would never want you to do this, Story. You must stay here and lead your people to finish this quest."

"I don't . . . ," she started, but then stopped, deciding she'd had enough of an audience.

Turning back toward the messenger once more, she asked, "How much time do I have to decide?"

"Until tomorrow morning. You can find my camp at the foot of the forest entrance, where the veil does not yet start. If we have no answer by then, why the Wolves will enjoy a nice meal. They'll especially enjoy The Witch—I hear it's like a high for them when there's magic in the blood."

Story bit back a growl and instead jerked her head in a quick and dismissive nod. "Now please leave us."

The messenger bowed, his squinty dark eyes glittering cruelly as he turned and strutted away.

"We need to call a meeting." Nicholas turned urgently to Story. Beginning to direct traffic, he started shouting orders. "Jess, you'll accompany me, Lance, and Kestrel . . . "

"Nicholas," Story said, placing a gentle hand on his arm. "I have to go. You must see that. I can't let him murder Ninian and Jemma, I can't."

"Of course you can't," Kestrel said, stepping forward and looking pale and resolute. Story breathed a sigh of relief. At least someone was thinking rationally.

"Kestrel," Racell hissed. "You can't think to send her to him."

"Yeah, and how do we even know he's telling the truth?" Adam chimed in reasonably, having joined the inner circle in their discussion.

Hope bloomed in Story. How did they know the Wolves really had them? It could be a trap. Elliott came up behind Story and slid a comforting arm around her. She looked up into his face to nod her thanks, but noticed the grim look in his warm brown eyes. Smiling sadly, he looked at Adam. "They have them, I saw it only moments before he spoke."

Jess nodded in agreement. "I got close enough to smell Ninian on the Wolves. She always had a hint of magic and owl to her."

Shaking her head, Kestrel ignored them all, taking Story by the shoulders and looking down at her earnestly. Story noticed for the first time that Kestrel wasn't actually much taller than she. She just seemed that way because of her status as a warrior and queen. Kestrel of the Seven Forests they had called her, Story remembered, and she realized that Kestrel had a story going on too. She was a leader, a leader of the forest's creatures. Story started to speak, but stopped as a small lizard-like creature landed on Kestrel's shoulder.

"A flying lizard?" Story asked, gazing at the small creature that sparkled blue and purple, with tiny scales that looked like sequins.

"A dragon," Kestrel said, reaching her hand up to pat the creature on the shoulder.

"But he's so little," Story protested.

"Yes, they are all around this size."

"So why are you showing him to me then? Although he is a cool little guy."

The little dragon blinked black eyes at her and flicked his forked tongue into the air.

"Because he will be accompanying me when I go save Ninian and my mother."

"What? You will do no such thing. I will give myself up before I let you risk yourself for me."

"You will not, Story," Kestrel said, her nose practically pressed against Story's in a battle of wills. "You will not give yourself up, not when we've come this far. I am a warrior, I have wings in the form of Pegasus, and I have dragons to guide me to our goal."

"How does he help? He's tiny." At her response, the small glittery creature hissed at her.

She stepped back, putting her hands up. "Sorry little guy, but seriously, Kestrel."

"Dragons need only an image to find their target, and they can take it right from our own minds. They can track anyone, and their teeth are sharp." As if proving Kestrel's last comment, the small dragon stretched his mouth in what appeared to be a semblance of a smile, revealing tiny toothy knives.

"With one song, he can call his entire clan with all their sharp little teeth," Kestrel said with a feral grin, her aqua eyes glittering in the mid-morning light. Story could see the warrior that lived inside of her as well as the forest queen that she was.

"I don't know, Kestrel. I still don't like it."

"You don't have a choice here."

Arching her brows, Story crossed her arms over her chest. Out of the corner of her eye, she saw Adam lean over to Elliott and whisper, "Oh no she didn't." Elliott nodded sagely in response.

"I seem to recall a prophecy naming me The Dreamer, and the leader here in this little fairytale."

"You may be the leader here, Story, but I'm a queen in my own right, and as much as I love you and respect you, I am going to save my mother. And no one here is going to let you give yourself up for what is most likely a trap. They are not going to free Ninian or my mother. So if you go, not only will our hopes in you be destroyed, but their hostages will be as good as dead."

Story stared down Kestrel, who refused to yield. After a few long moments, Story looked away only when Racell placed his hand on her shoulder and squeezed. "She's right, Story. You are much too important, and Kestrel has a stake here. It's her mother," he said softly.

Story looked around at her friends and family, from Racell and Adam to Elliott, who nodded his encouragement to her, and Bliss, who smiled compassionately. Finally, she turned her gaze to Nicholas, whose dark eyes told her all she needed to know. She met her adopted sister's gaze and nodded.

"I don't like it, not at all. So you had better come back in one piece. And you're not going alone, no matter how many dragons you can call."

"Of course, Story. Lance will accompany me."

"But what about Robin?" Story asked, her gaze finding Jess, who cradled the babe to her chest while uncharacteristically cooing down at him. Story would have laughed at the Amazonian queen coddling a baby, had the scene not been so sweet. Smiling, she started to nod but Jess glanced up and caught her look.

"Are you insane? I'm going with them." She strutted over with a toss of her wild red mane and a wink, then handed Robin back over to Kestrel.

"Ophelia," Lance said with a grin, his eyes looking up as a pearly pink shape came into view, floating above the tree tops. Her light yellow wings caught the last of the breeze before she circled down into the clearing.

Kestrel smiled widely and turned to Story. "Ophelia," she said matter-of-factly.

Throwing her hands up, Story sighed. "I give up. Go, but be careful."

Ophelia, who was now wearing her human shape, sauntered toward them. Her long pink hair bounced and her cream-legging-clad hips swayed, a black belt riding low on her slender hips while her corset-styled yellow top appeared to be made of much more supple and breathable fabric than Story's own.

"OMG," whispered Elliott. "If I liked women, she would be it for me. I just love the hair."

Obviously having heard him, Ophelia turned to him, winked a large almond-shaped amethyst eye, and smiled. "I'm very sure I would like you back," she said in her sweetly high-pitched voice before turning to her brother, who swooped her up and planted a wet kiss on her cheek.

"You called?" she said, wiping her slimy cheek with the back of her hand and shooting Lance a playful glare before embracing Kestrel. Then she turned to Story, placed her index finger against her lips, and bowed, giving the Tresslan greeting that signified respect.

Smiling, Story returned the gesture.

"Dreamer," Ophelia said with a soft smile. "Do you remember our times together?"

Story laughed and stepped forward, embracing her in a warm greeting before letting go and nodding. "Of course, you taught me to fly. I sometimes dream about it."

"That I did. And you taught me to play hide-and-go-seek and evade my parents, which for me was much more fun."

Story blinked, a melancholy feeling of sadness washing over her. Those innocent days were so long gone, and here she was, wishing she could go back to a time that was simpler.

"Oh, but it was never simple," Ophelia said, serious now, her small face grave.

"How . . . "

Beside her, Racell wrapped a comforting arm around Story's shoulders. "The female Pegasus are telepathic at close range."

"Yes, don't you remember, Story?" Ophelia asked with a small frown marring her otherwise sweet features. "I always used to read your thoughts."

Shaking her head, Story sighed. "Yes, I guess I just forgot."

"Not to break up the reunion here," Nicholas suddenly piped up, "but we should probably come up with a plan."

"Yes," Story said, looking around at her following. "Let's get this party started."

"What party?" Jasper piped up in his gravelly voice. "Aren't we getting ready to go to war?"

Story shrugged, "Yes, it's just a figure of speech."

Elliott smoothly slid an arm around the earth troll. "I'll explain it to you."

Shooting Elliott a grateful smile, Story clapped her hands together and then rushed to cover a yawn. Her friends' dreams had begun to cramp her style, haunting her nights with their fears and regrets. She'd lain awake for several nights now as pictures from their sleeping brains infringed on her own, especially her father's. Images of Racell's murky nightmares, in particular—where he dove into Lake Sandeen time and again, only to reemerge in Tressla each time—were depressing. Witnessing his grief-stricken cries as he called out to the youthful image of her mother on the shoreline had grown old fast. Edie never heard him, and Racell never found peace. His broken-hearted pleas for Sandeen to open the way to him resonated so heavily in her chest, she no longer felt any anger toward him. She only felt sympathy. He really did love her mother. "First things first," she said, turning to Racell, "We need to talk."

Chapter Thirty-Two

Edie's Kitchen, Real World

GAZING OUT INTO THE DARK from where she sat at her kitchen window, Edie tried hopelessly to balance her checkbook, but the hum of the computer screen did nothing to help her focus. She sighed and glanced at the barely-touched cold pizza that she had tried to choke down. She peeled a piece of pepperoni from the hard cheese and put it in her mouth, wishing she had any sort of appetite. Derek had been over several times to see how she was since Story's disappearance, and every time he commented on her dwindling frame. Even Edie knew she looked bad. But if she looked in the mirror, all she would see was lank, unwashed black hair, dark circles, and a pile of bones that used to have a daughter and brother but had failed to keep either safe.

For the first couple of days, she had just cried. She didn't have the will to go on. But a spark of hope glimmered inside of her when no evidence of Elliott, Adam, or Story could be found in the lake. It wasn't a huge lake, and there was no way three bodies could just disappear, so she believed that Story was alive. The bad news was that if she was alive, she had been sucked into whatever alternate world Peter had vanished to so many years before. In a crazier moment, she had even went out to the lake and swam around for hours until she was exhausted and spent, weeping and cursing the lake for not taking her too.

But there was hope. Although small, she felt she might be onto something. Unfurling her palm, she studied the silver necklace that Story had worn from the time she was a child. Clicking out of the spreadsheet she had been working in, or not working in, she brought up the search engine and typed, "Secrets of the Veil."

When Story hadn't returned, Edie had gone to a colleague at the college who was firmly invested in studying the occult. He had checked out the origins of the necklace and had been able to tell her that it was very old, but not much more than that. It was then that he had directed her to a woman he knew of, an expert on occult matters and relics. Who was it but none other than Dr. Harvey, the doctor Story had visited as a child.

She had been reticent at first. After all, the doctor was a bit more intense than Edie liked. But apparently, she was well-known in the area for her expertise, and so Edie had sucked it up and sent a picture of the necklace to her in an email. It took all of five minutes for Harvey to respond, and when she did, there was an eagerness in her message that told Edie the necklace meant something to her.

Since then, they had met several times over coffee, and what the doctor told Edie had made her head spin. But then her brother and daughter had disappeared, and her lover had appeared to her one night like magic that saw into her soul.

So now she had purpose: working to reveal the secrets of the necklace and to see if they could somehow open a door to this other reality that Edie believed had stolen away all the people she loved best.

She was just thinking about giving the piece of pizza another go when she heard what sounded like her front door opening and creaking shut. Instantly on the alert, she grabbed a bat she kept in the kitchen for a weapon and started to creep to a hidden corner where she could crack the intruder's head if it came down to it. Her blood raced, and she wished that she'd grabbed her cell phone.

She flicked the kitchen lights so only the full moon poured in through the window. The green clock blinked on the stove, from when she had lost power a few nights back during a freak storm, and it still glowed the wrong time. She raised the bat above her head as she heard his footsteps draw near. Her tongue felt swollen, sticking limply against her teeth as all moisture evaporated from her mouth.

Edie saw only his silhouette when he entered the room, outlined by starlight. He had a strong jaw and a slightly larger than average nose, a profile she remembered well as she saw it always like that, in the dark of the night and light of the moon.

But she only dropped the bat when she saw his long golden braid swing. "Racell," she whispered, her voice strangled in a sob of disbelief.

The large man turned toward her. Even in the shadows, his golden eyes gave her a pang as they were so like their daughter's. He stepped toward her quickly and left no room for accusations or questions, pulling her to him before she could even think to protest. Not that she wanted to. The full strength of his presence flooded her senses with his woodsy musk and warmth. "Are you really here, or have I gone completely nuts?" She looked up at him as he drew her closer.

"I'm here," he answered back thickly as if overcome by his own tide of emotion. "Story's safe. She's fine, she sent me back here for you." And then, before she could start asking the twenty or one hundred questions that had instantly popped into her head, his mouth descended on hers, and she again remembered the wild abandon that he ignited in her peaceful soul so long ago.

They barely spoke, so consumed were they by twenty years of unspent passion. The carpet became their grass and the moonlight shining in from the window greeted their lover's' embrace with its rays as would an old voyeuristic friend.

Racell's lips crushed against hers and cradled her small frame to his own wide chest while delicately laying her down as if he might crush her petals. She said nothing, consumed by her need for him. The hole in her heart that had never closed up started to feel less empty as his hand touched her once again, moving away her clothes in an all-consuming need to be with her, inside her. It was a sentiment she echoed.

Her arms wrapped around his waist and she cried out as he thrust into her, his fullness filling her up in a way that hadn't been satisfied in a long time. He pressed his moist mouth to her nipples, and she shuddered at the exquisite joy of his lips on her, all over her.

He thrust against her again and moved them into a rocking motion that sent her mind into oblivion, so all that she could feel was his body wrapped around hers and his kisses lacing her skin with fire. Their passion mounted quickly, and both their cries of ecstasy punctuated the night, their bodies and souls mingling in the moment.

They lay quiet for only a few moments before Racell stood and lifted Edie up once again. "Where's the bedroom?" he mostly growled. Wordlessly, she pointed toward the stairs transfixed by his sudden and consuming presence in her life. He marched into her room and laid her down on the bed, his hungry eyes taking her in. Her cheeks grew hot and she bit her lip. It had been twenty years since she'd been with a man. This man.

Lowering himself into her once more, his lips found her ear, making her senses vibrate. "I love you, Edie. I've loved you all these years." Then they commenced to work out two decades of pent up passion. And for a while, she was able to lose herself for the first time since Story had disappeared.

By the time they were spent, the room had lightened considerably. As they both drifted off to sleep in their exhaustion and contentment, Edie felt relief and a sense of momentary peace. Racell had returned to her, and most importantly of all, Story was safe.

CHAPTER THIRTY-THREE

Racell's Rood, Tressla

IT WAS SOME TIME LATER when Adam and Elliott found Story in Racell's Rood by herself, staring blankly at the prophecy once more, and from the looks of it, getting nowhere. The grove was a part of the Rood, and it was supposedly where Racell's mother, a human who had been trapped in Tressla when the worlds divided, had birthed him.

Story was sitting down, leaning against the biggest tree in the grove, an ancient they had been told. Adam could attest to that since he could hear the trees talking, and this one spoke in terms of centuries.

Both men dropped down next to her and were quiet for a few moments. Elliott found her hand and took it, and Adam realized he was no longer jealous of their friendship. He had his own thing with Story, and he actually had his own connection with Elliott as well—in a strictly platonic way, he amended to himself.

Story didn't seem to mind their company, although she didn't say anything at first.

"So he's gone for now?"

Story looked up at Elliott and nodded. "I should have known you had seen it. I saw you looking all psychic-y earlier."

Elliott opened his mouth as if to respond, but Adam interrupted. "Who's gone?"

Both Story and Elliott looked at him as if he was daft. "Racell," they said in unison.

"Gone? Where did he go?" he asked, starting to panic. One reason he thought they had a good chance was that they had this demi-god on their side. Now he was gone?

"I sent him through the door," Story said, folding the prophecy and slipping it into the pack that lay in the grass at her feet.

"Why?" Adam asked, not understanding.

"Because, dimwit, Story's mom is on the other side." Elliott spoke as if he were talking to a child.

"Okay, yeah, I get that," Adam said, feeling annoyed. "But why right now? Aren't we going to need him when we storm the castle and save the world?"

"It's not really a castle," Story corrected him with a light smile. "And anyway, I need him to be with my mom. I can't worry about her right now, and I've been having nightmares about it. And Racell, he needed to go. He wasn't at peace. His dreams were starting to suffocate me at night. In fact, a lot of your dreams are starting to merge into mine, and I'm having a hard time sleeping," she said, looking up.

For the first time, Adam really looked at her and saw that her expression was muted. Her cheeks were chalky and dark circles ringed her usually moonlit eyes.

He was jerked from his thoughts by Elliott, who looked far away. "You have to find her. It's the only way."

"Find who?" she asked, leaning forward and staring intently into Elliott's face, which Adam noticed for the first time was devoid of all expression. Elliott was in a trance.

He was staring straight ahead of him, his eyes unseeing or actually seeing into the beyond, when he turned to Story so quickly it was creepy. "The dream girl. She's the only way to save this," he continued in a monotone voice, his blank eyes still staring at Story, who clutched Elliott's limp hand in her own and shook her head in confusion.

"But I'm the dream girl."

"No, there is another. You know her."

"But I don't . . . " Story dropped Elliott's hand and put her face in her hands, shaking her head. "I don't know!"

Adam reached forward and tucked an arm around the distraught heroine, feeling as confused as Story.

"So we can't stop Brink without her?" Adam asked.

Elliott didn't even blink. "You need her to save the worlds. She must be joined."

Adam opened his mouth to ask another question, but the seer in Elliott was gone, and life once again flooded his eyes and face.

Elliott dropped his head, rubbing his temples and grumbling about a headache.

"I'm not The Dreamer," Story murmured, and Adam could have sworn he saw a momentary flash of relief in her expression.

Appalled, Adam shook his head, denying all they'd been through had been for nothing—that there was still someone out there that had to save the world and probably didn't even know it.

Elliott too shook his head and looked at them, regaining his composure. "No, I didn't feel like that's what I was saying. I feel like there was just another Dreamer."

Story shook her head and rose. "I have to tell everyone that I'm not it." And then she paused. "Did you say another Dreamer?"

Elliott nodded.

"Spirit," she whispered without looking at either one of them, seemingly lost within her own abstract thoughts. "I've gotta go." She hurried out of the clearing without a backwards glance.

Adam turned to Elliott. "Nice going, psychic boy," he said, and then he turned and followed Story.

Behind him, Elliott sighed and sat there for a very long time.

Adam went after Story, confused by the revelations only Story seemed clued in to, but he found her making rounds and looking in on everyone's activities. The Trolls were busy making weapons. Story sat down next to Grady and acted as if she was actually interested in his techniques as he used his fiery beard to melt metal into arrows. Adam watched her as she moved on to the Elves, murmuring about tactics, inquiring whether any more Elves might join them.

"Oh good, Adam. Could you see to it that Elliott knows he's on wood for dinner?" She was already turning from him before Adam could bring up Elliott's vision, and Bliss's sudden annoying entrance further distracted her.

"Oh god, do you hear that buzz?" Adam asked, waving his hand in the air as if swatting a fly.

Bliss stopped long enough in her flight to send Adam a seething glare, her large electrical eyes shooting sparks. "I doubt even a mosquito would dare bite the likes of you," she retorted.

Before he could stop himself, Adam found himself asking why.

Snorting, quite cutely since she was so small and dainty, she responded. "Because you smell."

Story, who had stopped to wait for Bliss, turned to Adam and smiled apologetically. "She's not lying. Maybe you should take a bath." She wrinkled her nose, not so cutely, Adam thought as he glared.

Bliss allowed herself a spiteful smirk Adam's way before turning to Story. He rolled his eyes and discreetly lifted an arm to smell his armpit. Grimacing to himself, he nodded. Okay, he did need a bath.

"Bliss, have you seen Nicholas?" Story asked, all business once more.

Wringing her hands together, Bliss nodded. "I'm sorry, Story, but he went with Jess and Kestrel. He didn't want you to know because he knew you'd worry too much."

"What." The word was not a question, more like an angry statement. "That is it. That is it," she said succinctly, gritting her teeth. "I am the leader here. Does no one respect that position?" Her eyes were lit with a golden fire. "This is not a democracy."

"Oh, do they have those where you're from?" Bliss asked wistfully.

Ignoring them both, she turned and stalked away.

Part III

But she was broken . . .

CHAPTER THIRTY-FOUR

Big Bad Wolves' Camp, Tressla

HE KNEW IF HE'D TOLD STORY he was going, she would have refused. So now here he was, belly down in the brush near the Wolves' camp and covered in unicorn shit. It was the one animal the Wolves wouldn't hunt, and so when Jess had told them all to cover themselves in it, he hadn't complained. He knew once the Wolves picked up their scent, they were dead. Even Miss Red wouldn't be able to take down the entire clan down, which was guarding Ninian and Jemma now.

The truth was that he was just selfish, Nicholas thought as he lay still in the night waiting for a signal from Jess. He needed Story to take down Brink because he couldn't do it himself. He could not kill his father. But he couldn't allow his father to continue on as he did any longer. Something deep down in his soul reviled the man so profoundly that Nicholas actually feared him. From the time he was a child, he'd had to force himself into the man's presence, and only then because it was what his mother had wanted. The subterfuge was required to help The Dreamer reach her potential untouched by Brink's hand. The song in Nicholas's spirit had never felt quite right, as if Brink's very existence kept him from his true potential. The hatred burned too deep for his comfort. Brink had to go, so that he could be the man Story deserved. One filled with light, not tainted by darkness.

A movement in the tall grass alerted Nicholas, who cocked his head to the breeze and sniffed the air. His smell might not be as good as the Wolves', but he knew what to look out for, having spent many a night sharing a campfire with them—when the only way to cover their animal stench was to let smoke from the burning wood seep into his clothes and skin. He didn't think for a moment they would spare him because he was Brink's son. He was pretty sure Brink would kill him himself if he would ever lower himself to outright murder.

Nicholas stiffened as the sound grew nearer. His hand went to the knife in his belt, but smell told him it wasn't Wolf.

"Hey Wolf lover," Jess hissed with a smirk the dimness of the night did nothing to cover. She had big lips and a wide, white smile that was almost as wolfish as the creatures she hunted.

"Hey," he whispered back, grinding his teeth only for a second at the barb, instead focusing on the scene only twenty feet or so beyond. They had to be careful. If the breeze blew a certain way, the Wolves could snatch their whispered plans from the wind.

The Amazonian redhead had belly-crawled next to him, her red hair dragging in the dirt behind her. Nicholas had to admire how she didn't bat a pretty eyelash at the filth of shit and grime. But then again, she was a Red Riding Hood, and despite her acerbic personality, he knew she was tough. The smirk was gone by the time she reached him, replaced by the expression of a plotting predator. She jerked her head to the camp below as a greeting and arched her brows in question.

This was the Wolves' main camp, located near The Capital. Tents dotted the landscape and it looked like any military compound, except the number of Wolves was nowhere near what they had bargained for. No, it was much greater, here where Wolves slept like men. Nicholas could not comprehend it at all. There hadn't been this many of them at the other camp, where they'd held Story only days before. But then again, he'd never actually gotten a chance to look around.

"There's a lot of them," Jess whispered seriously below the fortunate din of the breeze.

Nicholas nodded, but turned a devil-may-care grin on her. "Yeah, but they're stupid," he whispered as stealthily back.

"How do ya gather?" she asked.

"They're Wolves, and yet they sleep in tents. Back under Nigel's leadership, they slept and subsisted as Wolves, living and breathing their animal counterparts. Here they're sitting ducks in slumber, waiting to be picked off by hunters looking for the nicest hide."

Jess seemed to take his comment into regard and nodded seriously. The snideness was gone as the hunter had come out to play. "I see what you mean," she murmured. "Nigel always was the smart one."

"Yes, I'm sure it makes you proud he was your Wolf," Nicholas said sarcastically, unable to help himself at the stab at her ego.

"Listen, I don't like you for Story—or like you in general for that matter—but I do think you should know, since we're going down there as allies, that the *only* thing that matters to me right this moment is seeing Ninian and Jemma out of there. And yes, it's a turn-on that I offed the alpha to these sorry excuse for Wolves, but they're all equally as vicious and equally as likely to kill our quarry and us. So this is my peace offering. Don't mess up and I won't tell Story horrible things about you." She offered her hand with a feral smile.

"Oh, well, how could I say no to that?" Nicholas retorted, but then grinned lightly in the night and shook her hand. "And who knows, you might get your wish after this since I left without Story's permission."

Jess chuckled low in response, pointing one long finger toward a lone man who was checking the perimeters. "It's now or never," she said with a nod, and then as fast as he'd seen any Wolf ever move, Jess was on the man. She had her knife to his neck so tight that there was no way he would be able to howl an alert, or his jugular would be cut with the slightest motion. The most he might illicit would be a gurgle. Nicholas quickly joined her, checking around to make sure no other Wolves were in sight.

Staring into the glinting, yellow eyes of the Wolf, Nicholas smiled like he thought his father might smile right before he ordered someone to death or worse, torture. He knew he must look horrible, because the yellowed whites of the Wolf's eyes rolled back.

"Raise an alert and I'll make sure you die slowly. I've watched my father enough times to know the best way to kill a man gradually." Nicholas was pretty sure that Jess's presence alone would have been enough to make him talk, such had her reputation preceded her. This particular Big Bad was pretty scrawny, and he knew fear when he saw it. The Big Bad was quaking in his fur, his sneer trembled, and if he'd been in Wolf form, his hackles would have been up.

"Where are our friends?" he asked as Jess continued to hold the Wolf tightly.

Their captive laughed, bits of saliva dangling from his mouth. "I tell you, I die in pain; I don't tell you, I die horribly," he growled, spit spraying. "Just kill me." Nicholas realized what he was about to do and started to warn Jess, but it was too late. The Big Bad threw himself into the knife at his neck, cutting his jugular. His blood gushed out onto the ground and he gurgled, thrashing in Jess's arms. She pushed his body away disgustedly and glanced quickly at Nicholas. "We do not have much time. If they smell blood, it's all over. For them and us."

"You're right, there's not much time at all."

Startled, Nicholas looked behind him to see a dark shape step out of the night. He blended in with the darkness, and only his green Wolf eyes glistened out of the night. Nicholas's hand was on his weapon ready to go, but Jess remained calm.

"Darvish?" she asked comfortably.

The man turned to her and flashed sharp, white teeth, reminding Nicholas of what they could do when in Wolf form.

"Ah, you've heard of me," he said. "And I know you, Red. But this is not the time for pleasantries. If you want your friends, they're being kept in the tent closest to the middle. You'll know it because it bears Nigel's flag."

Nicholas squinted against the glare of the torches lit around the camp, and sure enough, there it was.

"Why should we trust you?" Jess asked warily, her eyes narrowed and her stance defensive.

Nicholas too was wary of this Wolf. But for whatever reason, Story seemed to have some sort of trust in the man. She'd told them what had happened when she'd been captured and in her faith that his loyalties did not lie with the Wolves. They really didn't have any alternatives. They couldn't pick off the Wolves one-by-one, there were too many. And eventually, the smell of blood would reach the Wolves and then they'd be dead.

"Because, Little Red, Story told you to, didn't she? And really, I think you're out of options. If the wind changes, the smell will bring them down on you so fast you won't know what's coming."

"Jess, we have to trust him right now, we don't have a choice."

"You have no idea how much I would really like to kill you," Jess told the Wolf. "It's boiling my blood, but Nicholas is right. So how do you suggest we get in there? It's completely guarded by a hoard of Wolves." Nicholas could almost hear the arch of her brow.

"It's strategically impossible," Nicholas agreed shaking his head, dismay falling over him. They couldn't leave Ninian and Jemma to the Wolves.

Darvish smiled. "It just so happens that a Daughter of the Will is staying with us right now, and she was nice enough to whip me up a potion from an Incognitos Silver Bell."

"Don't move," a voice whispered from behind Darvish, and Nicholas saw Lance, face grimly set in the moonlight, nudge him with a long sword. "Unless you want to die."

Kestrel suddenly appeared beside Jess. "We must go now. I'll kill him."

"No," Nicholas whispered vehemently. "He's on our side. Lay down your arms, Lance."

The Pegasus prince hesitated, obviously torn by the command. But with a nod from Jess, the expert on all things Big Bad, he listened. Nicholas could tell it cost Jess to give a Big Bad her safety approval.

"Story told us to trust him," Nicholas said, turning back to Darvish, who stepped away from Lance and eyed the Pegasus Prince and his queen with wariness.

"So Ninian gave you some potion, how will it help us?" Jess continued with the questioning.

Smiling now that a knife was no longer in his back, Darvish chuckled. "I will send out two from my ranks to check out the perimeter. Dispatch of them, but don't kill them. And do not draw blood. Once you have, take a drop of their saliva and put one in each potion. Then drink it."

Beside Nicholas, Jess made a gagging noise.

"You will take on their likeness. I will then send out two more men, who you must do the same to, except this time, do not drink. Save your vials and head back down into camp. Find the tent and give Ninian and Jemma each a vial. If anyone asks why you're going into the prisoners' tent, tell them Darvish told you to see to their wounds. I'm the closest thing the pack has to a doctor. Say that the better kept they are, the more fight they'll put up later on when Brink lets us have them.

"As soon as you can, get out of camp. Got it? Oh, and one more thing. Don't get separated from each other or the potion will lose its power."

They nodded in response and Jess jerked her head at Kestrel. "We'll meet you by the hollowed tree we saw up the hill. If you hear the hunting howl, get out."

Kestrel shook her head. "No way, Jess, my mother is in there, I should be going with you."

"No," Jess said with such authority, Nicholas could see why the Wolves were scared of her. She wasn't afraid of much. "You may be a queen in your own right, and I understand it's your mother, but this is my territory. I'm the Little Red Riding Hood here, and I've trained to kill these monsters my entire life. And Nicholas knows them—he has spent more time with them than even I have. We go. You stay here. Her tone brooked no argument, and Kestrel nodded her assent, although he could tell she wasn't happy. Too many alpha females. It was amazing they all got on so well, Nicholas grimaced.

"Besides, you have a little boy that needs his mother, so stay alive another day, Kestrel."

Although Kestrel still seemed unconvinced, Lance appeared to like the plan, relief smoothing his handsome features as he took her arm. "Let's go," he murmured.

The rest of them watched as the couple headed back into the brush. Darvish was unabashedly grinning in the darkness, his strange canine greens almost glowing as bright as Bliss's eyes sometimes did.

"What are you smiling at?" Jess growled at him.

Darvish chuckled and shook his head. "Just you, Little Red."

Jess's face twisted into a snarl, but Darvish winked a gleaming Wolf eye and nodded. "They'll be up soon. Be on the lookout."

"Oh, I will," Jess hissed. "I will."

Chuckling, Darvish walked down the hill, leaving them to hide and wait. "Green, but he's annoying," Jess muttered as they crawled back into the brush, obscuring themselves from view. "I don't know why Story wouldn't let me just kill him."

She was silent for a moment and then glanced at Nicholas. "You ready for this, Wolf lover?"

"Oh, I think you'll find I don't love them so much."

The night grew silent after their final exchange, with only the sounds of an occasional animal moving or insect chirping, but even insects didn't like to be too close to the Wolves. Jess's breathing was imperceptible to the ear, but then he guessed it was all part of being a predator herself.

They were crouched down in the brush for only a few more minutes before they heard the footfalls and the two Big Bads stealthily making their way up the hill. From what Nicholas could hear, they were in man form, and for that he was thankful. They were much more lethal as Wolves, and if Nicholas and Jess could get the jump on them, they might be able to dispatch them before they had time to change form.

Nicholas could see now that Darvish had sent up some of the scrawnier Big Bads, and he started to wonder what the story was with this Big Bad Wolf. In his experience, Wolves didn't help the good guys.

"I don't smell nothing," the skinnier of the two said in a canine-like whine.

The stockier shape grunted. "I'd rather be back at the tent where the witch is being kept. I think I'd like to get a little taste of her."

They were drawing closer when the shorter one sniffed the air. "Hey, you smell that?"

Lanky stopped and took a big long sniff in as well. "Yah, it smells like . . . "

Jess glanced at Nicholas and in fluid motion, she was up on her feet, stepping behind the shorter one as if in a dance. Her hands sailed through the night like white hands of judgment as she grasped his neck and snapped it.

"Me," she finished his sentence with a scary smile.

Lanky's eyes rolled back as if he sensed a predator stronger than he, but Nicholas was on him before he could react. Taking the blunt end of his dagger, Nicholas conked him on the head hard enough to knock him out.

"Get his saliva," Jess commanded.

Nicholas put a vial near his Wolf's mouth as Jess did the same with hers, and he was able to collect a drop as the Wolf drooled in his unconscious state. Shaking the mixture, Nicholas turned back to Jess.

"Darvish said not to kill them," he hissed.

"No," Jess said with a smug smile before she downed her drink, her face twisting in distaste before she looked back at him. "He just said 'don't draw blood.'"

"And he also said 'don't kill them.'" He clenched his jaw, wanting to shake her.

She shrugged carelessly. "Ooops. Oh well, too late now." She laughed to herself. "We already killed one, what's one more?"

Nicholas felt himself begin to change, a tingling sensation like he'd felt when Ninian had given them the Incognitos Silver Bells before. "Don't kill the next ones," he retorted as they hid once more after dragging the bodies out of sight. Nicholas only hoped the Wolves wouldn't catch the scent of death before they could get the jump on them.

Jess said nothing as they waited, which was a little bit longer than the previous time. But soon enough came two more. These ones were also not very big, but they seemed less stupid. That was until he noticed one was walking with a bit of a sloppy swagger, lacking the grace that made Wolves such great hunters.

As they got closer, Nicholas caught a whiff of alcohol and grinned. The Wolves might be bigger, but Darvish had sent them up a drunk.

"Don't know why I hash to come, I's jest fine where I was," whined the inebriated Wolf in a half-slur.

The other guy, with an average build, shrugged. He didn't seem overly concerned about being backed up by a drunk Wolf, and he looked as if he was about to turn back around before they even got close enough. But he suddenly stopped and sniffed, a slow growl sounding in the back of his throat.

"Wa's ish it?" the other one drawled, looking around with hooded yellow eyes in the night, his movements slow and sluggish.

Jess jerked her head at the sober one, staking her intent to take him. Before Nicholas could protest, she was out of the brush and on him, but this Wolf was more alert than their previous victims and he blocked her assault, sending her dagger flying into the grass. Nicholas took the moment to grab the drunk Wolf, who only seemed to comprehend what was happening as Nicholas brought his sword down and easily dispatched him with a thud to his skull.

He turned, hoping to find the other on the ground as well, but Jess was struggling. This Wolf was stronger than he looked and was blocking all her attacks, stopping her roundhouse kick in mid-air with his massive hands. The Big Bad leered at her surprise and sent her flying through the air. Nicholas looked for an in, feeling the urgency to quell the disturbance on the hill before they were noticed. He flew toward the Wolf. His opponent reared up, and Nicholas felt the impact of the Wolf's feet to his chest, his breath gasped out of him as he lost it and went flying to the ground. His chest heaved as he tried to suck in air, but all he could hear was the sound of his own wheezing. He was too late—the Big Bad was morphing into beast form, and once he changed, there was no way Nicholas would be able to defeat him. The Wolf would send out a howl and the entire horde would be after them.

Helpless, Nicholas glanced over to Jess, who was staring at him as if she'd never seen a Wolf before. All he could manage was a gasp and a wild gesture. "Wolf—you kill . . . Birthright."

She appeared confused, her skin tight against her face in the pale moonlight, but he saw her steel eyes gather storm. In the moments a Wolf changes, there is a lapse where he is vulnerable, and she took the opportunity. Rising to her feet in one swift leap, she released her axe. It went singing through the air with a whisper of steel on the breeze, the razor edge sweeping the Wolf's head from his neck just as the change completed. So much for not drawing blood, Nicholas winced.

"Dammit Jess, more death, and now blood?" He got up from where he'd fallen, his breath collected, and he quickly gathered the saliva needed from the decapitated head.

"We'll have to bury him," she whispered calmly, her confidence seemingly restored. "It will help mask the scent."

Nicholas didn't argue. It was a good idea, but they'd have to work fast or else all their trouble would be for nothing. Without speaking, the two gathered the head and the body, dragging them as far away as they dared. Then, using sharp rocks, they proceeded to dig as much as they could. They soon realized they weren't going to get very far without a shovel, but figured they could gather as much leaves and grass as possible, cover the body, and hide the scent that way.

When they were done, the shape in the darkness merely looked like a mound of grass and branches, camouflaged as it was against the tall brush.

"Well?" Nicholas turned toward her as she sniffed the air. One of her gifts as a Riding Hood was her ability to smell as well as a Wolf.

"It's better. Plus, *I'm* looking for the smell. It will work well enough that it won't alert anyone in camp. But if anyone comes out this way, they'll smell it for sure. We'd best get going."

Nicholas nodded. "Don't leave my side. If we're separated we'll change back."

"I don't remember Darvish saying that," she whispered back.

"Yeah, just like you don't remember him saying not to kill anyone?"

Jess was silent as they started down the hill, and Nicholas felt bad for a moment, but he was too busy concentrating on walking like a stealthy Wolf.

As they entered the compound, Nicholas made himself remember what it was like to travel with the Wolves. A feeling of calm washed over him as he pretended he was just a boy and they would never dare touch him. In fact, during that time in his life, they had been scared of him, scared to make Brink's son mad.

Jess looked every bit the role, sauntering past other Wolves with a sneer and a nod here and there. Plus, she had already been gifted with their preternatural grace. Nicholas was assaulted by the smell of Wolf—he forgot how strong it could be. It was musky, with the faintest hint of sulfur. They were everywhere, laughing and talking. Nicholas glanced to his side as they walked past a ring of men shouting. A small crowd was making wagers over two Big Bads in Wolf form, who lunged and snarled at one another. Wolf fights.

"Hey Barton!" Nicholas was focused on the tent ahead of them, the one flying Nigel's flag only ten feet in the distance. It was simple, purple for the color of Wolf royalty. As alpha, Nigel had taken on the role of leadership to his pack, but he had also somehow grown his pack to hundreds, which was pretty much unheard of.

"Barton!" The shout came again and Jess elbowed Nicholas, who turned toward the voice.

"Yeah?" he called back, doing his best to impersonate the whininess of the real Barton's voice.

"You want to wager tonight?" called the man. Nicholas had never seen him before, but he could see there was viciousness in his Wolf eyes. He was also tall, maybe six-foot-eleven, the tallest Nicholas had ever seen. He imagined with an inward shudder that he must be massive when in Wolf form.

"Nah, not tonight, I've got me some drinking to do."

The big man laughed. "Next time then," he said with a slow growl and turned back to the crowd. Nicholas and Jess shared a nonchalant glance, but he didn't need her to tell him. That was the new alpha in town, and he looked scary. And unfortunately, he was awfully close to the tent they needed to get to.

But as sly a Wolf as he seemed, he didn't seem to be paying them much attention as they continued toward the large burlap tent next to the deep, royal purple flag bearing the emblem of the Jaws of the Wolf. As they approached, the guard, who had been sitting at a table with another Wolf playing cards and smoking cigars, glanced up.

"No one goes in," he snarled.

"Darvish sent us—said the one woman was sick," Nicholas whined.

Stabbing out his cigarette, the Wolf shrugged. "Why should Darvish care whether they suffer?" he said with a leering laugh.

Nicholas realized pretty quickly that the Wolf wasn't going to budge easily—suspicion was already slitting his sickly yellow eyes.

Nicholas remained calm and split his lips into a wide, lascivious grin. "Brink wants them healthy I guess. You know, for the torture," he whispered, casting a nervous look around. "'Sides, the blondie looks mighty toothsome, mayhaps we'll get a chance at them later. It'd be more fun if she gave a bit of a struggle."

The large Big Bad laughed mockingly. "As if you would get the chance. But go on in, wouldn't want to deprive Lord Brink of a good torture."

Nicholas scowled at him, and along with Jess, ducked into the tent before the guard dog changed his mind. The tent was deceiving from the outside and was much larger than it looked, containing a basin of water, a table, and a decent sized bed that harbored at least one sleeping woman. Nicholas stood back, scanning the tent for any sight of the other woman while Jess headed toward the bed, whispering Jemma's name.

Well, if that was Jemma, where was Ninian? He didn't see her anywhere, until he noticed a silent shape in the back of the tent. She was completely still as he drew closer, and she sat with her back ramrod straight, her chest barely rising and falling. Her golden blonde hair hung loose down her shoulders, stringy and dirty-looking, while her face was smudged with dirt and a large bruise in the shape of a handprint over her right cheekbone. Nicholas gazed at her and turned just in time to put a restraining arm on Jess, who was moving quickly to Ninian's side.

Jess shook Nicholas off. "I want to check on her."

"Don't," Nicholas said, nodding to Ninian. "She's in a trance, and it's not a good idea to disturb a Daughter of the Will when she's communing with nature and the spirits. Things can go wrong."

Jess turned her borrowed, craggy façade of a face toward him and arched a brow quizzically. "How would you know, Wolf lover?"

Nicholas met her gaze for a moment. "My mother is a Daughter," he said shortly and moved toward Jemma, avoiding the surprise that blossomed across Jess's temporarily masculine features.

"How is she?" he said while gesturing to Jemma, cutting off the questions he knew Jess was dying to ask him. Jemma's frail frame was curled up in a fetal position, her angular features sharp and tight in the pale light that flickered from a single candle in the center of the room.

"She's sleeping," Jess said.

"Get away from her," a voice hissed behind them, causing Jess and Nicholas to jump as they turned to greet the voice. But it was Ninian, who had come out of her trance and found the two figures lurking over Jemma.

"Ninian," Jess said, starting forward to embrace her, but the pale Daughter backed up, stepping away from Jess. "Does Keir know you're in here? You know he said that Brink did not want us harmed. Come near us and I will scream for help," she said, holding her chin up like a queen and arching a brow, her gaze meeting Jess's in a challenge.

"Ah," Jess said with a grin and nodded comprehendingly. "What big ears you have."

Ninian relaxed, a slow smile curving her lips as her shoulders sagged in momentary relief.

"The better to hear you with, my dear," she finished with a nod and opened her arms for Jess to embrace. "I must say, I'd rather hug you as yourself," she said, smiling and stepping back to embrace Nicholas.

"Nicholas," she whispered, "I am honored you came to rescue me."

"How could I not?"

"So I see that Darvish got you the potion. Shall we get out of here?"

"Yeah, we've been in here long enough," Jess said, casting a glance toward the door and moving to Jemma's side with the swiftness of a Wolf in motion. Nicholas decided he would keep that observation to himself as he was sure she wouldn't be too appreciative.

Just as quickly, but without the preternatural grace, Ninian grabbed Jess before she could wake Jemma. "If she sees a Big Bad looming over her, she'll most likely scream and we can't have that. Allow me."

Jess stepped back, a blush creeping up her cheeks for not having thought of that herself. "Yes, of course," she said, glancing down at the floor. Nicholas was surprised—Jess had more pride than a cat and just as much snarl.

"Jemma dear," Ninian said softly, gently shaking her shoulder. "We have to go." Jemma stirred, opened bleary eyes, and blinked in confusion while glancing at Nicholas and Jess.

"Ninian?" she asked quietly while staring at the men.

"We must hurry, Jemma, we don't have much time. Do you have the potions?" she asked, turning toward Nicholas.

Nodding and fumbling in his coat pocket, Nicholas withdrew the small blue bottles and gave them to Ninian, who handed one to Jemma.

"Drink this. What are our names?"

"You are Moth and Jemma is Spider. You're brothers and you never go anywhere without one another," Jess said softly, talking below the level of the Wolves' hearing outside the tent. "Jemma, you're the dumb brother." Jemma smiled in response and downed the contents of the vial.

"It'll be hard for these smart bones to play a dimwit, but I'll see what I can do," Jemma said as she started to change, a sparkle in her eye. Ninian had done the same and within a minute, two familiar-looking Big Bads stood before them. Nicholas wondered idly how Jess had known the two Wolves' names, but he figured it didn't matter at the moment.

Nicholas nodded. "Let's go." He lifted the flap and stepped out into the night, finding himself face-to-face with Keir.

"Grab him," Keir said, the growl a deep vibration that accompanied everything he said. Before Nicholas knew what was going on, he was being hauled off by the neck and manhandled by two very big Wolves.

"You owe me from your gambling debts, Barton, and I'm sick of waiting for you to pay up," Keir said, paying no mind to Jess, Ninian and Jemma, who had crept out of the tent unnoticed after him. Nicholas cast Jess a single look willing her to go. She started to shake her head, but then thought better of it and nodded, herding the other two into the milling crowd of Wolf men.

Nicholas was relieved that she had listened despite the predicament he was now in. At least they could get out. Time to play the part, he thought grimly. Howling as if in pain, more for show than any need to yell, Nicholas whined like he believed his Wolf counterpart would. "I can get it, I swear."

"Take him to my tent," Keir snarled.

Terror gripped Nicholas's chest. Damn The Will, they were going to see that Ninian and Jemma were gone. But the Wolves were moving him away from that tent and heading toward a bigger one some feet away, and Nicholas drew an inward sigh of relief. He couldn't let Story lose them. It would utterly defeat her, and her grip on this reality was tenuous already.

Once inside the tent, the Wolves sent Nicholas flying so that he slammed to the ground. He grappled for breath, trying to inhale lungfuls as he gathered his ability to take in air once again. Above him, Keir loomed with a disturbingly calm and sadistic smile curving thin lips, revealing his big, shiny white teeth. He looked remarkably like a Wolf even in human form. He was bigger than Nigel, and easily as cruel. But Nicholas could tell that he wasn't as cunning as the smaller alpha had been.

"I don't like weak links, Barton, and you're my weak link. You drink, you gamble, and you lose. You owe me three Pigs."

Nicholas tried to get to his feet, but one of the Big Bad henchmen kicked him in the stomach. He almost laughed at the currency requested, but decided against it between gasping breaths of pain.

"I can get them," he said through his groan.

"Really, because last I heard, they had gotten into the Wolf hunting business."

Oh, *those* three pigs, Nicholas thought. That made more sense.

"And since your deadline is up, I'm going to make you a deal. Call in Darvish," Keir continued, turning to the Wolf at the tent door, who nodded and disappeared into the night. The Wolf returned a moment later with the dark-skinned Big Bad who had helped get Nicholas into this mess.

He hoped Darvish was still on his side because otherwise Nicholas was dead. One more minute and Jess and the girls would be out of range, rendering the potion useless and leaving Nicholas showing his true face.

Darvish nodded in respect to Keir, standing almost as tall as the new leader, while not quite as massive in bulk. Instead he was leaner, more cut, and poised. "Yes, Alpha?"

Keir bared his teeth, and Nicholas got the impression this Big Bad was definitely more Wolf than man. "I want you to treat him."

Nicholas glanced at him sharply, unsure if he had heard him right.

"Treat him?" Darvish asked, sounding just as confused as Nicholas felt.

"Yeeaaaah," Keir drew out in his deep, growly voice. "I want him fit to fight. He goes into the ring tonight."

Darvish's eyes barely flickered as he nodded. "Yes, Alpha. Why don't I do a quick examination here, and that way I can let you know my best estimate for when he'll be able to fight in your ring," he said in a brusque, professional manner.

Keir narrowed his eyes and nodded, dropping down into a chair. Turning to a pile of what looked like raw beef, he tore into it. While most Wolves acting as men would eat as men, Keir used his fangs, the gore from the animal reddening his face.

Nicholas turned away lest he be sick. There was something unnatural about watching a man become an animal. But Wolves weren't animals, they were beasts, he reminded himself.

Nicholas stayed where he was as Darvish approached, trying his best to block out the sounds of Keir slavering away at his food.

"Hey Barton, I'm going to just check you real quick and make sure you don't have anything broken," he said, and he began to press lightly against Nicholas's rib cage, causing him to wince. But nothing hurt more than when Darvish pressed hard against the area of his torso where he had been kicked. He gave an honest howl, and Darvish patted Nicholas on the head before turning to Keir.

"He has a broken rib," he notified the giant Wolf, who was dabbing at his mouth with a cloth—as if he were fine-dining and not wiping shredded flesh and blood off his face.

"Can you fix it?"

"I can, but I'll need to take him back to my tent to heal him. My Bone Grafter Shrooms are there, and I'll need to mix up the potion."

"How long?" grunted Keir, who was now picking his teeth with a small bone. Gods, how long before someone noticed that Ninian and Jemma were gone, Nicholas worried.

"Two hours at best."

Scowling, Keir nodded and jerked his head at one of his guard dogs. "Go with them and stand outside the tent in case this one gives Darvish trouble. Not that the little rodent would be able to take our good doctor," he said laughing.

Painfully, Nicholas got to his feet with Darvish's help. "Be ready to feel what it's like to have your throat ripped out, Barton," Keir growled as they walked out of the tent followed by his guard.

When they got to Darvish's tent, Dr. Big Bad motioned for the guard to stay outside while he and Nicholas went inside. Darvish got to mixing some herbs together while Nicholas sat in a chair, wondering if he had really cracked a rib.

"Here, drink this," Darvish said quickly.

Eyeing it, Nicholas looked up at him warily. "What is it?"

"It will fix that broken rib," Darvish said levelly, not a trace of impatience or malice evident in his calm exterior.

Sighing, Nicholas grabbed the mixture and downed it fast, nearly gagging on the putrid stench, although the taste wasn't as bad as it smelled. As soon as the liquid was in his system, he felt it warm his limbs, and the sharp pain in his ribcage subsided.

Nicholas opened his mouth to ask him what the plan was when Darvish took three purposeful steps toward the door. "Hey Yeti, could you help me with something?" he asked.

"Sure, doc," Yeti said, stepping all the way into the tent just as Darvish waved a smoking stick of Night Leaf in Yeti's face. The guard dog didn't have time to struggle as the drug took effect almost immediately, and the lithe figure of the blond Big Bad dropped to the floor. Nicholas hadn't even seen Darvish light the sleep-inducing herb.

The green-eyed Big Bad glanced at Nicholas and beckoned him over. "We have to get out of here before they discover the tent is empty. Follow my lead and try not to talk. Oh, and just in case we get stopped, you now have a temporary case of Fire Pox."

"What?" Nicholas's hands flew to his nose, feeling the large, oozing, deformed bumps that now covered his face.

"You poisoned me!" he exclaimed in a whisper, still conscious that all those big-eared Wolves might be able to hear them.

"It was necessary—the potion wore off several minutes ago."

Nicholas looked down and realized he could see his own clothes again, his own hands. He only hoped the reason it had worn off was because Jess had gotten them out.

"Oh, and put this on," Darvish said, turning and wrapping a cloak around Nicholas's shoulders.

Nicholas pulled the hood down and bowed his head, following Darvish out into the darkness. Creatures of the night as they were, the Wolves were in revelry mode and didn't seem to pay Nicholas and

Darvish any mind as they wove through the tents toward the tree line. As they walked, Wolves parted for them, and Nicholas realized that Darvish commanded respect from the Big Bads. It was interesting because the man exhibited none of their animalistic behavior, although Nicholas knew that not all Wolves were as terrifyingly primitive as Keir. But Darvish walked among Wolves, and out of them all, he seemed more man than beast. And yet, Nicholas sensed the man was capable of savagery beneath his cool exterior.

Nicholas's face was starting to itch, and he knew that itch would turn into a burn sooner than later. He inwardly cursed Darvish for giving him this particular ailment, but as they rounded a corner and nearly ran into another Wolf, he decided that if he got out of there with his life, he'd deal with it. He really wanted to kiss Story again. Her golden gaze and sweet but solid strength had been haunting him since he'd left. He'd felt an ache that had begun to burn worse than the Pox when he had thought for a moment that Keir was going to have him killed. He didn't know when she had become his very reason for life. Actually, that was a lie, he did. The moment he had met her, something had passed through him that he had never felt before. His cravings for other women had completely disappeared, and now all he wanted was to get her alone and make her his own forever.

A Wolf stopped them and glanced at Darvish while nodding to Nicholas. "What's with him?"

"He's got the Pox, I have to get him out of the area," Darvish said.

The Wolf backed up quickly. "Get him out of here before he infects the rest of us," he hissed and moved away from them as fast as possible.

Then they were away from the tents and fading into the night. "I might hate you for the pain you've caused me tonight, but it sure as hell worked."

"Well, Fire Pox can kill a real Wolf," Darvish said.

As they made it to the tree line, Nicholas held out his hand. "Thanks for getting us out of there. I guess Big Bads aren't all so bad."

"Don't be fooled, I just hide it better," Darvish said with a wolfish grin and a firm handshake.

"So will the Pox go away then?"

Nodding, Darvish started up the hill. "Yeah, in about an hour. But there's no time to talk, we've got to get out of here," he said urgently.

"They'll be checking in on the women to feed them soon, and then they'll discover they're gone."

"You're coming with us?"

Turning, Darvish looked at him as if he was daft. "I can't go back now. They'll know I was involved. They'll kill me."

"Now that wouldn't be such a bad thing, would it? A Big Bad finding his timely end?" Jess asked, appearing from behind a tree.

Darvish grinned. "Oh, I definitely like you better as a woman," he said with a whistle, causing Jess to scowl in the moonlight.

"I must enlighten Story to the benefits of a Wolf-free Tressla," she said with a slight tilt of her head and a superior smile before turning and glancing over her shoulder as she started up the hill. "Come on, the others are waiting up the path."

"You should have gotten out of here," Nicholas reprimanded her as he clumped up after her, trying his best to ignore the burning on his face that was growing worse by the minute.

Jess ignored him and concentrated on climbing up the steep path to their waiting friends. As they neared the top, Jess cast another glance over her shoulder at Darvish.

"Thanks for your help and all, but we'll be fine from here. You might want to join the rest of your pack."

Rarely looking anything but amused, Darvish's easy smile appeared and he laughed. "While I'm sure you would like to be rid of me, you're stuck with me. If I return, Keir will have me killed—slowly. And I rather like being alive, with my body parts intact. Besides, Story owes me a favor."

While he talked, Jess looked increasingly unhappy—bloodthirsty, really. But she couldn't very well kill the man who had just saved her and her friends' lives, so she snapped her mouth shut before answering as if to calm her fiery tongue. "How do you figure?"

"Well, first I saved her, and now I've saved you. I'm sure your pretty little red head can do the math," he deliberately patronized, obviously enjoying himself as a gleam lit his green canine eyes.

Nicholas was sure he was going to have to save Darvish from the now royally pissed off Red Riding Hood.

As they came to the top of the hill, Nicholas could see that Kestrel clutched her mother's hand, the reunion obviously having had already happened.

Ninian turned to them all from her spot near Lance. "Well done. Now, we must get to Story because I'm sensing that we are about to be in some trouble," she said with her familiar formal lilt. To give impact to her words, a piercing howl filled up the night—a cry to hunt. Nicholas had heard it many nights before when the Wolves rampaged towns.

"That didn't take long," Lance said quietly with his normal patience, but Nicholas could see he was as agitated as the rest of them.

"Longer than you know," Nicholas murmured before turning to the group. "We're going to have to run. Kestrel, take Jemma and go with Lance and warn Story. Once we get to the sanctuary, we should be fine, but tell her."

Kestrel nodded. Wasting no time, she turned to Jemma and helped her mother up onto a now horsey-looking Lance. Swiftly leaping up behind her, she grinned. "I think you're going to like this, Mom." Jemma grabbed Lance's mane, her sharp face set in anticipation. If they weren't running for their lives, Nicholas would daresay that a gleam lit up her small, dark eyes.

Kestrel glanced down at Nicholas. "Start running, we'll send help."

Turning quickly to Darvish, Nicholas jerked his head. "I saw you as a Wolf before and you're pretty huge. Can you carry them both?"

Darvish's green eyes diamonded, always so startling in the face of a man. He wasn't grinning now—his expression all business as he nodded. "It will slow me down, but I'll still be faster than on two feet."

Nicholas nodded sharply. "Then do it."

Darvish wasted no time and morphed into a gigantic chocolate-colored Wolf. Ninian looked at Nicholas uncertainly, but quickly climbed onto his back and glanced at Jess.

"No way, I am not riding him and leaving you to be eaten by Wolves, Nicholas."

"Get on him, Jess, and don't argue. We don't have time."

In the dark, she turned her lightning blue eyes to him and stared. "I. Said. I'm. With. You. Nicholas," she ground out succinctly between clenched teeth. Sighing in frustration, but knowing she wouldn't listen to reason, he looked at Darvish and waved his hand.

"Go—get Ninian to safety." Without a backwards glance, Darvish bounded into the night while Nicholas and Jess began running for their lives on foot. Behind them, the night filled with howls as the beasts came out to play.

Nicholas had never run so fast in his life. The moonless night was a blur, and he wished he had Jess's night vision. Most of all, though, he just wanted to see Story. That wasn't the first time he had thought that tonight. Jess kept length beside him, but even her breathing was slightly ragged.

They both had their magical inheritance going for them. As a Red Riding Hood, Jess had Wolf-like abilities, such as night vision, stealth, and the ability to run long distances at a relatively abnormal speed. Nicholas had trained all his life, so he had endurance, but she was faster. Sooner or later, the Wolves were going to catch him. Hopefully, Jess would make it in time. He knew she was running slower so as not to leave him behind. His own breath came out in wheezes, and his chest was already beginning to burn for air. The uneven field sent muscle cramps racing through his legs as he tried to run faster amidst the yips and yowls haunting their shadows.

It was fortunate the Wolves' camp hadn't been too far away from Racell's sanctuary, and he hoped that already Lance was touching ground into the protected grove. The howls were growing louder, making his hair stand on end. It sounded like the entire hundred or so hell beasts were right behind him.

"Jess, go ahead, I know you can run faster," he gasped. But she ignored him and continued to run beside him, the night doing nothing to mute the vibrancy of her legendary red hair as it whipped in the wind behind her.

They probably had a half-mile left to run, and he knew their head start had diminished greatly. He slowed his running for a mere moment to cast a glance behind him and saw a horrifying image as the Wolves' looming shadows broke forth into sight, the moonlight gleaming off their wicked eyes and making them look like the demons Nicholas knew they truly were. He started to really run then, but felt despair set in as their hot breath radiated in the night, drawing closer.

In those moments, his mind flashed back to Story, that child he'd seen staring scared up through the cracks of the floor. She had just witnessed her papa die, and had Nigel or any of the Wolves looked down, they would have seen her. He had kept quiet and tried to herd the pack out, but not before he saw her literally wink out of existence, or reality. He had been struck then by her wide golden eyes, so filled with pain. He'd thought of her every day since, and he was determined that a lifetime of yearning—of searching—was not going to end tonight, without one last moment beside her.

The sound of teeth gnashing together made him jump forward and pick up his speed, feeling the rabid spittle of Wolf seeping through his clothes. Jess had surged ahead out of necessity, and he was glad to see she might make it to the camp, which was only a small distance ahead.

"Nicholas, grab hold!"

He looked up as Adam held out an arm from atop the back of a Pegasus that must have been Lance's mother. He leapt up, grasping Adam's forearm, and was lifted off the ground and hauled onto Landria's light blue back. As they lifted off, he remembered Jess and was relieved when he saw she was safely behind Kestrel, and that Lance was well out of range of the Wolves, who had stopped to look into the sky with howls of spite. Some leapt into the air, snarling as if they could pull the Pegasus from the sky.

They left behind the Wolves and landed a few moments later in the sanctuary, where their once-small band of followers had grown in just a day. As they touched down and Nicholas slid off Landria, he saw Story head towards him. He smiled despite having the creeping feeling that she was probably livid with him. Oh The Green, he hoped the Fire Pox spell had worn off. He touched his face quickly and sighed in relief that the Pox seemed to be gone, and he was back to normal.

He stepped forward to embrace her, regardless of any oncoming wrath, but howls broke the celebratory cheers and greetings. Kestrel, Nicholas knew, had wanted Jemma to meet her grandchild right away, and mother and daughter were busy crooning over the infant. Near the fire pit, Adam was laughing with Jess while Elliott was greeting Ninian, who was trying to calm a worried, flitting Bliss. But everything stopped as the low rumble of a hundred Wolf growls caused even the breeze to shudder. Hundreds of paws thundered against the ground and the earth shook beneath their feet.

"They shouldn't be able to get to us here," Story murmured, her face devoid of color, golden eyes wide. She turned her stricken gaze to Nicholas. "They shouldn't be able to get to us here," she echoed herself.

"Where's Racell?" he asked, the howls growing closer while everyone, even Jess, remained frozen in shock. "Story, where's Racell?" Nicholas grabbed her shoulders and shook her, trying to snap her out of it.

"He went . . . I sent him to my mother . . . through the portal," she whispered, sucking in a large gulp of air.

"The Will it all to hell!" he cursed and shook her again. "Story! You have to get everyone ready. You have to prepare for war. They're coming."

Story stared uncomprehending a moment longer, her trance only broken when Jemma let out a scream. The Wolves answered back their intent with the barking howl of predators come to slaughter.

Story nodded at Nicholas and turned sharply. "Everyone, we don't have time to be afraid. Get ready, the Wolves are coming. We are no longer protected here. Fight for your lives! Fight for your world!"

As she was talking, Nicholas was running toward the swarm of Wolves. The spirit of the warrior his mother raised him to be came alive as he swung his sword and sliced through the neck of a Wolf who had been leaping for his throat.

All around, people were running—warriors throwing themselves into the throng of the fight, Fairytales using whatever tools inspiration gave them—to take down as many Wolves as they could.

But the most beautiful sight of all was Kestrel, Queen of the Seven Forests, taking to the sky on the back of her trusted steed and greatest love Lance, his wings like a halo of death around her as arrow after arrow rained down on the Wolves with deadly accuracy. And when she started to sing, it was as if the world stopped.

Animals, big and small emerged from the forest to help beat back the Wolves. Nicholas grinned and swung again and again. After a few moments, he noticed that Jess was beside him, covering his back. He caught her eye for a moment and she nodded. They were a team.

Darvish had joined the fray and was leaping with brutal ferocity at Wolves he'd once called brothers, while Adam, a practiced bow and arrow huntsman, shot from a tree. Elliott brandished a sword in one hand and a torch in another, slicing and flinging fire in the direction of any Wolf who came near the women and children he guarded further back into the trees. He was helped by a storm of Thumbelina Fairies, who circled their victim in swarms and attacked with thorn-tipped daggers. Kestrel called to the sky and the dragons came, bombarding Wolves with their sharp, razor-like teeth.

Nicholas grinned as Jess ducked so he could take down a Wolf in midflight who was aiming for the back of her neck. His sword arced up and sliced through the Wolf's torso, spraying a haze of blood down on him. The Wolf dropped, and Nicholas turned to meet his next foe, a large black Wolf whose yellow eyes diamonded in on him for blood. Gristle? Fear seized his body at the thought of encountering the old foe he had relieved of a paw. But a swift glance at the Wolf's left foot showed him that this one still had his limbs intact.

Out of the corner of his eye, Nicholas saw Jess duck as a paw came flying at her head. She turned back with a kick and stabbed with one sword as if she were a harem dancer, her other hand wielding an axe that arced through the air. Her movements were quick, fluid, and sensual, so that Wolves fell to her, hating her and wanting her at their very end—a rightful curse to all Big Bads.

Nicholas stood in a standoff with the midnight colored Big Bad, the Wolf's hackles raised, its head lowered as it growled deeply. It took Nicholas a moment, but he realized why the beast seemed so familiar—it was Bastion, Gristle's brother. Even worse because this one had four working paws with razor-sharp claws. Nicholas danced around him, never taking his eyes off the Wolf in front of him, trusting in Jess to take care of his back.

Nicholas could tell that Bastion was aware of who he was. Blood clumped the Wolf's dirty coat, and his lips pulled back from his teeth in a terrifying snarl. But Nicholas had fought these beasts many times, and he knew that he would take this one down, just as he'd taken down Gristle. "Scared I'll take your paw like I took your brother's?" Nicholas taunted with a sneer, zeroing in on the Wolf while maintaining awareness of his surroundings.

Bastion growled and leapt, his paws splayed out, claws gleaming in the light cast by the torches that lit up the field. Anticipating the Wolf's move, Nicholas ducked in a roll under the airborne creature, propelling himself up and twisting his battle-trained body in a one-eighty just as Bastion landed and turned toward him. Without hesitation, Nicholas pulled his arm back and plunged his sword deep into the Wolf's breast, the beast's eyes going wide as he fell.

Stupid Wolves. Nicholas shook his head. They always give in to the taunt. He pulled his sword from Bastion's chest and wiped the blood from it before turning and leaping back into the fray with Jess, his unexpected ally, by his side.

Wolf after Wolf fell to the ground so that The Green's verdant earth was bathed in red. When Nicholas had a moment, he looked up from the furor of the war and death and frantically searched for Story. How could he have forgotten her welfare for even a moment?

His head swiveled about looking for her. In that moment of distraction, fire sliced through his back as a Wolf's claws raked him from behind, shredding his shirt and flesh. Jess skewered the Wolf with her long sword while flipping a dagger into the eye of another. She grinned and flipped back tangled red hair clumped with blood. Despite her war-torn appearance, her eyes gleamed. If it hadn't been obvious before, it was to him now: killing Wolves was definitely her calling.

Cringing from the pain, he nodded his thanks and turned around to look for Story once more, choking on bile as the bloody shreds of his back stuck to the cloth of his shirt. His grabbed his chest when he spotted her, a pain shooting through his heart that was so palpable, he thought it might break. She was in the furor of the fight and was surrounded by Wolves on all sides. He knew they probably wouldn't kill her because Brink wanted her alive. But then again, they were also under the spell of blood and war lust aroused by the fighting around them. He was on his way to her before he even thought about it. Dashing through the fray, he was almost hobbled by the pain in his back as he dodged mini-battles that were taking place all over the battlefield, and then he stopped short. Kestrel was circling the sky with her arrows, and taking down one by one the Wolves surrounding Story, swiftly, like a bird of prey.

But there was one Wolf who took no heed of Kestrel's or Brink's wishes, and he was closing in fast on Story, his yellow eyes gleaming in the night as it faded into dawn. He was slinking closer, and Nicholas didn't have to see the bloodlust in his eyes—it was emanating off him like an odor.

Nicholas started to fight his way through, no longer aware of the pain in his back. From across the way, he saw a green-eyed Wolf leaping toward Story and hope surged through him. But it was Kestrel who was close enough to save Story from the rogue of doom, and she swooped down. Too close. Story looked up to smile gratefully at her sister, relief easing her features, but then her face contorted and she started to scream as another Wolf—Keir, thought Nicholas—bunched his muscles and propelled himself through the air onto Lance's back and took Kestrel down to the ground. Before Lance could recover, the Wolves were on him.

Keir tossed Kestrel to the ground, and with one large paw planted firmly on her chest, he lifted his other and took one swipe. Nicholas turned away and looked instead to Story, who was screaming Kestrel's name over and over, her pain and rage let loose on the masses. Even the Wolves cowered beneath it. Nicholas tried plugging his ears, but he could feel her screams reverberate through his soul, and then he knew nothing.

When he came to only seconds later, dawn had turned black and Story's golden eyes were the only thing visible in the night. That and the hundreds of dark shadowy Nightmares broiling up through the crevices of The Green, come to do their Dreamer's calling.

It was all her fault. That's all she could think as she heard the Wolves' howls closing in on them in the night. She had sent Racell to be with her mother because she couldn't deal with his dreams any longer, and she also couldn't stand to think of her mother being alone. And she had left everyone unprotected—innocent people who had come to follow her. The Stupid Dreamer. She'd forgotten that without Racell in their world, his Rood was no longer protected.

She joined the fray with a lance in hand, flanked by the two Elven sibling warriors who refused to leave her side. And so the three fought, and the fight was going their way, or so it seemed to Story, with Kestrel in the sky looking like an angel of vengeance. While Story fought, she tried to conjure up any magic she could. A hole in the fabric of reality, sure, but how was that going to help? Perhaps the Nightmares could help, she thought, trying to conjure them forth. But she struggled as she swiped with a lance and knocked a Wolf out of the air, luckily. Her fighting talent was mediocre at best, and Bliss had tried begging her to stay out of the battle and to try helping through magic, but she was too stressed, and she couldn't get a handle on it. And there was no way she could stand by and do nothing while everyone fought for her. So there she was, protected by Elves and doing a poor job of calling up any helpful magic. Story wished she were home, curled up by her mother on the couch and watching a movie with popcorn. Being a superhero was exhausting.

Just when it seemed as if the Wolves might stand down, the Big Bads lived up to their name. Somehow, she had become separated from her two Elven bodyguards and surrounded by Wolves. All those games with Adam as a child flooded back to her, and she felt her throat thick with fear. Slavering jaws yapped and quivered, creepy yellow eyes zeroed in on her throat, and she was sure that the end had come.

But when she looked up to the sky, she saw Kestrel taking Wolves down as if they were dominos, her arrows singing through the breeze. Story smiled a thanks to her big sister for saving her and started to turn to begin fighting back as well, when she saw Kestrel's smile falter.

A massive gray Wolf had grabbed Lance's tail with sharp claws. The Pegasus had flown low in his attempt to save Story, and the Wolf was able to leap onto Lance's back with ease, smashing Lance to the ground below and taking Kestrel with him. As Lance hit, Wolves launched onto him as if he was their last meal and devoured him, the sickening crunch of his bones and flesh making the ground move beneath Story's feet as her legs threatened to give out. Kestrel hit the ground as well. The large Wolf lifted up one paw and slashed her neck with one swipe, casting all life and love from Kestrel's once-beautiful, soulful eyes.

The pain hit and lanced through Story's body—beyond even emotional or physical pain. But even as her screams flooded the breaking night with power, it was her rage that put out the lights and allowed her to free the Nightmares.

The black came fast to her soul, and she quickly realized that darkness had always been a part of her as the fury took over her senses. She easily altered her mind state and created a portal that yawned open and brought forth the Nightmares by the hundreds. At first they just surrounded their queen, worshipping the Bringer of dark dreams. It had been so long since she had shown her true face to them. They had tried to find her before, bringing her nightmares of her own to remind her that they needed their mother back. But she hadn't listened. Now she was here, and they fawned beneath the cruel golden glow of her eyes.

"Kill them," she whispered in the silence of the dark as all creatures lay still in the presence of such malevolence. And that's when the Wolves ran, their frightened howls filling up the night as they were dogged every step by their worst dreams come true.

CHAPTER THIRTY-FIVE

Racell's Rood, Tressla

WHEN LIGHT CAME TO the grove once more, Story kneeled down and lifted Kestrel's head and placed it gently in her lap, caressing her sister's blood-soaked, straw-colored hair. Tears rolled down her face freely, and the pain breathed inside of her as if it was a living creature. From behind her, Story heard Jemma cry out and come running to her daughter's side. She lifted Kestrel's limp hand and choked quietly on her grief. Story wrapped her arms around Jemma's slight form, and the two wept, rocking together on the forest floor.

Story wished she could stay like that forever. But she was the leader, she realized, even though all she wanted to do was fall apart, agony chewing at her heart. Elliott was the first to approach her with a gentle hand on her arm. She looked up and shared a look with him through her tears. He didn't look surprised, just guilty. That's when she realized he had known—he had seen Kestrel's death. She wanted to be angry with him, she wanted to scream. Rage boiled inside of her and she felt the Dark Dreamer living within her. She had always been there, Story realized. She'd just been ignoring her.

But instead of losing it, Story took Elliott's arm and rose to her feet, wiping her moist face and nodding to him that she was okay. Inside, she felt the Dark Dreamer quiet, although she still hovered within her soul. There would be time for her later, away from the eyes of her followers.

Elliott seemed to see something in her eyes because he stepped back quickly, concern flashing across his handsome features. Story didn't care. Her mother had raised her to not make a spectacle, but she wasn't done with him.

At the moment, she had Jemma to worry about. The grief-stricken mother had collapsed over her daughter. She was inconsolable, refusing to be helped away from her daughter's still form. It took a baby's cry, ripping through that particularly dark morning, to still the childless mother. Jemma lifted her head and blinked her swollen eyes as a red-eyed Ophelia came forth cradling the now-orphaned child in her arms. Story felt the loss start to well up in the back of her throat at the unfairness of it all, but she pushed it back down. There would be time for more tears eventually. The thought didn't quell the ache that seared through her chest.

Jemma lifted her creased face and reached out for her grandson. Ophelia placed him in Jemma's arms, and she cradled him to her chest, staring down at him in love and pain. Story and Ophelia flanked Jemma and stared down at the infant's small little face, his eyes closing sleepily as he yawned, safe in his gram's arms.

"He will need you to raise him now, Jemma," Ophelia said softly, smiling gently despite her own sadness.

Jemma lifted her gaze for the fleetest of moments to Ophelia, and then her eyes were drawn back down to the little bundle in her arms. "Won't the Pegasus want him? You're his family too. And he's royalty," she said in a barely controlled voice.

Ophelia shook her pink head and reached out to stroke the child's tiny nose with a delicate finger. "He belongs with you, I believe. We would like to visit and teach him our ways as he gets older of course."

Jemma nodded, a reason to live once again resting upon her spirit—a grandson in need of his gram. Story looked down at his face as well and wondered if such innocence would always exist. She wasn't a psychic like Elliott, but she could guess that when he grew up, he was going to want to exact vengeance on the ones who had deprived him of two loving parents. She knew that's what she'd do. At the thought, the Dark Dreamer lifted her head. Story shuddered and pushed her back down.

Story wasn't surprised when Ober and Landria touched ground a few moments later and morphed into their human forms. Both had already been grieving, Story could tell. Ober walked over to Story, put his hand on her shoulder and squeezed.

"What can we do?"

Story nodded and forced an appreciative smile. "There are wounded lying on the far side of the fire. They could use some Pegasus magic."

Ober nodded in response and Landria started to follow, but paused in front of Story, her sad amethyst gaze meeting Story's golden one.

"Do not grieve too long, Dreamer. They died as heroes, protecting you," she said softly. Landria had always been the gentlest of souls, and Story felt ashamed for a moment, nursing the darkness that lived within as she did. Perhaps Landria would not be so forgiving if she knew the urges that warred within Story right now, the desire to allow the dark part of herself full reign—so that she wouldn't have to think about Kestrel's last flight through the air, her straw yellow hair, and the childish laughter that had been Story's companion on so many childhood adventures. It didn't matter that they weren't related by blood. Kestrel had always been her sister.

Story nodded. "Yes, well, let's hope that I was worth saving," she murmured and then turned away, ignoring Landria's frown as she headed toward the injured to see if she could help.

Chapter Thirty-Six

Racell's Rood, Tressla

IT WAS HOURS LATER, when the injured had been tended to, that Story was able to sneak away. As she started to slip off, Nicholas approached her. She had almost forgotten him with Kestrel's and Lance's deaths, and making sure people got taken care of. She had known he was alive, and that is what had gotten her through.

She sighed as he approached. Story just needed to be alone with her darkness, and here was the source of all light in her life, coming to head her off. She wasn't in the mood to be consoled.

"Story," Nicholas said, his dark eyes searching hers as she stopped to greet him.

"Nicholas," she nodded, and then fell silent.

"How are you?" he asked, reaching out a hand and clasping her smaller one in his own. She felt the calluses on his fingertips and was comforted for a moment. It didn't last long.

"I'm fine," she said shortly and looked longingly off into the woods, where she yearned to be alone. The Dark Dreamer wanted to come out, and Story didn't really want to stop her.

"Story, I . . ."

Slipping her hand from his, Story sighed. "Nicholas, I just need some time right now to be alone. Okay? Do you think you could back off for just a few minutes for The Green's sake?" She didn't mean it to come out as harsh as it did. But suddenly the hum of people around her was suffocating, and before he could answer she turned sharply and headed to the grove, hoping for some silence from the doom of the impending night. The day had gone so quickly, it felt as if her friends' lives had been snuffed out as rapidly as the sun's passage across the sky.

As she headed away from the thrum of the quiet camp that grieved for the dead, she felt calmer. Their safe haven was no longer a haven, so they were going to have to get moving, but not until the morning. Story figured the Wolves would need to regroup and that the Nightmares had given them something to be frightened of. All the same, she had assigned a guard of Kestrel's dragons, which had taken to following her around since the death of her sister, and they were keeping watch on the outlying areas. She had also secretly posted a few Nightmares. No use freaking people out by letting them know the dark dream creatures were nearby. They wouldn't touch anyone's sleep unless she said so, and her people needed a good night's rest.

She entered the grove and sank down to her knees by the tree, wishing for more than a couple of reasons that Racell was there to talk to, that her mother could be there too. She had yet to change out of her clothes, and she was still covered in Kestrel's blood. But when she finally was alone with her thoughts, she couldn't grieve. She felt cold. There was an emptiness inside of her that the Dark Dreamer wanted to fill.

She needed quiet, she needed to meditate, or she was sure she was going to lose any light she still held onto in the dark recesses of her troubled soul. Sitting down in the grass, she leaned her head against her knees and tried to quell the internal trembling.

She felt them before they got there, so she wasn't surprised when Adam and Elliott entered the darkening grove a few moments later. Story sighed. So much for being alone. Deep inside her, the Dark Dreamer perked up: Elliott.

Story tried to keep her in check, but she felt rage and something dark fill her up. But she didn't say anything as Adam and Elliott dropped down on the grass beside her. They also didn't say anything, and minutes ticked by while Story felt herself grow quiet once more. She kind of liked having her two best friends by her side on this night, this lonely godforsaken night.

But the silence didn't last long, and it was Elliott who spoke first. "Story," he said softly. "We're here if you need to talk." Slowly, Story lifted her head and glanced first at Adam and then at Elliott, the quiet within her also broken.

Story's fingers clenched, and she gripped the grass beside her and ripped from the roots, feeling the rage inside her ignite with a black fire. Adam and Elliott waited as she stayed silent, although she seethed within. Perhaps they noticed her strangeness though, because in the descending twilight, Adam went to speak, and then seemed to think better of it.

"Story?" he finally asked quietly.

Snapping her head around, she glanced at Elliott, and her hand clenched as she fought the desire to call on the Nightmares to take him away from her, away from her sight.

"You knew," she hissed.

Elliott frowned and looked away. "I tried to tell you, but there was just so much going on."

"Tried?" she said, looking up at him and feeling the light within her waver. "You should have tried harder."

Adam's brow furrowed and he looked back and forth between the two friends. "Okay, you lost me. What did Elliott know?"

"He knew Kestrel was going to die. He saw it in a vision."

Adam turned to Elliott and held out a hand in question.

Sighing, Elliott nodded. "Yes, I saw it, but . . . "

"I don't want to hear your buts. Save it for your own conscience," Story said venomously and rose to her feet, smelling the copper of the blood that clung to her skin and clothes. "You could have saved her, Elliott, but you were too busy flirting with the Elves to take the time to save my sister."

Adam's mouth gaped at Story, but Elliott was shaking his head. "No, Story, I couldn't have done anything. I see visions, I don't get to play God and change the outcome."

"You have before," Story exploded, all the anger erupting, so much that the night rippled around her as Nightmares hovered on the edge expectantly, feeling their dark queen near. "How do you know you couldn't save her when you didn't give me a chance to try? You stopped us from going out that night. Why am I busting my ass trying to figure out this damned prophecy if it's just pointless?"

Even in the moonlight, Story could see Elliott's features pale. Maybe it was the demons that lay waiting on the edge of the night, perhaps it was the realization that he had done nothing to stop a death, or perhaps it was the darkness that hung around Story like her own personal shadow in the deepening dark.

"Story, I have different kinds of visions," he began, but Story stopped him with a hiss.

"Oh, stop right there, you sorry excuse for a human being."

Adam's head jerked to Story. Having watched the scene in silence for the last few moments, he now intervened.

"You wait just a minute, Story. What has gotten into you? I know you lost your sister today, and I can't imagine what you're going through, but we all lost someone today. We all grew to love Kestrel in the time we've known her, and you have no right to suggest that Elliott would sit idly by while she was murdered."

"Oh yeah?" Story said, the danger like velvet in her voice. "Well, that is what I'm suggesting. I'm also suggesting you get out of my face, Adam. As if you have any real worth here. At least Elliott is psychic, but you just run off and get lost in the woods and get captured by Fairytale vamps. I should have left you to them," she sneered.

Story stopped and glared at him, the moonlight reflecting down on both Adam and Elliott brightly. She felt no such glow on her own countenance. Adam stood still as if he had been slapped. The air was rife with tension before Adam spoke and broke it.

"I don't even know you right now," he said in his familiar even voice. "But I can tell you one thing, these people need a leader, not someone who is going to throw blame around," he said and got to his feet and turned, stalking into the night without a backward glance.

Elliott started to follow him, but then turned to look back at her once more. "I know you may not believe me right now, but I really would have done something if I thought something could have been done. I see things in abstract, sometimes. I didn't even know it was going to be Wolves. I love you, Story, I would never want to see you hurt," he said softly, smiling sadly at her before following Adam back to camp.

In the darkening gloom, Story dropped to her knees and cried tearless sobs. "What is happening to me? This can't be me, it can't be me," she whispered.

CHAPTER THIRTY-SEVEN

Lake Sandeen, Tressla

GAIA. MOTHER EARTH. THE GREEN. She had been called many names by different cultures and different worlds even. They thought of her as a goddess, a spiritual being who could destroy them all or give them resources to live and love. She was all that, but when boiled down to her purest form, she was the essence of the earth. When it had been torn asunder so many eons before, she had found that it weakened her. But now she was starting to die. They could blame the crazy storms and unpredictable weather on global warming and man's destructive nature, but in the end it was merely her inability to exist in two worlds.

She could feel that Racell had left Tressla, but at this point she couldn't deny him his own happiness. She had felt Kestrel's death, kin to her from some long distant past, sown by the girl's heroic deeds and connection with the land. For every death, The Green grieved, but none more greatly than those who helped keep the land alive. Kestrel's death had more impact than anyone knew.

She had come here to Lake Sandeen to find out what her daughter was hiding within her watery kingdom. Nothing was going as hoped.

When The Green parted the waters and beckoned Sandeen above the waterline, her daughter came up looking wet and annoyed. Dripping water from her straight black hair, angular features, and eyelashes, she scowled at her mother as if she were a surly teenager.

"You could have at least let me dry off."

Pulling her hood down, The Green met her daughter's glare with a tired smile. "I apologize, Daughter, I only meant to summon you, I have not the strength to journey down below," she finished as she took a seat on a rock, which gladly transferred what energy it contained to its creator. She perked up a bit, but not enough to assuage Sandeen's suddenly concerned look.

"Mother, you do not look well," she said.

Arching a now-silvery brow, The Green smiled wryly. "You always were talented at stating the obvious."

Sandeen's scowl set in once more, causing The Green to smile. Good. She could take surly, but the worry and pampering would drive her mad. She might be old, but she wasn't completely devoid of hope. Yet.

Growing serious once more, she touched a finger to her lined skin. She had been eternally beautiful and young for so long, it was hard to believe that she was starting to look aged. She had taken it for granted, all those years wandering the world and yearning for Him, her long-forsaken consort. Frowning at the direction her thoughts were taking, she cast a serious eye to Sandeen. He was gone from this world, so good riddance. "You know I love you, right?"

"Yes, I guess that's why you banished me to this watery existence right? Because of love?" Sandeen spit out spitefully, making The Green smile once more. Ah yes, this is why she loved being a mother.

"Your father was the one who did that, you know that. And that's not why I'm here. I know you know something, dear, and I need to know what you know about Story that the rest of us don't."

Sandeen had by now dried herself off and once again looked her elegant gaunt self, but The Green did not miss the uncertainty in her eyes before she quashed it down with the cold glimmer of the deep dark.

"I have no idea what you're talking about," she murmured, looking off into the distance.

The Green felt her longing, her desire to be anywhere that was not wet.

"Sandeen, something dark is happening. Kestrel is dead. And the Wolves have been chased away by Nightmares, who did so at the bequest of their queen, Story. And yet, she still doesn't seem to be The Dreamer I remember."

Sandeen laughed, although she quieted quickly when her mother sent her a scathing glance. "I am sad to hear of Kestrel's passing, Mother, but if I may, that's what heroes do. They fight, they sacrifice, and then they die, usually when they're young. As for the rest, have you gone mad? She just discovered who she truly is. She can't be expected to save the world just yet. Perhaps she merely needs to find her own path," Sandeen said, her eyes looking away furtively.

"Sandeen," The Green said simply. And yet, her tone reverberated within the deep earth and shook the still waters into waves.

Sandeen sighed and rolled her eyes toward her mother. "You more than anyone should realize there's a dark side to everything and everyone. Does it surprise you that The Dreamer, who also is a harbinger of nightmares, would have darkness within her?"

The Green was chastened by the insight. Yes, of course, she thought. "But why did we never see it before?" This time Sandeen looked away and The Green was sure she saw that uncertainty flicker in the depths of her deep black gaze.

"That I'm not sure. But," Sandeen sighed, a heaviness settling on her bony shoulders, "it could be because she's a split soul."

"A split soul?" The Green echoed, confusion and dawning hitting her aging expression at the same time.

"Well, it's really just a phrase," Sandeen hurried. "Story's soul is really quite intact. It's the Spirit she's missing. That part of The Dreamer has been missing for a long time."

"How did her Spirit go missing, Sandeen?" The Green was able to exact as parental a look as she had when her daughter was young.

Sandeen frowned, meeting her mother's green gaze, the only thing that remained young yet. Sandeen opened her mouth as if to object and then poured out the entire tale instead.

The Green rubbed her temples, and wariness settled in once more. Perhaps she should find another rock, she thought, when a tree limb gracefully bowed down and lent her some strength. She nodded gratefully to the tree and whispered her thanks.

When Sandeen was done, The Green felt more tired than she ever had before, but she also felt a renewed hope. Now they could fix things, now they knew. Turning an eye to Sandeen, she opened her arms to her daughter. "Come dear. I don't blame you. You did what you had to, and in the end all we can do is hope."

Sandeen had been written into stories as well—in some she was the Lady of the Lake, in others a siren luring good men to their watery graves. But here she was The Green's daughter. And when it came down to it, "Mother" was really the name The Green liked best.

CHAPTER THIRTY-EIGHT

Racell's Rood

IT WAS QUIET when Story finally made her way back to camp from the grove. She had spent most of the night trying to squash the Dark Dreamer. But darkness still pervaded, although she was sure dawn hovered close by.

Fairytales and Tresslans milled about, speaking in hushed tones. A fire roared as she approached Ober, who turned to her from where he had been speaking quietly with Ninian.

"They would like to honor the dead," he said, gesturing to the followers who had grown even quieter as she approached. "We would like to honor our son and daughter," he finished gently, turning his kind eyes to Story.

"Yes, of course," she nodded, feeling her cheeks color from shame that she had disappeared when she was most needed. "I'm not very practiced in this sort of thing, and I don't really remember Tresslan custom. Ninian, would you like to lead a memorial or . . . "

"No, it should be you," Nicholas said, joining them and meeting her gaze. She hoped he could see by her expression how sorry she was for earlier. He nodded gently and reached down and took her hand.

"He's right," Ober said, placing a firm hand on her shoulder. "They need their leader."

Nodding slowly, she tried to hide how flustered she felt inside. Lead a funeral for five dead Tresslans? "Well, ok . . . " she said slowly. "What has been done with the dead?"

"They have been gathered, but some remains have been torn apart," Adam choked out softly, having joined their conference along with Jess only a few moments before.

"The idea is to burn them and purify them in the fire so their souls can be set free," Ninian said, gesturing with her delicate hands to the air and sky around them. Story envisioned the spirit of Kestrel racing along the wind on the back of her true love Lance, who would fly her up free as a bird into the sky, where they could always be together. Wiping away a tear that slipped from her eye, she looked at Ninian.

"Will you help me?"

Ninian smiled gently, her lightly lined face as lovely as ever, and nodded. "Of course. Perhaps music would be fitting?" she said and looked at Nicholas, who nodded tersely.

Story glanced curiously at Nicholas as he squatted down to open his mysterious pack. From within, he pulled out a violin that was polished to perfection and engraved with intricate lines and patterns. He ran his hands lovingly over the instrument, his hardened fingers delicately plucking a string. It reminded Story of how Faulks used to caress the stems of his plants, pouring life into them with just that one, earnest touch. She knew right away that like plants had been Faulks's passion, music was Nicholas's.

"I didn't know you played," Story said softly as she took in the beauty of the instrument.

Nicholas looked up and met her eyes with a half smile. "Now you know my secret; I'm a poet musician at heart, although you may be sorry to have found out after you've heard me play," he said.

Ninian laughed and nudged him, shaking her head with a smile and a good-natured roll of her eyes. "He's not usually this modest about his playing," she said dryly.

"Okay, so we have music." Story cast a sideways glance at Nicholas once more as he began to tune the instrument, his dark head bent in concentration. She wanted to brush back the shock of hair that fell over his forehead and obscured his studied expression from her view. "Any volunteers to run the funeral pyre?"

"We will," piped up Grady and Gordon. The two stocky fire trolls approached, their matching red beards sparking at the mention of fire. "Won't hurt us if we get too close to the flame," Gordon added, and caught a spark in his hand before it could leap onto Ninian's white riding outfit.

Story smiled gratefully at the two men. "Thank you."

"'Sides, Jasper sacrificed himself today to protect us, so we feel it's fitting we help our brother on his way," Grady said, brushing a tear away.

Story placed a hand on Gordon's shoulder before removing it very quickly. Ow, he was hot. She pressed her fingers to her lips and sucked on them, reminding herself to sleep near them on cold nights.

The two fire trolls nodded as if synchronized, sniffing and moving toward the spot near the fire where their friends' remain lay. Story was silent as the trolls clasped hands and nudged the fire higher with their elemental energy. When it was roaring, Story called the Tresslans to gather around her with Ninian by her side.

Taking a deep breath, she lifted her gaze from the brightly burning fire and met Ober's eyes. His deeply kind, silvery eyes glowed with his own grief, but she felt strength infuse her from his steady presence. He nodded at her to go on, and she sucked in a breath, trying to ignore the pain that had claimed her heart. What could she say? She was just a girl barely out of her teens, and yet she felt as if the expectation lay heavy on her shoulders to help them move on, to say goodbye. But she had one thing on her side. She knew death. She'd lost Faulks, lost her uncle Peter before she was even born and seen how his disappearance had weighed on her mother, and she'd lost her sister today. So she grieved with the rest of them, and that she could hang on to.

She looked out on the crowd and saw the way they looked at her, as if she truly was their leader, as if she was their hope. She felt shame they were even in this predicament. If she'd only kept Racell by her side . . . But she couldn't think of that now. Jemma, a thin-looking withered woman, had lost her only child today, but Story only saw love and forgiveness in her dark eyes. Jemma nodded at her, the baby now sleeping against his grandmother's chest, quiet and snuggled safe.

Although she was horrible at public speaking and hated giving presentations, Story sucked in her grief and let it flow off her tongue as an accompaniment to the crowd's mourning.

"When I was a little girl, I wanted to be just like Kestrel, my big sister. The cool thing about Kessie was she wasn't my blood sister, so it's almost as if we got to pick each other, pick our own sisters. She grew up strong, and one day the royal Pegasus showed themselves to us and called her Queen. They told her she was needed for a task, and in that task she was told she needed to protect me . . . " Story paused for a moment, feeling nausea rise from her grief, but Adam, suddenly by her side, rested a hand against her back as if supporting her against a strong wind. Nicholas's steady dark gaze met hers from where he sat with his fiddle. She knew she could go on.

"I don't agree, or believe that my life is worth any more than Kessie's, but she took that task to heart and spent the next half of her life becoming a warrior and protecting me as well as Tressla's wild places. And in the end, she saved my life. I . . . I only wish I could have saved hers. We have all lost today—family, friends . . . parents." She glanced again at the sleeping form of Robin and took a shaky breath before turning back to the people.

She almost expected them to hate her. She hadn't been ready for the onslaught of the Wolves' attack. Although the guilt weighed heavily on her, the dark part of her whispered that she didn't owe anyone anything. Pushing back the troubling thoughts, she continued looking into the crowd of open, but sorrowful faces. "We grieve for them all, our brave warriors," she said glancing at Ninian, who took her hand and spoke.

"I believe I speak for Ober and Landria and Ophelia when I say that Kestrel and Lance would have wished to die in no other way than as warriors fighting for a brighter future. And I think we can agree that everyone who died here today was fighting for that same thing. As Story said, they were brave. But they were also something else. They were believers," Ninian said in her vibrant, yet elegantly lilting voice.

Story glanced at her in surprise, seeing Ninian's pale features set, strong within the glow of the firelight jumping on her face. "They believed that they were fighting for something greater, that they were fighting to restore the First Dreamer to her rightful role, to bring down Brink, and to restore our land to freedom."

Gordon nodded, his beard like a living flame on his face. "Ay, Jasper convinced Grady and I to join him. His family had been killed by the Wolves when he was just a young troll, and he lived for the day when The Dreamer would come and dream a lovelier existence."

Sylvaine had lost her brother, and her sorrow had been deep, but now she looked up. "As Elves, we are privy to the lands of dreams in a way that most are not. We have an affinity with sleep, as some wayward humans may have learned," she said in her proud voice, a mild smile lighting up her usually solemn face. "The moment Sylvester saw her, he said he knew. He could feel that she was the one, and he was determined to serve her until the very end. I am ashamed now that I was the one who doubted. But I doubt no longer. My brother died for the First Dreamer and I will too if The Green decides it to be so."

Stunned, Story watched as one after the other spoke of their loved one's devotion to her, and her guilt nearly overwhelmed her. Who was she to have such loyalty? It was her fault they were all here in the first place, according to Brink. She had split the world apart in her grief so long ago, and she had ripped all hopes and dreams from someone, a truly horrific action.

She wanted to deny their devotion and cry at them to leave her be, to let her just be a young twenty-year-old girl with her own hopes and dreams to . . . She stopped her train of thought, perplexed. What dreams did she have? To be an artist? She liked to paint, and she was good at it, so she'd thought she could be an art teacher—maybe sell a few pieces in her lifetime. But she'd never had any great aspirations. Fall in love? Yeah, sure, but her heart had never been in it until Nicholas. Then what? What did she, Story Sparks hope for? She wanted vengeance for Kestrel, yes. She wanted to take Brink down, yes. She wanted to . . . She wanted to love Nicholas, she thought, turning her gaze to him. Her heart thumped in her chest, and she knew she was following it despite her better sense. But there was more. She'd never had purpose until now.

Ober stepped up and smiled sadly, his great presence soothing and awe-inspiring at the same time. The great Pegasus king. His giant wings were folded around him like a cloak. Landria stood beside him, her small hand held within his massive one. His voice was as melodic as the first time Story heard it, and it was heavy with the wisdom of eons.

"When Story first came to us years ago, it wasn't hard to believe that such a self-possessed and strong-willed child would one day be known as the First Dreamer. From the moment Kestrel took her rightful place as heir to the Seven Forests, she knew that one day she would die in the service of our land. And she was aware that service would be protecting Story, who is precious to us and our people. But she lived life, easily winning Lance's heart, who also knew that one day he too would sacrifice himself for something much greater. They were brave, they were dedicated, but they were also doing what they had been raised to do—fight in the name of the First Dreamer and the true Tressla. So let us not grieve but celebrate our fine warriors' lives, and the service they gave, and the faith they had, which has made us only stronger to face the darkest of our foes." Ober finished to silence. Turning to Story, he kissed her brow. "Do not let your guilt and insecurity shame their sacrifice," he whispered before stepping away.

Nodding, she wiped tears away from her cheeks and gathered herself before speaking lest she start sobbing uncontrollably. "We have all lost a lot, but none so much as the ones who lost their lives. So, as Ober said, let's celebrate their lives. But first, we'll say goodbye."

Turning to Grady and Gordon, she nodded. The two men picked up the first of the still bodies, which were now nothing but empty shells, and cast it into the fire. It burned brighter than any fire Story had ever seen, bigger than any crazy bonfire party she had ever attended. But the fire's heat didn't bother her. She stood close by the troll brothers as they cast off their friends into the freedom of the flames. The light soothed her aching soul and kept the darkness at bay.

Turning to Nicholas, she nodded at him and he picked his fiddle up. Resting it expertly under his chin, he began to play. Most bowed their heads, while others like the elven and trolls watched their brethren's last journey into the flames. But from the first note struck, Story was rapt, her attention fully on Nicholas.

The music he wove was like nothing else she had ever heard. It flooded her soul as if it were rain cleansing the land. The firelight lit up his face, and Story studied the planes of his features, the depth and width of his dark eyes. His brow was high, accented by two dark slashes that arched so perfectly she would have thought he plucked them if she didn't know better. His jaw was strong and angular under the shadow of a beard. When he crooned sad words into the night, shock rippled through her. She felt as if she were seeing him for the first time . . . in centuries. Yes, she knew him.

"And tonight we lift up our eyes to the stars above, and we thank them for their lives, which go on and on and on," Nicholas sang. The connection, when it came, would have brought her to her knees if it weren't for Elliott's sudden appearance by her side.

"Story, you don't look so good," he whispered.

"I feel great," she said with a hysterical giggle, feeling her legs almost give out beneath her. Frowning in the glow of the fire, Elliott directed her to a nearby boulder. He watched her warily, obviously a bit taken aback at her laughter. They were, after all, having a funeral for their dead.

Story leaned forward and watched Nicholas, unable to take her eyes from him, hungry for the feel of him, crazy to taste his lips. She felt slightly unhinged, and she wondered for a moment if she was just going crazy. But she knew. Deep within, a memory had stirred, and she grasped it now, loving the feeling of the knowingness that spread through her. The realization brought her fragmented personality together for one moment. She felt the heady effect of bliss lacing her blood like an aphrodisiac. She didn't want to look away, she didn't want to . . . blink. Story gasped in protest as Nicholas disappeared from her view. Her eyes flew around her. She was no longer in the Rood by the fire, but in a barren room with a bed and bars on the windows. She'd been there before.

Darting toward the door, she went to bang on it, but her hand passed right through. Panic started to creep into her chest, and she was about to scream when a female voice spoke from behind. "You came back, I see. Come to keep your promise?"

Turning, Story's eyes widened. The girl's hair was stringier and more unkempt than the last time she'd seen her. She was paler if that was possible, and she had dark smudges under her eyes. "I don't even know what promise I'm supposed to keep," she whispered, backing up without looking where she was going and catching her foot on something. Trying to grab onto anything so she didn't fall, she suddenly felt arms around her. Her eyes flew open, and she was looking up into Elliott's concerned gaze.

"Story?" he asked, brow arched high.

Looking wildly about, Story pushed herself to her feet with Elliott's assistance and glanced over to where Nicholas was still singing softly in the night.

She looked away, still trying to get her footing after the transition and turned to Elliott, confused. "How long was I gone?"

"Gone?" he asked, his brows arched even higher if possible. "You didn't go anywhere, not physically anyway. But your expression seemed vacant." Shaking her head, Story sat down, trembling again and trying to make sense of what happened. Actually, adding some sense to the whole night would be nice.

"What happened, Story?" Elliott asked, kneeling beside her.

Glancing at him she shook her head. "I'm not sure. I was here, and I was listening to Nicholas. And then this knowledge—this intense feeling of wholeness came over me, and I felt like everything was okay with me, like I was finally myself, but a self I'd never been before. Then, suddenly I was in a room. I've been there before, just not like this . . . " she trailed off, remembering the headache the girl had given her before and the promise she'd made to fix her—them? Yeah, way to go making promises to a dream girl when she wasn't even sure what she'd promised. It had to be her subconscious trying to tell her something, she reasoned to herself. Or her Spirit? No, that wasn't possible. This girl seemed alive—in her dreams, anyway.

"Been where before, Story?"

"The institution," she said so softly she wasn't sure he heard her, but when she sneaked a glance up at him, he was regarding her with a look that told her he thought she might actually need an institution. "I'm not crazy, Elliott. There's a girl in an institution and she looks like me, and she keeps coming to me in my dreams. Or maybe she is me—I don't know. But there's more. When I heard Nicholas play, I think I unlocked a memory of some sort. It's not like a visual, but I know who he is," she whispered fiercely, glancing around to make sure no one overheard, but everyone else was intent on their farewells and Nicholas's beautiful playing.

"Who?" Elliott said, frowning and searching Story's face.

"Nicholas," she answered passionately.

"Brink's son?" Elliott asked, confused.

Shaking her head, Story laughed softly. "No, he's the Fiddler. The one The Dreamer loved. The one I love," she whispered. "For a moment, I felt her, The Dreamer. And she was me, and I was her. And we were one."

"But you are The Dreamer," Elliott argued.

Shaking her head again, Story looked at him intently, feeling the gravity of her voice as she spoke. "I'm not, Elliott. I feel it."

"But you just said Nicholas was the Fiddler. You'd have to be The Dreamer then to even understand that." He dragged a hand over one eye and down his face as if the exhaustion and the complexity of their current lives was taking its toll. His strong jawline was covered in a beard when he was usually clean cut, and she noticed that his familiar light-hearted quips were rarer. A pang tugged at her heart, but she knew she couldn't change things—nor would she have wanted to. She only wished her friends didn't have to suffer in the process.

"I mean, yes, a part of me is her," she answered. "I believe that—boy, do I believe that," she emphasized to a curious look from Elliott. Not wanting to go there, she rushed on, "But I don't think I can fix everything they want me to fix. I mean, after I deal with Brink, it's like they expect me to fix their world, our world . . . My worlds," she smiled fleetingly. "But I'm not right. I don't know what's wrong with me, but I feel it in my whole being that I'm not right. And I don't think I'll be able to live up to their Dreamer until I'm the me I'm supposed to be. Does that make sense?" She glanced at Nicholas longingly, the soothing sound of his music like a balm on her tired soul. "Maya said . . . she said in the valley that she thought I was missing my Spirit . . . What if she's right? I think she is."

Elliott crouched down so he was level with her, a sparkle of the old, romantic Elliott back in his eye as he took her hands in his. "If that's true, then we'll find it. And you do know one thing. You and Nicholas are like soul mates. You can't fight it anymore. Some part of you, or I guess all of you, loved him at the beginning of the world. And you love him again. It's destiny," he finished with a longing-filled sigh. Story smiled in response, glad to see their journey hadn't jaded him beyond redemption. Of course, she also couldn't fight the light that filled her at the mention of Nicholas.

"Elliott, about earlier . . ." she said after a moment, realizing an apology was overdue. But he stopped her with a gentle smile and shook his head.

"I wish I could have saved her too," he said.

Story smiled tremulously and nodded. Although she'd never been quite so horrid to him before, their tiffs usually ended soon after they had begun and were quickly forgotten. She was grateful Elliott was so forgiving now. It was more than she deserved.

The song ended, and the fire burned brighter than she thought possible. Nicholas came over and clasped her hand, and she felt the connection between them grow even stronger. She met his soft smile with one of her own. Adam and Jess stood close by, and she reached out her hand to Adam, mouthing, "I'm sorry" to him. He nodded in response, his friendly eyes telling her all was forgiven, and took her hand as well. From his other side, Jess met Story's eyes with a wink, and she winked back. Bliss flitted over and landed on her shoulder. Turning to the blaze, Story lifted her eyes to the sky and thought for perhaps a moment she saw Kestrel's shape emerge from the flames, bright and new, riding on Lance's back and laughing into the night as they disappeared above them.

"Tonight we say goodbye. Tomorrow we head to the holding of Morgana and Guinevere, who Grady and Gordon said will welcome us," Story announced. There were mutters of surprise, and then the sound of a cork releasing as the revelry began—the celebration of life lived and of life past.

She brushed an errant tear from her cheek and turned towards Nicholas, uncharacteristically falling into his arms and pressing her lips to his warm cheek. The fire would burn all night, as would she.

CHAPTER THIRTY-NINE

Racell's Rood, Tressla

STORY AWOKE WITH A START, shuddering from a chill caused by the absence of the fire's blaze. Blinking her eyes, she slowly sat up, warily taking in her surroundings. She was in a room, but not the institution. Slowly turning her head, she combed fingers through her curly waves and rubbed her eyes. How the hell did she get here? She remembered falling asleep after many hours of muted celebration and tales and songs of their deceased friends. Nicholas had been by her side as she had drifted to sleep.

There were no windows in the room, merely stone walls and another bed. The only light flickered from a number of torches hanging around the circular tower.

"Finally," came a familiar voice from behind her. Story quickly swiveled to the source of the sound and narrowed her eyes as she peered into the dark corner, where a figure emerged. "I've been waiting long enough for you to get here."

"Wha . . . ?" Story started to say when the woman came into view. Gasping, she looked up into a face that could have been her twin, aside from eyes like charcoal and hair to match. "Who . . . Who are you?"

"Seriously?" The girl asked with a roll of her eyes and a toss of her hair that was much more unruly than Story's normally was. "I'm you of course. Your darker aspect, you could say. And we need to talk. This fighting me every step of the way is so not going to work." The dark girl, draped in a black robe, paced and knocked on the wall. "See? No windows. How am I supposed to see out and know when you need me if there are no windows?"

Story gaped at her for several moments. "I don't understand, how are there two of me? How am I here? Could you catch me up on that first?"

Sighing, her darker self smiled, and Story imagined it looked a tad bit more sinister than her own. "You're dreaming, dear. No need to worry, our body is safe at rest right now, snuggled in our love bug's arms. Where you are is inside your consciousness. Here's the story, Story." She stopped and laughed to herself as if she'd said something terribly clever, and then went on. "When you called the Nightmares, you set me free. I'm a part of you, always have been. But I've remained—untapped, you could say. I'm the part of you that cursed the bastard who killed Nicholas so many years ago. Since I was set free, I decided to name myself. You can call me Senka."

Seeing there was no door to escape through, Story quietly seethed from the bed she sat on. "Well, if that's the case, I don't want any part of you. What you did was horrible. I would never do that now that you're not a part of me. And as for the Nightmares, you can have them. I'll find other ways to save Tressla from Brink."

Senka merely smiled thinly, crossing her arms over her chest. "I'm the strong part of us, Story. Do you really think you can win this war without me? At one time we were unified, we worked as one."

"Yeah, and look where that got everyone," Story shot back, feeling heat rise to her cheeks. "Now we're on a quest in a magical land for The Will's sake instead of worrying about what bar will let us in with our fake I.D. Now I know I partially grew up here, and I am going to save Tressla if I can, but it's your fault we're here in the first place."

"My fault?" Senka scoffed. "Wake up and smell the reality, Story. It's Brink's fault, the one who killed Nicholas. If he hadn't destroyed our heart, no one would be here in the first place. How can you hope to defeat such an unrepentant foe, huh? Ages have gone by and he doesn't care what he did," she said, walking slowly toward Story until she was just a foot away.

Story shook her head and put her hands over her ears. "No, I won't listen," she yelled, feeling rage creep into her and knowing the girl was feeding it to her. Just as she felt her anger might burst from her in a tidal wave of hatred and anguish, she shoved the girl back. And screamed, feeling herself tumble backwards as the dream fell apart. As sleep overtook her, she heard her own voice follow her, demanding she take the wall down. But Story envisioned a tower thick with walls and vines, making it stronger.

CHAPTER FORTY

Forest of Sylum, Tressla

AS THEY STARTED OUT the next morning, the procession of Story's followers was surprisingly quiet—especially with the likes of their growing population of trolls, who usually bickered amongst themselves, given their elemental opposition. Grief still hung thick over the followers, despite the quiet celebration of lives that had taken place the night before. Even Robin was quiet, cradled against Jemma's chest.

They were headed due north toward Morgana's and Guinevere's Holding. It was close enough to The Capital that they could get there within a few hours if needed, but also secure enough to keep them safe from the Wolves while they figured out their next move. As least, that's what Story's plan was. Gordon had mentioned that the legendary women might be able to help, and that they had been secretly building their own army for the better part of ten years.

Story rode atop one of the few horses they had picked up along the way, despite her protests that she could walk. She could have opened a portal and walked them all through it to the foot of the holding, but she begged exhaustion, claiming that doing so would sap her of strength. In truth, she couldn't stand the thought of using any of her powers and letting Senka take over once again. She shuddered, remembering the darkness that overwhelmed her only the day before.

Story had been up late, although she hadn't been doing what she wanted to do—which was get Nicholas alone. Story felt her face color as she pushed torrid thoughts away. And then the dream. She had woken up to find Nicholas staring down at her, his dark eyes concerned. Story admitted to herself that despite her worries, waking up to him had sent a thrill through her. Everything about Nicholas caused her sensors to go off. But when he had asked what was wrong, she hadn't been able to tell him. She wanted to, but she could feel the darkness hovering in the back of her mind, and it scared her in a way that she wasn't willing to share. Not yet anyway.

Instead, she had smiled and brushed his concerns aside, playing up her reputation for being self-possessed to the best of her abilities. She was so good at it, she found she was disappointed that he believed her so readily. They were ancient soul mates—shouldn't he know when she was lying?

"Story!" Blinking, Story turned to look at Elliott, who rode next to her. He had managed to finagle himself a horse by claiming to be The Dreamer's personal seer. Story and Adam had nearly choked on their own laughter, but she wasn't going to deny him this. He had followed her loyally to this world and stayed by her side even when she had acted like a shit. Besides, he really hated walking. And the outdoors. Plus, his little Elven boy toy had flitted back to Maya's Valley, claiming visitors were in need of a guide.

"What?" she offered mildly, trying to find Nicholas's back, which she'd been staring at for the last hour, only to have him disappear the moment she took her eyes off of him. The part of her that remembered his soul didn't want to risk losing him again. How many lifetimes had her soul come back looking for his? She had a feeling it had been many.

"I was saying that Bliss has been acting strangely lately. Like last night, she didn't so much as snarl at Adam when he batted at her like she was a fly."

Story nodded to Jess and Adam. "It doesn't take a genius to figure it out." The two lovebirds were walking so close their shoulders brushed while hands lingered, fingers just barely touching. Frowning, Elliott glanced at them and shot Story a look of confusion.

Rolling her eyes with a playful grin, she said, "I might be in the market for a new seer."

Shooting her a look of pure fury, Elliott looked back at the two, taking in how Bliss flew along behind them with a scowl twisting her little rosebud mouth. Elliott's heavy, dark brows shot up into his hairline. "Seriously? She's like as big as my hand. How could that ever work?"

Shrugging, Story slid her fingers through the horse's silky mane, trying to imagine falling in love with a man who was a horse fifty percent of the time. At the thought, Kestrel's face surfaced in her mind, but she shook it away, reminding herself of the free spirit Kestrel had hopefully become.

"The heart wants what the heart wants, right? I hardly think sanity has anything to do with it . . ." Her voice tapered off as she said the sentence again in her mind, something clicking away behind the veil of her consciousness. "Sanity," she whispered.

"What?"

Turning toward Elliott, all thoughts of tragic love triangles vanished from her mind. "Sanity, something to do with sanity right? My dream girl was in a mental institution. There were bars on the windows, and I remember thinking it was strange that it was so sparse."

"But she's not real, right?"

"I don't know . . . I mean, she feels so real. She certainly acts crazy." My spirit, she thought. The more she played with the idea, the more she thought she was on to something. But despite her feelings, she also knew it was pointless. Where was she going to find a random girl who lived in a mental institution, a girl she'd only ever met in her dreams?

It was late in the day when Jess pulled herself away from Adam long enough to sidle up to Story, who decided she needed to stretch her legs. Story tried giving Tuscan to Jess, but she just scoffed at the idea. Instead, a crone had taken the perch, causing Story to wonder when she had joined them and why the old woman hadn't been given a horse to begin with. The old woman had the whitest hair that spilled down her slightly hunched back like soft snow, and the softest, wrinkly-looking skin. It made Story want to run her hand down the old woman's cheek like most women wanted to caress babies. Damned Fairytale magic.

Frowning slightly, she turned to Jess, who had dirt smudging the curve of her high cheekbone. Her fitted pants were stained from traveling and her red curls hair looked more unruly than usual. But none of that marred her natural beauty nor touched the happy glow she radiated as she laughed at something Adam said. Story smiled tiredly. It was nice to see two of her friends so happy. It was a simple relationship, one that wasn't tainted with ancient curses and forgotten promises.

"Hey Jess," Story murmured as her friend joined her. Man, she was thankful that Sandeen had the foresight to give her such nice walking shoes. She didn't have a single blister and those shoes had seen a lot of miles.

"Story!"

"Huh?" She looked up from where she had been staring at her shoes.

"Where did you go? Thinking of something deep?" Adam asked.

"Shoes," Story responded through gritted teeth while silently saying goodbye to heels for a long time.

"Trust a woman," she heard him say from behind them.

"Never underestimate the power of a good pair of shoes," Elliott responded in her defense.

Feeling in good spirits for the first time, well, since Kestrel died, Story arched her brows at Jess and nodded. "The man is right. When we get through all of this, I'm taking you for a holiday to our side, where you will meet the finer side of shoes, namely Christian Louboutin, Jimmy Choo and Marc Jacobs."

"You name your shoes after men?" Jess asked in confusion.

Laughing, Story slipped her arm through Jess's and nodded. "Just wait till you meet the boys."

Jess shrugged. "Sure, why not. But first we have to save the shoes of the world from Brink's plan of ultimate destruction."

"He has a plan for ultimate destruction?" Elliott asked from beside them, where he still rode astride a tall brown gelding that had been brought to their army by a Fairytale Extra.

"Well, I'm just assuming," Jess said with a roll of her eyes.

"You assume rightfully I'm sure," Story nodded resolutely and dropped her arm. "So what's up? I'm sure you didn't tear yourself away from your lover's arms to talk shoes with your best gal pal."

"You always talk so funny," Jess responded with affection. "But that's not the reason. You were saying we need more fighters to help us against the large pack of Big Bads and whatever Brink throws at us. And now, well, without Kestrel and Lance, we're significantly weaker."

Story nodded, keeping her face composed. "Yes, I was hoping when we got to Morgana's and Guinevere's they would have enough fighters to sustain us."

"Yeah, but what we need are some fighters who know how to take down a Wolf. I know three. Last I knew, they were hanging out in Sherwood, which isn't too far from here. If you'll give your permission, I'll ride ahead to the town and recruit them to our cause. They love to take down Wolves, trust me."

"If you're going to get the Pigs, you'll need backup. They're not to be trifled with," came a new voice to their discussion. Story glanced over at Darvish, who was staying out of Wolf form at the moment so as not to frighten the rest of their growing procession. Jess instantly went from friendly to on-guard. Her hackles rose and she narrowed her eyes at the green-eyed Big Bad who wasn't all that bad.

"What would you know of it?"

Darvish smiled his easy, toothy grin, reminding Story that he was a formidable opponent and a well-won ally.

"Enough." Turning to Story, he bowed his head in respect. "If you'll allow me, I would accompany Jess."

Story could see Jess screwing up her face to protest, her eyes almost going as red as her hair. But Story stopped her with a dark look.

Turning back to Darvish, Story shook her head. "I'm sorry, Darvish, but we need you here. Letting both you and Jess go would put us all at risk since you two are our strongest fighters against the Wolves."

"Well, that's not entirely true, Story. You're our strongest fighter—you have the Nightmares at your beck and call," Elliott added from above.

"It's true." Darvish looked at Story seriously. "You are the strongest."

Story felt panic rise at the thought of calling the Nightmares to her. Because it would release *her*, who Story had built a ten-foot wall around. She could almost hear the echo of her laughter reverberate in the back of her head. No, she couldn't release her. She didn't know what would happen to her if she did. She might lose herself. Forever. "No," Story said harshly—too harshly. Even Nicholas heard and glanced back at her, his brows rising in question. Story read the concern in his face, but she didn't respond. Feeling claustrophobic, Story pinched the bridge of her nose as a massive headache settled into her skull.

"Jess, you go. Take . . . "

"I'll go," Nicholas said, having walked back to join them when he saw Story looking distressed.

Story started to shake her head, but he cut her off. "You're going to see the Pigs, Jess?"

She nodded, her impassive expression barely managing to hide the glee from her eyes after Story had told Darvish no.

Turning to Story, Nicholas met her golden gaze with his black one. "I know them, Story. Not only that, but Jess and I have a good fighting chance together. Losing me from the group for a few hours won't leave you as vulnerable losing Darvish would."

"I don't want you to go, Nicholas," Story whispered, unable to communicate into words how the very thought of him being out of eye distance made her feel despair. She didn't care that her friends watched, she only cared about Nicholas in that moment.

Pausing in their march, he pulled her off the path and touched her face, tucking a strand of her hair behind her ear and smiling gently. "I will always come back to you, my love." And for a moment, Story could swear that he knew, that he remembered their legendary history together as she did. But it was gone before she could be sure. Leaning in, he brushed his lips against her own, causing that fluttery feeling to race in her throat and chest.

As they broke the kiss, she sighed, resigned. "Fine, but make it quick. Any sign of Wolves, and you ditch the mission and get back here as soon as possible." She met Jess's gaze and nodded.

"It's really close, Story. We'll be back before you know it with three warriors who are well worth the risk," Jess promised.

Glancing around the sun-dappled path they traveled on through the woods, she reached out and squeezed Nicolas's and Jess's hands. "I hope you're right."

CHAPTER FORTY-ONE

Morgana & Guinevere's Holding

THEY REACHED THE HOLDING by sundown, much to Story's relief. The thought of being out in the open with such a large number of people in their procession made her no less than terrified. A Big Bad attack in the absence of the Big Bad Wolf slayer would be disastrous. Plus, Story could not even fathom the idea of calling on her darker self. No sir, she liked her locked behind a big wall and in a metaphorical tower without windows.

The holding was just what she imagined. It was a fortress protected by high walls made of stone, and the only way to cross into it was to go over a bridge. Story wondered idly if there was a serpent in the moat as they drew the horses to a stop.

Her group stared in silence, many among them hopeful they would find peace within the solid walls. But Story knew that if Brink wanted in, nothing was going to keep him out for long. Story glanced over at Elliott, who was staring into the water that circled the fortress. Blinking, he looked over at Story. "You think there's a serpent in there?"

Grinning, she tossed back her head feeling like a wild warrior, like Jess. "I hope so." Glancing back at the people who had chosen to follow her, she started forward once more. But before they could pass the gate to go over the bridge, two miniature-sized men stepped out from what seemed like thin-air and clanged their spears together. Trolls.

"Who dares cross Morgana's Bridge?" they asked in unison. They were almost identical. Both wore grey tunics that did nothing to hide lithe muscles. While Gordon and Grady's beards were red, these two were clean-shaven, with pointy features that more resembled elves—if elves had been three feet shorter. Their eyes were steel grey and both had bushy, silvery blue eyebrows. Their long blue hair released steam every few seconds. Story smiled. They were water trolls.

"I do," she responded, lifting her chin and squaring her shoulders proudly. "The First Dreamer."

"You say that with conviction," noted one, whose voice was as light and silky as his hair looked.

Story noticed the speaker was a bit shorter than the other troll, and she nodded. "Should I not?"

"Well," amended the other one, who was not only taller but whose voice was even more lyrical if possible. "The First Dreamer is a large role to fill. Are you willing to take on the world?"

"I didn't know trolls were such riddlers," Story heard Adam mutter from behind. Hiding a smile, she met both trolls' gazes for a moment. "I am sure of who I am. And I am willing to take on this world and the next to right the wrongs from mistakes my past self made."

"Why have you come?"

"These people would ask for Morgana and Guinevere's protection. The Wolves attacked us and we lost some of our people. I won't let that happen again."

They studied her for a moment and then the taller one nodded. "Who will witness?"

Story opened her mouth to ask what they would need to witness when the fire troll brothers stepped forward and nodded at the water trolls.

"Wily, Dunker," Gordon nodded to them. The water trolls greeted them back and then waited.

"We will offer witness to her crossing."

"Very well," nodded the shorter one. Wily, Story thought.

Stepping back, the two trolls lowered their spears and stood motionless. Glancing at Gordon, Story raised her brows in question. *What the hell?*

"May we all cross then?"

"You first," Dunker said stoically.

Grady leaned forward and patted her back. "You must cross on your own and see if the river accepts you."

Bliss landed on her shoulder and tugged at her ear. "It is said that the river will eject anyone who claims to be someone they are not."

Story flexed her fingers and then clenched them against now-sweaty palms. What if the river didn't accept her? It would sense if she wasn't whole. What would happen if it ejected her? Story's heart picked up pace, and she felt her stomach drop with nerves, like it did when she had to give a presentation or take a big test. Except more was at stake here than a mere grade.

Deep in the back of her mind, she could feel the dark one moving around, and she knew that she was going to have to embrace that part of herself to some degree if she was to prove she was The Dreamer. She heard a cry of triumph as she lifted the wall enough so that she could feel Senka nearby, but she was damned well not going to let her take over again. Senka's victorious smile vanished when she realized she wasn't going anywhere at the moment and Story smiled. She was in control. Taking a deep breath, she nodded her thanks to Bliss, who flitted off her shoulder to land on Elliott's. Those two had become sudden friends recently, and Story was glad for it. She'd been so tied up with Nicholas and everything else going on, she had paid little attention to her oldest friend.

She glanced back at Adam, whose angular jaw, now covered with the start of a reddish blond beard, was tense. He was worried too. They'd always had a connection, and she could tell he sensed that all was not right in First Dreamer land. But he nodded to her, and the faith in his gray eyes gave her the strength to push forward. She would cross this bridge. She was the First Dreamer, even if she was possibly missing some parts.

Giving a short nod to the two water trolls, she placed one booted foot onto the wooden planks and then slowly, the other. Fully on the bridge, she nervously eyed the moat for any telltale signs of serpent. A tail? A wing? Despite her earlier bravado, she was quite sure that she didn't really want to meet a serpent, especially with so little separating her from it.

She was about halfway across when the murky depths of the water cleared up and instead became a swirling blue. Just when Story was sure a humongous serpent with blue and green scales was about to emerge, something glittering jumped from the water, arcing through the air and diving back down.

The golden creature was a blur as it swam about and arced through the air once more. It definitely wasn't a serpent. Instead, when it finally slowed down, Story could see it was a golden fish.

"Greetings, Dreamer," it said from the water below.

A talking fish? It sounded like a fairytale she'd read before. "Hello," she said, tentatively. Somehow talking to a fish seemed strange. But really, one of her best friends was a rose that became a fairy, and since she was a child she had been trained by flying horses that turned into men. And yet the talking fish suddenly made her think twice about all the seafood she'd eaten growing up. She was a sucker for some good salmon.

Shaking her head lest her thoughts leak out and anger the golden fish who had the power to expel her from the bridge, she turned her focus back to him.

"I am the spirit of the moat. Not my best gig, mind you, but it's something. I was once the golden fish of the entire sea. When I was upset, the sea would churn with me . . . "

From behind her, one of the water trolls cleared his throat.

Story nearly laughed aloud when the fish rolled his eyes. "Whatever, so here I am. Fish King of the moat. But it has its perks, namely getting to offer the First Dreamer a wish."

A wish? Story thought. "Like, anything?"

"Like anything," the fish echoed back with a chortle.

"Well, I . . . " she started, but then stopped to think. What would she wish for? She wanted to wish for Brink's demise, and to be able to hold back Senka, who hovered strong and dark on the edge of her consciousness. She wanted to wish for a safe return to her own world, especially for Adam and Elliott, who hadn't asked to get sucked into all of this. She wanted Faulks back, to tell him she was sorry for ultimately being the death of him. She wanted to go back and be the First Dreamer in the beginning and never make that awful curse to begin with. But most of all, she wanted to wish for Kestrel's life. She wanted Robin to grow up with a mother, and for her sister to laugh again and run through her forests. But she couldn't, and she knew that. To make a wish, any wish would be self-serving. And she'd certainly read enough stories about wishes.

"I would decline a wish," she answered, feeling the rightness of her choice as she said the words aloud.

The fish shook its head and jumped into the air sending a spray of mist, which she felt settle on her face and skin, easing the prickling heat. "Although an honorable choice, you must wish."

"Well then, I would wish for many things, but some would be wrong. The safety of my friends or the downfall of Brink would not be so bad of me, I don't think, but I ultimately have to make them happen myself. I think in the end I would wish for the confidence in myself to see this through, to be a better Dreamer and leader."

The fish seemed to contemplate her wish before nodding. "A noble wish indeed.

I will let you through, on one condition: when you get to The Capital, you free my mate from Brink's collection of pets."

"What does she look like?"

"You'll know her when you see her. She will be silver all over and have eyes like the deepest sea."

Nodding, Story promised she would.

"Then you may move forward as the proven First Dreamer, minus her Spirit."

Story started forward, and then stopped, realizing what he'd said. "Umm, what?"

"I said you may move forward as the First Dreamer."

"No, that last part about the spirit."

"Oh yes. Minus the Spirit."

"Minus my Spirit?" So it was true, she thought. She rubbed goose bumps on her arms, suddenly cold.

The golden fish dove down and back up in impatience. "Yes, that's what I said. Did you not know?"

"I only guessed," she said softly.

Swimming in circles, the fish suddenly stopped and slapped the water with his tail, sending more droplets through the air. "Well, now you know. I do not sense your spirit anywhere within you."

"Do you know where she is?"

Ninian, who had been standing beside her, looked at her oddly. "She?"

Story wasn't ready to share her theory, so she shrugged as if confused herself. The fading sunlight cast glaring lights off the fish's scales, blinding Story for a moment. When she looked back the fish looked sad, his great black eyes glistened more than usual. "Many stories begin with a dream, but it is rare when the dream is the story itself," he said before disappearing back into the water, the brilliantly blue depths turning murky once again.

"You knew this, Story?" Ninian asked, with an arch to a slender brow.

"Maya said something about the possibility," she murmured. Unwilling to say more, she avoided Ninian's gaze and took the last few steps to the other side.

"Could a talking fish be any more cryptic?" Elliott muttered as he joined her. Story didn't answer, the fish's words ringing like truth in her mind. She'd told Elliott only the other night that she knew she wasn't whole. And here was her proof. She truly didn't have a spirit. But how did one go about finding one's spirit—namely a girl in an institution? Her thoughts were cut off when the last person crossed the bridge. They were in the holding.

CHAPTER FORTY-TWO

Morgana & Guinevere's Holding

WHAT THEY FOUND when they arrived was like a small town. People littered dirt streets, some training in combat, while happy children laughed and played. In front of them lay a massive building of stone resembling a miniature castle. Within, Story imagined it could sleep every member of their rebel gathering.

"Well, I guess we try the door?" Story glanced at Bliss questioningly, who had floated back to her shoulder. After the fish was done with them, it seemed they weren't going to be getting any other tour guides. Bliss nodded helpfully, and Story stepped forward. But before she could lift her hand to knock, a short, well-dressed troll wearing spectacles and a look of disdain stopped her. An air troll, of course.

"Excuse me, but do you have an appointment?" he asked, taking his glasses and blowing softly, the dust lifting away as if by magic. He examined them for a moment and then slipped them back up the bridge of his thinly boned nose before looking at Story.

"An appointment?" she asked, confused and glancing at Ober and Ninian for help.

"You do know who these people are, right? King of the Pegasus? A Daughter of the Will?" Ninian asked.

"Yes, I am very aware of who they are, but that does not answer my question as to whether you have an appointment with the Ladies Morgana and Guinevere. They're, um, quite busy," he said, his cheeks coloring but doing nothing to mute the condescension that hung heavy in his voice.

"Well no, we don't have an appointment, but I'm sure . . . "

"No appointment, no entry," he sniffed.

"Well, they're certainly high and mighty these days," Landria said imperiously. "Turning away Pegasus royalty and a Daughter of the Will, not to mention the First Dreamer."

"Yes, well . . . " he began, but stopped mid-blow of his glasses. Sliding them quickly back on his nose, he leaned forward. "Did you say the First Dreamer?" His eyes grew wide as he really looked at the group for the first time.

"In the flesh," Elliott answered haughtily from beside Story, nodding his head toward her.

"Well, I would be remiss if I did not check with the ladies to see if they were interested in visitors. I'll just be right back." With that, he turned, fumbling with the door handle in his haste to get inside and shooting an apologetic look at Story, all disdain having disappeared from his face.

"That was so smooth, Lady Landria," Elliott said, putting his hand in the air for a high five.

Landria merely arched a delicately curved blue brow and awkwardly pressed her hand gently to his. "And you," she nodded with a smile.

"Don't worry, you'll get it at some point."

Elliott started to show Ophelia, who was much more interested in the Real World's bizarre rituals—that's how she'd said it, anyway—when the air troll returned, smiling apologetically.

"They would love to see you, but they thought you all might be more comfortable after you have washed up. We are preparing snacks and baths for as many as we can. If you don't mind, please follow me," he said, talking through his mouth in such a nasally way that Story was pretty sure he was trying not to breathe in their fumes.

Although she urgently wanted to see the two legendary women and find out if they knew anything about any weaknesses Brink might have, she hadn't bathed since swimming in the lake before Sandeen had dragged them down.

Despite the disrepair of the crumbling castle, the room Story was taken to was spacious and airy, and must have been one of the last rooms that remained intact. As they had walked through the upstairs hall, she'd noticed that in many areas the roof was completely gone as if it had just crumbled away one day, leaving a constant view of the sky.

But she paid no mind to any of that because standing in the middle of the room, filled with soapy water, was a basin. She barely had time to nod that she would call if she needed anything and close the door before she was undressed and in the tub. Ah, she would never take running water and daily baths for granted ever again. She slid into the bubbly goodness. Inside her mind Senka sighed as well, and she figured even the Dark Dreamer liked to be clean.

A short time later Story was dressed. Apparently, little elves called brownies lived within the castle and had managed to clean her outfit while she'd bathed. Story didn't really care how they did it, all she knew was that she felt like a new woman. She wished Nicholas could see her with her hair clean, although her curls had taken over. She glanced in the mirror and smiled at her reflection. The person reflected back smiled at the same time, but her smile was cruel, and her eyes were black, not gold. Crying out, she jumped back and almost toppled backwards over a stool behind her. At the last minute, she caught herself. Glancing into the mirror once more, she frowned. It was her again, but for a moment she had looked like . . . Senka. Shuddering, she checked the mental walls keeping her darker self in check, releasing some tension when she found them intact. She was still in control. Time to meet the ladies, she thought, glancing at herself once more and heading out the door.

As she came to the entryway, which must be where Guinevere and Morgana planned to receive them, Elliott, Adam, Bliss, Ninian, and Ober joined her. She glanced at them thankfully and then headed into what was probably once the throne room. But now it was . . . a garden? Story glanced around and felt a pang at the familiarity of the flowers blooming.

Like so much of the castle, the roof was gone and breezes swirled temperately through the room. Sunshine warmed the stone floor and cast natural light, reflecting through prisms of stained glass that adorned the intact windows and reminded Story of a church. The floor was a mix of stone and life. Through cracked pieces of floor sprung grass, flowers, and other such fauna that Story had only ever seen within Faulks's unique gardens so long ago.

The scents were overwhelming as flowers bloomed out of the very walls themselves in white, red, blue, green, yellow, orange, teal, magenta, any color imaginable. Flitting about were flower fairies tending to the gardens, singing songs, and stroking roots to grow. Story breathed in and her senses were assaulted. Tears sprung to her eyes when she found a garden of Thumbelinas, still small and quiet, not yet ready to be plucked and repotted for a little girl. All those years ago, she remembered Faulks painstakingly growing a Red Rose Thumbelina just for her, grumbling that if she were smart she'd have stuck with a Morning Glory Thumbelina. But she had insisted she be red. Despite a bad rep, not all Red Rose Thumbelinas took off and married fairy princes. In fact some became the best of friends. Story glanced at Bliss, who flew beside her. Meeting her longtime friend's large dewdrop eyes in understanding, Story smiled.

"Faulks would have loved it here," Bliss said softly.

"I agree, but that's not what I was thinking. I was thinking, 'Who would have thought a best friend could be grown?' But Faulks did just that when he grew you for me."

Blinking, Bliss shook her finger at Story. "Don't you dare make me look like a Briar Rose, all dramatic and sappy and full of themselves because Shakespeare wrote about them. I am a Red Rose, you hear me? I have a rep to protect. Do not make me run off with some damned prince. I really don't think I could stomach it."

Laughing, Story blinked back. "I love you too."

Bliss harrumphed and crossed her arms over her chest, but Story saw her glance out of the corner of her eye and smile softly.

"I see you like our garden," a husky, yet feminine voice said from behind her. Turning, Story met deep brown eyes that seeped with arcane knowledge, set in a face with plump, high-boned cheeks and a wide, full mouth that was smiling at Story. Her wild brown hair fell to her hips and was adorned with flowers woven into the curls. Her bare feet were soiled as if she walked often in the dirt, and she had an earthiness about her that reminded Story of The Green for a moment, but that's where the resemblance ended. She wore a shapeless yet attractive sort of dress and reminded Story of a seventies flower child. She expected the woman at any moment to hold up two fingers and say "Peace."

"Yes, it's very nice. It reminds me of the gardens my papa used to grow when I was a child. He was a Green Thumb," she offered.

"Oh? Who was your father?" she asked in such a laid back way that Story fully expected her to start crooning like Janis Joplin.

"His name was Faulks."

A wide smile curved her mouth and she nodded. "I knew him well, we were friends when we were younger. He actually tutored me for a while in the way of the Green Thumb."

"But weren't you too busy being a priestess and trying to take down King Arthur?" Elliott asked, although Story had no idea when he had joined their group.

A bubbly, girlish laugh joined them in the guise of a well-dressed blonde woman. Where Morgana was mellow and serene, this one was all golden and fused with energy. Her blonde hair had been carefully woven into a complex style of braids and curls, pinned and neatly coifed. The longest lashes fringed her bright blue eyes, and her tan cheeks were colored like roses. Whereas Morgana wore nothing on her feet, Guinevere's feet were adorned in matching slippers beneath a silvery gown fit for a medieval queen. She looked like a fairy-tale princess, except for a glint in her eye that told Story this princess was not to be trifled with.

"Fairytales live a long time, dear," Guinevere said in a high-pitched girly voice and knowingly smiled at Morgana, taking her hand. "Our lives are really much different from how they were written. Right, dear?" she asked, looking slightly up at Morgana, who was taller and more statuesque next to Guinevere's diminutive stature.

Curling her fingers around Guinevere's hand, Morgana turned toward the blonde beauty and smiled adoringly. "Much different," she replied and then leaned in and pressed her lips lovingly against hers.

"It might just be me, since I'm gay and my gaydar is pretty right on, but I'm going to say that in this story, there is no Lancelot," Elliott whispered in Story's ear, making her have to choke down the laughter all over again.

Pulling herself together, she silenced Elliott with a look. "Thank you for seeing us—we realize you only see people by appointment."

"Oh don't thank us. Gale is really just a bit of a ninny. He likes to act as if he's important by making it seem as if we are very busy. In truth, we're usually just in our gardens," replied Guinevere, lightly casting a secret, flirtatious smile toward Morgana, who returned her smile with a gentle one of her own.

"Actually, we are quite honored," Morgana said, meeting Story's gaze. "I never thought to lay my eyes on the First Dreamer. We owe our very existence to you. You are our creator. Our god."

"To deny you entry would be sacrilege," nodded Guinevere solemnly. One of her hands was now looped through Morgana's arm.

Story was taken aback. A god? Her? She couldn't wrap her head around the idea. Feeling Senka hovering in the background, she decided thinking too hard might not be a good idea.

Story shook her head, nervously tugging at her slightly damp hair that fell in loose curls to her shoulders. "I . . . I don't know what to say. I am no god. I'm just a girl."

Reaching out her hand, Morgana squeezed Story's out of sympathy or comfort, Story wasn't sure. "You're much more than that."

Later, they were sitting around a large, wooden, roughly hewn table. It looked like it had been a giant tree that had just been sawed in half. In fact, Story was pretty sure that's what it was. Morgana and Guinevere had graciously served them wine with some bread and cheese before they got down to business. Story had been reassured that the rest of her followers had found food and comfort within the broken castle's many rooms. Roofless or not, Story realized Morgana must have created a protective barrier around the castle so that none of the elements could get through unless she wanted them to. Even the temperature remained just right, despite the open sky over much of what remained.

"Although I cannot imagine a more exciting day than having the First Dreamer stay with us, how can we possibly help you?" Guinevere asked, sitting primly in her seat beside Morgana, who relaxed in more of a lounging position, her long tapered fingers wrapped around a mug, her fingers covered in silver and jeweled rings. In contrast, Guinevere wore no jewelry aside from a simple band that circled her right ring finger, and the pins that held her hair in its complex style.

Morgana nodded thoughtfully. "I too am perplexed. You have great power, how can we help you? And let me add that we will help you in any way we can if that is what you seek."

Story nodded gratefully, meeting Bliss's gaze before responding. "We're in need of protection to regroup. We were hit hard by the Wolves a day or so ago, and we have lost . . . a lot," she said softly, glancing at

Ober, Landria, and Ophelia, who had joined them for the discussion. Ober met her eyes and he smiled lightly in response, but sadness touched his warm expression. Story turned back to their hostesses and tried to shrug off the sorrow that weighed heavily on her heart.

"We're sorry to hear that," Guinevere's voice was heavy with compassion. A sudden melancholy had come to visit, leaving no one in the group untouched. "Yes, of course, you can stay here as long as you like. Morgana has created barriers around the holding so that no Wolves and no magic can get in. I believe even Brink would have a difficult time tearing down these walls."

Relieved, Story took a nervous sip of her wine and tried not to choke as the liquid burned all the way down. She instantly felt her cheeks flush, her skin grow warm, and the sadness lift just a little, but enough to keep the darkness away. She turned her focus back to the discussion at hand.

"Thank you," she said. "We have several friends who should be joining us at any moment. Could you please make sure they are allowed entry?"

Guinevere nodded. "Yes, of course. I will let Gale know at once." She rose from her chair and exited the room.

"I realize that you've had a rough time evading the Wolves, but you're the First Dreamer. You have powers, yes?" Morgana asked.

Story nodded stiffly, hearing Senka whisper to her about how powerful they could be together. "I can call the Nightmares, and I can open portals from this world to the next, but that's about all I've been able to accomplish." She didn't want to admit out loud that she would not be using any powers to call the Nightmares anytime soon. She didn't know how her portal opening powers would do anyone any good anyway, besides allowing them to move faster. Besides Brink, of course, who wanted to abuse that power.

A frown etched its way on Morgana's face, which was not altogether pretty as it was timeless. She could have been any age. She was both youthful and old at the same time.

"I'm not sure I understand," she said, and started to go on—but Story raised her hand and signaled for everyone to quiet. Elliott's face had gone blank, and she knew he was having a vision.

Adam, who was sitting beside her, nudged him. "Elliott?"

"Shhh," Story shushed Adam vehemently. "He's having a vision."

"He's a seer?" Morgana asked, her eyes widening in surprise.

"Yeah, I guess," Story responded distractedly.

It only lasted for a moment, but when Elliott returned to himself, he was a picture of fright. His face was pale and drawn, and his gaze instantaneously locked on to Story, horror erasing the blankness of his trance as if it had never been.

"Oh Story, I'm sorry," he whispered, just as the doors flew open and Guinevere returned, followed by Jess, two smaller men and one rather large, well-muscled woman who carried a spear. Story clenched her teeth. Jess's hair was more unruly than ever and her eyes were wide and harried.

"Are those the three little pigs?" Story heard Adam say, but chose to ignore him.

Story kicked her chair back and stood, meeting Jess's eyes. Her pulse hammered in her brain, while her throat was already thick with loss. "Nicholas?"

Shaking her head, Jess's usually grinning features crumbled. "I'm sorry, Story, they took him. They ambushed us on our way back and . . . We didn't stand a chance. They only wanted him. They gave us a message from Brink. He said if you want to see your Fiddler, you're to meet him at The Capital by dusk tomorrow or you'll lose him. Again."

"Again?" Ninian said sharply, turning to Story.

"Oh my," Guinevere whispered, Morgana beside her with an arm wrapped around her waist.

As if from a distance, Story heard Ober murmur softly to himself, "Again . . . Of course." Ninian quickly glanced over to Ober, who met her gaze and nodded.

"Story," Ninian said, starting over to her, but Story didn't hear her, nor did she care. All she could think about was Nicholas. He had died because of her once before. She couldn't let Brink's greed destroy their love again.

Blindly, she rose from her chair and without a word bolted from the room, running through crumbled passageways and hallways. Deep within her mind, Senka howled, tearing at the tower walls until her fingers bled. It filled her mind and merged with her own anguish. In this, their love for Nicholas, they were one.

Chapter Forty-Three

Morgana & Guinevere's Holding

WHEN NINIAN FOUND HER, Story was in her room, staring out through the cracked walls and gaping holes into what had become the first grace of nightfall. It came earlier than she liked. She had put Senka back in her place hours ago, but in those first moments of panic, she had felt so close to her as if they were one person. And of course they were—Story knew that. But she didn't like it. She didn't like to believe that she could ever be so dark.

She was curled up on the window seat, staring out into the twilight when Ninian knocked gently. "May I come in?"

Story nodded without looking at her, trying to peer out into the night and find him. She was The Dreamer, so shouldn't she be able to see? Morgana had called her a god for The Green's sake. She should be able to do something. Instead, she felt more helpless than ever.

Ninian's soft footsteps approached, and Story felt her gentle hand come to rest on her shoulder. "I never realized how strong love could be until I saw one of my dearest friends almost destroyed by it."

Slowly, Story turned toward her and met Ninian's quiet, crystal blue eyes curiously. "What happened?"

Sitting down beside Story, Ninian looked out into the darkening gloom before responding. "He died. He died before they could see their love blossom, before it could become what it should have been. She blocked the world out, almost allowed her son to be destroyed, but in the end, she came through the darkness and she stalled the ending." Turning toward Story, Ninian took her hand within her own. "I know in a sense you're much older than I am. You've been through this before and it has nearly destroyed us all. Love. It's just a word. But its essence is more powerful than anything. Use your love, Story. Use it to do what you need to do to see this through. But do it quickly because before you know it, it will be morning, my child," she finished with a wistful smile, remembering the girl Story had once been.

Tears flooded Story's eyes for the first time and she wiped them away. "The funny thing is, I don't feel like her. That Dreamer, the one who they say is like a god. I don't feel like that girl who cursed the world because her heart was torn to pieces. But I know I'm her, and I know Nicholas. I am in love with him and the love is so new. But it's old as well. We're connected, and I . . . " She swallowed the rising thickness in her throat, pausing for a moment to regain her composure. "I don't want to do something horrible if I lose him. Again. And I feel guilty for thinking that. But then, when I think of losing him, I feel myself go a little crazy . . . and I'm just scared, Ninian. What if I can't save him? What if I can't save anything, and I do it again, but this time I just destroy . . . everything?"

Gripping her hand hard, Ninian leaned forward and reached up to push Story's hair behind her ear, caressing her hand down her cheek. "You won't. I believe in you, Story. I believe in The Dreamer within."

Story nodded and tried to find some peace within Ninian's words. "Who was the friend you spoke of?"

"I believe it was me." Story and Ninian both turned toward the door, startled by the intruder's voice. In the doorway stood a woman with raven's wings for hair, it was so dark. She walked into the room without so much as an invitation and started towards Ninian, who looked surprised but not upset.

"Drianna," she whispered and met her embrace. "Sister," she amended, hugging her tightly. There was something so familiar about the woman. Perhaps it was her smile. It filled the room with light. It reminded her of . . .

"Story, this is Drianna," Ninian said. "This is Nicholas's mother."

That was it, she thought, looking to the woman once again. Initially she had looked so young, dark and haunted like Story's mother. But now that she was closer, Story could see the white in her dark hair and the crow's feet around her mouth and eyes—one brown the other blue—

making her wonder if her lines came from laughing or crying. Probably both. All the same, she was gorgeous in a dark, ravishing way. Story only wished she could look half as good as that at Drianna's age. She instantly felt guilty for having such mundane thoughts when the stake of her true love, and well, the world, was up to her.

Rising, she forced a smile. "Nicholas has mentioned you often," she said. Drianna turned from Ninian to look at her, so much that Story felt like she was being checked out by the most judgmental person someone could ever meet: a future mother-in-law.

But Drianna smiled instead and stepped forward, taking Story into her arms and stroking her hair. "Where is my son? I came here to meet him, but I haven't seen him."

Pulling back and glancing at Ninian quickly, Story uttered words that terrified her. "Brink has him. The Wolves ambushed them and took him."

Drianna visibly blanched, but she remained calm. "Don't worry, dear Dreamer, Brink will not kill my son. The prophecy says he is too important, and Brink wants to win."

"Yes, but do you realize who Nicholas is?"

"Yes, of course. He is my son," Drianna said with some confusion. "He is Brink's son."

"That wouldn't stop him from hurting him. But that's not what I'm talking about."

Ninian shot Story a look, and she backed off for a moment. But after a quick pause, she changed her mind and gave Ninian a look back that said if Ninian wasn't going to tell her, then she would.

When Story didn't let up, Ninian sighed and turned toward her friend, who bore an identical tattoo of a spider on her wrist, the symbol of a Daughter, one of The Will's priestesses. But these two had long ago forsaken The Will's unbending teachings. "Sister, what Story is trying to say is that Nicholas, well, he's special."

Impatiently, Story shook her head and smacked the wall with the palm of her hand. "What I'm trying to say is that Brink has killed Nicholas before, so what would stop him now?" She felt like banging her head against the wall.

Drianna looked mildly surprised, but remained calm, her brows merely etched in consternation. "What do you mean he's killed him before? Are you saying that . . . "

"I'm saying he's the Fiddler, the one the First Dreamer died for in the first place. The reason we're in this mess."

"But how can that be?" she whispered, her creamy skin turning as white as Sandeen's if it was possible. "And Brink knows this?"

Story turned toward her. "I don't know. Maybe not always, but I think he might now. But the prophecy says . . . "

"Forget the prophecy! I made it up, I made it all up," Drianna shouted, her desperation rising.

"You didn't make it up," Ninian said sharply.

Story looked between them, confused.

"She made a part of it up," Ninian explained gently, putting her arm around a now-distraught-looking Drianna. "To save Nicholas."

Turning toward them, her face in her hands, Drianna finally lifted her head. "Brink was going to kill him the moment he was born. So I made a prophecy that would prevent him from hurting him. I didn't know that my son was the Fiddler. But then again, all he's ever wanted to do was play that cursed fiddle. I had to make him a fighter. I made him who he is so that he could fight if he needed to." Shaking her head, Drianna seemed to come back to herself, and she turned to Story. "He will fight, I made sure of it. I made a warrior out of a gentle soul, and while I hate myself for it, I cannot be sorry that he is strong. But I am sorry that your once-pure Fiddler has known the blood of another."

Story was silent, looking out into the darkness that had come as suddenly as her heartbreak. There really was only one thing to do. Didn't all stories end this way? Turning toward the women, she first met calm blue eyes. Ninian had always steadied her, and she needed that. But when she looked into Drianna's challenging multi-colored gaze, she was spurned on. Lifting her chin, she felt Senka within her smile at her resolution. "If he wants me, he'll have me. It's time I paid Brink a visit in person."

"No, I must go, I'm Nicholas's mother. I'm Brink's wife. I can go in and out at ease," Drianna protested.

Story shook her head. "For all we know, Brink knows you're here now and has figured your part out in the making of the prophecy. He could hurt you—kill you. No, I will go," she said firmly, and neither woman argued. "But first, I have to sleep."

"Sleep!" Jess stalked into the room, her red hair very nearly sparking like the fire trolls' beards. "Story, you can't think to sleep at a time like this. We need to fight now!" she exclaimed, working herself into a frenzy. "We can't leave him there, we go now. The Wolves will eat him alive. Did he tell you there's one that has a vendetta against him?"

"Jess!" Ninian frowned at her, pale brows furrowing in a frown.

"It's okay, Ninian. I can handle it," Story murmured, raising a calming hand and meeting Jess's wild gaze.

"You would have me take on the Wolves when their powers are at their greatest, beneath the full moon?" Story asked softly.

Bewildered, Jess shook her head emphatically. "No . . . Well, I mean yes. We can't just sit here!"

Story reached out and grabbed the much taller girl's hands and looked up at her sympathetically. "You're not the only one who lost him, Jess. I'm the one in charge, and I let you go. I should have insisted you both stay with me, but I didn't."

"No, it's not your fault, Story," Jess said biting her lip and shaking her head again, red curls bouncing everywhere. "I'm Red Riding Hood! I should have been able to stop them. Instead I ran."

"You did what you had to, Jess. Listen to me. You are one of the bravest people I've ever met. You're a true warrior. You laugh when I'm hiding under the covers. I need that Jess. I need badass Jess. But I also need you to trust me. Because I have an idea."

Jess's eyes widened, and she nodded as Story directed the three women to take a seat. "Here's what I'm thinking . . . "

She talked for what seemed like the entire evening, but it really was only an hour of strategizing. Jess decided it would be best if she also got some rest to maintain her strength, and then it was time for Story to sleep. But she wasn't sure how much rest she was really going to get. Ninian followed Jess out with a quick kiss to Story's brow. "Sleep well, my dear," she murmured, and was gone.

That left Drianna and Story. "So you think I can do it?" Story asked as she slipped under the covers, almost crying over how soft the bed felt after she'd spent so many days sleeping on the hard ground and cold earth.

Drianna nodded, her creamy skin pale again, but she looked calm. "I haven't done what you've attempted to do, but I'm not the First

Dreamer. I have seen the future in my dreams before, and I know it is important to remember your purpose within a waking dream. Don't forget why you're there, and I have no doubt you'll find Nicholas—as long as he's sleeping, that is."

Nodding, Story nestled down further under the covers and sighed, wishing for a fleeting moment she was home in her own bed, and that Drianna was Edie telling her some story from one of her classes. Instead, she was here, with a thousand lifetimes of burdens on her shoulders. But Nicholas needed her. And she realized that despite the ache of homesickness, this is where she belonged. So many people wished they could change the world, but how many people could say they actually did it? She had a chance to make amends, and most of all, save Nicholas.

Glancing down at her hand, she stared at the ring Sandeen had given her. She'd told her it would keep her soul in her body while she was in Tressla. But to Dream Walk, Story was pretty sure she needed the freedom to leave her physical self. It seemed like ages since she'd emerged from Lake Sandeen, finding that Tressla felt brand new and like an old friend at the same time. She slipped the ring off and handed it to Drianna, who placed it on the vanity table before moving back to sit on the edge of the bed. She took one of Story's hands in her own and caressed her cheek softly. "Find my son, Story. I'll be right here if you need someone to pull you back into the light."

Her eyes were already nodding closed, and she yawned sleepily, feeling like a child for a moment, safe and warm. "Good," she answered sleepily. "She can't be allowed out."

Frowning, Drianna jiggled the hand she was holding. "Who, Story?" But Story was gone, and she had dreams waiting for her.

Chapter Forty-Four

Dreamside, Tressla

ALMOST AS SOON as she closed her eyes, she opened them. But she wasn't in Morgana and Guinevere's holding any longer. Blinking, she looked around and frowned. She was in that room again, the one with the crazy girl. Almost as soon as she thought it, there she was. The frail-looking creature stood by the barred window, her bony fingers splayed against the glass, looking chapped and worn.

Story hadn't kept her promise yet, and right now she needed to Dream Walk to get to Nicholas. She crept toward the door, hoping the girl wouldn't notice her this time and barrage her with more cryptic comments. How did she usually propel herself from this dream? Oh yeah, the insane girl usually started talking crazy. *Damn.*

"I know you're there," the girl said softly, not looking behind her. Story thought for a moment that she was mumbling to herself, but the girl finally turned and met Story's gaze. Stepping back, Story felt the cold, white wall greet her back, and that's where she stopped and stared. The girl's face was so like her own, just gaunter and more weathered.

"Who are you?" She knew, she just wanted to hear it.

"Do I have to tell you?"

"What is this?" she asked throwing her hands in the air in frustration. "How many parts of me are out there that I didn't know about?"

Wearing sweats that were too long and a long-sleeved shirt that hung on her like a sack, she moved closer to Story, her eyes widening. "I warned you about her. At least she's real. You did this to me you know. You condemned me to live this life. I should be going to school, hanging out with my friends. Instead I'm here, because of you."

Story would have backed up more if it was possible, but she had gone as far as she could go. "Maybe if I killed you here, I would be the one to wake up in your body, the Real Story," the girl said, a crazy light in her almost golden eyes.

Shaking her head, Story realized she wasn't scared of her, nor did she pity her. Instead, there was guilt. How horrible had her existence been? Story didn't know anything about who she really was or what this all meant, but she did know one thing. "I have to go. I have to find our love, the Fiddler." At the mention of Nicholas, all fury fled the girl's features, and what was left was a shell. Shoulders sagged and eyes drooped with the effect of the narcotics they must be feeding her.

"Yes," she whispered. "He matters most, you must go to him. Don't let anything happen to him again."

"I don't plan on it. But I promise you, I'll be back for you."

"You promise? You said you'd fix us. But you haven't yet."

The way the girl said the words made Story gasp. It sounded like what she'd heard from herself, talking on a tape recorder or home video—it was her own voice talking about fixing "them" as a collective. "You're my Spirit," she breathed, feeling the confirmation settle. It explained why she looked like her, why she kept coming back here, why she felt such guilt when she looked at her.

"I don't even know anymore, I've been here so long," the girl said forlornly, but her eyes brightened enough for Story to realize she knew more than she was saying.

"Try to remember. Do you know what state you're in?"

"I wish we all could be California girls . . . " she crooned with a crazed, half-lit smile.

"California?"

"You promise you'll be back?"

"I promise," Story whispered and reached for her, touching her hand to her cheek.

"I've been waiting so long," the girl murmured.

But Story wasn't listening anymore; she was focused on Nicholas. "Nicholas, Nicholas, Nicholas," she said aloud, imagining the smell of lemon-scented pine and wood that usually surrounded him. She could feel his strong arms around her, his lips insistently finding hers and molding with hers. She remembered the song he played, the one that made her realize the connection they shared from long ago. Oh Nicholas, please be sleeping, she thought as she closed her eyes.

When she opened them again she had left behind her insane self. Although despite her eccentricities and occasional inclination for violence, the crazy part of herself was easier to deal with than Senka, who remained looming in the back of her consciousness, threatening to take over. It was all very confusing, but she would have to figure it out later. Right now, it was Nicholas that mattered.

Grayness surrounded her, muting her vision. The air was soggy and cloying, and she knew if she hadn't been dreaming her hair would have been a frizzy mess. She was in a cell. What was it with her dreams? She kept finding bars.

Nicholas was there, huddled in a corner. She called his name before she could stop herself. His head jerked up from where he sat with his head bowed, and he opened his mouth and smiled, although it looked as if it cracked his face. "Story! Am I dreaming?"

"You are," she said quickly before running into his arms and clinging to him for a few moments. He felt so real. She inhaled lemon and pine, which pushed the gloom of their dream away.

"Is this what your cell looks like?"

He laughed half-heartedly and glanced around. "No, I think my dreaming self made it prettier. Honestly, you'd think I'd dream something better than this."

"I don't think you can," she whispered, her eyes darting around the cell from the tall ceilings to the dirt floor. Placing her hand against the bars, she felt a shock go through her, almost like electricity, as if the bars were trying to keep her within the cell walls now that she was here, locked inside of Nicholas's dreams.

Turning back to him, she caught his hand. "He knew I would come here, to your dreams. He spelled it so that when you dream, you can't leave. Even in your dreams you're a prisoner," she whispered. "What a bastard. And he meant for this to keep me in once I got here."

"Story, I'm sorry," Nicholas moaned, raking a hand through his hair.

"He can't keep me in," she said with uncharacteristic confidence and a grin. "I'm way too powerful for that." Just as she finished saying the words, she flung her arms to her sides, closed her eyes and dreamed the barrier away.

Nicholas's dark eyes widened slightly, his face an expression of disbelief. "Story?"

"You have no idea how powerful we are," she said, grinning.

"We?"

Story lost her smile almost instantly, and choked her words back down before shooting Nicholas a furtive glance. "I meant I," she covered quickly. Senka lifted her head and laughed, the richness of her throaty chuckle reverberating off her soul.

"Okay, well, can you get me out of here?"

Turning to him, she shook her head sadly, despite the fact that Senka was trying to beat back the new walls Story had erected. "We're only in our dream bodies, but don't worry. I have a plan."

"Story, you can't even think to come here in your physical form."

She crossed to him in a matter of seconds and took his hands, feeling the callused fingertips, a fiddler's fingers, and stared up at him fiercely. "You can't even think I would leave you here with that murderer."

"He's my father, Story. He won't kill me."

"Why not? He did it before," she said without thinking.

Nicholas's tan brow wrinkled in confusion. "What?"

Shaking her head, she lovingly tucked back a strand of his dark hair behind his ear. "It doesn't matter. What matters is that you listen to me. It's going to go down like this . . . "

"It's crazy, and I don't like it," he said a brief time later. "Is there any other way? One that preferably keeps you as far away from my father as possible?"

She smiled faintly and shook her head. "Nicholas, I have to go soon, I might wake up at any instant and I'm . . . " But it was Nicholas who faded first.

"What's happening?" he asked anxiously.

"You're waking up."

Growling as if he was more beast than man, Nicholas stalked to where she stood, paused from a half hour of pacing, and pulled her to his body. Pressing himself against her, his lips found hers and devoured her so that she was left breathless—if a dream version of herself even needed oxygen, she thought. One moment he was there about to ravish her, and the next moment he was a ghost. "I love you," he whispered, and then he blinked out.

Standing in the empty cell of his dreams, she fought back tears. If she started crying now, she might never stop, and she had someone else's dreams to visit before the night was done. "I love you too," she said quietly before closing her eyes and bringing another face to her mind. This time she only had to think of Brink's name, and she was transported to another gray world.

Unlike her own recent dreams, which were impossibly vivid with color and action, his were dank, gloomy and devoid of color. Nothing was happening. She was in a wasteland of death and absolute solitude. A cold breeze whipped about, and she rubbed her hands over her bare arms. She appeared in his dream as she looked in reality, wearing a nightgown Morgana and Guinevere had provided her. Shivering, she peered around the desolation, looking up into a colorless sky. It was like watching the beginning of *The Wizard of Oz*. She kept expecting the world to burst open with color and sound. But it was a muted dullness. Even the breeze was silent.

"So you came to haunt my dreams, did you?"

Story jumped, turning to see Brink, who was as colorless as the rest of this dream world. "You plan to kill me here I suppose? You could, you know. You're the First Dreamer and in dreams you are a god."

"Funny, you're the second person today to tell me how god-like I am and yet I don't feel much like one," she answered honestly. He laughed in response, his face almost handsome if it weren't for the cruel sparkle of his black eyes and the bitter turn of his mouth.

Spreading his arms out, he gestured to the scenery as if it were a forest of lush vegetation that surrounded them instead. "You made this especially for me," he said with narrowed eyes. For the first time, Story realized what was bothering her about him. He was wearing a suit. Not a medieval suit of arms or the medieval-punk style that passed for clothing around this place, but a Versace suit. It fit him perfectly, sharp and clean. She recognized the designer only because Elliott had stood outside the store many times in New York, ogling the men's wear and praying he would have enough money to afford such high fashion someday.

Frowning, she opened her mouth to question him about the suit when she realized what he had said. "I'm sorry, what did you say?"

"Oh no need to apologize," he answered, his voice laden with sarcasm. His dark eyes, so like Nicholas's, had a gleam that Story thought could be amusement. Not a good sign. She needed to regain the upper hand.

But she was thrown off guard when he somberly replied, "This is my punishment for so long ago killing your love. This dream world, it's all I ever see when I close my mind. No wishes, no hopes, and no dreams—isn't that what you decreed? I sit here in this bland world every night, and no dreams come. I would even welcome a nightmare," he finished through gritted teeth. "Can you imagine this for your entire life? No? Then imagine this for thousands of lifetimes, for that's how long I've had to endure this prison you created for me."

"I see I didn't destroy your ability to whine. A pity," Story quipped back, hiding behind her own version of sarcasm while trying to push the heavy sense of regret and responsibility from overburdening her. She needed to be strong.

Her response did nothing to calm his furor, his eyes growing wide with a crazy glint reserved for the worst kind of villain. Realizing that she would need to settle him down if she wanted to do what she came here for, she held her hand up to stop his tirade. The most he could do was give her a piece of his mind since she ruled the dream world, so her interruption only received a snippy, "What?"

"If I could, I would restore your ability to dream. Although I can't remember taking it away, I know it wasn't right."

"Can't? Or won't? I know you're scared. Scared I'll destroy your true love once again, and you're not wrong." He stared her down, a smile curving his lips so slowly and smugly, she realized too late he'd had the power all along.

Shaking her head, Story realized the dream was spinning way out of control. "No, I can't do it, I honestly would if I could."

"Lies," he said without a hint of fear in his tone, nor a wrinkle in his expression to connote anxiety. He was a mask of calm, a righteous villain who knew when he had won. "And you'll pay with your lover's life once again if you don't do exactly as I say. You will come to me tomorrow and surrender yourself to me to do as I please, and Nicholas can go. If you don't, he's dead."

"But he's your son," she heard herself plea, the gray world and the depth of Brink's hopelessness crushing her.

"He's his mother's son," he smirked. "She doesn't think I know, but I know. All I had to do was hear him play, and I could see the soul of the thief who stole my birthright. But I'd never heard him play until the other night in the wood for your little funeral. Oh yes, I was there. With Racell gone, I was able to observe your little gathering. When I heard him play, I knew."

Story swallowed her grief and narrowed her eyes. "He stole from you? Now I can see there is just no reasoning with you, Brink. You're insane. And this prison," she said gesturing around her, "you did to yourself when you killed a man because of greed."

"My, aren't we bold to say such things when I hold the key to your precious Fiddler's life."

Paling, Story stepped back and remembered herself. "I'll see you tomorrow."

His smile, when it came, was slow and lascivious, more malicious than even Nigel's had been. "I'll be counting on it. And then things will really change."

He didn't merely want to use her. He wanted revenge. She could feel the hatred seep from him, making his dream world even bleaker. She closed her eyes and wished herself away from the dream that had become a nightmare. She thought to wake herself up, but a dreamless sleep called to her weary and broken soul. And so she slept.

CHAPTER FORTY-FIVE

Morgana & Guinevere's Holding

"SHHH, SHE'S STILL SLEEPING," someone whispered. Well, it was too loud to actually qualify as a whisper, but Story was willing to give him a B for effort. She peeked through a slitted eye.

"Maybe she was before you walked in here talking like you're at a rock concert." That was Adam. He had undeniable snark.

"What's a rock concert?" She could see Jess was rummaging through her closet and eyeing the dresses Guinevere had given her, not that she'd ever wear them.

"Hush, all three of you are going to wake her up!" Bliss chastised, accidentally sweeping back the drapes with her wings so that the sun rushed in. It was odd, given sunlight already bounced around the room from the holes in the ceiling and walls. She could feel the sun from the window, but not from the gaps. Must be part of the charm Morgana had put on the castle.

Sighing, Story opened her eyes fully and tried to move her tired limbs from the cloud of the bed that embraced her drained self. "Any chance of me sleeping disappeared the moment the four of you decided to storm my bedroom."

Sitting up, she ran a hand through her tangled hair and smiled at her four best friends circling her bed. Not many people could say they had one true friend, and she had four. Now if she could only bring Brink down, rescue her boyfriend and save the world from annihilation, she could color herself complete.

"Hey guys," her voice still croaky from sleep. "How many hours until dusk?"

"Six or seven," Jess answered.

"That's it?" Rubbing the last bit of sleep from her eyes, she jumped out of bed, wincing at the way her muscles protested. She must have worn herself out jumping through dreams like that last night. Brink's dream especially wore her down, she thought, remembering the starkness of the landscape.

"I need to get dressed now. I have to get over there, I have to save Nicholas," she said, running to the closet and pulling at clothes that Jess had only moments before been admiring. She fingered dress after dress until she finally found a dark pair of riding pants and a matching tunic.

"This place would do good to be merged with its counterpart, where jeans and sweatshirts would make a nice alternative," she murmured. She found a black shirt and slipped behind the dressing screen, where she began to change.

"Okay folks, what's the story? Why did you storm my room?"

"Well, we were hoping you had come up with some sort of plan of attack," Adam admitted quietly.

"If it makes you feel any better, I've seen several futures where you win," Elliott chimed in helpfully.

Popping her head up, Story wrenched the shirt over her head. "Several?"

"Well, yes. And if you must insist, several where you don't win," he continued cheerfully as if not winning was merely a silly notion.

"What happens in the futures where I do win?"

Elliott shook his head, looking distressed, his forced brightness fading. "I don't know. There's just something different about you . . . You didn't look like yourself. You look like more." He was obviously struggling with his words.

"Yeah, well," Story stepped out from behind the screen and spotted a pair of tall, black boots. "I am more. I have a Red Riding Hood on my side—and a Red Rose Thumbelina, a psychic, a nature nut, and a gang of Fairytales. I think we can win." When Elliott arched his brow and made a face as if he didn't believe her, she ignored him and turned to the others.

"Come on, Elliott, bring back Mr. Sunshine. I'll tell you my idea, but it requires you all to trust me."

"I don't like it." Adam's sentiments echoed Nicholas's from her dream the night before. Adam, however, had voiced his dislike for her plan so many times throughout the day, he had begun to resemble a broken record. Only he was more obnoxious because he kept insisting he come with her.

"I need the element of surprise. He knows I'm coming, but he expects me to ride with my warriors and rush the Wolves. If I can get into the castle before the fighting starts, I might be able to at least get Nicholas out before Brink can use him as leverage against me. The moment we show up there waging war, he's going to do something awful . . . And besides, I won't be alone." She glanced at Jess, who met her eyes and nodded. Gone was the girl who had been admiring dresses earlier that day. The warrior was present, and she was ready to play, her silvery blue eyes flashing like lightning.

"What? Jess is going with you?"

"As am I." Darvish stepped forward, his dark, taut muscles rippling beneath his short-sleeved tunic. Jess was tall for a woman, but he dwarfed her. The Wolf and the Wolf killer, Story mused, admiring the way the two complimented each other, although she didn't miss the roll of Jess's eyes.

"I don't think I ever realized what a delicious monster he is," Elliott murmured in her ear, causing her to almost snort the water she was drinking out of her nose. "Alas, he has destiny written all over him."

Story merely arched her brows in response, but he knew what she was asking. Smiling knowingly, he shook his head. If he knew, he wasn't telling. Tressla had only proven to make Elliott an uber-psychic, one who saw the future around every corner.

"Listen, Adam. Jess, and Darvish can help dispatch guards within the castle, and they will be leading the fight within, so I need them on the front line to formulate an attack."

"I would do fine by myself, Story. I don't need a Wolf." Jess gritted her teeth and crossed her arms across her chest, her red hair rippling like she had bathed in fire. Story once asked her why she didn't pin her hair back when she fought, and Jess had grinned. *I look fiercer this way*, she had told her. And indeed she did, as if she were made of fire that had been set free.

Story pretended not to hear her. "And they know how to get us into the building. Besides, you won't be far behind. I just need some time to myself. Drianna gave me a spell to shield my entrance into The Capital in case he has it booby trapped, and I'll bet he will."

Adam sighed. He was unhappy that not only was his new girlfriend heading into danger, so was his best friend. Grabbing Story's hand, he locked gazes with her intently. "Just promise me that if it gets bad in there, you'll like teleport yourself out or whatever."

Story smiled gently up into his fixed stare and squeezed his hand before pulling back. "I'll do what I can." She wasn't going to promise him anything because when it came down to it, there was no way she was going to leave Nicholas in there alone. Turning to Elliott, she hugged him briefly.

"Make sure to fill in Guinevere and Morgana as soon as we're gone. And Adam, Bliss, get our troops underway the moment we're through that door. I can't bring everyone through the portal with me, so I'm counting on you guys to hustle. Dave, the air troll, can control the breezes to some degree so that you won't be heard marching in, and he'll try to keep your scent from hitting the Wolves before you're there. And you might not need to fight. If I can get the fiddle, I can maybe bargain with Brink.

"You ready?" She looked at Jess and Darvish, who begrudgingly stepped forward next to each other. They both nodded at Story, though Jess stonily refused to meet Darvish's amused glance.

Turning, she met Adam's eyes one last time and then, putting her finger out, traced a doorway in the air, imagining the room where Brink had kept his instruments. Adjusting the vision in her mind's eye, she made sure they would end up just outside in the hallway in case Brink was in his music room. Gesturing for the two to go through, she watched them disappear into what appeared to be a void, and then stepped through herself, blinking out of existence so that all who was left were Bliss, Adam, and Elliott, unlikely warriors put in charge to lead a hodge-podge of an army.

As soon as Story stepped out of the void and into the shadowy hallway, she knew there was trouble. A guard—not a Wolf, she was relieved to see—had been turning the corner when Jess and Darvish appeared. By the time Story even turned to help, Darvish had disarmed him and knocked him out cold. Glancing at Jess, Story raised her brows. "See, useful."

Crossing her arms under her breast, Jess pouted. "As if I couldn't have taken care of him? Please, I'm saving myself for the real danger."

Throwing her arms up in mock defeat, Story turned to the door.

"She just can't admit that I'm quicker and stronger," Darvish lifted his easy grin condescendingly, casting Story a wink. Stifling a smile, she put her ear to the door, listening.

"Oh, when this is all over I'll show you who your master is, and you'll obey me like a good doggy," Jess hissed.

Darvish's quiet but deep and hearty chuckle came from behind Story, and she knew Jess was probably seething. He was one of those people you just liked to hear laugh. It lightened an otherwise serious situation.

"Let me try," he nodded at Story. Shrugging, she stepped back. He probably had more practice than she did anyway, as she had zero experience with breaking and entering. Wrapping his large, dark hand around the door handle, he snapped it down. Despite the fact that the door now seemed very much unlocked, when he pushed, nothing happened.

"It may be ensorcelled." He gave her a sympathetic look and ran a hand over his shiny head as if brushing away an imaginary pelt of hair.

Sighing in frustration, she kicked the door and it flew open. Eyes wide, she glanced at Darvish in surprise. Wasting no time, she started to step in, very aware that at any moment one of Brink's henchmen could come moseying around the corner. But Darvish stopped her before she could go any further. "Let me. He could have set traps."

Story started to object, but he stopped her by putting a strong hand on her shoulder and squeezing while drawing her into his liquid green eyes. "You are important. I am not."

"You don't have to tell us that," Jess snidely interjected in the background.

Darvish just ignored her and kept peering intently at Story. "You're The Dreamer."

Shaking her head, Story put her hand against his stubbly cheek and smiled up at him. "You have proven that chivalry really isn't dead like they always say, but you can't go. If it's ensorcelled, you will be in danger, while I believe I'll be fine. I've been here before."

He looked as if he was about to argue, but Story pushed him and gave Jess an urgent look. "We don't have much time. Go, you know what you have to do." Quietly stepping inside, she waited for something to happen, but nothing did, so she closed the door behind her.

The room looked much the same as it had when she had been thrown through dreamtime by the Nightmares. It was like a shrine to all that was musical. There were beautiful, ornate golden harps and wooden guitars carved with intricate designs. Silver flutes, pianos, drums, banjos, and jewel-encrusted maracas. She saw the violin she had asked Brink to play during their first encounter, the beautiful one he had said belonged to his mother. But seeing it a second time, she knew it wasn't the right one and scanned the room for the other one. When she spotted it she saw that it was resting gently on its side atop a high table, the bow lay next to it as if it had been recently played. It was unremarkable. A plain, unvarnished wood surface that was cracked and peeled. The strings were torn and the tuners broken. From the snippets she'd heard over the last several days, she expected it to be cared for, loved. It was rumored to have been created from the tree of a dryad, who gave its life for the creation of the exquisite music the fiddle would make. If it held any of Brink's powers, she would have thought it would look . . . better.

Furtively glancing over her shoulder, she threw open trunks and looked under tables cloaked with long sheets, unconvinced that the remaining violin could in fact be *the* fiddle. Finally, she sat down on the floor and put her head in her hands. She still hadn't saved Nicholas, and now her one and only plan had backfired on her. Where could the fiddle be? Dust covered her chestnut curls and colored her black attire gray. How could she save the world when she couldn't even find one stupid fiddle? He'd probably hidden it somewhere else. She felt defeat hover nearby.

Sneezing, she wracked her brain in the middle of Brink's floor. She closed her eyes and pressed her hand against them so that she saw spots behind her lids. That's when things got hazy and pictures began to dance like a movie. First she saw faces, and then it was as if she herself was actually there.

She was in a clearing next to Nicholas. Except it wasn't. This man looked like Nicholas, but his face was more open, free of worry and sorrow. His eyes were dark and intense as always, yet weightless and bright as if he had yet to know pain. But it was the same soul that shone from the depth of his gaze. This was her original Fiddler.

She could smell the freshness of a new day and feel the dew beneath her knees as she crouched in the bushes, staring at the man who would become Nicholas. He was beautiful, and her breath caught in her throat as she gazed at his strong, angular jaw and the muscles rippling under his flawless skin. She could see why her previous self had fallen for him. Watching him made her ache for her own Nicholas, and when he pulled out a fiddle, her heart fluttered.

The instrument looked old and worn, and it was made from wood that looked cracked from wear. Narrowing her eyes, she leaned in closer. My god, she thought, it's the one in Brink's music chamber. It can't be . . .

When he put the fiddle to his chin and pressed the bow to the strings, the sweetest music she had ever heard poured out of it, filling the air like magic. Upon the first note, the violin transformed from a worn instrument destined for the scrap pile to a thing of wonder. A golden sheen erased the wear from the instrument so that it shined anew, the strings and the grains in the wood glittering gold. The song he played filled the grove so that even the trees stopped their swaying to listen. Held rapt, she couldn't move as he raised his voice to meet the music, soothing the insecurities and rage that simmered within her. She felt present and stable. Comforted while aching to touch him. When he was done, nearby animals remained silent in awe. Everything looked greener, newer, and more right.

Remembering herself, she realized she had to get back to the chamber now that she knew where the fiddle was, but she paused when a girl stepped out of the trees and headed toward the Fiddler as if in a trance. Story was shocked when she saw the girl's face, because it was almost a replica of her own. While she was getting mighty sick of seeing girls with her face, she realized more rationally that this was The Dreamer. Envy filled her. The Dreamer's step was light and graceful, and her hair was strangely tri-colored, gold, black and brown, hanging to her waist. But it was her face and eyes that got to Story the most. Her eyes were the same honey gold as Story's, but there was a completeness and rightness about her that Story felt she lacked. She was serene and obviously in love, whereas serenity and love had never gone hand-in-hand for Story, who now constantly felt the burden of being this legendary being. She didn't stick around long enough to see what would happen—the memory had returned magically as if it had always been there.

Closing her eyes, she pictured herself back in Brink's chamber. She didn't even question how she had blitzed through time; she hadn't put her ring back on that morning for a reason. She knew only that she needed to get the fiddle and get to Nicholas. When she opened her eyes, she was back, sitting in the same position in the middle of the floor, cloaked in dust. But this time, she had company.

"Dreamer, I see you've come at last."

Damn. Blinking, she took in her surroundings and met Brink's cruel, dark eyes. She saw the fiddle master in him, the one who killed her true love. He smiled slowly, and gestured to the two Wolves standing by his side. "I hope you don't mind, but I have other things to attend to before you and I can get down to business so . . . "

She was up and running, jumping for the fiddle before he was done with his sentence. If she could get it, he wouldn't be able to use it against them. But before she could wrap her fingers around it, a Wolf man grabbed her leaping form with one well-muscled arm and dragged her up and away.

Clucking his tongue, Brink smiled. "Now, now, all in good time," he said, glancing to the Wolves to give them a directive. "Throw her in with lover boy, so she can feel what she'll be missing if she refuses to help me."

The Wolves nodded and dragged her from the room. As she looked back at him, he almost smiled at her sympathetically. "So sorry your plan didn't work. Now you'll have to do things my way."

"She's where?" Ninian exploded, pacing the room where Morgana and Guinevere sat on their respective thrones, both looking equally stricken.

"That was a very foolish thing for her to do," Ober agreed more calmly. "She's the world's only hope, and Brink has impressive resources at his disposal."

Their reactions were making Adam increasingly anxious and angry at himself for going along with the whole thing in the first place. He glanced over at Elliott and Bliss and met their worried expressions.

"Yes, I can't imagine what she was thinking, going in there alone," Guinevere said. "His greatest goal has always been to use The Dreamer to his own devices." She nervously smoothed her hands over her already perfect updo. "If he uses Story to unite the worlds, our people, the Fairytale race, will cease to exist."

"But she plans on grabbing the fiddle, and if she gets that, she'll be okay. It's the source of his power," Elliott spoke rapidly as if to reassure himself.

"Who told you that?" Drianna lifted her head, shaking away whatever thoughts she'd been lost in.

"Well, Ninian did, I think," he glanced over at Ninian, who nodded.

"Is there something you know that we don't?" Ninian asked, a frown marring her elegant features. "It was you who said he coveted it, that it held great power."

"Well, yes . . . The fiddle is his means to an end, but it is not the source of his power. The magic he has is stolen power. But the fiddle, well, it's his connection to a time when the worlds were one. If anything, the fiddle is a danger to Story."

"You could have given Story a heads up, maybe let her know what she was getting into," Adam interrupted angrily.

Ninian started to open her mouth again, but Morgana held up her hand. "Let's hear Drianna out. We must remember that her son is in grave danger and Story is trying to save him. I am sure she bears Story no ill will," she pointedly looked at Drianna with slender arched brows. The power that existed between the two of them crackled in the air.

Drianna ignored the look and nodded her thanks. "First, let me tell you the legend of the fiddle. Not many truly know the entire story. It's a sacred object of power in this world and once belonged to the original Fiddler."

The Golden Fiddle

Legend has it that a king commissioned its making. He was a good king. But like all kings, he had lovers. When he met his wife and married her, he swore off all other women forever, and this angered one lover particularly—a powerful witch. In a fit of rage, she put his wife under a sleeping curse. But all curses must have a way to be broken. Knowing how much he and his wife loved music, she made it so that only the purest music played by the purest heart would break the curse.

Heartbroken, he sent out word, and soon every musician in the kingdom had gathered to play. But no one could break the curse, no matter how beautifully they played. Only one musician, a fiddler, struck the king as being particularly talented and particularly pure. So it was he that the king chose to go find a perfect fiddle to play.

The young fiddler searched high and low, for he truly wished to save the queen for the king. Being a musician and poet, he appreciated true love and wanted to help in any way he could. But no matter where he searched, no instrument would do. This one was out of tune, that one pure of sound but cracked. They were all imperfect. Merely a boy at the time, he began to despair as a year passed and then another.

He was barely a man when he decided if he could not find a perfect instrument, he must make one. So he went deep into the forest and visited every tree, praying to The Green to show him a tree that would do. Every night at the end of the day, he would sit down and play his own fiddle, a nice enough instrument, but not truly pure. Despite this, he played like an angel, and even if he did not know it at first, he had an audience.

When she eventually showed herself to him, he found her more beautiful than anyone he'd ever seen. Her eyes were leaf green, and her hair was a soft, silvery blonde. She fell in love with him, and he lay with her, entranced by her pure, seductive beauty.

He loved her in his own way, but he was bereft at the thought of returning to the king and telling him he had failed, so pure was his heart. And because she loved him and could not stand to see his tears, she gave him a gift.

After lying with him one night, she took his hand and led him through the trees, her long hair trailing in the dirt behind her, practically a part of the earth. He followed her, believing he would follow her anywhere, his heart was becoming so full with her.

Finally, they came to a tree. Kissing him, she promised him this tree was pure, that it would make the most beautiful music and would surely wake the queen.

He asked her how she knew. She merely replied that it was a tree made of magic and love, and surely that was pure.

They slept by the base of the tree that night, and when he awoke she was gone, like she always was. He only ever saw her by night, but he was so trusting, he never asked where she went.

That morning he set to chopping the tree down, and as he did so, his heart felt heavy. When the tree was felled, he caressed its bark and indeed felt that it was a magic tree, worthy to make the perfect fiddle.

He was the son of a fiddle maker, a great one at that, and so he set to carving the wood into an instrument that would be pure. It was glorious, with a golden sheen that clung to the strings and bark. But he didn't want to play it until he was in front of the king, and so he waited until nightfall to ask his love to accompany him on his travels. When she didn't come that night, he worried but thought something may have simply kept her. So he waited another night. By the seventh day, he was sure she hadn't really loved him, and he headed back to the castle heartbroken. Not even the thought of waking the queen and restoring true love could make him feel better.

When he reached the castle, he quietly found the king had aged during the few years the fiddler had been gone. But the king was overjoyed to see the fiddler, and his entire face lit up when the fiddler told him his story.

When the fiddler took the instrument out of his bag, the king delighted at the sight of it, for it was a thing of beauty. With a heavy heart, the fiddler sat down and for the first time touched his bow to the strings, and then he began to play a slow lament to his lost love. At first, the fiddler merely looked sad, but within a few moments tears streamed down his face. Those who were present that day, including the king, thought he wept out of happiness because after a few strokes of the strings, the queen began to stretch and yawn and finally opened her eyes. The kingdom rejoiced, and the king made him the royal fiddler, bestowing upon him the title and gift of his very own perfect fiddle. No one knew the reason he wept that day. But while everyone else heard music, he heard his true love singing to him with every note, telling him she loved him and that her gift to him was perfect music. And that's when he knew she hadn't been a woman at all, but a tree dryad who had sacrificed her life to him out of the purity of her love, so that he might fulfill his quest. Every time he played the fiddle thereafter, he would weep, for her voice was always singing that he was her truest love.

Years passed, and the fiddler married. There came a time when he put the fiddle away, although he never forgot his love nor the sacrifice she made for him and for the true love of his king and queen.

He eventually had a son, and when his son grew up to be pure of heart with the soul of a fiddler, he bestowed upon him the most perfect fiddle that was ever made. By the time he gave it to him, it wasn't as shiny and lovely as it had once been. It had been worn through time, but when the fiddler's son played the instrument, it would light up and become the beautiful instrument it had once been. And the fiddler was happy to see that when his son played, he was lit from within. He also noticed that it intensified his son's talent, making him an even better fiddler, perfecting previous flaws in his playing . . .

"His son, as it turned out, was the Fiddler we now know to be the true love of The Dreamer. The power of the fiddle, which had been made in perfection to break a curse, has been said to have healing properties to fix that which is imperfect or broken," Drianna finished softly.

Everyone was quiet for a few moments, stewing on the story. Finally, Ninian shook her head. "Yes, but that doesn't explain how Brink plans to use the fiddle and Story to unite the worlds."

"Ah yes, sorry, I sometimes get lost in that story. It's so sad, true love and all that," Drianna said with a glisten in her eyes. "You see, the magic of the fiddle lies in its ability to perfect flaws, having been created to be perfect itself. And dryads are nature spirits with healing energy. So if someone who was sick were to play it, it could potentially heal them."

"So, it may not be the source of his power, but it's like an amplifier," Elliott spoke up excitedly.

Adam felt hope and relief wash over him. If she got the fiddle, it really would help. But Drianna was shaking her head. "That fiddle doesn't work for him, it never has. He doesn't have any talent, and he's too broken to fix—he has no harmony or melody left within him. But mostly, his heart is impure. Remember, only that which has a pure heart can use the magic within. I only recently learned that he is the original Master Fiddler."

"How is that even possible?" Landria asked, her amethyst eyes disbelieving. "He is only a human with borrowed power. Not a god, not an Original Mythic, nor even a demi-god like Racell."

"No, but he was cursed by The Dreamer back when time was younger, and she stole his dreams and hopes and any chance for peace in the afterlife. So he lives on. I swear I did not know it until only a day ago when it came to me in a dream. He has lived a long life without love," Drianna said almost sadly, a touch of compassion lighting her multi-colored eyes before it drained away and she hardened. "But he has done much wrong. Sandeen and I believe Brink wants to get Story to play the fiddle, then her power will be funneled through the instrument, which will try to fix what is broken: the worlds. My husband wants to bring the end of life as we know it. The end of Fairytales."

"My god, if she's got the fiddle, we could all die." Adam exploded, banging his fist against the stone wall without so much as a cringe. "She thought it was his source of power."

"In a sense, it is Brink's power. If she were to destroy it, it would destroy everything he has been working toward these many thousand years. She's his only chance to regain his dreams and to eliminate Fairytales as they exist with us now."

"Did you put this in her head, Drianna?" Ninian narrowed her eyes.

"I told her where he was weak, and she made her own decisions." Drianna didn't lift her gaze away from Ninian's, as if refusing to show guilt.

"And I guess it never occurred to you that maybe you could have told her this entire story about how it's useless to him unless she's using it. No, you're just worried about your precious Nicholas, so no one else matters," Adam spit out, grinding his teeth so that his jaw looked as if it might pop out from under his skin. "If she destroys it, he could still kill her. He'll still have his power, and it seems to me he might be motivated by more than just power. Revenge, anyone? She took away his hope."

Snapping, Drianna's glittering gaze fell on Adam. "She was already going after the fiddle. Your seer spoke of it before I even said a word. I am a seer. I knew that if the fiddle was destroyed, it would cost him personally, but I had no knowledge of what would happen if she were to play it—not until this afternoon when I had a vision, and by then Story was already gone. And she was already aware of Brink's true identity," she finished tiredly, pinching the bridge of her nose as if in pain. Glancing up, she met Bliss's gaze. "You know she means more to me than just serving as Nicholas's savior."

Bliss held her gaze for a moment and then reluctantly sighed and nodded as if to herself. Then Drianna pinned Ninian with a look.

"I believe Drianna is telling us the truth," Bliss said. "I think we need to stop fighting and instead gather what forces we have and go. She's counting on us no matter what happens, and I'm not planning on letting her down," Bliss urged.

Adam's jaw still twitched, but he nodded and stood. "Everyone is ready outside. We need to go now—I don't know how much time we've wasted already."

Standing, Morgana smiled ferociously. "Happy endings, friends. That's our belief and our rule. Let's see it done." Guinevere rose next to her and slipped her hand into Morgana's, nodding resolutely.

"Whatever resources we have here are yours, but let's get to Story as soon as possible. I'd like to see that scoundrel's face when he realizes it's not only Story he has to contend with, but a legendary queen, her witch consort, two seers, Daughters of the Will, outlanders, a ferociously loyal Thumbelina Rose, and an army of Fairytales wanting to claim their land back." Several chuckles followed Guinevere's uncharacteristic outburst, her delicate features set in grim determination. Morgana wrapped an arm around her and gave her a gentle squeeze, her gaze lit with love.

"Are you in?" Ninian asked Drianna.

Looking hurt, Drianna nodded. "I'm sad you have to even ask. Not only is my son at stake, but my way of life and my land. Whether you believe it or not, Ninian, I was chosen to lead and I intend to do just that once he and his rule are disposed of. I want this to be a good place, one where Fairytales live in peace. After all, my son is practically a legend himself. I may have kept from Story that the fiddle wasn't as integral to Brink's power as she thought, but that's only because she needed something to grasp onto, something solid she could fight with. I saw that in her eyes last night. And if she is able to destroy it, it will hurt him. Only when she thinks she's strong do I see her truly embracing herself or her powers," Drianna said with conviction.

Ninian nodded, forgiving her friend for her secrets. After all, the two of them had kept many secrets from everyone else, and they knew Sandeen was keeping even more. Drianna looped her arm through her friend's, and the two priestesses hurried from the room to join the army already gathering outside. Adam had given the word hours ago for their weapons and any available horses to be ready and waiting.

He now turned to Bliss, and before she could fly out of the room, plucked her from her perch, relishing the indignant yell she gave. "I beg your pardon," she blustered.

In response, Adam merely smirked. He didn't know why pushing her tiny little buttons gave him such pleasure, but he just couldn't stop. It made him laugh to himself every time he got a rise out of the fairy with an attitude the size of Mount Rushmore.

"What was that whole thing between you and Drianna?" he asked while holding on to her lest she fly away.

"None of your business, giant ass, so let me go," she tried kicking him with her little foot, but he merely smiled.

"I don't have any reason to trust her, and yet you seem to believe we should, so I want to know."

Flinging back hair the color of rubies, she narrowed her eyes. "Drianna and Faulks, Story's papa, were once in love. Faulks knew all about the prophecy because Drianna told him about it. They had a covert affair for years, and she knew how much he loved Story, so she promised him to do all that she could to protect her. Got it? Now let me go." Leaning down, she bit him as hard as she could. Adam yowled and shook her off, putting his thumb in his mouth to suck the now-bleeding wound.

"Great, now I'll probably get rabies from the feral fairy," he growled.

"I don't know what that is, but I'm sure if you got it, I would get great pleasure from it." Then she zipped around his head and out the door, calling over her shoulder in a sing-songy voice laden with sarcasm, "Better get a move on, General."

Scowling, Adam continued to suck on his thumb and stalked out the door after her, hoping against hope that Story wouldn't play the fiddle and end time and their two worlds as they knew it.

Chapter Forty-Six

The Capital, Tressla

STORY HAD KICKED and screamed her whole way down to the cells, but to no avail. She hadn't really expected to get loose, given the Wolves had a grip on her like steel. But she felt satisfied that she had made their duty just a little harder, and she felt secure in the fact that although Brink wanted her behind bars, he didn't want her harmed—so she knew the beasts wouldn't be committing any aggravated assaults anytime soon.

The Wolves tossed her into the cell, with snarls emitting from their too-human mouths. She shuddered. It was a creepy scene she truly never wanted to see again.

She curled up in a corner for a moment, giving the appearance of being beaten—when in fact she just wanted them to go away as fast as possible, so she could start thinking of an escape route. At least she was in the vicinity of where she wanted to be.

"Story," a voice whispered.

Peering out through her hair, she saw a man slowly start toward her. He was covered in filth, and his clothes hung off him. But what she noticed the most was that his face, his beautiful face, had been beaten so that it was swollen and lumpy in some places and dirty in others. Only his eyes and his graceful hands told her who it was.

"Nicholas," she breathed and ran toward him, collapsing in his arms. The two slid to the ground and cradled each other. "What did they do to you?"

"Nothing I can't handle," he whispered, running his hands through her hair and down her back. "I can't believe it's you."

"I told you I was coming. Why didn't you let me see what they had done to you last night, when I was here in your dreams?"

"Oh Story," he murmured, pressing his lips to her cheek, even though it probably hurt him to do so. "I could hardly believe it was real, let alone want you to risk yourself coming here to save me. You need to save everyone else. I'm not a priority."

Opening her eyes, she grabbed his face delicately between hers and leaned forward, pressing her lips ever so gently to his swollen ones. "You're a priority to me," she whispered against his mouth.

His left eye was practically swollen shut, but his right eye, so lively and familiar, gazed soulfully back into her golden ones. "I don't deserve you."

Running a finger gently over his swollen cheek, she shook her head smiling. "Don't be silly, I've been looking for you for thousands of lifetimes," she murmured.

He arched his brows questioningly, although the effect with his swollen features was rather gruesome. "Lifetimes?"

Ignoring his question, she lifted his shirt despite his protests and saw how bruised he was. "You know, I knew Brink was a bastard, but I didn't think he would do this to his own son. Deep down, I really thought he wouldn't do this to you again."

"Agai—"

"I mean, you're his son. His flesh and blood," she raged, pounding a fist on the dingy cellar floor.

"Well, if it makes you feel any better, I don't believe he ordered this upon me. The Wolves felt a little betrayed. When I was a boy, they had at one time accepted me as one of their own, and my mother forced me to fight with them. So they had fun kicking the ever-living Racell's balls out of me. I'm lucky Gristle doesn't seem to be present. It would have been worse."

"For the love of . . . The Green, could you not use my father's name in vain."

Laughing, Nicholas wound his arm around her and pulled her in closer. "I love you, Story Sparks."

Story's eyes widened and her head slowly jerked back so she could look into his dark eyes—well, eye. It was the second time he'd said it, but she didn't count their conversation in her dream the night before.

He smiled gently and took her hand. "You don't have to say it back, I just wanted you to know that's how I felt."

Story laughed a little hysterically. If only he knew. "Oh Nicholas," she whispered. "I . . . I do love you. I just, it's hard to explain."

Nodding, he backed off a little, putting space between them. "No, it's fine," he turned his face away, a mask of stone settling over his now-lumpy features.

"No, you don't get it," she grabbed his face between her hands as gently as she could and turned it so that he was practically bumping noses with her, forced to look her in the eyes. "I've loved you even before I knew it. Some part of me has always loved you. You may not remember, and I don't remember a lot of it actually, but we've loved each other before."

His pained smile vanished at her words. "What are you saying?"

Sighing, she glanced around the jail cell and the dirty floor covered in straw, a metal plate kicked in the corner. Way to go for the jail cell cliché, Brink.

"When I first met you, I felt this connection with you, almost as if I couldn't stop myself from staring at you." Nicholas grinned licentiously, and Story blushed with a soft laugh. "Don't get too full of yourself. But the truth is, I started to fall for you not long after that. But it wasn't until I heard you play that I remembered who you were."

"Who I am? You mean when we were children?"

"No, I mean I remembered you . . . from before."

"I'm sorry, Story, but I'm still confused."

"Okay, I'll break it down. I'm the First Dreamer, right? That's established?"

"Well, yeah," he nodded gamely.

"You," she pointed at him, "are also someone from the past. Can you guess who that might be?"

He sat there for a moment, and then his good eye widened. The other one was too swollen shut to do much expressing. "No." He shook his head. "I don't remember anything of the kind."

"Well, be that as it may, you are the Fiddler. The very Fiddler the First Dreamer fell in love with."

Jumping back from where he kneeled near her, he got to his feet and paced. "How can that be?"

"Apparently, I've been searching for you. Well, my soul has been searching for you."

"And yet, you don't really know that for sure."

"Yes, I do. I can feel it."

"But you don't remember everything."

"No, but I remember you."

"If this is true, how come I don't remember?"

"It's been thousands of years. I don't remember all of it."

"And yet, now I'm supposed to believe that I didn't fall in love with you for who you are, I just fell in love with you because some guy from thousands of years ago and I share the same soul?"

Story rose to her feet and went to grab his hand, but he pulled away. "Why are you acting like this? Who cares why we're in love? I just know I feel it, and that's all that matters."

"But you're telling me we don't have free will, and that's just The Will winning again, taking away our choices and making it all about fate." She couldn't begrudge him his feelings—hadn't she said almost the exact same thing only days earlier at Ninian's cottage?

"Nicholas," she said demandingly. "I don't care about fate or destiny or free will at this moment. All I know is I love you, and I don't care where that comes from." And she didn't—not anymore. It may have been her soul's recognition of his that had drawn her to him in the first place, but what she felt for him now was all her. It was Story. And possibly Senka and crazy girl.

"Well, I do. I've lived my life by some prophecy my mother wrote about a Dreamer coming to save us all, and now you're here. I don't want to live by fate anymore. I want to live by free will. So if I share the soul of some Fiddler from eons ago, I forsake that. I refuse to love because The Will decides it must be so."

Tears stung Story's eyes, but she quickly blinked them back into oblivion and watched him in disbelief, unable to follow his rationality or reason. "So what does this mean? You refuse to love me?" She turned away, the pain in her chest wrenching, until she felt his hand on her shoulder. "I didn't know it was a choice."

"Story." His voice was rough, his good eye filled with pain. But her cheeks were dry when she turned to him.

"Knock, knock," a deep, slavering voice said from behind them. Startled, Story spun around to see two Big Bads grinning outside the cell door. "Lord Brink commands your presence now." The burly Wolf grabbed Nicholas by the arm.

"No," Story lunged for him, but the other Wolf put out an arm like steel to stop her. She locked gazes with Nicholas, searching his beaten face. But she couldn't see past the hardness in his eye when he looked at the Wolves.

"Brink said he'll require your company soon enough." The heavier set one smirked.

"Nicholas," Story said, despairing and reaching her hand out between the bars as they began to lead his defeated form out. "No, just take me to him. I'll give him what he wants. Don't take Nicholas."

The Wolf holding Nicholas grinned, his tongue lolling from his mouth as if he were actually in canine form. "Don't worry, you'll give him what he wants," he barked out with a laugh, his other friend slapping him on the back as if sharing in some great joke.

Shaking his head, Nicholas tried to make eye contact, but she avoided his gaze. "Story, don't worry, I know how to deal with my father."

He looked back several times as they dragged him away, but she was trying to ward off tears. She would save him even if he didn't want her. He'd said it—if he couldn't choose whom he loved, then he wouldn't love her.

Chapter Forty-Seven

The Capital, Tressla

IT FELT LIKE THEY HAD taken down half The Capital building's guards by the time Jess and Darvish made it to the underground entrance. Luckily, they hadn't met up with more than two at a time, and together the guards had been easy to take down, as much as Jess hated to admit it.

They found themselves in a dank chamber, where Jess found she was too afraid to make a move—there were easily more than a hundred Wolves stationed outside, and she wasn't sure whether their own army had made it yet. The sign, Adam had assured her, would come in the form of an annoying little insect. So far, Jess hadn't seen any "insects." She was starting to get nervous they had missed the sign and would have to take their chances and attack, which really wasn't ideal, seeing as there were only two of them, no matter their strength.

Despite being a kickass Big Bad warrior, her greatest fear was to end up as a Wolf's meal. She hated them with every part of her being, and she'd rather die choking on a piece of food, which for a warrior would normally be kind of pathetic. But all the same, that's how she felt. There was no nobility in these creatures; they were pure demon. Well, except if your name was Darvish, then you were just insufferable.

"What was the sign again?" He sounded annoyed, as if he didn't trust her intelligence.

"He said, and I quote, an 'annoying insect,' which is ridiculous since there could be any number of annoying insects."

"Oh for The Green's sake, he's talking about the Thumbelina. Bliss will find us to give us the signal."

"But she's not an insect."

"Oh, it's just his pet name for her." He sounded amused.

Glancing at him from the corner of her eye, she lifted her chin nonchalantly while looking out the window again as if she didn't care. "Pet name?"

He chuckled in response. "Don't tell me you haven't noticed the little thing those two have going for each other."

Looking disgusted, she turned to him and whispered fiercely, "He's like ten times the size of her! That doesn't even make sense," she scoffed.

She glanced at him again and was even more annoyed when she saw his incredibly white smile had gotten even wider and toothier. Those damned Wolves and their annoyingly humongous grins.

"I've heard of stranger things happening, such as a Big Bad Wolf killer and a Wolf working together."

She didn't even give him the satisfaction of acknowledging him, and she was saved when Bliss suddenly crawled up through a crevice in the wall, covered in dirt and looking somewhat pale. "I was meant to fly free, not dig through the ground like a rat." She ran her fingers through her usually ruby locks that now seemed to be the only color in the dimness they huddled in.

"I will definitely be taking the scenic way out," she muttered before looking up at Jess and Darvish. "Here I am, your sign. I apologize if you were waiting for an actual insect to announce our arrival. Seems Adam can't find it within himself to actually act like a grown-up for once, even when we're trying to save our best friend, the world's savior." She shrugged. "But who am I to judge. I'm just an insect." Shaking out her wings, she mock-saluted. "So consider yourself alerted. They're outside and waiting."

"Have you heard anything of Story?" Jess asked, ignoring the smile Darvish still had trained on her.

"We were hoping you did." Bliss responded, looking worried. "I have to go, I need to get into the palace and find Story. If she's in trouble, perhaps I can help."

Jess shook her head in agreement. "You go, we'll join the crew once we've cut our way through."

Flittering in the air between them, Bliss met both their gazes. "Be careful," she added seriously. "They're hungry."

"You too." Jess glanced at Darvish and nodded, his lazy grin replaced by the stoniness of a warrior.

"You ready?" He grabbed her hand and squeezed. Despite the seriousness of the battle that lay ahead of them, she found his hand, although ridiculously large, warm and comforting. She glowered to herself at the shiver that swept through her, and she slipped her hand from his as quickly and nonchalantly as she could. He grinned that annoying smile at her, making her stomach do a little flip. What was wrong with her?

"Come on, Wolf Slayer, show me what you're made of," Darvish said with a yawning smile.

She returned his grin for the first time. "Prepare to be in awe."

The two slipped from the cellar room and crept through the underground hallways that Darvish assured her would open up behind the hill, where the Wolves had gathered. It was there that Adam and the others were supposed to be waiting.

It got darker as they worked their way further underground. At one point, Darvish asked if she needed a torch, but she scoffed. "My night vision is as good as yours if not better. Keep moving, Wolf." He merely chuckled lowly in response, the sound of it grating on her already taut nerves.

They were moving at a good pace when Darvish stopped, causing Jess to gracelessly run into his back. Rolling her eyes, a snide remark was on the tip of her tongue when he shushed her by holding up a hand. "Shhh, I hear something."

Jess cocked her head to listen but didn't get the chance. Darvish shoved her back against the wall, putting himself between her and the three Big Bads that approached on both sides.

"Oh look, it's the traitor and the destroyer, all packaged up in one nice, easy-to-kill, no-escape bundle." The one who spoke was closest to Jess, and she saw the gleam of his Wolf eyes before she saw his face.

"You're right." She stepped out from behind Darvish and tossed him a haughty look before smiling at the Wolves. "There is no escape. For you." She met Darvish's gaze for a split second and mutual understanding flew between them. He nodded almost imperceptibly, and then Jess jumped, hooking her fingers around steel rungs hanging from the low ceiling and flinging herself feet first at the Wolf with the big mouth.

She knocked him down and somersaulted through the air into a graceful landing. Then she turned around just in time to duck as his fist came flying at her head. She spun around and dropped low, sweeping him to the ground with her leg, the sounds of growling and tearing flesh surrounding her. Before the Wolf could recover, she planted her elbow into his windpipe and straddled him, while with her other hand she slid her silver knife from its sheath in her boot. Looking down at him she gave him a feral smile. "My, what big eyes you have," she whispered, his gaze widening so she could see the whites of his glowing yellow eyes. Lifting her arm back, she brought it down into his chest, and continued to slice him down the middle.

Wasting no time, she turned to see how Darvish was doing and saw him struggling with the last Wolf, who was snarling on top of Darvish's massive Wolf form. Grabbing the attacker's tail, she whipped him off the other Wolf and flung him with a crack into the wall. He slid down, but she knew he'd recover quickly. Jess was faster and was on the Wolf before he could blink. Slamming her knife into his throat, she grabbed her ax from where it was strapped to her back and sliced off his head. Stabbing a Wolf in man form normally would kill them, but when they were in animal form they needed a bit more convincing to stay down.

Turning back to Darvish, she drew a hand across her chin, wiping blood away. He had already morphed back into human form and dismembered the other Wolf. He glanced over at her, unsmiling.

"They don't call me the Destroyer for nothing," she grinned.

He held her gaze for a moment and then finally smiled back. "Remind me again why I like to piss you off?"

Snorting, she started down the wide tunnel once more. "You must have a death wish," she called over her shoulder.

He chuckled behind her, but this time she found it less annoying, which annoyed her even more. "Maybe I just like to dance."

She did her best to ignore him—being friends with a Wolf would only get her in trouble. She could see a light ahead and knew they were nearing Adam soon. She hoped Story's plan would work.

Chapter Forty-Eight

The Capital, Tressla

LARK DARTED AROUND CORNERS expertly while dancing out of the way of any sunlight lest she be turned into a puddle doomed to fall through the cracks and crevices of The Capital. Story did her best to keep up with her, failing to exhibit the stealth that seemed to come naturally to the spritely little character. Despite Story's lack of sneaky grace, they managed to evade any guards, arriving at the Great Hall's doors in a matter of minutes.

"I can't go with you, unfortunately," Lark frowned, staring longingly into the room where sunlight sparkled through the windows, reflecting off three great prisms of glass that held The Three imprisoned. Tressla's true rulers.

"It's okay, Lark, you've done so much already."

Story had wracked her brain for a plan to get out of the cell after the Wolves had taken Nicholas. She had tried to open a door, but it was as if Brink had put some spell on the prison. She couldn't even call a Nightmare. She was so lost in thought that when she saw a puddle of water, she'd thought back to Lark, who as an Asrai was doomed to live without the sun's warm rays, and how she'd mentioned to call for her from a body of water if she were in need of help. Story figured this situation counted as pretty dire, so she'd crossed her fingers and said Lark's name several times. At first nothing happened, and Story had thought herself defeated. She'd barely managed to stifle a shriek when she'd seen the diminutive features of the elfin-like creature gazing up at her through a curtain of silvery blonde hair.

Lark had been her rescuer. Having spotted another nearby puddle, she'd disappeared and reappeared outside the cell with a piece of wire to pick the lock. Surprisingly, she'd been quite adept at the art and had gotten Story free in a matter of moments. Once she'd stepped outside the cell, Story found her power to open doors was back, and so now here she was. Plans had changed, and she no longer knew what to expect. But she had to save Nicholas. She had to save Tressla.

"Would you mind making sure Nicholas isn't being held anywhere else?" Just saying his name made her chest hurt.

The tiny merchant from Sandeen's caverns proved herself to be a true and loyal friend. "Of course. Be safe, Dreamer."

"You too," Story said softly. Lark disappeared back into the maze of hallways and Story was left alone. She cracked open the door and peeked her head in, confronted with silence. Her instincts had been right; this is where she needed to be. The Three looked as if they were sleeping behind the walls of glass that kept them in a stasis-like state. Story padded across the mosaic floor that caught sunlight and reflected back beams of colorful light.

She would find some way to release them after Brink was stopped. She walked over to one and reached out her hand, touching her fingers against the glass prison. It was bitingly cold. She was wondering if heat might help her release the prisoners, when she noticed something from the corner of her eye.

Her heart started to hammer in her chest. She just couldn't be this lucky. It was the fiddle. All ruined wood and broken seams, sitting on the table as if it were a centerpiece to Brink's throne room.

If she destroyed it, she could possibly cripple him. With single-mindedness, she started toward it only to stop when she was halfway there. It just couldn't be this easy. A tingling feeling crept over her flesh—the fiddle felt like it was calling to her.

"It's a trap," she whispered aloud. But her feet kept pulling her forward, until she could reach out and grab it. She recalled what it looked like when the Fiddler played it in the grove of her vision, the way it shone like the stars and emitted music that seemed to reverberate through her very soul, so pure it almost hurt to hear such loveliness.

When she came back to herself, the fiddle was in her hands, and she was stroking the strings like a lover caresses his true love the first time he lays with her. She was startled when she actually remembered what that felt like—when she was The Dreamer and Nicholas was the Fiddler.

She strummed a chord, but she was an artist, not a musician. *Wrong,* the instrument seemed to whisper to her. *You know me and I know you.* And it was right, because her fingers were moving along the strings as if it was natural, and the sweetest music poured forth. But despite the purity of sound, there was something she couldn't make out. Another whisper.

"So you've found the fiddle. I imagine it was hard tracking it down to my main hall." Brink smiled, steepling his fingers together and lounging in the high backed chair as if he'd been there all along. He was once again clothed in a designer suit from the Real World. The lines fitted his trim figure as he lifted one foot to rest on the top of his other leg. Story almost expected him to kick off his shoes. Shoes that were no doubt designer as well and would have had Elliott salivating.

Her fingers paused in their passage. But the yearning to play overtook her, and she felt a song seep from her heart into the strings and out into the world. Whatever music was relayed was lost on her because the whisper was louder now, and she knew what it was saying.

The bow came to a standstill, and Story lifted her gaze to the darkly grinning countenance of Brink. "What does she say to you when you play her?"

Brink stared uncomprehendingly at her for a moment or so and then finally blinked. "What?" he snapped.

"What does she say to you when you play her? I assume you've played her before. Oh wait, that's right, you have no talent. She doesn't play for you, does she?"

Brink was looking darker and darker, but Story didn't care. "If you haven't been using its power, then what good has it been to you?"

"Ah, so you figured it out." He nodded at her, his brows lifting as if he truly was impressed with her deductive skills. But Story knew as well as he did that she should have figured out that one small detail prior to this meeting.

She heard his laughter from far away, and then his voice. It was curling, like smoke in a room, inviting her to listen and explore. "Remember the day this was taken, the day that I stole this from your love? I want you to remember that day . . . "

That was easy. She had already remembered the day before, her fingers wound around the strings as she plucked them against all reason. She knew she should stop, should fight against what he was saying, but the image popped into her mind as if the memory was from yesterday. A dark shadow settled next to her, and the silken tone of Brink's voice was all she could hear, all she knew.

"I want you to go back. Go back to that time when you first loved your Fiddler. Go back, and I'll show you how to save Nicholas. You want to save him, don't you?"

She did. The desire to save her love made her gasp, but it was the energy that was building inside of her that left her shaking. The fiddle was working its magic as she played, and its essence sifted through her soul like silk. She could feel it looking for her imperfections while building on existing power. So that's how it works, she thought. It heals.

Brink was beside her, his hand on her shoulder, his voice soft and mellifluous, convincing her how easy it would be to go back, to go into the vision. She wanted to, and the urge grew stronger with each passing moment. Her body began to thrum with the intensity of her own power building up inside of her, with the desire of the dryad swirling within her, wanting to fix her and perfect all that was broken. She could also feel something else from the entity working its way through her soul. It wanted true love again, and so it clung to Story, urging her back through time to the purity of The Dreamer and Fiddler's love.

The essence of the fiddle continued its path within her, and she could feel its yearning, the yearning to be with the Fiddler once again as it began to merge with her own essence. It wasn't something she could fight, not the dryad's yearning on top of Brink's and her own.

Her vision blurred, and she felt a doorway beginning to yawn open, and the world rushed around them. Then there was a pause in the fluidity of the door's creation, and the world stood still as the fiddle's essence leapt away from Senka, who suddenly decided to make her presence known. Not knowing what to make of the darker version of Story that twined through her soul like a black thread, the dryad retreated until the world crashed in on itself and her fingers no longer strummed the fiddle. Senka had saved her.

As the spirit of the dryad disappeared back into the instrument, Story's mind merged with the dryad's for a moment, and she was able to sense how truly broken she was. Heaving breaths rasped from her lungs as the world came back into focus. She blinked her eyes and realized she still held the fiddle, but its power couldn't harm or help her now.

Broken, I'm a broken girl, she thought, forgetting Brink in those moments. He hadn't wanted her to just unite the worlds, she realized. He had wanted to go back to the beginning, to when it all started. Her head snapped to Brink. "Why?" she asked him.

Brink seemed calm at first, but it wasn't long before the storm started to take over his eyes. His face transformed from anticipation to a twisted shadow of a grimace. He laughed once, a bit maniacally. "Can't you guess?" He crossed to her, and before she knew what he was doing, he had snatched the fiddle from her hands. "This is useless to me. You've seen my dreams. I wanted to go back and kill the Fiddler before you had a chance to meet him. That way, I would have the fiddle, my hopes, my dreams, and possibly a muse." His smile retuned, but it was far from nice.

"You lie. You were leading me back to the night The Dreamer first lay with him. That would have been too late. I think you were going to stop yourself from killing him."

Brink glowered at her. "Forgiveness doesn't suit you. I should know."

"Oh, don't worry, I'm not forgiving you for anything. If you'd done that, stopped yourself from killing the Fiddler, then the worlds never would have been divided. History would have been rewritten, thousands of years squashed in one moment. You wouldn't have just annihilated Fairytales—the impact could have destroyed us all." Story trembled for a moment at the implications. Had a broken piece of herself not put the dryad off, had it not made it so clear that Story couldn't have perfect love or a pure heart when pieces of herself existed separately, it could have been the end. Looking back up at Brink, she smiled without humor. "I'm not so naïve as to think your efforts were in any way selfless."

Story noticed for the first time that he had a large staff in his hand, glittering with a bright and shiny black gem embedded in the knob at the top. Probably one of the magical artifacts he'd stolen from a Fairytale, she thought. If the dungeon was ever emptied, she'd bet her life that there were quite a few shady characters down there looking to avenge themselves against Brink. Which could work to her advantage.

"It would have been worth it. You have no idea what my life has been like since you cursed me."

Story rolled her eyes. "Whine, whine, whine, I'm so over your woe-is-me bit." She knew it probably wasn't smart to antagonize him, but he'd almost destroyed the world, so her hackles were up.

His heavy brows furrowed low and his dark eyes narrowed, staring at her with a hatred so intense she took a step back. She stared at the staff once again. If only she could grab it, she knew she could rid him of some of the power he had stolen from others. But she wasn't sure how to rid herself of him completely yet, so she needed to stall until Jess and the others made it there and could distract him. It was only a matter of time before the Wolves made an appearance.

"I would watch what I said, little Dreamer, or your Spirit may find an untimely accident waiting for her—hmmm, perhaps an overdose?"

Story's gaze snapped from the staff to his face, which was now twisted in a smug smile of satisfaction. He knew where her Spirit was? But how?

"I see you understand me. But I'll leave her be for the moment. You see, I have other methods of convincing you to see things my way."

Nicholas. All thoughts of her insane spirit self were vanquished to the back of her mind with the arrival of a hulking Wolf in man form, dragging a figure behind him. "Nicholas," she whispered aloud, her heart clenching in her chest so hard it was painful. Behind him, the Wolf easily toted another smaller figure. Lark. She'd asked the Asrai to help her and now she'd signed her death certificate.

Story started toward them with no thought as to how to help them, but she was brought up short at the sound of a sharp clap from Brink. Chains fell from the wall, allowing the Wolf to chain up Nicholas, who seemed only semi-conscious. His face was still swollen from previous beatings, and Story noticed now that he had a new bruise swelling his lip.

She glanced at Brink, who studied Nicholas impassively, but when he spoke, a steadied calm laced his voice. "What happened to his face?"

"He got rowdy, so some of the boys had to take him down," the Wolf answered. His name was Claw, Story remembered from her time at their camp.

"And you and all the boys, vicious animals to be exact, had to destroy his face all together? Because one human man was such a threat?" Brink asked mildly.

"Well, yeah."

Story almost felt bad for the Wolf. He looked like one of the meatheads from her gym in New York, all big muscles and bravado, little in the way of intelligent thought. *Almost* was the key word, she thought as she looked upon Nicholas's beautiful but ruined face.

Brink sat up from his lounging position and aimed his staff at the Wolf. "When I give an order, I expect it to be followed," he said lightly, almost as if they were having a friendly conversation. "I don't care if I'm going to kill him tomorrow. My prisoners, especially ones that happen to be my son, are to be treated like guests."

Story shot Brink a look, eyebrows shooting into her hair at this display of, well, almost fatherly concern. It was probably the best he could do, given that his mortal enemy was dating his son.

"Let this be a lesson to you and the rest of your filthy Fairytale brothers." Lowering his staff to eye level with the Wolf, a crackle of electricity charged the air, and in a blink all that remained of the Big Bad were ashes.

Story stared at where the Wolf had been and frowned, worryingly unfazed by his death. *Curiouser and curiouser.*

Brink turned to Story and smiled. "Now, where were we? Oh yes, here's my proposition. You take me where I need to go, and I'll let Nicholas live. If you don't, I will have him killed."

"I find that hard to believe since you just dusted a Wolf for beating him up." Story lifted her chin and met his gaze, attempting bravado and confidence she didn't really feel. He had decimated populations of trees, sent his Wolves to pillage towns, enslaved a race, and finally, killed her father and Kestrel as well as countless others. He may not have pulled the trigger, but it had been under his orders. She had no delusions that he was a good guy.

"Don't fool yourself, dear. I really just don't like Fairytales and I don't like to be disobeyed."

Wolves *were* Fairytales, weren't they? Story mused. Her thoughts were cut off when Brink lifted his staff at Nicholas and a beam of crackling blue energy hit his son's unconscious form. Nicholas's eyes shot open and his back arched as he screamed in pain, his muscles rippling and twitching. Beside him on the floor, Lark lay lifelessly.

"Stop it!" Story charged at Brink, her head a cloud of rage, her only thought to claw his eyes out for making Nicholas hurt so much. She was only a few feet away from him when he leveled his staff at her, his dark gaze meeting her golden one.

"Any closer, Dreamer, and you'll be in a world of pain far worse than what your dear Nicholas just felt."

Glaring at him, she concentrated, pulling at the magic that still reverberated in the air and drew it into herself. She'd never done it before, but her anger fueled her to action. It was hard work. A bead of sweat trickled down her forehead and into her eyes, but she blinked it away, holding his gaze.

"So what's it going to be? Shall we journey back to that ancient time when you and I first had the pleasure of meeting?" His voice, always laden with sarcasm, was beginning to fray at her nerves.

"Do you ever shut up?" she screamed the words, feeling Senka's violence take over for a moment before she could push her back down. The toll for using her power would be the end of herself—she could feel it and she was scared. How could she hope to defeat him when she couldn't even use what powers she knew how to use?

"I don't even know if I can do that," she stalled, holding on to what power she had managed to sweep from the room. "As you seem to already know, I'm broken."

Smiling darkly, he turned his staff once again at Nicholas and zapped him. But this time, Story was prepared and she threw the power she had grabbed back at him, striking him through the chest. She hardly gave herself a moment to enjoy his expression and his shriek as he went flying back into the wall, because she was running toward Nicholas and Lark. Quickly, she grabbed the still Lark and shoved her into the center of the room where the sunlight streamed in. Story watched as she melted into a puddle of water that was at once lively and quick, a living stream that found the closest crack and seeped through. Relieved that Lark was safe, she turned to help Nicholas, who was peering out at her through his swollen eyes.

"Story," he croaked. "Behind you . . . "

She turned just in time to see Brink's face screwed in hatred and a bolt of energy come flying at her. The pain filled her chest with fire and reduced her to tremors as she hit the floor.

Set me free . . . Senka whispered in the back of her mind, promising to devastate the overlord and his assault on her love. But despite the pain, Story refused, fortifying the tower walls of her mind with brick. Even so, the rage bubbled within her, and it was getting harder to keep her darker self quiet.

Towering over her, Brink looked down at Story. "You have no idea what power I command. I have dragons up my sleeve and evil stepsisters who have a taste for homicide. You can't hope to thwart me, Story. But if you give in, maybe we could strike a deal."

Finding she could control her limbs once again, she shakily climbed to her feet. "I'm not here to make a deal, Brink. I'm here to take back my boyfriend and put an end to your reign."

He chuckled. "No one has been able to yet, and you can't even find it within yourself to give into your darker nature and win." He smiled knowingly.

Story was at a loss for a moment. Did he know about Senka? She opened her mouth to ask him, but a voice interrupted her thoughts and lit a fire of hope within her. Story swung around, eyes widening at the sight of Racell.

"Dad!" she cried, the namesake rolling off her tongue as if she'd always known him as such, his golden presence an instant comfort.

His hard eyes softened when she said his name, but then he turned back to Brink, who laughed. "You have no magic, Racell. You're merely a figurehead for Tressla, someone for the poor and pathetic to pray to."

"I have the strength of a thousand men, and a millennia of you annoying me. Try me." Nodding at Story, Racell advanced and was met with a lightning bolt that barely seemed to faze him.

With Brink distracted, Story ran to help Nicholas. Glancing down in dismay at the ropes that bound him, she looked around for a weapon. When the Wolves had thrown her into the cell, they'd taken the dagger she'd been given by Kestrel. Eyeing the now-deceased Wolf's ashes, she noticed the glint of steel beneath the dust. Scurrying toward it, she bit back her distaste, wrinkled her nose, and plunged her hand into his remains. Grabbing the steel blade, she kneeled at Nicholas's side and started to saw away at the ropes that bound him. She hurried, knowing Racell could only keep Brink busy for so long before he would be too tired or too dead to be of any help anymore. And she didn't plan on losing another father.

As the ropes sprung free, she grabbed Nicholas beneath his arms and dragged him to a corner of the room. Propping him up, she whispered, "Can you hear me?"

"Story?" His voice was raw as if he'd inhaled too much smoke. Her own throat felt as if it had been burned as well. Probably from Brink's attacks.

"Nicholas." She gently touched his swollen face and bit her lip, glancing back at Brink and Racell, who was already looking beaten by the onslaught of magic Brink was using against him.

"Stay here and rest. I'll be back in a bit." She frowned, not wanting to leave him alone, but unable to see an alternative. She glanced back at Racell and Brink and was overcome with the need to help. Darting a look at Nicholas, she frowned, indecision keeping her from acting. Story glanced at the crystal prisons where The Three existed in a state of standstill, noticing the water that dripped from the crystals as if they were stalactites in a cavern. When a pale blonde head popped out from one of the puddles, she stepped back almost tripping over Nicholas.

Grinning, Lark materialized in solid form, talking excitedly. "I waited around once you set me free. Let me try and help Nicholas. As long as I'm in the shadows I should be able to work."

Relief overwhelmed Story, and she kissed the water sprite. "Thank you!" Turning, she knelt down by Nicholas once more and brushed her lips over his forehead.

"Story," he grabbed her hand weakly. "Story, I didn't mean before—I mean, I only meant that I don't believe fate is why I love you. I love you because of you. That's all I was trying to say—that I love you."

Tears sprung to her eyes, and she nodded as his eyes closed. "I know, Nicholas."

Story started to turn toward Racell, who was on his knees swaying and pale, when she was stopped by a humongous brindled Wolf. His hackles up and teeth bared, he stalked toward her. What could she do? If she called the Nightmares, Senka would get free, but if she didn't . . . No, she couldn't let her out. She didn't know if she would ever come back from it, her darkness was so strong.

Story grabbed the shortly curved broadsword she'd dropped by Nicholas's side and pointed it at the Wolf. As a child, she'd trained in sword fighting a bit with the Pegasus. Of course, she had always sucked at swordplay and recalled Ober rolling his eyes and telling her to use her magic instead. She just wasn't the warrior that Jess was or that Kestrel had been.

Even so, she had to try. The sword trembled in the air and she willed herself to stop shaking. She knew he could smell her fear. The Wolf grinned, and she felt her pulse leap to her throat. They circled each other, never moving their eyes from one another, both with golden eyes—hers like honey and sunshine, his the sickly color of jaundice.

She was no match physically for this monstrosity, but if she could keep him off his feet, she might be able to slice off a member. Sometimes the pain caused them to transform back to their human form. Different stories and creatures often intermingled when they came to life in Tressla, so Big Bads had some mythically based werewolf-like weaknesses.

She thrusted once, and he leapt over her, darting in with a vicious attack that she barely managed to escape by ducking and rolling. Out of the corner of her eye, she saw Brink look up in glee as he was about to finish off Racell, and she felt her chest lurch painfully. Senka beat at the walls, calling to her. The wall began to slip.

She wasn't sure she could hold her off anymore, and she didn't know if she even wanted to. The Wolf loomed on her, and her walls slipped further. But just as she was about to let Senka free, a red-haired Amazon queen came riding in, roaring a battle cry atop another giant Wolf. They leapt across the room in a matter of seconds, and before Story could even react, Jess had taken her attacker down and was slicing out his heart.

"Jess, Darvish, your timing rocks, but I've got to save Racell."

"We're all here, Story, save the world." Jess grinned, flipping back her curls. "We'll fight the good fight."

Warriors and Wolves flooded the room. The war had come to the main hall.

She started to run toward Brink, grabbing energy from the magic being used around her, so that she could create a barrier against his next attack on Racell. From above, Bliss zipped toward Brink, zooming around his head as if she were a really large, angry bee. Off balance, Brink swatted his hands around him before he got his eye on what was distracting him from his task at hand. Story grinned, only Bliss. But her smile faded as he went to zap her, probably out of existence considering her size. Story's mouth opened wide to scream, but Adam, who had been creeping up on Brink, swung at him as if he were a mere man, landing his fist into the taller man's chin. Brink stumbled back, and Story laughed at the sheer brilliance of his attack.

Barely affected by the punch, Brink's head snapped back up, and he set his darkly lit gaze on Adam. His arm came up and he sent out a beam of light that crackled wildly in the battlefield of the room. More powerful than any bolt he'd thrown yet, Story knew it would kill Adam.

Instinctively, she threw out the net of power she had collected and hoped it would reach him in time, but the energy swooshed from Brink's staff and caught Adam, who went flying back into the wall with a loud crack.

Oh no, Oh no, NONONONONONONO pierced through her head. It sounded like an explosion. No one could hit their head that hard and come through it alive. Story stopped breathing, and the world went still aside from the screaming in her head. The screams stopped, and she was left gasping, desperately trying to draw in air.

Story turned back to Brink just in time to see Gordon the fire troll fall beneath a Wolf's slavering jaws. Racell lay on the ground still as well, his face pale and waxy. She could see Ober's strong haunches stained red with blood flowing from a missing chunk.

They were falling all around her. They were all going to die. And it would be all her fault. The First Dreamer, the one who had torn the world asunder. Story, the girl who didn't know what she was doing but still led an army to their deaths. She was helpless, a failure. She couldn't save the worlds. She couldn't even save her friends. How could they all have thought she was so much more? They'd even called her a god. She laughed hysterically, the sound catching in her throat and almost choking her.

Wait. "A god," she whispered. Morgana's voice echoed in her memory, telling her she was practically the god of the Fairytales. Then Brink, saying the same to her in their shared dream the night before. Yes, a god. Elliott would have jokingly called her vain. But she knew a god would need her darker half. She wasn't scared anymore. The red had washed her fear away.

Darkness enveloped her. Her eyes flickered black and then gold again. The whisper she'd been hearing for days was louder now. *Set me free, sister.* This time Story obliged, letting the walls finally crumble. From the wreckage she saw her dark-eyed sister emerge with an exultant laugh. Senka reached a hand up and Story met it with her own.

First came the Nightmares. They flooded the room and joined the fray, taking down the Wolves by dragging them off into their worst nightmares. Dark creatures of lore and legend appeared, fairytale monsters and beasts, but they fought on the side of good, taking down Wolves alongside her army and her Nightmares.

Turning her head, she sightlessly saw into the depths of the jail cells below, and with a mere thought, flung open doors encrypted by sorcery and impenetrable steel. The true dark and powerful ones came, homing in on the beacon that was Story.

Brink was looking fairly stunned, but had begun to gather his power and was shooting Nightmares out of existence when they appeared.

The ones that ruled the dark corners of pages and literature, or had set legends into motion. They came in an angry cloud, calling for their objects of power to be returned to them. A sorcerer, impossibly tall, materialized first. He had a large wizardly hat on his head, adorned with stars, and a long robe and a beard that nearly reached the floor. With barely a flicker of his hand, a wand appeared as he took his power back. Brink's head snapped toward them, and he stumbled as if he'd taken a physical blow to the stomach.

A Wolf came leaping at Story. She merely lifted a hand and flung it away as if it were a doll. The wizard leveled his wand and began to engage Brink in magical combat.

But the wizard wasn't the only angry one. A green-faced witch wearing glittering shoes stepped up beside the sorcerer and let out a high-pitched shriek. At her bequest, a broom flew through the air, flinging itself into her hand as if it were a dog greeting a long-lost master. The witch, although certainly ugly, looked less so when she smiled gently at the broom as if she was equally touched to have it back. Then with small, dark, narrowed eyes, she joined the Wizard in the attack on Brink, whose face was set impassively as he held strong against them.

Next, a wizened crone, bent and stooped, joined the other two, a red apple clenched in her fist. Brink doubled over as another one of his magical artifacts was taken from him. Although haggard, he still had his most powerful object yet. He lifted the staff and fought back, bearing down on the three dark ones who seemed to shrink beneath the power he shot at them.

Story frowned. Where was the owner of the staff? Even Story's powers, what she could do with them anyway, were no match for the bejeweled item. Senka and Story screamed in rage as one, and the dark ones cowered lower. The crone's apple began to shrivel much as she did, while the witch's broom sparked and smoked.

Story took her eyes off Brink and glanced around the room to see Adam still lying motionless, and then swiveled to see Nicholas still looking beaten and bruised. She turned to look back at Brink just in time to see his smile vanish and his dark eyes light with fear.

A young, dashing man appeared and gave Story a cocksure smile and a wink, several timepieces hanging around his neck, a watch around his wrist. He touched his face and gazed at his strong, masculine hands. "I'm young again," he said, delighted. His smile only faded from his handsome face when he turned to Brink, his jaw clenched.

"That," he said, pointing at the staff, "happens to be mine. And I want it back." With a single gesture of his elegant hands, the staff flew out of Brink's grasp and into the young man's grip.

The show was almost over. But she had a few more matters to attend to. Reaching out with her mind, she touched each Wolf's thoughts until they were all cowering down before her. She was their true alpha, she only wished she'd realized it sooner.

"So you're The Dreamer, I would presume," the man said. He nodded and gave her a sexy smile. "Merlin, at your service."

She nodded back, her gaze flicking toward Brink, who was confined by a force field the magical group had erected around him as a prison.

"Brink has been our warden for many years now, having trapped each of us through trickery and greed. He has made everyone in this land suffer while he took what he would, but he has suffered as well. Has he not, Dreamer?"

Story frowned, not liking where this was going. Her fingers were clenched, and she was itching to strangle Brink with her mind, watch his breath quicken and then cease, his heart stop and his despicable face fade away. She glanced at Adam again. Loyal Adam, her best friend with his cocky smile and stern, kind eyes. Gone. She nearly sobbed, but she couldn't feel anything but vengeance.

"He deserves worse," she spat out.

"Story!" Bliss zoomed over, sounding shocked. Up until that moment, she had been huddling around Adam's still form like a worried mother hen. Coming close to her, Bliss stared into Story's gaze and saw the dark behind the gold. "Story?" she whispered a question. "Story," she repeated and smacked her with her small hand.

Story barely seemed to notice. "Adam is dead." Her voice was devoid of all inflection.

A concerned and haggard-looking Elliott came to her side, all other fighting in the room having come to a standstill the moment she took her place as alpha to the Wolves. "Story?" he asked as if uncertain she was still present.

"No, Story, he's not. Not yet. He might still live with some help," Bliss told her, a pleading in her great electric green eyes.

Looking around, Story took in the quiet room. Wolves lay on the ground, their noses buried in the floor as if waiting her command. Others lay wounded, being treated by Ninian and Drianna, who as Daughters of the Will were trained in healing practices.

But there were other bodies, dead bodies of those like Gordon, who had been the sweetest troll. And then there was the black-haired Sylvaine, her breast stained red. She had gone to join her brother now in the Summerland.

Turning back to Adam, she saw that Morgana, also a healer, was by his side. Then she glanced at Nicholas, who Lark had helped hobble over to Story's side. Reaching down, he took her hand and managed to stand on his own. She started to change her mind until she saw Nicholas's destroyed face. Glancing at Brink, who looked frightened in the bubble that was his prison, she narrowed her eyes, and Senka smiled with pleasure. But before she could snuff him from existence, a familiar voice called her name. A much beloved voice that even Senka could not deny.

"Mom?" Her mother with her long dark hair and wide, usually haunted eyes, lurched forward through the crowd of Wolves and Fairytales toward Story—who lunged toward her until the two women were crying, wrapped in each other's arms. "How did you get here? Oh, of course, Racell!"

Nodding, Edie stroked Story's hair and then pushed her out to look at her. "Story, oh Story, I knew you were alive. You look older, like you've aged. When did that happen?" she asked softly, fingering a strand of Story's hair that had gone silver.

"Probably around the time the weight of the world was handed to me," she half-joked.

They both laughed through their tears and only stopped when Merlin cleared his throat.

"I love a good mother-daughter reunion as much as the next wizard, although you definitely look more like sisters." He cast a wink toward Edie, who smiled.

"Watch yourself, wizard," Racell growled. Despite looking haggard, he had seemingly begun to recover from his battle with Brink.

Merlin looked even more pleased with himself if that was possible. She could practically hear Elliott salivate from behind her. She glanced back at him, mimicking herself wiping drool. Elliott rolled his eyes, but then nodded, mouthing, "OMG."

With her mother's arm wrapped around her and Nicholas's hand back in her own, she was able to push her darker self back down. Overcome with the appearance of her mother and Nicholas by her side, Senka didn't fight too hard. When Story looked back at Brink, her eyes were like honey again.

"Merlin is right. He suffered at my hand when I tore away his dreams and hopes in a previous life. Were I to do it over again, I'd take it back. But I can't, and Brink can't take back the wrongs he committed either. He has stolen magic, taken power that was not his, and committed the Fairytales to live in fear and servitude when this land is rightfully theirs. And he has killed.

"So his punishment is this. He is to be banished to the magic-less cells he forced others to live in. It is there that he will live out his life, a prisoner of his own making."

The barrier, which had been like a cloud around his form, disappeared. Brink stood staring hatefully at Story. "You should just kill me, Dreamer, otherwise you'll be keeping me there for an eternity. I will always come back to haunt you," he promised. Story believed him, but she also couldn't bring herself to kill him, however much she had wanted to do it moments before. That had been Senka talking.

Deep within her Senka laughed. *Don't fool yourself, you are me.*

Ignoring her, Story shrugged. "Sorry, I don't deal in death sentences I merely want this land restored to peace." For a moment, she thought about banishing him to another dimension if that was even possible, but he would just make trouble there as well, and she couldn't risk that. She'd have to come up with an alternative solution at some point. Keeping him in a cell for eternity seemed particularly cruel since he apparently couldn't die, but twenty or thirty years would be good for him.

"Perhaps I can assist you in binding him in his cell," Merlin offered. "After all, I am the most powerful wizard alive," he added, without any false bravado.

"I never knew the real life you would be so narcissistic." Her insult did nothing to faze the annoyingly perky Merlin, who merely smiled.

She laughed lightly, happy to be able to feel the weightlessness of the motion. "Yes," she nodded. "Your help would be appreciated."

"Don't forget that pesky Spirit. I'm sure you'll find her." Brink grinned darkly over his shoulder as Merlin, followed by the three dark ones, directed two Wolves to grab Brink.

"Spirit?" Edie said, confused, glancing at Story sideways.

"It's nothing, Mom." Thankfully at that moment, when she could see Racell about to close in on the questions as well, Uncle Peter sauntered in as if he did it every day, and her mother lost it.

"Peter?" Her mother's voice was barely audible, and she blinked her eyes as if she were dreaming. He moved toward her, his own brown eyes glistening. "Peter!" She shrieked and rushed him while he swooped her into his arms. They hugged for so long, Story thought they would never let go, but then they opened their arms and motioned for her to join them. Racell embraced them all moments later and the four of them stayed that way for some time. She hadn't realized she'd been missing it until they held her. Family.

CHAPTER FORTY-NINE

The Capital, Tressla

MUCH LATER, AFTER THE THREE had been released, the Wolves dispatched under Darvish's new leadership, the dead set free, and the injured tended to, Story was finally going to get a few moments alone with Nicholas, who was resting in one of the many rooms they now occupied at The Three's invitation. Merlin had been able to free the Three rulers, and they were recovering from their years trapped in glass. There was a lot in the aftermath that would need to be figured out, and a land that needed healing.

She had just had enough time to bathe. In fact, she had almost met her untimely end in the steaming waters by falling asleep out of pure exhaustion. Only Bliss had found her before she slipped beneath the surface. How silly would that have been? Save Tressla but then die by taking a bath?

Before stopping to see Nicholas, who she knew was alive and well, she visited Adam, who was still being tended to by Morgana. Her attractively lined face looked tired, but she smiled brightly when Story knocked and asked if she could enter.

"How is he?" Story glanced over to where he lay, pale and bruised. He was so still she was sure he had died, but then Morgana wouldn't have been smiling, so she drew some relief from that.

"He's been badly injured, Story. His brain has been injured, and he is hemorrhaging, but I am doing everything I can." That wasn't what Story wanted to hear, and tears slipped from her eyes as she drew near his bedside.

"Will it be enough?" she asked, placing a gentle hand against Adam's slack, white cheek. She couldn't live in a world where his dancing gray eyes and penchant for sarcasm wouldn't always exist.

She didn't even realize she was doing it at first, until she felt the power unsettle her defenses against Senka. In the last few moments sitting by Adam's side and watching him slip further away, she had begun to siphon the remnants of magic from the fight the night before. There was quite a lot just hanging in the air, and she felt it like an energy coursing through her body.

The power hung so heavy, she felt as if she would start sparking at any moment. Placing her hand on Adam's third eye, she sent the magic into his head like a healing brand, doing in mere moments what doctors would have done in surgery. She could see the inner workings of his brain, almost as if she were looking at a clear x-ray.

The magic poured out of her so quickly, she couldn't put a plug on it. She knew that if she didn't get away from him quick, she would kill him, but it was as if her hand was stuck fast to his head. The magic seeped from her like a tidal wave that kept turning and turning. Strong arms came from behind and wrapped around her, pulling her away so roughly, she stumbled and hit the wall, sinking to the ground in a horrified heap.

"What did you do?" Morgana demanded, finally looking like the witch the legends always made her out to be, her dark eyes narrowed and her lips puckered. But her eyes glittered with fear.

Shaking her head, Story shakily jumped to her feet. "Is he okay?"

"You could have killed him!" Morgana checked her patient and then gasped.

"What?" Story flung herself at her side just in time to see Adam grin.

"Hey," he drawled sleepily. "Have I been out long? Did I sleep through the war?" He yawned and rubbed his eyes with his hands.

"How do you feel?" Morgana asked, shooting Story an incredulous look that was partially awe and partially wariness.

"I feel like I got hit in the head with a baseball bat, but other than that, dandy."

More tears sprung to Story's eyes, but they were out of joy as she lurched to hug him.

"Hey, don't crush me too hard, my ribs feel a little cracked."

"That's because they are," Morgana affirmed.

"Wow, did Brink do this to me? I must be lucky to be alive."

"You most definitely are." Morgana shot another look at Story, this time with questions on her face. But Story barely noticed, she was too busy crying.

"I thought you were going to die."

"Hey, you know I would never do that. There are too many chicks . . ." He didn't finish the sentence, but Story rolled her eyes.

"Now I know you're doing fine since your one-track mind seems to be back in focus."

He grinned his rakish smile. "Would you rather I came back spouting poetry?"

Laughing, she shook her head and wiped her eyes free of tears. "Although that would have been refreshing, I much prefer you just the way you are."

Story laughed with Adam, who winced from the pain it caused him. But it was healing for them both. Eventually he grew tired and Morgana shooed her out. But he grabbed her hand before she could turn to go and met her gaze seriously. "I know what you did. I could feel you in my head fixing things, making me whole again. I knew deep down I wasn't going to come through this, but you saved me, Story. Thank you."

"Well, you saved all of us because if it hadn't been for you, I wouldn't have went all super chick and beat back Brink. So, *thank you*." Kissing his forehead, she escaped the room before he could ask her any more questions.

Before she could quite make it fully out the door, Morgana was behind her and had followed her into the hall. "I know there's a lot going on right now, but later, you, Ninian, Drianna, and I need to sit down and talk about what just happened in there." Her dark eyes were more serious than Story had ever seen them, and she sighed.

"Yeah, sure." Story brushed her off, begging exhaustion. Really though, she was feeling wired after the power she had grabbed, and she wanted more than anything to go see Nicholas.

When she found his room, he was sitting up in bed strumming the fiddle. He looked up guiltily when she entered, his face still puffy and black and blue. She stopped when she saw what he was holding. "Where did you get that?"

Setting it aside, he beckoned for her to join him on the bed, which she did willingly. As she sat on the edge, he took her hands in his and tried smiling, although his face was so swollen it looked more like a grimace. "Brink left it just lying on the table, and I thought it would be a good idea to take care of it."

"Yeah, good call. I wouldn't want anyone else getting their hands on it. Besides," she squeezed his hand gently, "I think it belongs to you."

He started to shake his head, his one hand releasing hers to gently stroke the strings as if it was already precious to him. "I couldn't take it."

"Well, what does she say to you when you play her? She does say something, right?"

Startled, Nicholas nodded, picking up the instrument in both hands and gazing at it. "Yes. She's asking me to set her free."

Nodding, Story put her hand on his arm. "Then I think she does belong to you, at least until you decide to free her."

"That's what I'll do, although I'm not sure how."

"Then we'll look for a way." She smiled softly. Lifting a hand, she touched his face gently. "Listen, Nicholas. I think I can heal your face if you'll let me."

The change of subject seemed to startle him and his puffy dark eyes met hers, searching to see if she was serious. "You're not a healer."

"But I can syphon power, and I have a lot left over from healing Adam."

His eyes widened if that was possible, given their current state. "You healed Adam?"

"Yep, I just left him before I came here. Although tired, he's as good as new. Well, not quite, but at least he's not about to die anymore. So can I try? I just need to avoid the third eye area."

He nodded, watching her intently as she laid her hand on his face and let the power hum from her fingertips, taking the swelling from his features. When she was finished, his face looked almost normal again aside from a few scrapes and bruises. "I best stop there, last time I lost control a little."

Frowning, he nodded and then brought his hands to his face, running his fingers over the smooth planes and hard feel of his jaw. "It's amazing." he marveled. "I can see normally again, and I don't feel like a monster."

Easing down so that her head was on his chest, she nodded sleepily and closed her eyes. "I think I'll just rest for a moment."

Her nap was short-lived. He was stroking her hair—and she felt herself about to drift off to sleep—when a knock came at the door. Sighing and yawning lethargically, she sat up. "Can't I snuggle with my boyfriend? Shouldn't I get that?"

He laughed, shrugging. "You're too important I guess. But later . . ." He fixed her with a stare that made her heart flutter and her cheeks flush, and she looked away, suddenly shy. Crossing to the door, she opened it, ready to bite someone's head off until she saw it was Elliott.

"Story, you need to come down to the dining hall. You're going to want to see this."

Ten minutes later, she entered the dining hall with both Nicholas and Elliott at her side to find her mother, Racell, Uncle Peter, Bliss, Ninian, Drianna, Landria, and a sore Ober gathered around.

"What's up?" Story asked as brightly as she possibly could, given the fact that she had been cuddling up to her man and taking a great big and much-needed snooze only moments before.

The group parted to reveal two women of mythical proportions, but two Story had met before. "Sandeen," she nodded and then moved forward to approach The Green, whose rich brown hair fell around her like a curtain of earth, except for the white that now streaked it.

The rest of the group, save her mother and uncle, who was looking at Sandeen longingly, bowed to The Green.

"I am honored," Story murmured. "Please, take a seat," she gestured to the comfiest-looking chair around the long table, biting her lip when the earth goddess slowly and arthritically eased herself down.

Shooting Sandeen a look, Story mouthed. "What's wrong with her?" Sandeen merely shook her head, her deep, abyss-like black eyes looking sad and her face looking gaunter than ever.

"I'm afraid everyone should probably sit down," The Green murmured.

One by one, the group slowly took seats. Everyone save Edie, who didn't know any better, seemed distressed at The Green's aged appearance.

It was quiet for a few moments until finally The Green sighed. "Sandeen," she said rather pointedly. Scowling, Sandeen finally took a seat, elegantly crossing one leg over the other and meeting Story's gaze.

"You may think you know the story of how Tressla came to be separate from the Real World, and a part of that comes from the essential aspect of yourself that is missing."

"What do you mean?" Edie was like a mother on defense in an instant, but Story smiled softly at her.

"Thanks, Mom, but it's okay. Sandeen, I do know this. I'm missing my Spirit, or so I've heard."

"Yes, well, what you might not know is that it was your idea to separate your Soul from your Spirit in the first place."

Gaping, Story silently cursed the holes in her memory. "What do you mean it was *my* idea?"

"When The Dreamer, you, came to me after the Fiddler had been killed, you planned to throw yourself into my waters and drown yourself."

Story nodded and was comforted when Nicholas took her hand, stroking her fingers soothingly. Although she was growing more disturbed by Sandeen's story, it did not escape her notice that her mother zeroed in on their interlocked hands.

Story pretended not to notice and turned back to Sandeen, growing uncomfortable by the number of eyes boring into her.

"You couldn't stand the thought of not being with him. You wanted to die and be reincarnated when he was so you could be with him again. As a muse, you were very passionate, and were ruled by those passions." Funny, Story thought, she had been trying so hard to go against her passions and where did it leave her? Fragmented.

"But we couldn't know if you would come back. Not even you were sure of your own origins. You'd just been found one day sleeping beneath a tree. You had a theory, however, that if I were to sever your Spirit from your Soul, then you would have to come back because the soul's natural state is to be with its spirit. You insisted it would work, and I couldn't say no to you. None of us ever could. So I did as you asked." Sandeen blinked her eerie black eyes as if trying to expel an eyelash, but Story could tell there were tears.

"There were so many wrongs that night, so many events that were never supposed to take place. The world couldn't take it. When The Dreamer's Soul was severed from its Spirit, the world was also severed from its own Spirit, thus creating these two realities."

The room was so silent for so long, Story was afraid she had gone deaf. When the hush was broken, the voice came from an unexpected source, one who could pull off the wronged party role better than anyone she knew.

"And why are you just telling her this now?" Elliott asked accusingly. "Don't you think this would have been good to know, I don't know, like when you dragged us into your little underwater wonderland? You could have saved Story some of the recriminations."

Sandeen appeared untouched by Elliott's outburst, and she met the accusing gazes of everyone else save The Green, who actually looked like she was napping.

"And what does it mean if she doesn't have her Spirit?" Ninian added.

"It means that there is a living, breathing girl living in an institution somewhere that belongs to me. That's my Spirit. I've known it for some time."

"Have you dreamt of her then?" Ninian asked. Story merely nodded in response.

"Well then, yes, she is a human being, but without her soul I would imagine she is quite mad," Sandeen murmured.

"How could you condemn someone to live such a life?" Nicholas gaped, his face like stone. "I've seen what it does to the Shadow Fae, the ones without their Spirits. And I've seen Fairy Spirits without a Fae to call their own, and they're some of the saddest creatures to live."

"Nicholas," Story looked at him. "If Sandeen is to blame then so am I. After all, it was my idea."

"But you're not her. You're Story, not some ancient Dreamer. You may have been her, but you're you now."

"How do I even know who I am when I am missing an integral piece of who I'm supposed to be? I don't even know who I am." She had known she wasn't complete for some time, but hearing it from Sandeen was making it all seem so much more real and honestly, unbelievable. As if her entire life had jumped out of a storybook. *And of course there's me,* Senka said with amusement. But Story ignored her, unable or unwilling to tell everyone about her darker self at the moment. Soon, she promised herself.

"Why tell her now?" Nicholas seemed chastened, but he had a hard angry glint in his eyes when he looked at Sandeen.

"Well, I had hoped that when Story was sent into the Chamber of Dreams, she would have remembered. And then I supposed I thought she would eventually regain her memories, but I see now that without her Spirit, she cannot be truly whole."

"Duh," Elliott muttered under his breath, his adulation of Sandeen obviously past tense.

"She also feels guilty," Sandeen said, her inflectionless tone finally softening.

Lowering her eyes, Story nodded and gave her mother a sidelong glance. "Yes, you're not wrong."

"So why now?" Nicholas was vocal tonight. Story stifled a grin despite the seriousness of the situation.

"I think that would be obvious—the worlds are dying." Story nodded toward The Green, who had opened her eyes once more and nodded sadly.

"Indeed they are." Although aged in appearance, she still had the gift of song that lit her voice like green leaves swaying in the breeze on an early summer day.

"So what," Story turned back toward Sandeen, "I have to find this girl, right?"

The underworld goddess merely nodded gravely, her black gaze lost in thought, or perhaps she was just staring at Peter, who watched her adoringly. Who would have thought they'd be so in love even after she had kidnapped him to her watery world?

"Where would you even start?" Edie asked rather calmly for someone who had been thrown into this world only twenty-four hours before—and had learned her daughter was some great mystical legend born at the beginning of mankind.

"Her dreams, of course," Sandeen said, focusing again.

At once, everyone began debating how they would find the girl who could help Story somehow save the worlds, but then they heard the loud howl of the Wolves.

"I thought we had them domesticated," Elliott scoffed.

"Wait," Story said, silencing everyone by raising her hand. "Do you hear that?"

It started as a rumble, then vibrations rocked the room. Adornments on shelves began to fall and break, while glasses on the table rattled violently. Then stone started to fall. Nicholas dive bombed her and dragged her under the table while Story screamed for her mother as more stone and wood crashed around them.

The earthquake seemed to last a century, but it was only mere moments. When the world finally stopped shaking, Story slowly crawled out from beneath the table and waved dust away from her face, coughing. Everyone seemed to be all right, although Ninian had sustained a nasty bruise to her left cheek, which Drianna was inspecting.

Guinevere, who had been crouching beneath a doorway, straightened up, looking proper as usual. The girlish lilt to her voice was absent, and instead the imperiousness of a queen shone through. "I believe you should begin this journey quite soon, Story. As soon as you can."

Story looked around the room at everyone she loved, her mother and father together for the first time in her entire life, her best friends, her new friends, her ancient friends, and her truest love. She pushed aside her doubts, her worries, and her misgivings, and she held her head up as proudly as she'd seen Guinevere hold hers. And she accepted it. The weight of the world truly was on her shoulders. There would be time to break down later, to cry about not being able to sit down with ice cream and watch reruns of *Friends* as any college student should have been able to do. She remembered her childhood training enough to know that she had always been working toward this. Whether she had forgotten it or not, it had always been there. And she had been hearing her Spirit self call out to her for some time, trying to wake her up to the reality of her life.

Looking at everyone, she nodded. "I promise, I'll save us. I'll save her." She glanced at The Green, who seemed be suffering from narcolepsy. "I'll be the Dreamer you need."

"When will you leave? Where will you go?" Her mom had paled.

She hated to worry her so, but she couldn't do much about it. "Tomorrow. I have an idea of where to look. There's just a few things I have to do first."

Nicholas walked with her to her room. He caught her hand and delicately slid his fingers down the side of her jaw. "Can I stay the night?"

Shivering, she nodded. He followed her into the room, and before she could even turn around, he grabbed her hungrily and pressed his lean body against hers. She started to melt against him as she always did when he touched her, the spark of their chemistry undeniable. But when he pressed his lips to her, she felt the connection between them intensify. If there were any doubts as to who they were and what had been, they were gone with that simple kiss. The years flew away and the past and present memory of her love for him seemed to merge. In the morning, she would not be left untouched by their night's passion. He slid his fingers over her bare arms and lifted her top from her body, pressing his lips to her flushed skin.

Tomorrow she would be gone, but tonight she would play. Sleep was for the dead, and she was very much alive. All she needed now was her Spirit, and she would be complete.

Deep within, Senka opened her eyes and smiled.

Here Ends Book I.

GLOSSARY

(Includes terms from books I, II & III)

Banshee Island—Once attached to mainland Tressla, the large mass of land broke off a century ago in the first beginnings of the two-world collapse. Since then, it has been home to criminals and refugees and has served as a place for Brink to banish Fairytales. There is little communication between the Island and the mainland aside from the traders, who dock regularly. The island is named as such because of the omen it represented to Tressla, which was the beginning of the world's demise.

Banshee Woodlands—One of the original Seven Forests, these woodlands are located across the Silver Sea and on Banshee Island.

Bellow Dings—A yellow flower that gives a loud bellow when intruders happen into a garden and a beautiful ding when friends come to visit.

Black Forest—It is in this of the Seven Forests where Nightmares lay in wait. It is always as dark as night, and the Nightmares cower until the sun sets each day so they can find their victims. The Wolves often frequent these trees, which are said to harbor all that is dark and twisted.

Chaos Creek—A creek in the Eldridge Mountains named for its proximity to the entrance to Maya's Valley.

Daisy Pillows—A large, soft, cushiony plant that grows close to the ground and is often used as a pillow.

Daughters of The Will—Priestesses who follow the Way of the Will, committed to upholding order, peace, and the barrier between worlds.

Elder Trees—This forest begins at the Eldridge Mountains, which leads to Maya's Valley. The trees may harbor dark Fairytales within their wooden depths, but happy endings rule the wood until the traveler reaches Maya's door. Then all bets are off.

Fairy Spirits—The spirit belonging to the Shadow Fae.

Fairytale Extras—Every fairytale has characters not central to the story, but who exist to move the story along or fill in small roles. These, too, are given life in Tressla, but they are lesser known and often can blend with regular Tresslan folk or Original Mythics.

Fairytales—The living and breathing essence of the fictional stories created by those living in the Real World. Once written, they come to life in Tressla and live real lives, although not necessarily how they were first dictated onto paper.

Field Mice Arugula—A leafy, lettuce-like plant good for eating and much loved by mice.

Fire Pox—A serious ailment that causes blistering, burning sores and bumps to break out on the bearer, and which can be fatal to Big Bad Wolves.

Forest of Light—The most central forest in Locksley, where Story grew up in Tressla, and one of the Seven Forests. This forest is especially known for the breadth of space between trees, allowing for sunlight to feed their roots and making them among the tallest trees in Tressla. It is also the Pegasus's favorite haunt.

Forest of Sylum—One of the Seven Forests, this is also where Racell's Rood is located. By grace of the Rood, the section of forest nearest this sacred spot is mostly untouched by evil and darkness, keeping even the Wolves out. It is one of the last few places left unfettered by Brink's rule.

Gargoyle Blossoms—This pearly pink flower, noted for its opalescent sheen and its sugary fragrance, is often planted with the Night Boggle. Although on its own the Gargoyle Blossom is only desirable for aesthetic purposes, when planted with the Boggle it works to enhance the repelling scent that keeps Nightmares at bay.

Gryphon's Eyeballs—A kind of grape found in most basic Tresslan wines.

House of Destiny—A sect that worships The Will and follows the ideology that although their lives are predestined, they have a measure of free will.

House of Fate—The teachings state that life is predestined and there is nothing you can do about it aside from live the life you were meant to lead.

Huntress's Thicket—The most gnarled and overgrown of the Seven Forests, the Thicket is home to the Weeping Queen's Wood, a grove located deep within the trees. It is nestled far from The Capital and any town, and is rumored to only be reachable by women who have remained chaste. Here, the soul of the original Queen of the Seven Forests is said to sleep within an ancient tree.

Incognitos Silver Bell—This flower is noteworthy for its glittering, silver petals as well as its ability to cast a powerful glamour. Whoever ingests the petals will take on the appearance of someone else, including their scent and tone of voice, throwing off even the best trackers. It can also be boiled into a draught that, when mixed with a person's saliva, allows the drinker to look like said person or beast.

Maya—She is the goddess of chaos and opposing face to The Will's religion of order. Maya changes form, most often taking on the appearance of a child or young girl. But there is no doubt, she is ancient.

Morgana and Guinevere's Holding—Located north of Racell's Rood, not far outside The Capital, the two iconic female figures from Arthurian lore rule a well-organized community of Fairytale and Tresslan rebels, who have been fighting their own underground war against Brink's oppression and waiting for The Dreamer to arrive.

Night Boggles—A vivid purple flower that blooms all year long and smells like lilacs. It's a good source of nutrition in soups and repels Nightmares. The Boggle only repels, however, when planted. Once they're harvested, they're only good for cooking.

Night Leaf—A leaf harvested from the Trees of Thanos that induces sleep when lit with fire.

Nightmares—These shadow creatures feed on the dreams of the sleeping innocent, plaguing them with nightmares. Generally, they can only come out during the night and can be repelled by Night Boggles, a plant that causes them to dissipate.

Original Mythics—These are the mythical creatures and races that existed before Fairytales— including your garden-variety trolls, fairies, Fae, dwarves, unicorns, Pegasus, and a number of other races and species borne of magic. They were a part of the original magic that existed in the world before it became two.

Pegasus—Although not all Pegasus can take human shape, the royal four are the very first of their kind and have both human and horse-like forms. There is Ober, king of the Pegasus, and Landria, who is queen. They have two children, Lance and Ophelia.

Purring Posies—Only available in varieties of black and white, Purring Posies are good plants for the gardener going for a simplistic look. Although low maintenance, if left unattended they go feral, hissing and scratching with hidden thorns that can leave a passerby sadly sore. If properly tended to, however, they are noted for the softness of their petals and the sweet purr they emit on a breeze.

Racell's Rood—The Rood is a grove that exists in the Forest of Sylum. It is a peaceful sanctuary, where legend has it Racell was birthed by his mortal mother. The power of the grove is its ability to shield those with good intentions from those who would wish them ill.

Real World Descendants—These are the descendants of humans who once lived in the world when it was whole and were on the magical side of the divide when it split. These mortals were some of the first Tresslan pioneers. Their descendants are the legacy of humans living in Tressla.

Sandeen—The daughter of The Will and The Green, she lives within her lake, guarding the passageway between worlds. She is often mistaken for the Lady of the Lake, but has more rightfully been called the Queen of the Sirens, luring would-be heroes into her underwater depths. Her father banished her to the lake when the First Dreamer died, blaming his daughter for not better guarding the lake.

Shadow Fae—This species of Faery folk are born with only a soul. When they come of age, they are sent on a journey into the Eldridge Mountains, where Maya's Valley lies. There, they go on a spiritual quest to find their Fairy Spirit, who is born at the same time a Shadow Fae first opens their eyes. This Fairy Spirit is their lifelong companion, and only when they find their spiritual match can they be whole.

Silver Sea—The main body of water that almost all other rivers and lakes lead to. The harbor is located in The Capital and is a docking port for merchants coming from Banshee Island.

Slow Bloomers—A large, white plant grown in swampy marshes that, when harvested and ripened, explodes. If left on the vine, they turn a bright red and then finally shrivel and die.

Stone of Souls—This ancient charm was forged by three magical races to keep the wearer bound to the world, in soul and in body.

The Capital—The main hub of Tressla. This is where The Three ruled the land until Brink overthrew them.

The Gardenia—A place where mystical plants and flowers grow in abundance, once tended to by Faulks, known for his green thumb abilities. This was Story's childhood home.

The Green—The essence of the earth, Gaia or Mother Earth, and mother to Sandeen.

The Green's Solace—This is one of three sacred groves in Tressla, the others being Racell's Rood and the Weeping Queen's Wood. In this particular grove, earth and rock soak up grief to give the bearer a brief respite from their pain.

The Three – Tressla's rightful rulers are made up of the three major races who are the blood of the land. The current Fairytale leader is the Queen of Hearts, known for being kind and insightful, if a bit promiscuous and too relaxed. Griffen the Centaur, a rigid rule-follower who is also highly intelligent, represents the Original Mythics, while Maggie is a Real World descendant and represents the mortal element.

The Will—The Green's long-ago consort, father to Sandeen and Racell. He is ruler of free will, but in the last thousand years favors the philosophies of destiny and fate.

Three Brothers River—This is a river that runs alongside the Forest of Sylum, emptying into the Silver Sea.

Thumbelina Roses—These fairies begin as roses and are a hybrid Fairytale plant that are grown and raised to be a girl's best friend. Each Thumbelina Rose variation, of which there is a number, tend to have different characteristics. Red Rose Thumbelinas, for instance, are notorious for running off with fairy princes, and are thus usually undesirable friends for a child. Morning Glory Thumbelinas, on the other hand, are known for their steadfast loyalty. But there are always exceptions to this rule.

Trees of Thanos—One of the Seven, this forest leads to The Green's Solace. Here, time can play tricks on passers in the woods, slowing a journey down by weeks or speeding it up to mere minutes.

MORE GREAT READS FROM BOOKTROPE

Billy Purgatory: I Am the Devil Bird **by Jesse James Freeman** (Dark Fantasy) Billy, A sweet talkin' badass skateboarder with attitude, fights supernatural forces while in hot pursuit of the girl of his nightmares. Wait, I mean dreams.

Changeling Eyes **by L.A. Catron** (Fantasy) An epic tale of loss, self-discovery, revenge, and magic. The first book in the Aesir Chronicles.

Dead of Knight **by Nicole J. Persun** (Fantasy) King Orson and King Odell are power-stricken, grieving, and mad. As they wage war against a rebel army led by Elise des Eresther, it appears as though they're merely in it for the glory. But their struggles are deeper and darker.

Doublesight **by Terry Persun** (Fantasy) In a world where shape shifters are feared, and murder appears to be the way to eliminate them, finding and destroying the source of the fear is all the doublesight can do.

In Starlight **by February Grace** (Fantasy) Young Fairy Godfather Gus Duncan must make the decision of his life: shatter the most sacred rule in the fairy code, or lose his beloved Till forever. Can true love save her when even magic fails?

The Chosen (Book One of the Portals of Destiny Series) **by Shay West** (Fantasy) To each of the four planets are sent four Guardians, with one mission: to protect and serve the Chosen, those who alone can save the galaxy from the terrifying Meekon. An epic story of life throughout the galaxy, and the common purpose that brings them together.

12535353R00246

Made in the USA
San Bernardino, CA
20 June 2014